DASH & THE MOONGLOW MYSTIC

DASH & THE MOONGLOW MYSTIC

PRU WARREN

QUI
LEGIT
REGIT
PRESS
She who reads, rules

Cover design by the Killion Group

Published by Qui Legit Regit Press
Alexandria, VA

ISBN: 978-1-7359919-3-1

Discover other titles by Pru Warren at pruwarren.com

090821wch

❀ Created with Vellum

BLISS & GIGGLES

Sign up for my newsletter, sweetpea! Go to
https://www.pruwarren.com/

My newsletter philosophy? Never take yourself too seriously. Skip the boring stuff. Amuse yourself; maybe others will be amused, too.

There's generally a smoochy gift to thank you for signing up. Maybe a free epilogue, maybe a peek at the next book, maybe something that gave me the giggles. C'mon and check it out; we'll have much delight together!

I was catching up with Jan, my former boss. She mentioned that her daughter had married a wonderful guy named Dash Ashleigh. "That's the greatest name ever! I must immediately write a romance with a hero named Dash Ashleigh! No, wait. Wouldn't Dash Ashwood be even better?!"

This book is dedicated to lovely Jan, and her slightly-misnamed son-in-law.

DASH & THE MOONGLOW MYSTIC

FEDERAL BUREAU OF INVESTIGATION
WASHINGTON, DC
CONFIDENTIAL

THIS COMMUNICATION IS PROTECTED UNDER THE LAWS OF THE UNITED STATES. ANY REVIEW, RETRANSMISSION, DISSEMINATION, OR OTHER USE OF OR TAKING ANY ACTION IN RELIANCE UPON THIS INFORMATION BY PERSONS OR ENTITIES OTHER THAN THE INTENDED RECIPIENT IS PROHIBITED.

INTERNAL MEMORANDUM

From: Jones, Owen, Director Eastern Division

To: Ashwood, Dashiell, Special Agent Financial Crimes

Good news, buddy—the Secret Service was so impressed you spotted those counterfeit hundreds that they want you on their joint task force. Good thing your niece and nephew picked that Podunk town for a pee break, huh? Even on vacation, you're an outstanding agent.

Here's what we know:

The Secret Service has been tracking a growing incidence of counterfeit bills, mostly through the Southwest region. It apparently began with overprinting fives onto bleached one-dollar bills (which no one checks) but recently jumped up in a big way to some pretty good hundreds.

The three you pulled out of that ATM in Wyoming all have the same serial number (as you noted), but in all other respects, the fakes are skillful. Your haul was the largest concentration of fakes the Secret Service has come across, so they did their research.

The last cash deposit before the ATM was restocked was for $883.16. It was two past-due payments on a truck owned by a Paul Abbott (minor rap sheet—mostly vandalism and public drunkenness), who works at the Triangle-K, a luxury dude ranch. That alone would not have raised eyebrows, except Abbott's boss (one Wolf Koenig, no criminal record) apparently tried to retrieve the hundreds Abbott paid with.

Background research found Wolf Koenig served in the Army with William Tilley, who was later fired from his job at the US Mint for suspicion of theft. Tilley died two years ago of cirrhosis of the liver. The Secret Service offers this theory:

•Tilley passed on to Koenig some confidential printing processes before his death.

•Koenig has been printing hundred-dollar bills and slowly distributing them through the American Southwest, far from his printing operations.

•His employee Abbott, needing his truck payments, lifted a few spare bills from the pile and deposited them at the bank.

That's where you had the good fortune to spot them on your vacation to Yellowstone. This is the biggest break in the case to date.

So now you and your new partner are being deputized to Wyoming. Enrique Martinez, US Secret Service, is already working undercover at the ranch. Your job is to pose as a vacationing accountant. Get a look at the ranch records. See what you can find out. You leave day after tomorrow. See Sherm Henry for details.

Before you go, let's make time for a meeting. I've got an opportunity I want to discuss with you.

Giddyap, Dash. Happy hunting.

ONE

DASH

I felt the Moonglow Mystic like electricity on my skin before I ever saw her.

I stood in the registration line at a luxury dude ranch, my "wife" at my side. (Rose Bennet had been my partner at the FBI for all of five weeks.) Rose bit a thumbnail and murmured to me, her low voice hidden under the hum of new guests recently released after a two-hour drive through the utter emptiness of Wyoming.

"Maybe I should change my name to Roz. Roz inspires respect, right?" she asked.

A buzz on my skin caught my attention. I sharpened my surveillance. The main lodge had a low ceiling, a stone fireplace (unlit on this summer afternoon), and antler chandeliers. Western chic, if you liked that sort of thing.

"Your name doesn't give authority. The toughest agent I know is named Percy. Do you feel that?"

She looked up. "Feel what?"

I plastered a smile on my face while eyeing the room. My skin was definitely tingling, and I could almost hear a faint hum, a tiny vibration through my bones.

And then I saw the woman.

She was across the lobby. Caucasian, early thirties, above-average height. Slim build, long silver hair. Eyes . . . blue. Violet, really. Those unusual eyes were fixed on me.

She didn't look away. I didn't either.

It's simple human psychology. If you're staring at someone and they catch you at it, you drop your eyes. You turn away. Maybe you flush or squirm or offer an abashed grin.

That's not what she did—and caught by her gaze, I didn't turn away either. The murmur of other guests continued but was suddenly far away. And I could still feel the electricity dancing on my skin.

"What? Do I feel what? Dash?" Rose tracked my stare and found the silver woman on the other side of the lobby. "Do you know her?"

I shook my head and fought to regain my focus. I pulled my gaze away. Looking at Rose, I clarified. "You don't feel . . . something? Electricity? Or something?"

She shook her head, her brunette bob swinging with the movement. I showed her my forearm, the hair standing on end. My skin was pebbled with goose bumps.

Rose looked at her own arm. She wasn't having the same reaction. "Huh," I said. Brilliant assessment from an experienced FBI agent.

I looked up again. The woman still stared at me. But whispers had started in the line for check-in.

"Who's that?"

"Is that one of the new ones?"

"Isn't she lovely! I want her to tell my fortune!"

The woman behind me gasped. It was Kimber. We'd met her on the bus ride from the airport. "That's her! That's the one who helped me!"

She shared her story with the fascinated guests—how, upon meeting Kimber a year ago, the Moonglow Mystic had diagnosed Kimber's cancer. "She was the receptionist at my vet's office in San Diego. She reached out and took my hand and told me. And she was right! My oncologist said we'd caught it really, really early. I owe her my life!"

The crowd *ooh*ed in appreciation, but the woman—the Moonglow Mystic—ignored the growing tide of curiosity. She kept her eyes on me. Was she judging me?

"Do you still feel it?" Rose wore her we're-so-happy-to-be-here smile, but her interest had been piqued, and she scanned the room.

"Like an iron filing next to a magnet. I feel . . ." The comparison died on my lips. I was going to say I felt like the tide pulled by the moon. Too close to the mindset that would allow a so-called moon goddess to con me. "Someone switched on a field generator—a powerful magnet," I said. "You don't feel it? Here—stand in front of me."

But no matter where she stood, Rose couldn't feel the electricity.

"I suppose it could be under the floor. Or in the attic. Shift around."

No luck.

I kept my eye on the silver-haired woman, and she watched me in turn. Then she pivoted on her heel and vanished through the double doors at the back of the lobby.

The buzzing on my skin faded.

I was confused until I remembered these "psychics" were con artists. That cleared my head. A con man's tricks could be extremely sophisticated. Had someone learned how to focus the effect of a large electromagnet so I was the only one feeling a strange pull toward the woman on the other side of the room?

Sure. That would explain my sensations. As soon as I figured it out, I felt better.

I turned back, refusing to shake my head in disbelief. It wouldn't do to appear immediately suspicious when surrounded by guests who were—according to all indications—eager to be conned by "prophets" and "mystics."

The fact that the entire ranch had been rented out for

"Prophecy Week" hadn't been lost on my bosses at the FBI. "You're going to look for evidence of a counterfeiting operation, Dash," Owen had said to me. "We have reason to suspect Wolf Koenig is running the operation, and he's the son of the ranch owners. It's dumb luck you'll be there while six charlatans are fleecing some wealthy believers. As far as Prophecy Week goes, if you don't witness a crime, don't worry about it. The fake bills are why we're helping the Secret Service—not the con men."

Fair enough. I'd keep my focus on the mission and ignore the con. But that was no reason to be careless or unobservant. Someone was using an electromagnet on me to fizz my skin while the silver-haired woman eyed me. They turned it off when she left the room. Nice technique. Not my problem.

We'd inched slowly forward to the check-in desk, where Bob and Marcia Koenig greeted returning guests and met the new ones, both with equal amounts of down-home hospitality.

Our joint task force partner at the Secret Service, Enrique Martinez, was already undercover at the dude ranch as a trail hand. The assumption was it wasn't Bob and Marcia Koenig who were printing out fake bills somewhere. It was probably their son, Wolf, who ran the ranch while his parents ran the inn. Both Enrique and Rose were junior agents where I was a senior agent with long years of experience, and I'd draw my own conclusions based on the kind of evidence that would stand up in court.

Those long years of experience weighed on me now. And they weighed exactly as much as the small case in my hip pocket, where a shameful folding pair of reading glasses now resided. Permanently.

A millstone around my neck.

I knew what they meant. They meant youth was now and forever lost to me. I was a field agent. I belonged in the field. At least, I used to. Now I was washed-up and useless. Probably going gray. Nothing left in my future but old age, isolated and alone in a perpetually weakening body.

As I'd been doing for the four days since the optometrist

gave me the news, I shook out of my blue funk and focused on the case.

"Next? Yes, sir?"

We'd made it to the front of the line, and Marcia Koenig exuded a cheerful welcome. Caucasian, short, plump. Early- to mid-sixties. No distinguishing marks. Short hair, bottle-blonde to cover the gray. Brown eyes. Air of happy innocence. Mother of our primary suspect.

"Dash and Rose Williamson," I said, holding out my ID and a credit card.

"Oh, the Williamsons!" Marcia Koenig cooed. "Our last-minute guests! How remarkable you called for a reservation moments after the Robinsons had to cancel!"

I had it on good authority that Bitsy Robinson had a small crystal meth lab in the basement of her summer home at Tahoe. She and her husband had gotten a provident knock on the door from the DEA as soon as we knew Rose and I needed a room at the Triangle-K, but I let none of that show.

"Well, their loss is definitely our gain!" I gave Marcia a big smile, which she returned.

"Oh, you're going to have such a good time! Here's the Prophecy Week agreement you need to sign. Every year, the mystics have us make all the guests sign it. Silly, isn't it? But each year the ranch sells out, so we love those prophets!" Marcia put the agreement on the desk before us, and Rose suddenly betrayed me by stepping away and gesturing to the paper with a grin.

And suddenly the small weight in my hip pocket threatened to drag me six feet under the ground.

"Damn it," I ground out.

Marcia was startled and looked at me.

"Sorry," I said and grumpily fished out the reading glasses. It was like holding a scorpion in my hand, or a vial of curare. This was death. Unwilling, I unfolded the glasses and put them on.

Rose laughed out loud and explained to Marcia, "First pair of reading glasses. He thinks he's dying of old age."

She and Marcia laughed merrily. Heartlessly. Marcia's hand reached out to pat mine. The Grim Reaper in an embroidered cardigan. "I remember when I got my first bifocals. It's a bad day. You poor sweetie. I promise—aging isn't all bad!"

I feigned a smile, and this time her husband, Bob, joined in the hysteria. "Don't worry, son. There's life after presbyopia!"

Funny. They were all charming. Like sledgehammers were charming. I scanned the agreement as Marcia told Rose about Prophecy Week private readings and group events. Buried in tiny, vision-defying legalese near the bottom of the contract was the reason why no law enforcement agency would intrude on the con artists' week-long scam: the all-important phrase "For entertainment purposes only." Of course. Now we were all legal and aboveboard.

I signed my name. Marcia beamed at me. "On behalf of those prophets, we thank you. Now, can I sign you two up for any of the ranch activities?" We leaned our heads together as she went over them. "We've got campfire cookouts and roping lessons—not on a living bull," she confided, "and trail rides. You'll love our trail rides."

"I don't much like horses."

"You'll like our horses! How about I sign you up for the beginner ride tomorrow? Short and easy. Everyone gets a personal guide. Get your fears all taken care of?" I opened my mouth to rationalize away my fears, but she was having none of it. "Your wife would like it, wouldn't she?"

Beside me, Rose was wreathed in eager smiles. "I used to ride as a girl! Let's go, Dash!"

"All right." My dislike of riding had to be overcome. Rose and I needed to spend time with Wolf and his ranch hands, our most likely suspects.

"And glamping—glamorous camping. Oh, it's wonderful. You take an all-day trail ride. Or," she amended, seeing my face, "you can go up the jeep trail with the staff. We have luxurious tents set up in Smuggler's Basin, and there's a gourmet meal, and you can sleep under the stars and sometimes see the northern lights! It's the most beautiful part of the world. Like a fairy tale. I know you want me to put you down for that?"

"I'd be a fool to miss it."

She beamed. "And skeet shooting. And what about fly-fishing in our rushing river?"

"Marcia, why don't you sign me and the missus up for everything and let us know where we're supposed to be?"

"Oh, you are going to have such a good time! And don't forget the square dancing in town on Thursday night. It's a Triangle-K tradition!"

Time for me to insert the first probe. "Say, Marcia, what accounting software are you running on that thing?" I nodded to the laptop visible behind the registration desk.

"Accounting software?" she said, surprised.

Rose nudged me. "Dash! You said we'd take a real vacation. No more accounting, please!" She turned to Marcia. "He's such a nerd!"

Marcia smiled in commiseration, but the hook had been set. Bob turned away from the family he was checking in to verify what he'd heard.

"Accounting software? Are you into accounting, Mr. Williamson?"

Rose laughed, the long-suffering wife, and pushed me away to talk to Bob while she and Marcia completed the registration.

"Call me Dash. I'm curious—what are you running there? Don't tell me it's QuickBooks, please."

He laughed and leaned in, interested. "NetSuite, actually. You're in the business?"

"I'm a CPA. If you're running NetSuite, do you have the macro for the new tax laws?"

"What's that now?"

Rose put a determined hand on my shoulder. "Dash, really. Leave it alone. Could you back off for once?"

I shrugged and smiled apologetically at Bob. "Have you looked into Patriot? They've got some great features."

"Well, I love the name. And God knows I hate paying those taxes!" Bob grinned.

Rose wheeled and glared at me through her smile. She was perfect. "Dash. Stop."

She mouthed "sorry" to Marcia, and I mouthed "talk later" to Bob, making a me-and-you gesture between us with my finger. He grinned and gave me a thumbs-up. Bait taken. Hook set.

"We'll have your luggage delivered to your cabin. It won't be a moment before the prophets do their welcome. You can wait right here in the lobby," Marcia finished with a smile, and Rose and I turned to mingle with the other guests.

"Well?" Rose asked me when we had a quiet space to ourselves. "How'd I do?"

"You were perfect. I'll have full access to their computers in no time. There's no hiding from us now."

And then the double doors were thrown open, and the Sun God stepped out.

TWO
EVADNE

I was a fox chased by hunters. My body was too big for my skin. All my nerve endings were sending out panic signals. *Stay quiet. Don't attract attention.* I grabbed Artie from where he was giving last-minute instructions to his prophets.

"I need to talk to you," I said, trying to keep my voice even and calm.

"In a bit," he said. "Let me—"

I dug my nails into his forearm, and he jerked in reaction and looked at me. "Now. Please?"

He must have known I was seconds away from bolting. He drew me with him across the room and out the side door, to where a sun-drenched afternoon waited.

I stood on the lawn at the side of the lodge and inhaled the dry, clear air, trying to quiet the percussion section whacking away in my heart. *Fly beneath the radar.* A lifetime strategy upended for one agonizing week.

"What's up, Evadne?" he asked.

All my fears welled up in me, choking me so no words could come out. I shook my head—the height of articulate.

His large hand came over my eyes, startling me. The other

hand fell to my shoulder. "Breathe," he said. "Just breathe. You can tell me later. For now, inhale. Now exhale—slower this time."

Without realizing it, I'd grabbed his wrist—not to pull his hands away from my eyes, but in fear he would do it himself.

"It's okay," he said. "I'm here. You're okay. A little slower. Breathe easy. Inhale. Good. Now let it out."

He talked me through the panic attack. The tide of my anxiety slowly went out, and it was easier to breathe. At last, I tugged on his wrist, and he let me draw his hand from my face.

My friend was very tall, and he stood in front of me, mostly blocking my view. I stared at his throat, at the collar of his blindingly white shirt, and waited until the restrictions in my throat had eased. Then I told him what he needed to know.

"Two of the guests are police. Or some kind of law enforcement."

His chin went up and the muscles of his neck were taut, but he remained calm. "We can handle that," he said. "If they sign the agreement, we're covered."

"*You're* covered," I protested. "I could be arrested." *Don't attract attention. Head down.*

"No." His calmness washed over me. "Elbert drew it up, and I've had it reviewed by two different lawyers—practicing lawyers who haven't been disbarred." *Poor Elbert.* "It's airtight in the state of Wyoming. You're safe too."

"I can't do this, Artie. I'm too scared."

"First, don't call me Artie."

"Sorry. Phoebus Apollon."

"Thanks. Second, you're going to be fine. You're reading people, anyway. Why shouldn't you profit from it?"

"I haven't been doing it for money."

"That's because you're a fool," he said soothingly. "I've been telling you for three years that you need to get in on this. You're going to make my Prophecy Week infinitely more successful. Next year, we'll be able to charge twice as much."

My wince was involuntary. Profiting from my "gift" was .

. . tawdry. And liable to draw attention to me. But I stiffened my spine. I needed some stability in my life. I needed to be able to pay more than the monthly minimum on some heavy bills. And I trusted Artie. Mostly. Plus, thirty guests waited for us on the other side of the wall. *Time to buck up, Evie girl.* "All right. I can do it. I can be brave." I inhaled to see if it would help set the sentiment into my soul. "And don't we have to get back? It's time for your welcome, right?"

"Can't start without you or me. They'll wait."

He'd turned me, and we walked along the waist-high meadow grasses that bordered the lawn. The air was rich with sage and sun-warmed freshness under the endless arch of the far-distant sky. His confidence helped.

"I'm a genius," he said. "The only thing Prophecy Week has been lacking has been the Moonglow Mystic to dazzle our guests and mesmerize them with her readings and her beauty. Every year, I rent out the Triangle-K for this outing, and every year, I've invited you to join us. This is going to be our best year ever, and you're the reason."

I gulped. "But no pressure, right?"

He laughed. "Honey, you're a natural. You're the only one who really can do what we all promise."

"I can't tell the future," I protested.

"Tell what you know. It will be enough." His voice was soothing and low. I don't make friends easily—well, I don't keep friends easily—and Artie (I mean, Phoebus Apollon) was one of the very few. If he needed me after all he'd done for me, I'd help him.

But I didn't want to. I didn't want to attract attention or have to be brave.

And I really didn't want to be arrested for fraud.

"Okay. I'm back on board."

"Thank you, sweet thing." Artie gave me an affectionate kiss on my head. I sometimes got that he'd be interested in more, but he'd never once pushed me, and I added that to the reasons I was grateful to him. "Which ones are the fuzz?"

"Tall guy. Dark hair. Lean. Great eyes."

Artie watched me with a smile, and I realized the heat I felt on my face was a blush. He grinned.

"Sounds handsome."

I shrugged casually. "I guess." The man had a swimmer's body, long and lean with broad shoulders and almost no hips. Good-looking—and more than that, he was mesmerizing. I was lost for a moment in the memory of all I could read in him.

"Anyone with him? You said two of the guests."

"Yeah—a woman."

"Looks like?"

I made a face. Busted. "I don't know. I didn't notice."

"Too busy looking at Tall, Dark, and Handsome, huh?" He was teasing me, even if he was mildly offended. Phoebus Apollon was tall, blond, and gorgeous.

I ignored his banter. "If you searched their luggage, you'd find badges. Probably guns, too, although they aren't carrying weapons today."

Phoebus ran his fingers through his long hair. His strong, white teeth bit at his lip as he thought. "We'll be fine. You're sure they're not just cops on vacation?"

I laughed. "At the prices you're charging? They'd have to be corrupt to afford this place, and they're both oozing integrity. Him more than her. These are two upright citizens."

"Think they'd accept a small bribe to leave us be? In case someone complains about us."

I scoffed. "I'm not kidding. That guy is Dudley Do-Right. Prince Valiant. A real Captain America type. Trust me, don't try a bribe."

Artie chuckled as he turned me to the lodge. "You are so damned helpful to have around. Why don't you marry me, and we'll conquer the world?"

"How about I don't and we just conquer Prophecy Week?"

"Good enough for now. Okay—here's how we play it. We're going to pick on your cop right off. Turn him into a believer. Then he'll leave us alone."

The thought made my stomach twist. "Let's leave him alone."

"Nah. We'll convert him. It'll work—you watch."

"You know, it's possible he's not here for us."

Phoebus Apollon was arrogant. It had never occurred to him someone else might be the center of attention, even for a reason that might draw the attention of law enforcement. But he wasn't a fool and gave the notion some thought.

"Well, let's see. There are some returning guests this year. Maybe it's one of them. We know that Rettinger guy is scamming his business partner. And Bitsy Robinson has something going on in Tahoe she doesn't like to talk about."

"You forget I know none of these people."

"You will. You could be right. After all, I'm perfectly aboveboard as long as they sign the agreement. An honest and upright citizen: that's me."

"That'll be the day." I nudged my friend. My turn to tease.

"You know it." He favored me with a particularly sunny grin. "Come on. Let's go fleece some sheep."

He'd gotten far enough ahead of me that he missed my wince. I really didn't want to be a part of cheating anyone . . . even though I was pretty sure I now was.

THREE

DASH

Rose and I both straightened when the double doors opened. The man who came to welcome us to Prophecy Week wasn't, of course, the Sun God, but he was a pretty good stand-in. Caucasian, late-twenties, unusually tall (I'm six-foot-two, and he would tower over me), extremely fit. Blond hair worn in a dramatic, rippling mane. Blue eyes. He wore embroidered golden robes open over a white shirt and pants.

This guy was seriously into manscaping. *Yep. Here's the master of the con, come to see if he's reeled in any fish.*

People gasped. Even Rose sputtered an impressed "Jeez!" A spontaneous round of applause broke out.

He favored his acolytes with a blinding smile. "Welcome, my friends. I am Phoebus Apollon, the leader of Prophecy Week. Please come into the Hall of Mysteries for our welcoming ceremony."

We followed him into the "Hall of Mysteries," which was a plain old meeting room with a stage at one end. Native American textiles of indeterminate origin hung from the walls, and large windows looked out on a green valley ringed by mountains. Dust motes drifted in the afternoon sunlight. Hard to imagine a space less likely to be called the Hall of Mysteries, but the guests crowding in behind us saw what they'd been told to see. They were excited and eager.

I was now in range of whatever electromagnet had been used on me in the lobby. My skin had a faint hum. Not painful. It made me aware of my body. I looked around. No one else reacted visibly.

Once we'd all filed in, Phoebus Apollon (a name I dimly remembered from high school English class. A unit on Greek mythology?) stood before us and gestured to one side. "We have an unplanned treat," he said, and the silver-haired woman stepped forward to stand beside him.

"I will do a reading," she said. Phoebus nodded at her encouragingly. "Him." She pointed to me, and the crowd drew back as if she had a laser and they didn't want to get hit. The electromagnet's pull increased.

Phoebus looked at me and then at her. "Of course, Priestess. If the celestial spheres call to you, who are we to deny them?"

The celestial spheres. The guy had the patter down, no doubt. I admired his glib ease.

"Sir, will you come forward?" He stepped down to escort me.

Though unwilling, I was urged forward by those around me.

"Go!" cried Kimber. "That's the Moonglow Mystic! You have to hear what she says!"

Kimber had the eyes of a fanatic. How many prophecies made by the Moonglow Mystic had failed to come to pass, forgotten in the glow of the one lucky guess? If Kimber and her husband wanted to believe someone had a line to the beyond, it wasn't for me to disabuse them.

But now it was Kimber's husband who nudged me forward. "Go on," he said. "I know you don't believe. I didn't either. Give her a chance."

Reading the room, Rose saw the inevitability. "Yes, honey. The spheres are speaking, and you'd better listen."

I glared at her but moved into the showmanship radiance of

Phoebus Apollon. He put a benevolent hand on my shoulder to usher me onto the stage.

Phoebus gazed upon the crowd. His honey-rich voice filled the room. The guy had professional training.

"My brothers and sisters, I have a welcome planned for you and a blessing, and I want to introduce this year's prophets"—he gestured to a man and four women standing near the stage—"but our plans are as nothing in the face of great destiny."

The man had a tremendous stage presence. He was easy in his skin and held their attention effortlessly. Everyone standing within his gaze nodded seriously. Great destiny. Got it.

He went on. "Evadne Nym, the Moonglow Mystic, has been called to make a reading. We cannot know which gods will speak through her or which voices from beyond are clamoring for her attention. But we stand in testament to her uncanny and occult powers. Will you hear her?"

They would. Clearly, they would.

He turned to me. "Brother, tell me your name."

The name slipped from my mouth. I've been undercover before. "Dash Williamson."

"Thank you, Dash, and welcome. May you find peace and acceptance here. You are in the presence of Evadne, the Moonglow Mystic. I leave you in her very good hands, but I won't be far. Know that when you are with me, you are always safe. Do not fear what you learn."

The man gave the mystic an encouraging pat on the shoulder and a significant nod. She watched him without moving. Then he had the cojones to raise his hand to me in some modified blessing. I resisted rolling my eyes as he stepped off the stage and stood in front of the room. His boots were as snowy-white as the rest of his outfit (whatever wasn't gold), with suspiciously thick white soles. Why would a guy that tall want to appear taller still?

I gave myself a mental shake. The man was mesmerizing, but not my target. I wasn't here for con men and false prophets.

Still, standing on a stage wasn't exactly helping me blend into the background. I'd definitely lost control of the situation.

Phoebus nodded to me from the audience, arms crossed over his mighty chest, to witness the miracles of the spheres.

Or whatever.

But I forgot him. I even forgot the counterfeiters when I turned to Evadne. She still stared at me, and whoever controlled the magnet must have dialed it up to ten. All the hairs on my body rose. It was almost maddening. The fillings in my teeth hummed.

"Face me, please, Dash," she said. I turned. The audience was rapt and silent. "Hold your hands out. Palms up."

She demonstrated the pose, and I copied it. She stepped in and cupped her hands under mine—and at the contact, the magnet suddenly shut off. The pulling sensation stopped, and a wave of intense relief and gratitude washed over me.

I shook my head to clear it. Had to give props to this con. They were pulling all the right strings to make me trust that this woman deserved her place in the Hall of Mysteries. Heck, give her a nice penthouse in the celestial spheres.

She closed her eyes, breathing slowly and deeply. Her calm was deceptive. Her hands trembled lightly under mine. Scared? Anxious? Wound too tightly?

She said nothing for a length of time that tightened my neck muscles as the situation became awkward. Well, *more* awkward. Then she whispered to me much too quietly for anyone else to hear, "You are the most honorable man I've ever met."

I startled and tugged on my hands, but her grip tightened. The assembled masses leaned in to hear better—what had she said? They whispered to each other to see if their neighbor had caught it, and distantly I admired the theater. Interest was now at a fever pitch.

And what a smart opening. Who didn't want to think of themselves as honorable? Who didn't start out believing in their own goodness until life proved the opposite? She'd startled and flattered me, setting me up for whatever was to come. After a long career in law enforcement, I despaired of lawbreakers—but I wasn't indifferent to the artistry in a skillful con. And between them, ethereal Evadne and movie star Phoebus Apollon were pulling out all the stops. I wanted to applaud, but my hands were being held in long, slightly chilled fingers that trembled no longer.

And then she opened her eyes and spoke in a carrying voice, "There's something in your pocket that makes you unhappy."

She nodded to my hip, and I had to smile. Nice try. I gave back nothing.

"Not enough to convince you?" She assessed me with a look and tried again. "When you were young, you spent time with . . . what was it?"

I knew this fishing technique. She would offer an open-ended question and then read my body language, measure the movements of my hands, watch the microexpressions on my face until she identified something that would lead her to the next suggesting question. Onward and onward until I unwittingly led her to an answer she could not have known any other way. FBI agents should be as skilled as the best cons when it came to interrogation.

And none of this had anything to do with the counterfeiting case.

But her gaze was hard to break. She continued fishing.

"It was someone—no, some*thing* important. So important. You were . . . oh, about fourteen years old. A boy on the edge of manhood."

Her focus was intense. If she read a microexpression on my face, it was the hint of a grin. *Keep trying, lady. You're making the audience slobber in delight.*

And then she ripped out my sanity and tossed it on the floor.

"Was it an eagle? An American bald eagle?"

FOUR

DASH

I YANKED MY HANDS AWAY FROM THE MOONGLOW MYSTIC and backed up. "What the hell." I didn't even realize I was still retreating until I walked into Phoebus. He'd come onstage, silent in his deceptive, white boots, and he stopped me with a hand on my shoulder.

"Safe to say she's right about the bald eagle?" he asked kindly, a smile in his voice. He didn't need an answer. No one needed an answer. My shock proved she'd uncovered something hidden in my past. "Our Moonglow Mystic is quite remarkable, isn't she?"

I wanted to wake up. My mind was frantic, trying to figure out how she could have known.

In the audience, Rose wore an uneasy smile, and her brows were drawn into a V. She telegraphed her question to me as the others watched. *True?*

Defeated, I nodded.

Collectively, the audience sighed in satisfaction. Prophecy Week had proven its worth once more.

Phoebus put a sheltering arm around Evadne. "Is there more, gracious one?"

She looked at me. "There is. But the gentleman isn't ready to hear more now." Slim, fragile, and proudly upright, she watched me still—but now without the steel-hard intensity or the zing of electricity surging under my skin.

He gestured toward the steps. I found I was obediently leaving the stage, my head still spinning. A few arms reached out to stop me, but I held up a hand to forestall them and joined Rose.

Phoebus went through his welcome speech, but Rose and I were whispering, and more people listened to us than to him.

"What the hell, Dash?" she hissed, linking her arm with mine in wifely fashion.

"I don't know."

"So it's true? You had a bald eagle when you were a kid?"

"Well, sort of." I shushed her and gestured to Phoebus. We'd listen to his greeting, and I'd take a moment to calm down. There had to be a way for the seer to know. There was no such thing as mysticism.

Because that was not a random coincidence. No one stumbled on the idea of a bald eagle in a young boy's life. This wasn't a vague presentiment of cancer in a woman from the right demographic range.

This was disturbingly specific.

Phoebus had a greeting ceremony and a blessing set up and he went through the motions (burning sage was the least annoying part), which gave me time to piece together some kind of theory.

When my boss had assigned me to this joint task force with the Secret Service, he'd asked what I wanted my name to be. Undercover, I stuck with my first name whenever possible. It avoided the glaring mistake of not responding when someone called you. I'd said I was born Dash Williamson, and that would do. So Rose Bennett and I became Mr. and Mrs. Dashiell Williamson of Bethesda, Maryland—one CPA, one personal trainer.

I was fifteen when my mother married for the second time to Carl Ashwood. My mother and stepfather let me choose: Did I want to stay Dash Williamson? Or did I want to change my name to the far more annoying Dash Ashwood?

By then, I loved Carl Ashwood. More, I was disgusted by my father, by then into the second year of a twelve-year sentence for child pornography. He'd only printed the filth in his shop, but he knew what he was doing and deserved his prison sentence. I ditched his name gladly, even if my new name made for some pretty ugly teasing at school. But before they'd married, during the summer when I was fourteen . . .

. . . when I'd been shattered and hurt by my father's incarceration and my parents' divorce . . .

. . . I'd volunteered at the Red Rocks Canyon Natural Conservation Area. And possibly because the rangers knew I needed something to focus on, I'd been one of the kids allowed to help rehabilitate an eagle caught in a poacher's snare.

I named the eagle Trap. I feared him. We all did. You couldn't look into the eyes of a bird that big, couldn't look at raptor claw talons and a fierce hooked beak, couldn't acknowledge the undeniable wildness in an eagle and not feel fearful respect. But I was drawn to him too. And although we followed the naturalist's orders to ensure we didn't accustom this massive bird of prey to humans, Trap somehow took to me.

On the day he was released, I didn't cry. I was fourteen; of course I didn't cry. But watching those mind-blowingly large wings unfurl and carry that bird to freedom raised a lump in my throat. I was glad for his recovery, but I sure did miss him in my life. Another prop in my universe had been withdrawn.

Until the afternoon I came home from school and found a large bald eagle in the tree in my suburban front yard.

There was no doubt it was Trap. I knew every missing feather on that bird. He hung around my house for weeks. A few days in and uncertain how to handle an offering of friendship from something as wild as lightning, I bought a whole fish at the grocery store after school and walked home in the glaring Las Vegas sun. I brought my offering to Trap, who sat as usual in a small tree that made him look even more impossibly large. I unwrapped the fish. He turned his predator eyes on me, and my scalp crawled in atavistic reaction.

No neighbors were watching. My sister and brother were elsewhere, absorbing their own misery at the shattering of our family. I took the fish by the tail and flung it as high into the air as I could.

Trap watched the silvery dart of light ascend and did his impossible calculus, figuring the perfect moment to snap his massive wings out and land on air that held him aloft with a grace almost too painful to witness.

He caught the fish neatly and held it for a moment as he stirred the air. Then he dropped it. He wasn't there for food. I felt like he was sending me a message in a language I didn't speak. I hoped he was saying thank you, but I had absolutely no way of knowing.

For weeks, the neighbors were unnerved. Occasionally, a cat would go missing and people would glare at me.

And then, one day in the fall, Trap flew away and didn't return. And I tried not to miss him.

Looking back on it, I decided it was possible some mention of the boy with the eagle visitor might have made it into the local press. It would have been the sort of thing my mother would have saved, and neither she nor I ever saw such a write-up, but it wasn't impossible we missed it.

And some clever con artist could have done some deep research into "Dash Williamson" and found it.

On forty-eight hours' notice.

With thirty-odd other guests on their way in.

I'd come to decide it was possible, if highly unlikely. And that was barely enough to hang my sanity on.

It settled something in me, like an unmade bed had been

tugged aright. I preferred an orderly, understandable life—it was part of what made me a good agent. Things that didn't fit nagged at me. I wanted to solve the unresolved. With that mystery (potentially) settled, I could focus again.

Phoebus was introducing the Prophecy Week psychics.

"As you know, you can buy an in-depth reading with one or more of our mystics. I already have reservations for many of you. Today, you've witnessed the power of the Moonglow Mystic, and I assure you she can read just as deeply into your life. I have several reservations for private readings with her already, so I urge you to tell me as soon as possible. She can only channel for so many people each day."

Next to us, Kimber wore a smug smile. "You have an appointment with her?" I whispered.

"Perry and I both do. I booked them as soon as we heard she would be at Prophecy Week. She's the reason we're here."

The forensic accountant in me stirred. "Do you mind my asking how much?"

She thought I wanted to know because Evadne had impressed me. "I knew you'd become a believer! She's amazing, isn't she? It's five thousand for an hour with the Moonglow Mystic."

Next to me, Rose eavesdropped, and she cursed at the steep price. Phoebus Apollon was definitely making his con pay off.

"It's totally worth the cost," Perry leaned in to whisper. "It could save your life." He looked at Kimber, his heart in his eyes. She ducked her head with a pleased smile.

"I've heard the other mystics aren't as expensive, but they're not proven the way she is either," she said.

A portly businessman—Quentin Somebody from Tallahassee —glared at us for whispering during the presentation, and we fell silent.

"You've already met the lustrous Moonglow Mystic, Evadne Nym." Phoebus let Evadne take her bows to eager applause. She glanced at me as she stepped back, and a shiver ran along my spine.

"Those of you who were here last year will remember the Sunset Soothsayer, Elbert Frothingham-Smythe. Elbert is our phrenologist." Phoebus gestured to the lone man waiting on the edge of the stage, and he stepped forward with a smile. He was cadaverous, with a great deal of forehead and an assortment of baggy clothes. I had a cynical moment to wonder if Phoebus Apollon would have allowed a handsome man to stand onstage with him.

"I will read the bumps on your head," Elbert said in what I was sure was a phony British accent, "and together we will discover what the future holds for you."

The crowd applauded. Elbert clearly had a following. I assumed he was a hair stylist named Dave in the off-season.

"And Sister Annette is here again. The Sybil of the Mists of Time will reach your loved ones beyond the grave."

A plump, angelic woman wreathed in gray curls bustled forward. "With Martine too! She's always with me, and she'll help us speak with those who have gone beyond the veil!"

She looked familiar, but I couldn't place her until Rose struggled unsuccessfully to suppress a giggle. "It's Professor Sprout from the *Harry Potter* movies," she whispered.

Once she said it, I couldn't *not* see it, and I had to hold in my grin.

Professor Sprout the Sybil took her place by the hairdresser.

"Also new this year, I am honored to welcome Madame Zoe, the Romany princess who will read all the mysteries of life in the tender palm of your hand."

The thin young woman who stepped forward was clearly not up to the quality of the others. She had attempted to beef up her drama with a swirl of bright colors and a bold attitude but had been only marginally successful. "Well," muttered Rose, "she's got the eye makeup for the job, at least."

"And also new this year is a powerful practitioner from

Mobile, Alabama. Don't let her powers frighten you—she assures me she uses her power only for good. This is Lady Celeste, the Voodooienne."

Lady Celeste was African American, at least six feet tall, with an impressive presence. She glared at the assembled victims. "I shall cast the bones for you. And maybe more." It seemed as much of a threat as a promise, and the stir of delighted unease in the room was palpable. These people didn't mind being scared as part of the prophecy experience.

"And I," Phoebus intoned, "am the Helios Oracle, in service to the sun and all the orbs of the celestial spheres. For those who wish it, I will read the entrails of a goat or a sheep to divine the supernatural auguries. If you are more tender-hearted, I will seek mystical answers in the wisdom of the Tarot."

So you could pay extra to watch a big blond guy slaughter an animal and make stuff up about the occult truths he divined from the folds of bloody intestines. Jeez. Prophecy Week was a laff-riot of excellent opportunities. I'd bet anything he did his slaughtering shirtless with a dramatic ceremonial knife and a horrified, delighted crowd, possibly with hidden speakers playing mad monks chanting for maximum effect.

"Of course, we don't want you to miss any of the more earthly delights available here at the lovely Triangle-K Ranch, so we promise to be available to you as you enjoy the amenities." He gestured grandly to Bob and Marcia Koenig, smiling near the door. "Go on a trail ride. Try fly-fishing in that fast-moving river —I assure you, it's quite an experience. Shoot some skeet. Don't miss the 'glamping' in Smuggler's Basin to see the northern lights. We'll be right there with you. We'll even go square dancing with you!"

In other words, he'd booked himself to earn some serious cash for Prophecy Week, but the Helios Oracle wanted a vacation too. Even con men needed a break. I shook my head in admiration.

"Much will be revealed this week, and lives will be changed.

Welcome, my friends." He wound up for a powerful conclusion and sent his voice thundering into the space. "Welcome to Prophecy Week!"

The con man was skillful. I wasn't here for him or his crew of fortune-tellers—but let them put one foot out of line, and I'd be ready to haul him in. Watching him put a possessive arm around the Moonglow Mystic, I thought I might even enjoy it.

FIVE
EVADNE

"HOLD IT TOGETHER FOR A WHILE LONGER, MY GIRL," Phoebus breathed in my ear as he turned me to face the onrushing crowd. "You were brilliant."

Hands reached out to touch him. Some of them hoped to touch me too. My heart rate increased. No chance of staying quiet, of going unobserved.

Phoebus nudged me behind him and gave a look to Elbert, who drew me back as Phoebus focused on charming his guests.

"Impressive," the Sunset Soothsayer said as he guided me to the nearest wall. That way, at least people could only come at me from the front. "You're extremely skillful."

Elbert, a disbarred lawyer who now "read" the bumps on peoples' heads, looked at me with respect. I'd met him and the other prophets when we'd arrived the day before. Elbert was second-in-command at Prophecy Week, and while the boss pressed the flesh, he took over directing the troops.

"Madame Zoe, I want you to meet Hal and Audrey. They were here last year, and I know they'd love to hear about your palm reading." Elbert plucked faces from the crowd to ensure each prophet spoke to someone. "Milt and Oscar—how nice to see you again. Let me introduce Lady Celeste."

He'd thinned out the people clustered around me, but hands still reached out. I slammed down my internal filters and murmured as calmly as I could, "Greetings. Yes, welcome. Nice to meet you, too, Cheri. How do you do? Thank you. Thank you."

I had to overcome my fear of crowds, or of the sensory over-load I experienced in crowds. I'd agreed to help my friend and I needed the money, and now was not the time to agonize over the moral failings of deciding to support a con man.

So I maintained the Moonglow Mystic persona—cool, distant, serene. Like the moon, even though I was sweating and my fingernails were carving crescents into the palms of my hands.

The lawman—Dash—stood on the fringes of the crowd. I couldn't help but notice him. He and the woman he was with watched everything.

After an eternity, Phoebus clapped his big hands together. "My friends, we thank you for your enthusiasm. It's time for you to get settled in your cabins and for the prophets to join me in an occult and sacred ceremony of purification. We will meet you tonight at dinner. Yes, that's at six here in the main lodge. No, I'm afraid our ceremony must be private. Yes, absolutely. Thank you. Blessings upon you."

Through a combination of his outspread arms and the force of his will, he herded the guests out of the room and closed the doors behind them. Then he turned to the five of us, and the silence in the space was an immense relief.

Phoebus put his finger over his mouth to remind us to remain silent and gestured to Elbert to close the curtains. The light-filled room plunged into gloom and sunbeams on the red curtains created an eerie, hellish light.

"Annette," Phoebus whispered, and the plump woman pulled back a corner of the curtain to watch the path beyond.

"They're leaving now." From her perch, she could see both

paths to the cabins, spread in a wide V along the valley floor. "Stragglers, but they're mostly . . . yeah. We're clear."

"Okay. We'll give them time to settle in, and then we'll see what we can find out."

Part of the setting-up chores yesterday had involved leaving welcome kits in each of the cabins. Bob and Marcia (the innkeepers at the Triangle-K) thought that was charming, and so they let Phoebus have a master key. They were blithely unaware Phoebus and Elbert had delivered the kits of healing crystals, a sage smudge, incense, and river stones "to cleanse the mind" while also installing small microphones affixed to the lamps. Voice-activated recorders waited in the cabin Phoebus shared with Elbert, and our "ceremony of purification" would take the form of earbuds in and notepads on our knees.

Electronic eavesdropping crossed a line with me. After a lifetime of knowing far more about people than I should, I valued privacy. But this was how Phoebus made his living. This was how the others (and I) would get through the year. And although I needed no bugs in guest cabins, it wasn't for me to instruct the others on moral behavior.

I was here to help. I was here to profit. I would do my part and quell my misgivings. For once, my "gift" would work to my advantage.

I stiffened my resolve.

"All right," Phoebus said. "We can leave now. Meet in my cabin in twenty minutes."

We emerged, blinking in the strong light. Wild, open, empty air rushed into my lungs. I had a sudden vision of sprouting wings—eagles' wings?—and leaping up and out, soaring free and alone over the meadows and the river and then up over the palisades of gray rock that formed a wall far ahead of us, evidence of some ancient geological disaster.

Celeste's voice pulled me back to earth. She and I shared a cabin, and she'd been pacing me as I walked on autopilot down the path toward the barns. "Your reading was intense. You're good at this. Why were you so scared?"

I'd met the "Voodooienne" the day before with the others and had felt a surprising kinship with her. Under different circumstances—if I didn't know what I'd always known—we could have been friends.

"I've never done this before. I told you."

"Yeah, but you had that guy in the palm of your hand. Ha." She laughed at herself and held out her hands, mirroring the position I'd used to read Dash. "Literally—and figuratively. Why don't you do this all the time? You'd make a fortune."

Her admiration was open and sincere. "Has it made you a fortune?" I asked, knowing the answer.

"I'm good, but I'm not that good, little one." She chuckled and I smiled, particularly at being called *little one*. I'm quite tall for a woman, but Celeste towered over me. "If you're not running a game, then how do you spend your days?"

I made a face. My resumé was nothing to be proud of, but there was no malice in Celeste's question, so I gave her an honest answer. "Okay. Let's see—I did medical transcriptions in Elk City, Oklahoma. Before that, I was a dog walker in Las Cruces, New Mexico. A home health aide in Gilbert, Arizona. I did park maintenance in the Kofa National Wildlife Refuge—"

She cut me off. "How far back are you going?"

I did the calculation. "About half a year. Maybe more."

"What's wrong with you? Why have you got to be moving around like that?"

I reached out to her and again found no malice, only curiosity.

"That thing I did with the guy? The Eagle Guy? Sometimes I forget and attract attention. I do readings like that with other people, which usually leads to people freaking out and me getting fired." It also led to me losing friends or being the subject of terrifying fixations, so often that I generally didn't try to make friends. *Stay below the radar. Don't get noticed.*

"Shit," she said succinctly. "So it's real? It's not a con?"

I shrugged. She'd make up her own mind about me eventually.

"Well, why now? How come you're in on Prophecy Week this year?"

My worries bubbled up, and I answered her more frankly than I should have: "Because I'm flat broke. Because my last two bosses refused to pay me severance. Because I deserve to make some money, too, and if people are stupid enough to pay for this crap, then for once, I'm not going to lay low. *I'm* going to take advantage of *them*!"

My voice had risen as we stepped onto the porch of our cabin. Each building housed a pair of suites, and I realized too late the empty suite next to ours was now filled with Prophecy Week guests. And—just my luck—the door to the connecting suite was open.

And who had stepped through that door and onto the porch, watching Celeste and me with intent focus?

Of course. A tall and lanky man who moved with quiet strength. Dark hair worn conservatively, dark eyes set deep in a handsome face, a mobile mouth that had quirked easily into unconscious skepticism as I'd held his hands in mine and then opened in astonishment when I told him what I'd learned.

It was the lawman. And there was no doubt he'd heard me.

"Hey, Eagle Guy," Celeste said, braving her way through the awkwardness. "Are you our new neighbor?"

SIX

DASH

I NARROWED MY EYES IN CONTEMPT. I'VE SEEN IT AGAIN AND again across my law career: money was always the driving motivator. I'd let her act fool me, but now the silver woman's words reminded me: every con artist worked the same way. They distracted you from what you should have been looking at. And what I needed to focus on were not the mystical purveyors of knowledge of the spheres, no matter how beautiful or theoretically magnetic.

"Yes," I said coldly to the Moonglow Mystic and Lady Celeste, "we're neighbors. If you'll excuse me." I left them on the porch and closed the door.

The suite was luxurious. A woodstove stood out into the room with a stovepipe chimney, the functional heat source for when cabin residents realized the stone fireplace looked good but didn't warm the place up much. The plush, king-sized bed meant my wife and I wouldn't have to sleep like sardines in a can. And the lavish bathroom featured a massive tub, as well as a walk-in shower. A large window over the tub opened onto the dense pine trees lining the endless driveway. A card with the password assured us the Wi-Fi would reach most of the way through the ranch property.

I did my sweep for implanted listening devices and almost immediately found a low-quality microphone attached to the lamp by the bed. I silently pointed it out to Rose, who nodded. No surprise. The question was: Who was listening?

Was it counterfeiters bugging the rooms on the off chance some guest was looking for something more than trail rides and fortune-telling?

Or was it the con artists who had arrived at the ranch the day before with plenty of time to plant bugs in the cabins of those they hoped to fleece? I'd take a walk around the ranch, earbuds in, listening to which cabin received the transmitter's signals, but I was betting it came from one building away, where Phoebus Apollon lay his golden head.

We'd find out.

I sent our initial report by encrypted email to Owen and the counterfeiting joint task force. His reply was swift. Condensed, it essentially said, "Glad you've arrived. Ready to accept the mentoring post?"

Christ. I refuse to be put out to pasture. I'm not that old yet. Back off, Owen.

Rose caught my wince and asked what was going on. I shook my head at the microphone in the lamp, using it as an excuse to avoid telling her about Owen's offer.

Before we'd left for Wyoming, my boss Owen had told me what he passed off as good news: I was being offered a director-level position with a new focus on teaching more-experienced agents how to be better mentors to younger partners.

Owen couldn't understand my reluctance. "This is a natural for you, Dash. Every partner you've had, you've mentored into an outstanding agent."

Except for Owen's own son, Rhys—my partner until he decided to quit the Bureau. He was now legal counsel to several nonprofits, painting every day, and over his head in love with his girlfriend—soon-to-be wife, unless I missed my guess. I hadn't thought Owen resented my part in that romance, but maybe he had.

"Your skills make you a real asset," Owen had said, and I had seen no revenge in his eyes. "And now we want you to teach those skills to others."

I couldn't help the question that had slipped out: "Then is this because of my optometrist report?"

Owen had looked at me in surprise. "The reading glasses?"

"You're taking me out of the field because I can't see, right?"

He hadn't masked his scorn. "Did I miss something? Is there anything wrong with your distance vision?"

"No. Still perfect."

"Can you hit the minimum distance target at the shooting range?"

"Quite a bit farther than the minimum."

"Then shut up about the reading glasses. Everyone goes through it. Get over yourself. Be proud, Dash. This is a good deal for you. You want to take this job."

I'd asked for some time. I knew he thought I was too old to stay in the field. Too old to be trusted with the responsibility of investigations.

And that meant I was too old to repair all the other aspects of my life I'd always meant to find time for: buying a house instead of renting an apartment, maybe getting a dog.

Finding someone to settle down with.

I would die alone.

I sighed, foolishly speaking out loud. "Bifocals."

Rose laughed. "Reading glasses," she corrected. "You don't need bifocals, old man. You can see everything else perfectly well."

This was probably my last field investigation, and I was spending it with an annoyingly perky cheerleader in the middle of the damned wilderness.

I straightened my spine. If this was my swan song, I would go out in style, aware of my surroundings and alert to all details.

Rose got our equipment settled and out of sight, including securing our service weapons. I held out my phone, which included an app to track the receiver for the listening device in our room. "Let's unpack, honey, and then take a walk. I want to see more of the Triangle-K."

"Good idea, sweetie. I'll be ready in a jiffy."

It wasn't long before we strolled up the wide path away from the barns, Rose's hand clasped cozily in mine. I tucked the earbuds away after the app confirmed a veritable storm of signals all went to the next cabin. I was confident Phoebus Apollon was indeed huddled over headphones and picking up anything he could use to con his wealthy patrons.

We'd studied the satellite photos. We knew the ranch layout of main lodge, cabins and bunkhouses, barns and stables. A second barn behind the lodge served as a large garage for the ranch's many vehicles, big enough to hide twenty Ferraris (the vehicle most counterfeiters can't seem to resist). A gas pump was visible in aerial photos, indicating an underground storage tank.

The property had other buildings, but based on wear patterns on the paths and roads, they were less- or little-used.

"The counterfeiting operation could be anywhere," Rose said quietly, taking advantage of being alone on the path to speak openly about our mission. "Anywhere big enough for a large offset press."

I corrected her. "Inkjet and LaserJet printers would do it if you know what you're doing. All you need is electricity and a Staples card."

"And privacy." She waved to a pair of guests enjoying the afternoon on their porch. "It's beautiful here." Rose was obedient to her training, observing without assuming. I ran my own assessment, inhaling and again noticing the smell of pine and grasses warmed by sunshine and the low dust we kicked up under our feet.

"Hm," I replied shortly.

"What?" She grinned at me. "You don't like it here?"

"It's beautiful." And it was. It just wasn't what I was used to. No Uber or Lyft. No subway system. The distance to the nearest Starbucks measured not in minutes or miles, but in tanks of gas. Why people lived outside a city was beyond me. The Triangle-K was both peaceful and alien—tranquil and unknown.

"Go on." She suppressed a laugh. "What's your problem?"

I made a face. "There could be timber rattlers coiled up in the grass over there. Or moose in that forest. Or . . . I don't know." Now Rose laughed at me openly. "You can't see the threats out here. This is not where I'm comfortable."

"Oh, you are such a Western hero!" she hooted. "What a brave man!" I didn't mind her teasing. From a distance, we would look like any loving couple. "You know there are bears out there," she challenged.

"Oh. Well, see? That's my point. What kind of bears? Cuddly teddy bears? Yogi Bear? Smokey the?"

"Big Billy, they call him. I heard about him on the bus. Grizzly."

"Grizzly!" I gestured, feeling this alone should make my point. "I'm going to need an elephant gun!"

She now laughed so hard we earned answering smiles from the "friends" in suite ten (Milt and Oscar. I was pretty sure they were a couple, but if they wanted to be friends in conservative Wyoming, I didn't care). Bob Koenig was chatting with them on their porch, and he said his good-byes and joined in Rose's laughter as he came to join us.

Excellent. Our best avenue of investigation had ambled up for a chat.

"It's Dash and Rita, isn't it?" he asked, beaming.

"Rose." She smiled. They shook hands.

"I'm sorry. I promise I'll have all the names down by tomorrow. You look like you're having a good time already."

"Rose was telling me lies about grizzly bears around here," I said. Bob offered another warm laugh. "Well, not around here.

Bears don't much like people unless they leave garbage lying around, and we never do. But up in the mountains?" He gestured vaguely with a sweeping arm that took in all the forest-covered hills around us. "Yep, sure."

I winced. He waggled his eyebrows.

"They were reintroduced into the Bitterroot, over in Idaho. We've had one or two come this far east. It's a good sign, you know. Means our habitats are healthy."

"Healthy. I'm sure." I was unconvinced.

"Don't you worry, Dash." He chucked me on the shoulder. "We'll keep you and Big Billy far apart from each other. The way you both want it!"

"He's really named Big Billy?"

"That's what the hands call him. They've seen signs of him up by Smuggler's Basin."

The name was disturbingly familiar. "Smuggler's Basin is where you do your glamping, isn't it?"

He and Rose were having a wonderful time laughing at me. "You betcha! But don't worry. We know how to bearproof the place. You're safe, young man. You have my word on it."

Great. I'd be sure to tell Big Billy that while he mauled me. What was the matter with a mugger? Street toughs? A roving gang? Those I could handle.

"I'm a city boy," I said. "It's going to take a while to make me comfortable out here."

"You'll change your tune, my friend. I'll ask you at the end of the week, and then you can tell me!"

"Great." I mustered a fake smile, and they laughed at me all the harder. Then Bob slightly angled himself so he blocked Rose. "And maybe you and I can talk about those macros for NetSuite?"

Rose rolled her eyes with an audible huff because that was the role she was to play, and I straightened and offered a real grin. (And really—whether it would give me access to ranch records or not, accounting would always beat bears as a topic of conversation for me.)

"Anytime! But you don't want to get them from me. Ask your accountant. I'm sure he or she will have them."

Bob brushed my statement away. "I only use that guy at tax time. I'd like to hear what you have to say."

"You run this place on your own? Without an accountant to back you up?" This was a weakness we'd identified early. Bob was not a particularly astute businessman, and the joint task force was interested in how his records measured up to projected expenditures. It was easy to make a mistake amid the enthusiasm of printing your own hundred-dollar bills.

"I do okay. At least, I thought I did! I didn't know about any macros and new tax laws, though. And I sure would like to do what I can to avoid sending my hard-earned money off to the feds, you know?"

Rose had wandered off to examine a cluster of wildflowers so her eye-rolling wouldn't bring this productive conversation to an early end. I was proud of her for how neatly she played her role.

"Well, call your accountant. Ask him for the macros. He'll help."

"How about you do it for me? I'll knock a hundred off your room for a night."

I smiled. "You don't want to give a stranger access to your accounts, Bob. Let the guy you know and trust do it."

"I want you."

Either Bob was innocent, or he was an idiot. If we hadn't had excellent reason to suspect the Triangle-K as the source of the funny money turning up across the United States, I'd have gone with innocent.

I feigned capitulation. "Tell you what—I'll email you a client contract. You look it over. If you're okay with it, you can autosign it and give it back to me. I'll charge you the friends-and-family rate of one hundred fifty dollars an hour." I eyed him pointedly to let him know I was upping his offer of money off our room rate.

"How long will it take?" Now he and I were shrewd negotiators, which put him on comfortable ground.

"I won't know until I get a look at your books. But I won't go over two hours without clearing it with you first."

"And I can pay by discounting your room rate?"

I stuck out a hand. "Deal."

He shook mine firmly and Rose offered a huff of annoyance.

"Dash—really? Another client? Can you not give it a rest?"

Bob and I exchanged a commiserating look, and I turned to guide her down the path.

"Bears." I pointedly changed the subject as Rose and I moved away from Bob. "Very large bears. And psychics. What else are you going to spring on me? Are you expecting a renaissance fair? Maybe some Civil War reenactors?"

Rose snorted. We teased each other until we were well out of hearing range. "You got it?" she asked quietly.

"Bob is about to sign a seven-page contract he's not going to read." As the psychics could tell us, the fine print details made all the difference in contracts. "Any judge on the planet will agree he's signing over full access to his computer files. And then we'll see what we can see."

"Even if we need our little folding reading glasses to see it." Her smirk was a sharp dagger to my heart. I'd forgotten once again that I was aging rapidly and probably growing a vigorous case of arthritis as we strolled along.

"Shut up about it, will you?"

She nudged me. "You did good, old man."

I shook my head. "Your turn now. Keep your eyes open for opportunities to talk with the staff. You're going to be great at this."

She nodded, but her brow creased in a frown. "It's hard for me when I've been treated as a cute little thing all my life. No one has ever thought of me as a badass. You sure I shouldn't change my name?"

"Your name is fine. And you want to be sweet and friendly. A badass would raise suspicions. You'll get to your natural authority. Don't rush it. Experience will help with that."

This time her nod was vigorous. "My instructor at Quantico said you were the best partner to get and I was lucky. I should learn from you."

Her instructor had thrown me repeatedly on the same hip the last time I went back to refresh my hand-to-hand combat skills. He was a lethal son of a bitch, but I appreciated his good recommendation.

Even if it did remind me my bosses wanted to lock me to a desk in DC and train others how to do the job I thought I'd been doing pretty well.

Focus, Dash.

We waved to guests we'd met on the bus. Kimber and Perry were enjoying their noncancerous state on their porch rockers, and twelve-year-old Melanie had gotten into the stream to her knees as her older brother, phone still in hand, looked on. They were the only kids at Prophecy Week, brought by parents with (I thought) too much money and not enough sense.

"Oh, God, this water's freezing!" Melanie shrieked happily. "Come on, Skip! You gotta try it!"

"Yeah—no," he said in feigned disinterest, but he was still more "boy" than "cool teen." It wouldn't be long before he put the phone down and tested how much freezing water he could endure. I remembered that age—from painfully long ago.

And then the kids spotted us.

SEVEN

EVADNE

WE'D BEEN SUMMONED BY OUR MYSTERIOUS LEADER. PHOEBUS had convened the Sacred Convocation of Soothsayers in the Inner Sanctum (which meant the suite he shared with Elbert).

He wrapped it in mystery, and the guests loved it. He managed to imply we would be prostrate before our gods, breathing hallowed, purple smoke and interpreting messages from voices whispering on the wind.

In fact, we interpreted messages from voices on Phoebus's bank of digital recorders. The six of us, earbuds in, hunched over notepads or laptops, taking notes on the conversations recorded in each room as the guests moved in.

It was creepy listening to people. People rarely say, "I hope no one discovers we buried Aunt Maude's emeralds under the azaleas." Mostly they say, "Did you pack the antacid?" and, "Shit, my shampoo is all over this suitcase," and, "Are you really going to wear that?" Things that not only should I not hear, but things I don't want to know.

But last year's veterans (Phoebus, Elbert, and Annette) listened industriously, and Celeste and Zoe tried to keep up. I was in this too far to object now.

The new kids had been assigned returning visitors because

Phoebus said they already knew enough about those people and our inexperience wouldn't cost much knowledge. The only exception was that I'd been assigned to listen in on Kimber and Perry. Phoebus knew she'd made her reservations because I'd told her to get checked for cancer last year when she came into the veterinary clinic where I'd been working.

She'd been dogging my steps ever since, following me from job to job, eager to thank me, as well as make sure she was all right after her treatment. She and Perry were in their cabin, keeping each other calm and telling each other they were sure Kimber's doctor had gotten all the cancer. I already knew I had good news for them.

Phoebus kept a helpful eye on the newcomers, particularly watching over Zoe, who gamely noted every word spoken by her assigned couples.

Celeste was the last to finish her review. Phoebus gaveled our meeting to order.

"At dinner tonight—who's got that seating chart? Ah, thank you, Elbert. All right. You're going to be at table one, Zoe. Also at your table is Oscar of Milt and Oscar. Who's got them?"

"That's me," Annette peeped. Even away from paying customers, her voice was high and childlike. "Oscar's easy. He and Milt are a married couple, but they're keeping that quiet as long as they're in Wyoming, so whatever you do, don't refer to Milt as Oscar's husband."

Zoe nodded and took notes.

Annette went on, "Oscar is launching a new business. You remember, Phoebus—he was worried about it last year."

Phoebus, who never forgot anything, nodded. "Online consignment shops for those who want to dress like the one percent. Good business plan."

"Well, he got investors, and now he's launching it. He wants to know if it will be a success."

Again, Zoe wrote it down. Phoebus smiled at her indulgently.

She couldn't take notes to dinner with her, and she did her best to mask her nerves.

"Don't worry about the notes," Phoebus said. "Listen. Look at his photo in his folder and listen to what Annette is telling you. You don't have to be perfect tonight. Stay as quiet as possible. Silence is mysterious. You'll be fine."

We went through all six tables, each of us giving reports on what we'd learned of our guests. Phoebus got to my table.

"Evadne, you're at table five. You'll have Val and her son Skip, Dan, Scott B., Heather, and Jack."

"Okay," I said.

He consulted the list again. "And at my table will be—"

"Hang on," Zoe interrupted. "What about reports? I can tell you about Heather."

Phoebus shook his head. "She doesn't need our help."

"What?" Zoe was confused. My heart sank. This would be the first sliver of distrust in this tiny community. It would happen time and time again until I stopped trying to be part of a group and just avoided detection. "What do you mean, 'she doesn't need our help?'"

"She'll know everything she needs to know about Heather— about all of them—before they sit at her table." Elbert and Annette watched Phoebus carefully, but they weren't surprised. Phoebus must have explained to them.

Zoe looked at me, as did Celeste. "How? What do you know that we don't?"

The only other person who could have even partially answered that question—my friend Artie, now Phoebus Apollon —was silent. Naturally, so was I.

"I don't get it," Zoe protested to the boss. "I've been listening to these people, and I know stuff that will help. She doesn't want to know it?"

He shook his head. "Let it go, Zoe."

"Let it go?" The Romany princess suddenly had a Jersey

accent. "Why let it go? We're trusting each other here, aren't we? What's the big secret?"

Elbert patted her arm, but she pulled her hand away. "Evadne doesn't need our help. That's all you need to know," he said in his gentle British accent.

"Oh, bullshit." She stood, a tiny woman in a pugnacious pose. "I'm not working a con with someone I can't trust."

"My dear," fluttered Annette.

Zoe rounded on Celeste. "How about you, Other New Girl? Are you down with these secrets too? Life taught you to trust blindly much?"

Celeste regarded me impassively. "I'll hear what the girl has to say for herself, I guess."

Any warmth—any sense of family, no matter how transitional —had fled. The cold winds of reality blew around me. I looked to Phoebus, who shrugged. I sighed and spoke. "That guy I read at the lodge? Dash, the Eagle Guy?" They nodded at me. "He's some kind of policeman." The uneasy shifting almost drowned out my follow-up. "The woman with him isn't his wife. She's his partner."

"Phoebus?" Elbert looked to his leader, who shook his head.

"Evadne doesn't think they're after us. Remember, we've got the clause in the agreement."

"For entertainment purposes only." Elbert nodded. "We should be covered."

"Right."

Zoe was nervous about the presence of law enforcement, but she wasn't ready to let me off the hook. "How do you know they're cops?"

"I know."

"I'm sure. You have no proof."

Here we go. "Zoe," I said, "you're older than you look. Maybe twenty-seven, twenty-eight."

"Oh, great. Maybe you can guess my weight next, and I'll win a Kewpie doll. This is country-fair bullshit. Aren't you going to make me put my hands in yours?" She thrust her hands out, mocking the pose I'd taken with Dash.

"When you were younger—midteens, I'm guessing—your sister drowned in a swimming pool. You were supposed to be watching her."

She jerked back but regrouped. "You could have read that in the newspaper."

"Could I have read you were inside the house when she died, buying weed from the kid who lived there? Was he your boyfriend? No, he was gay. Just a dealer, then."

"How do you—"

"You told us you'd been working out of New York City for the last two years, but that's not right, is it? You were farther north. Syracuse? Funny for someone who hates the cold to spend so much time up there. But if your father's sick, that's where you go, right? Especially if you feel guilty about being the only child now."

I could have been far gentler with her. I could have done the last-night-you-dreamed-about gig. It's as effective at making skeptics into believers and thoroughly shatters any possible friendships without forcing the shocked recipient into a weak collapse back on her sofa. Zoe had dreamed she was onstage, naked. It's classic preperformance anxiety. I could have told her that.

I'd overreacted. Between taking on Prophecy Week and discovering a man who pushed integrity before him like a Mack truck pushes air, I was off-balance.

When Zoe had risen to her feet, she'd changed that feeling of being accepted, and I'd reacted badly. I regretted my words as soon as I finished. But once the toothpaste is out of the tube, no amount of apologizing will get it back in.

This is why the rule is to stay low. Don't get noticed.

"How did you . . ." Zoe couldn't finish her question. Phoebus rested a hand on her shoulder.

"Don't worry about it. It's who she is," he said. "You'll come to accept it. And she'll help you with your readings too. She's quite remarkable."

Zoe looked up to Phoebus as he moved to lean against the bureau again. "There are no such things as psychics. Right? That's not real?"

His response was a raised eyebrow and a long pull on his water bottle. Then he turned to Celeste.

"Any questions from you?"

She held up one long hand. "I've seen stranger things in my time. I'm good."

"Okay, then," Phoebus said. "Zoe, you'll learn you can trust Evadne. You can trust all of us. If you want to be a part of this group, you'll be welcome. But you have to let this go now."

Elbert reached to put a comforting arm around her shoulders, but she shrugged him off. He masked his disappointment. Elbert looked like a scarecrow before the stuffing went in, and he perpetually longed—unsuccessfully—for a little scarecrow sweetie of his own.

She finally raised her eyes to mine. "I can let it go."

"I apologize," I said. "I was too rough."

"That's okay." But her eyes fell again, and I knew things would be prickly between us from now on. Story of my life.

Still, Celeste might become a friend, and I treasured every potential connection I might have.

We finished up our preparations and settled on who would lead the presentation that evening. Phoebus selected Zoe and Celeste, not only because they were new to Prophecy Week and thus of particular interest to the guests, but also to show them he trusted them. Celeste was impassive as usual, but Zoe straightened with a smile.

Phoebus opened the door to usher us out, and I was struck by an inrushing message of confusion. "What is that?" I asked involuntarily.

Annette and Zoe were already out the door. They turned and

looked at me, as did the others. Phoebus was at my elbow quickly.

"What is it? You're pale, Evadne."

I shook my head and stepped away from him. On the porch, I gathered in as much information as I could, but it made no sense to me.

"That's so familiar, but it's wrong . . ." I was so focused on what I sensed that I was blind to the glorious afternoon. "I don't know what that is. But it's strange, Phoebus."

I looked to him, my vision returning. My oldest, best, and possibly only friend—who else would I tell?

"What kind of strange, Evie? Give me something here."

"It's like a door has been opened . . . to . . ." I tried to put words to emotions and came up short. "To the wrong place," was the best I could do.

He relaxed. "Wrong place? What's that mean?"

I shrugged. "I don't know." It was frustrating. The information I got was so familiar, and yet I couldn't place it.

Phoebus didn't care. "Then let's not worry about it yet. I'm sure you'll know if something bad is about to happen, right?" He smiled at me, willing me to relax and move on.

I gave him an automatic smile, and he turned back to the cabin he shared with Elbert. "All right, then. Onward, my friends!"

Zoe and Annette disappeared into their room one door down, and Celeste and I stepped off the porch for the short walk to our suite in the next building.

She had a close eye on me. "It's not all right, is it?"

I felt a burst of gratitude. "It's really not. Something strange is going on here. I think there might be trouble coming."

"Soon? Do we need to get out of here?"

She wasn't doubting me. She was ready to hit the road on my word, and her confidence made me irrationally happy.

"We're okay for now. It's hard to know, though."

She nodded. "Can I help?"

I shook my head.

"Can *anyone* help?" Her question tugged at me. We'd reached our cabin's porch and the door to our suite. Twenty feet further was the door to the suite shared by Dash and Rose. They were gone, but maybe I could wait for them.

I remembered his goodness.

And I remembered his scorn when he'd overheard me admitting I was here to make money off the guests.

"Maybe," I whispered. "At the least, they deserve to know."

EIGHT

DASH

T HEY WEREN'T EXACTLY JUVENILE OFFENDERS, BUT THE TWO youngest guests at the Triangle-K were suddenly youths with a mission. Skip and Melanie abandoned their attempts to drown themselves in the rushing stream and headed toward me. I don't fear kids, exactly (my brother has two, a boy and a girl, and I like them well enough), but these two came at me like they were about to chew out an employee.

"Hey," said fifteen-year-old Skip. "Hey, Eagle Guy!"

This was the first time I saw young Skip with his nose out of his phone. He and his sister, Melanie, had been dragged to Prophecy Week by their parents, Charlie and Val. I'd had a soft spot in my heart for Skip since the bus ride in, when he'd made it clear no one would tell his fortune and how soon before he could go skeet shooting? My kind of annoying teenager.

But after the Moonglow Mystic had ripped my sense of balance out from under me by identifying my past with a bald eagle, Skip came out of his phone to give me the third degree.

"Man, did you used to have an eagle?"

It's hard to get a sense of wonder out of a fifteen-year-old. Kids who spend their time on computers slaughtering aliens, zombies, and other socially approved bad guys don't have a lot of room to be impressed with things in the meat world.

I hedged my answer. "Well, sort of—"

Skip elbowed his younger sister, an automatic gesture she paid no attention to. "What's that mean?"

Several guests had come off their porches to join the gaggle on the path. They'd abandoned any pretense they weren't eavesdropping.

"I helped to rehabilitate an eagle when I was a kid. He liked me."

"So you had a wild eagle as a pet?"

"He liked you?" Melanie was now in on it, elbowing her big brother in her turn to get in front of him. Their scuffling was on autopilot. This was a dance all brothers and sisters performed. "Like *The Jungle Book*? Could he talk to you?" Her eyes were wide.

How did situations with kids get out of hand so quickly? I laughed as I told her no, but clearly, I let her down.

The growing cluster of adults cared less about the bird and more about the reading.

"The Moonglow Mystic—how did she know?"

"That's incredible."

"Is the eagle your spirit animal?"

"I bet it is. I bet the eagle is your spirit animal."

Rose sputtered at that. We did sensitivity training at the FBI, and she knew an unintended microaggression when she heard one. "Spirit animals are sacred to Native American cultures. We shouldn't bandy the term about—"

"Oh! Native American culture! Are any of the prophets from a Native culture?"

"Well, the Moonglow Mystic knew about Dash's eagle. How did she know? Does she do spirit animals?"

"No kidding," Rose protested, "you have to drop the spirit animal idea. It's . . . rude." She might as well have been talking to the blue sky above. They paid no attention.

"I don't know. I don't think so. It didn't say so in the Prophecy Week information. Maybe she'll tell me what my spirit animal is!"

"Could *you* talk to the *eagle?*"

"I want to be a jaguar. Can I be a jaguar?"

"Pretty sure you don't get to choose, honey."

More guests, attracted by the crowd, had joined us, and the excited discussion swelled around us. I had no control over the conversation, and as long as I didn't volunteer anything, the assorted guests were content to throw their questions and comments at each other. Rose realized she'd made no headway against the unwitting abuse of Native cultures and listened to the debates with the air of a dog who couldn't understand the sounds he was hearing.

Melanie tugged at my arm, regaining my attention. "Could the eagle pick you up? Like, fly with you? Could you ride the eagle like a pony?"

Wasn't she too old for these questions? Her brother cut her off before I had to answer. "Jeez, that's stupid. You're stupid, Mel."

His mother shushed him automatically. "Did you feel anything when she did the reading? Did you feel the brush of the afterworld?"

"Did I *feel* anything?"

"Kimber says she felt something last year when the Moonglow Mystic did her reading in her vet's office."

Interesting. Perhaps the con woman had used the electromagnet trick the year before. I searched the crowd and found Kimber heading down the path toward me, Perry at her side.

"Dash!" she said. "Did you feel it? Did you feel when she did your reading?"

"Ah," I hedged. "Maybe? What did you feel?"

She stood in front of me, now the center of attention. She held her hands out, palms up, ignoring the room key she held.

"I was cold. So cold," she said, her eyes going distant. "And she stepped up and put her hands under mine. Like she did for you!" Kimber's eyes flew open in excitement. She nodded to encourage me to nod back and join her in the mysteries. "And then I felt . . . oh, a rush of warmth all the way up my arms! She wrapped me in her aura. It was silver and shone all around me."

The crowd around her sighed.

"Was it like that for you, Dash? Did you feel it too?"

Kimber held my gaze, longing to welcome me into the brotherhood of believers. She was so earnest. So hopeful. If I were a different man, I would have wanted to con her myself because the low-hanging fruit was so easy to pluck.

"I don't know," I said with a weak smile. Not the electromagnet, then. "Maybe?"

The crowd sighed again. My response was enough for them to continue to believe.

Their chatter was now so animated that Rose and I were able to back physically out of the circle and return the way we'd come, leaving the gaggle to exchange stories of the occult without us.

The air was dry; the afternoon was warm. The scene was markedly different from the landscapes I was most familiar with from my childhood of growing up in a Las Vegas suburb or from my recent past, spent either in the glorious confusion of New York City or in the metropolitan sprawl of swampy Washington, DC.

The fields ahead of me were annoyingly green, as if groundskeepers had sprayed them in the night. Mountains were grouped artistically around a vast, flat region where trees popped up in clusters that must have indicated water. The nearest mountain sheared off into stark cliffs, a stony wall to obstinately hold back the sweet rush of civilization beyond the borders.

Or not. We'd driven for two hours from Jackson Hole to get here, and the "rush of civilization" meant diesel palaces for long-distance truckers and the occasional national park entrance.

Wyoming was a whole lot of *nothing*. I didn't have to check my Uber app to know I couldn't catch a ride out of here.

"You need to get over those reading glasses, Dash."

Rose's comment was so intimate, so wifely, that I looked around for whoever was eavesdropping. We were alone on the path.

"Yeah," I said in the way that meant *drop it*.

She didn't. "You're not dying, Father Time. You're, what, thirty-nine?"

"Thirty-eight." She cut me.

"So you're young for reading glasses. It's no big deal. What about Lasik? Can't they correct for that now?"

"They can do one eye for distance and one eye for up close. The brain adjusts, but that's not a good option."

Rose understood. It wouldn't be good for someone who needed to be able to shoot a gun. She gave me a grimace and tucked her arm into my elbow in unspoken support. We continued our walk along a distressingly unpaved path.

The afternoon smelled strange. I could identify the scent of pine and dust but couldn't name the faint tang of some spicy plant. We walked past large log cabins, each housing two suites and a porch with rocking chairs.

An electric gator beeped politely behind us, and we stepped to the side as a so-called cabin girl puttered past us, the storage area filled with fresh linens and extra towels.

"Let's wander to the barn. Maybe meet Wolf before tomorrow's trail ride."

Rose agreed with that idea. "Check out employee parking, see what he's driving—what all the ranch hands are driving when they come to work. Any evidence they have more cash than expected."

Rose and I strolled past the main lodge. Rocking chairs lined a long, rustic porch. Every Cracker Barrel in the United States tried to recreate this scene—or maybe the Triangle-K tried to recreate the Cracker Barrel. I wouldn't admit I regarded the chairs with suspicion, but I would say I'd spent more time on subway benches than rocking on a porch. And that was the way I liked it.

"The printing presses are most likely close to here," I mused quietly. Maybe we'd find them and wrap this up before I had to get on a horse.

NINE

EVADNE

HAVING A ROOMMATE WAS SORT OF LIKE HAVING A FRIEND. Celeste and I sat in the pair of rocking chairs on our side of the porch and watched two ranch hands in the field across the path. They were checking hooves, probably because the trail rides would start the next morning.

We were waiting for Dash and his "wife" to join us.

The quiet was soothing, but I still read something out of place at the ranch. I hadn't noticed anything the day before, nor in the morning. It was probably something that came in on the bus from Jackson Hole with the guests.

Trying to figure out what I sensed was like trying to work a tiny fragment of food out from between my teeth with nothing but my blunt, stupid tongue. I'd give up only to realize a few minutes later that I was at it again, trying to place what I was sensing.

So it came as a great relief when Dash, his partner's hand through his elbow, came down the path from the lodge. But when he saw us, his pace slowed. I could read his suspicion from a distance, and it stung me.

Celeste, rocking beside me, didn't get the same vibe. She

gave out a smile a great deal less alarming than the one she'd visited upon the guests in the Hall of Mysteries.

"Hi, neighbors. Step on up."

"Hi." We introduced ourselves and hands were shaken in civil fashion. Dash's partner was named Rose. She was a cute brunette who looked vaguely familiar. She waited for Dash to take the lead in our chat.

"You already know Evie, of course," Celeste said. "She did quite a reading for you today, didn't she, little man?"

Dash drew himself up to his full height. He was taller than Celeste, but not by much. "Very interesting," he said guardedly. "Well, we were heading to the barns. Maybe meet some horses." No special senses were needed to tell that when Dash said *horses* he meant dangerous *things I'd rather stay away from.*

"Horses are out in the field," Celeste said easily. "See? The hands are checking them now, making sure they're ready for a trail ride tomorrow." The four of us turned to watch distant figures lift massive hooves and examine mouths. "So I can show you around if you want. We got here yesterday, and I've got the lay of the land."

She moved to the railing and pointed with a long arm.

"That's the barn, and then past the paddock are the stables. Next building down is the ranch hands' bunkhouse. And that window there"—she didn't point, but her chin was a clear beacon showing the way—"is where Abbott and Costello live."

"Abbott and Costello?" Rose asked.

"Not their real names, but that's what they call them. Those two are the jokers who think they got the better of me. We'll see about that."

Her tone had gotten colder. She was back to the scary Voodooienne persona. And this time, it was apparently real. Rose raised an eyebrow at Dash.

Then Celeste's mood broke. She grinned at us. "So that's the working end of the ranch. Now I think you might like to hear what my girl Evie has to say."

The turn of conversation was so abrupt that my eyebrows were still in my hairline when the three of them turned to me.

"Oh?" Rose said politely. "About what?"

Dash was silent, but I could read his suspicion and distrust.

"Nothing," I said. He wouldn't believe me anyway. But Celeste wasn't having it.

"Go on, Evie. Tell them what you told me."

It was so easy for her to encourage me. She hadn't had a lifetime of people either mocking me or chasing me for more until my only option was to pack up and move in the middle of the night. Agitated, I stood and took a lap, walking to the far end of the porch and back in an attempt to work up the willingness to be humiliated.

Once again.

When I returned, Dash and Rose both thought I was unbalanced, and they looked their questions to me.

"All right," I said with a sigh. "I know you don't believe in my abilities, and I guess I don't blame you."

"Well," Rose said, "I don't know—"

Dash cut her off. "What do you have to say, ma'am?" he asked me coolly.

I couldn't bear to keep his eye, to face his rejection. I looked down and fought a fidget. "I can sense something . . . strange."

I stumbled to a halt, and Celeste nudged me with her elbow.

"Strange like how, honey?" She nodded at me to encourage me.

Dash and Rose at least still listened, so I heaved a sigh and continued. "Strange like . . . filing cabinets."

They processed that, and then Dash clarified.. "Filing cabinets?"

I shook my head. "I know. It's weird. I can't come up with any better description. It's like a storage cabinet or a supply room. Whatever it is, it's not—" I'd been about to say it wasn't right, but Dash had straightened, his focus on me now like a burden.

"A supply room? Do you mean . . . ink?"

Ah—the fragment of food, the annoying raspberry seed, the tiny flicker of parsley had at last worked its way out of my mental tooth. "That's it exactly! I can sense ink! Thank you!"

"Ink," Celeste said, stumped. "You sense ink? What does that mean?"

"I don't know," I said, watching Dash and Rose, who had a conversation with their eyes. "But maybe you two do?"

Dash took a step forward and his hand came up as if he would hold my arm to restrain me. He pulled back, but not from lack of interest. "What do you mean, you *sense* this? Sense it how?"

I nodded, suddenly tired. "I just do. That's my gift. I can't explain it, and you wouldn't understand if I did."

"Try me."

Celeste came to my rescue. "It's the mystery of the spheres, baby, and not for you to understand. You've got my girl's message to you, and obviously it means something to you. So now she and I are going to go into our room and rest up before dinner. Okay? You got anything more to say, Evie?"

I shook my head.

"Okay, then. You can maybe talk at dinner. Let this go for now." She pushed me into our room and stood before the door, arms crossed like the bouncer in front of a club's VIP section. "I think we're done here."

Dash wondered if he wanted to press the situation, but Rose took his arm. "Come on, Dash. We'll talk to them later. Come on."

He surrendered and let her draw him away, but his eyes promised this would not be the last time we spoke about ink. I definitely wasn't going to be able to fly under the radar with this guy.

TEN

DASH

The barn doors were closed and the large, open paddock (like a forecourt to a wooden castle) was empty. Probably a good thing there was no one around, as my observatory powers were offline.

No agent worth his salt would believe anything a so-called psychic told him.

But how had she known?

Pulling "ink" out of the blue sky was pretty . . . strange. Eerie. Weird.

It's a common failing among novices. You want something to be true so hard you start believing it. You start arranging facts to suit a theory instead of determining a theory based on facts. That's a surefire way to get a court case thrown out.

And now that I thought about it, I was the one to supply the word "ink," not her.

You don't believe the con man—or con woman—when she tells you she senses ink on a ranch, even if you're looking for evidence of a printing operation that can counterfeit astonishingly good facsimiles of US currency.

Rose was deep in thought too. "Maybe she's in on it. Maybe that's how she knows."

"If she was in on it, she wouldn't tell people she could sense ink."

"And what does that mean, she can *sense* ink?"

"Damned if I know."

"Maybe the Secret Service would have some thoughts. When do we meet our contact, the ranch hand?"

"Enrique," I said. "He'll get in touch with us when it's safe. We've got his report, anyway. If he suspects he'd be blowing his cover, he won't check in at all."

We wrestled uselessly with our thoughts until it was time to head to the lodge for dinner. Whether she spoke more to us or not, I'd be keeping an eye on the Moonglow Mystic. She'd suddenly become a part of the larger case.

Rose was mobbed as soon as we walked in the lodge door. Suzette held a phone. John was right behind her. "Excuse me— you're 'Running with Rosie,' aren't you?"

That was fast. Rose had disclosed to me and our superiors that she'd made a series of videos while in college to help a friend be a better runner. The friend had slapped on an opening sequence and made the videos public. Rose had a small but dedicated following, and she'd worried this might blow her cover.

She'd never given any personal information, so we'd included the fact that she was a personal trainer in her cover in case the videos were discovered—as they now had been.

Rose nodded and was soon surrounded by guests interested in her physical regimen. They bombarded her until the arrival of Phoebus, dressed in a crinkly gold shirt and flowing white pants. His feet were bare (in violation, I noted, of health code policies about footwear in dining establishments). Now he was only about three inches taller than me. He'd made his impressive entrance in his platform boots, apparently, and could now appear at a mere six-foot-five.

"Tonight you have assigned seats!" He smiled widely. "We all meet someone new tonight. And every table is hosted by one of our psychics, who will guide the conversation. Please, enjoy your meal!"

Rose had been seated with Lady Celeste. Although I'd hoped to be at Evadne's table, I was with Professor Sprout. I had a moment of panic when I realized I didn't remember her actual name, but a high-energy woman named Heather addressed her immediately as Sister Annette. I relaxed into my seat and let the conversation flow around me.

Eventually, however, Annette turned to me. "And now, let's get to know you, Mr., er, hrm . . ." My name was on display on a tent card easily readable from both sides, but it had rapidly become clear Sister Annette might be able to communicate with a sixteenth-century French waif named Martine, but neither Martine nor Annette could see much farther than her nose.

"Dash," I supplied. "Dash Williamson."

"Oh, Dash!" she said happily. "You're the man with the eagle!"

The other faces at my table were so fixated on me now that I surrendered to the inevitable. Explaining something they clearly didn't want to understand would be swimming upstream—or ignoring the music of the celestial spheres. "Sure," I allowed.

"Lovely!" she said. "You have already communed with the mystic realms. You are in tune with the occult world! Could you pass those biscuits?"

I could.

Basket now in hand, she continued to smile upon me benevolently. "And such an unusual name—Dash. What does it mean?"

She peered at me myopically, a large biscuit clutched in her hand.

"It means my mother was a fan of mystery novels. I was named for Dashiell Hammett."

"Oh, indeed! Touched by mystery from the first!" The table *ooh*ed, pleased with Professor Sprout's deft turn. "And have you brothers or sisters?"

"One of each," I said.

"Wait!" she cried with instinctive drama. "Martine wants to guess!"

She held one finger imperiously aloft and listened to the air. The table hushed in anticipation. I refrained from asking why, if Martine was so all-knowing, she would need to guess at all. Finally, Annette returned her gaze to me.

"Martine wonders if you had a brother named Philip Marlowe."

Heads swiveled to me as if at a tennis match.

"Chandler, actually." I smiled. "For Raymond Chandler. Would you care to guess my sister's name?"

I broadened it out to the whole table and a fierce discussion broke out. These people *did* like a mystery. "First of all," opined Hal from Arizona, "Philip Marlowe was a character, not an author."

We all nodded, impressed.

"Secondly"—Hal had the habits of a schoolteacher—"your sister's name was . . . Agatha?"

Oh, said the table. *Good one.*

"Christie. You were close." We exchanged smiles all around.

"And could all three of you talk to eagles?" Sister Annette asked brightly.

"No—not talk to eagles," I protested.

"So only you, then?"

"Wait—no—"

"Could I have the biscuits?" asked Hal.

"Could you talk to other birds of prey too?" asked Cheri, sitting next to Kimber's husband, Perry. My head was swimming. "You know, if you wanted to. Have you tried?"

"Have I tried talking to other birds of prey? Like what?" The conversation devolved, and I was soon left out of it entirely, to my great relief.

"Oh, I don't know. A hawk?"

"Is a hawk a bird of prey?" Foster asked.

"Well, a falcon is." That was Suzette.

"But what about a hawk?"

"Are there any more biscuits?" Hal regarded the empty basket with sorrow.

"I think you could try talking to a condor," said Cheri.

"Oh, that's a big bird," Perry agreed.

"That's what I'm thinking."

"Martine says a condor would not be a good conversationalist."

"What does she think about a hawk? Would a hawk be good to talk to? Dash, are hawks good to talk to?"

"And what would that mean, I wonder? A sense of humor, perhaps. Which one is funnier—a hawk or an eagle?"

"Couldn't be a condor."

"No, not a condor. Definitely not."

"Excuse me—can we get more biscuits?"

I longed for some counterfeiters to battle.

"An osprey! I've thought of one!"

"One what?"

"Bird of prey."

"Is an osprey a bird of prey?"

"It's a sea eagle."

"Well, that's just another eagle, then, right? Right, Dash? Can you talk to ospreys?"

"Of course he can. It's an eagle. I think we've established that."

"Can I get a drink?" I asked hopefully of a passing server.

Across the way, Rose's table was far more in control—no doubt because Lady Celeste had lost her friendly attitude and cast a foreboding air. Those at her table were not discussing the presence or lack of humor in birds, or the role of the psychic arts in the ability to summon extra biscuits to a table. Their conversations appeared to be happening at the level of a whisper. I longed to be seated there.

In desperation, I flung my napkin over my shoulder. *Better retrieve that.* I pushed away from the table for a few blissful minutes. Behind me, young Skip the teenager had found something more interesting than his phone. He was fixated on the Moonglow Mystic, utterly luscious in a blouse with the color and drape of an alabaster sculpture. Even at a glance, I could see kindness in her eyes as she answered a question from the boy.

And then, as if my gaze had brushed her skin, she looked at me.

All the chatter of the room fell away, and for a moment, there was nothing but peace.

Peace and deep-violet eyes.

Skip touched her shoulder gingerly, and she looked away. The world rushed in. She was a con artist, in it for the money, and I was too experienced to be her dupe. I was called upon to confirm the debating skills of birds of prey and other large birds that made a great deal of noise, most of the table agreeing a sea gull would almost surely win an argument. But was a sea gull a bird of prey or not? Ah, that was the question.

I decided I would rather face Big Billy.

But eventually, like all nightmares, the meal did end. Rose and I pleaded headaches and jet lag and begged off the after-dinner opportunity to witness Madame Zoe's palm readings or benefit from the voodoo spell Lady Celeste would cast to protect us all from malevolent spirits. Any malevolent spirits in the region had probably been imported for the occasion by Lady Celeste herself so she could smack them down publicly.

We spent our evening with the curtains drawn. The bedside lamp with its microphone to Phoebus Apollon was moved into the bathroom with my phone and a classical music playlist. Let Phoebus enjoy some culture.

I'd emailed my "professional" client contract to Bob so he could sign away his right to privacy, and then we huddled over Rose's phone as she maneuvered the quadcopter around the property. The night-vision cameras were good, and we found unexpected heat signatures in the back barn and on three far-flung outbuildings on the property. All but the back barn could be reached from the road that ran past the ranch. We marked those for investigation.

All other aspects of the Triangle-K were as expected. The employees were either at the lodge watching the psychics or in their respective quarters. No men waved uncut sheets of twenties to dry them in the mountain air. No grizzly bears patrolled the boundary line.

All was quiet. We disassembled the drone and had it hidden away before the evening's entertainment at the lodge was finished. We'd done all we could for the day. I emailed our encrypted report. Then, worn out, Rose and I fell into bed comfortably apart from each other and went to sleep.

If only the next morning had been so relaxing.

ELEVEN

DASH

I WAS FLYING ON A SEA GULL BESIDE THE MOONGLOW MYSTIC, who was naked and riding an eagle. This was a pleasing image, and I greatly resented being awoken by a painfully chipper Rose.

"Get up, hon," she chirped as she shook me.

"Rose."

"Come on. We're going for a run."

"No. Back off." I tried to pull the covers over my shoulder and roll away from her, but she was relentless.

"Babe—you promised you'd let me train you on our vacation."

This was so improbable that I opened one bleary eye. She kneeled on the bed next to me in black-and-teal underwear, and she gestured with her chin to the bedside-table lamp sending its signal to Phoebus, the con man. "Come on. We're going for a run."

"What time is it?" I yawned, struggling to extricate myself from the covers.

"Quarter to six."

"In the morning?" I was horrified.

She grabbed my arm and stopped me from returning to my dreams. "You're jet-lagged. It's a quarter to eight in Maryland.

You'd be on your way to work if we were home. Let's go. Get in the bathroom! Shorts and sneakers—hurry up!"

She would have made a fine drill sergeant. Who was the senior partner here? Long before I was awake enough to defend myself, she'd announced we were doing five miles out and five miles back.

"Driving?" I said hopefully.

"Dash!"

"How about half a mile out and half a mile back?" I opened negotiations. By the time she'd jollied me onto the driveway and out of range of the transmitter, I'd woken up enough to be restored to a quasi-human state. Still, I could feign weakness to make my morning easier. "There's no way I'm running ten miles. And what are you wearing?"

Rose's underwear turned out to be high-performance running gear. It might have been appropriate in a DC gym, but out here in Why, oh Wyoming, she looked like an alien from another planet.

"Quit your griping, Grandpa. Let's go. We're heading east to check out the two buildings we saw on the drone last night."

I wasn't a fan of running as a form of exercise, but I'd endured it over the years. By the time we reached the end of the driveway, I'd warmed up, and my joints felt oiled and easy. *Better appreciate that while I still can.*

When the driveway met the road, we turned east, where the road rose into the mountains. Running with Rosie was complimentary about my stride, but I was not appeased. The uphills began to degrade my soul. I noted grimly that the path was hilly enough that the return trip would be as horrible. I contemplated selling my soul to get out of the rest of the run. Rose, still in possession of unblurred eyes, ran easily. *I ran like that when I was a young man.* Long, long ago.

Running with Rosie, indeed.

And all that effort was for two shacks that, judging from the evidence, were hangouts for area kids. Dirt bike trails had plywood jumps and banked hills in a course around an abandoned quarry.

"No tires through here bigger than a motorcycle," Rose said. "No power lines either. Unlikely there are printing presses out here."

I leaned gratefully against the side of the shack. "It's damned dry here."

She unzipped her efficient runner's pack and extracted a squeeze bottle of blessed water. "Here. Let's head in."

"Oh, good." *Christ, I hate to run.*

The sun finally crested the mountains, and actual light poured in on a slant, casting long shadows before us as we began our return journey.

In a field, I saw the strangest, leggiest cow I'd ever seen. I was pointing it out to Rose when it lifted its head and I realized I was looking at a moose.

"A moose!" I said stupidly. "Right there! Where is it supposed to be? Surely not right there?"

The moose, unimpressed, moved away, heading for the cover of the nearby woods. I felt almost offended. What were we doing out here in the middle of nowhere, where moose roamed around as if they owned the place?

"No antlers," Rose commented, still running easily at my side. "Must have been a lady moose."

I had no words. I was far from home.

The thought of random moose wandering about kept my annoyed mind occupied until the need for oxygen drove the image away. Rose allowed me to walk before we reached the long driveway to the Triangle-K because "otherwise you'll faint on the way in, and what would that do for our reputation?" I almost had the strength to glare at her. Her poor self-confidence had faded in the rush of physical exertion, at which she (damn it) excelled. She didn't understand the painful burdens of advancing old age.

We took the barn exit and jogged along the corrals and stables, heading for our cabin. The staff parking area held nothing flashier than Ford pickups and old beaters. No one was spending counterfeit bills on flashy autos—not that they were parking here, anyway.

We jogged past the barns. Lady Celeste and Madame Zoe approached from the other direction, probably having finished breakfast. The scene was peaceful until two ranch hands came out of the bunkhouse to head to the barn.

It was the tall, skinny one who leaned over to examine what he'd discovered lying on the porch in front of his door.

"What the hell is that thing?" he asked.

The shorter one stopped to join him in consideration. The first one reached out and picked something up.

It was a dead prairie dog—gray and lifeless and stretched to an impossible length. It wore a strange crown (or maybe it was a wreath) of dead flowers in a disturbing daisy chain.

"The fuck?" he said.

And that was when Lady Celeste froze in her tracks. One long arm shot out and pushed little Madame Zoe protectively behind Celeste's back. The tall woman, eyes wide, lifted her chin, opened her mouth, and let out a blood-curdling scream.

TWELVE

EVADNE

A SMALL, STUFFY OFFICE OFF THE LOBBY WAS TO BE MY OWN personal Hall of Mysteries for the week. I did my best to take that seriously, if only to give the paying customers what they expected. My first private reading of the day had been with Kimber. No surprise. Her gratitude was only outweighed by her fear. As soon as we sat, I ended her strain.

"You're clear," I told her. "I'm not reading any cancer at all."

She burst into tears and buried her face in Perry's neck.

"Her doctor said the same," he said to me, his relief resolving in a huge sigh and a grin that did nothing to deter his own tears, "but we knew we had to hear it from you before we believed it."

There are days when my gift (and the inevitable loneliness it causes) weighs on me, but this wasn't one of them.

Kimber had paid a premium for an hour-long session, but it rapidly became clear they were going to have a hard time concentrating. Phoebus wouldn't have approved, but I made an executive decision.

"Let's carve out forty-five minutes before dinner tonight. You guys need to go run around. Or dance. Or"—I was suddenly overwhelmed by the love and lust rolling off both of them—"something. Burn off that energy."

They stared at each other, electricity and need surging between them, and then at me. "Thank you! Thank you, Ms. Nym!"

They all but ran out of the lodge, hand-in-hand. In the silence of their departure, I tried to clear myself of the lust and longing their emotions had set up in my solitary soul.

Isolation crashed down on me. They were so fortunate to have found someone to trust, to care for, to love. Too many people wrapped themselves around the weakest sham of love and were then surprised when their relationships failed. I'd seen it too often, and it made me cynical. But witnessing the love and devotion Kimber and Perry had for each other was almost worse. It cast my life into a harsh, brutal light that created only one lonely shadow stretching out before me.

I shook off my self-pity. I now had almost an hour of free time before Quentin's reading at eight. Phoebus would want me to check in with the other novice prophets, Celeste and Zoe.

I came out of the coolness of the lodge into the brilliant sunlight of a new summer morning. Could I repair my relationship with Zoe? She'd been watching me with suspicion. I was used to it, but given the enthusiasm Phoebus showed for having me with him this year, Zoe would earn his scorn and be cast out of Prophecy Week if she couldn't accept me.

I was halfway to my cabin when a terrifying shriek ripped the air.

I cast my sense out to measure danger and was confused when I found nothing but powerful determination, surrounded by confusion.

Ahead of me, beyond our cabins and nearer to the barn, a scene unfolded.

Celeste was on the path, legs planted firmly. Zoe, wide-eyed, was with her. The two ranch hands known as Abbott and Costello stared at her in surprise. One held a strip of gray fur in his hand.

Beyond them, other ranch hands gathered. My eyes caught

for a moment on Dash and Rose. They'd clearly finished up an early-morning run, and I saw his legs were long. Fit. Deliciously naked from the sneakers all the way up to the brief running shorts. I tamped down on a burst of lust, no doubt an aftershock from Kimber and Perry's desire.

Celeste's scream still rang across the pastures when she switched to shouting. "Oh my god!" she cried. "Oh my god!" Her voice had taken on a surprising Southern lilt entirely unlike her normal speech. She patted ineffectually at the air around Zoe. "Get back, honey—you go get in your room! And you lock that door!"

Celeste was as new to Prophecy Week as I was, but unlike me, Phoebus had insisted Celeste was a pro. He'd worked with her before and promised she was an ace. It was clear the professional was now working her skills.

A crowd gathered. An air raid siren couldn't have drawn people more effectively than her scream. Soon I had guests on either side of me, their curiosity and fascination preceding them like spice.

Lady Celeste cautiously approached the bunkhouse, wringing her hands.

"Now, sugar," she said, plastering a fake grin on her face, "which of you two fellows found that thing there?"

Costello dropped the strip of fur and pointed at Abbott, who was pointing at Costello.

"He did," they both said.

Now lying in the dust of the path, I could see the gray fur was a prairie dog, bizarrely circled in a string of dead flowers. Since I'd watched Celeste string those flowers at the table in our room the night before, I was pretty sure where the prairie dog had come from. But I was almost certainly the only one.

"All right," Celeste said, making large calm-down gestures with her hands and then screaming, "Get back!" at Madame Zoe when she crept forward to see better.

"What is it?" asked Abbott nervously. "It's a prairie dog, right?"

"That's right, honey. That's right. That's all it is—sure. I'm going to take care of everything. Now, don't you worry—no!" she screamed when Costello crouched to examine it. "Don't you get too close! You didn't touch it, did you? Oh, Lord!"

Costello wiped his hands on his jeans. Fear and fascination grew in the crowd. I kept a careful lid on my admiration. Lady Celeste was giving a master class on selling the con.

A new player entered the field: Phoebus Apollon burst from his cabin. The assembled women murmured appreciatively. I fought to not roll my eyes. The man had such a flair for the dramatic. He wore neither shirt nor shoes, and his hair fanned out over his broad, tawny shoulders. The hero had arrived.

I had enough distance from the scene to marvel that Phoebus's chest, no more clothed than Dash's legs, wasn't nearly as naked to me. If I'd had a brother, I suppose I wouldn't have been able to see him with lust either.

Celeste proved her improv skills. She saw Phoebus and turned to him. Her screams got louder. "Oh my god! Phoebus—my god!"

He raced to her, his long legs eating up the distance. He wore his high-waisted, slim-cut black pants because he knew they emphasized his chest. When he wasn't scamming people, he was working out. Why shouldn't he show off the results of his gym routine?

It was a safe bet he was late on the scene because he'd taken the time to choose his costume and make sure his mane was perfect.

"Lady Celeste! What happened?"

He was probably the only one tall enough to not stagger when she threw herself into his arms and rested her head on his broad chest. Her dreadlocks were calligraphy against his skin. "Phoebus—it's George! I never knew he could get this far so fast!"

My friend Artie is addicted to adrenaline. He admires anyone who can make up a good scene on the fly, and in Lady Celeste, he'd found his natural match. He didn't know what she was talking about, but he kept up gamely. "Not George!" he cried as he held her protectively. He scanned the valley around us. We all looked around, too, eager and scared to be the one to spot trouble lurching our way. The sunny serenity now seemed untrustworthy.

"Yes! How could it be?" She drew back and regarded him, horror writ on her face. "And we crossed the Mississippi! How could he get over the river?"

"We crossed many rivers, my lady. I thought we'd be safe here." None of the assembled people asked what rivers had to do with it.

"Oh, Lord—I did too!"

"Who the fuck is George?" Abbott called out, masking his unease with belligerence.

Celeste wheeled out of Phoebus's tender embrace.

"He's no one! Don't you worry about that George—he's nothing. I am going to handle this!"

Dan, the lawyer from my dinner table the evening before, called out from the crowd, "Is it voodoo, Lady Celeste?"

She threw her hands into the air and screamed again, an impressively shrill sound that made us all wince. Phoebus was right; she was completely mesmerizing. Abbott and Costello backed further away from the small corpse in front of their door. The crowd drew closer—but not too close.

"What the hell do we do?" Costello cried.

"You don't touch it. Don't touch that evil thing!"

Small Madame Zoe peeked around Celeste. "Don't you touch it! Don't go near it!"

"What are they supposed to do with it?" Lenny, the ranch hand, stepped forward, uncertainty written on his face. "Go throw that thing on the manure pile, Costello."

"No!" Lady Celeste stepped to him pleadingly—and impressively. Lenny was a big man, but Celeste was taller. He backed up a step. "No, you have to bury it by running water. Even better"—she wheeled to Costello—"is there a river? Can you put it in the water? Can you throw it in so it's carried far, far away from here?"

Costello nodded. "Over there a ways. Two pastures from here."

"Take it on a shovel. Don't touch it. You understand me, young man? You treat it like it's poison. Don't you touch it!"

"Take it on a shovel," agreed Phoebus.

"Then throw the shovel in too!" chirped Madame Zoe.

"Aw, jeez," Costello whined. He looked to Lenny. "Can't someone else do it? Where them Mexicans at?"

"This is your problem, Costello," Lenny barked. "You handle it."

Costello stomped off the porch to find a shovel, giving the prairie dog a wide berth. He jumped when Lady Celeste suddenly stopped him.

"Son, now you listen good to me, because this is important. Are you listening?"

Mesmerized, twenty people leaned forward to make sure we all heard every word.

"You hear something? Like . . . crashing through the woods? Like . . . crash, crash, crash?"

Costello was rigid with fearful attention, Abbott at his side. "Yeah?"

"You're going to want to sing his favorite song. Get him in a good mood."

"Who?" Costello asked, as if he didn't want to know.

"George, you ijit," Abbott barked, elbowing him sharply.

"What's his favorite song?" a voice called from the crowd. It was Robin, clutching Frank's arm in excited dread.

And this was where Lady Celeste proved herself some kind of genius.

THIRTEEN

DASH

THE COUNTERFEITING CASE WAS THE REASON ROSE AND I were at the ranch in the first place. We assessed the ranch hands as they called out to each other and Lady Celeste spoke to them. But as hyperaware as we were that the counterfeiters could be standing right in front of us, it was impossible to ignore Celeste.

She never broke eye contact with Costello. "Sing the song he loved. Sing it loud, boys." Then she sang in a low, powerful alto, "'Is this my real life? Is that just fantasy? Caught in a slipslide, no escape from reality . . .'"

Next to me, Rose murmured, "Hang on. Those aren't quite the right words, are they?"

"Whatever." I was enjoying the spectacle.

Dan said it. "George's favorite song is 'Bohemian Rhapsody'?"

"That's the one!" Lady Celeste wheeled away from Costello, who all but collapsed against his partner in relief. She addressed the throng now ringed in around her. "You sing that song! You sing it loud! Maybe it will reach him—down here!" She planted a palm across her heaving bosom. "In his heart. If he still has one!"

"Oh my god," breathed Dan's wife, Sue.

Celeste turned to her. "Honey, he isn't coming for you. Did you get one of those charms on your porch this morning?"

Dan and Sue looked at their cabin up the path. They could see their porch. No one else could see their cabin, but they all tried anyway. "No," Sue answered.

"Then you are as safe as houses," Lady Celeste said consolingly.

I wanted to applaud the beauty of her art, the skill of her craft. This was a con artist any FBI agent would admire.

Celeste turned to Abbott and Costello, compassion and regret coming off her in almost-visible waves. "I'm sorry about this, boys. I am." She set her emotional knife. "I don't mind those hurtful words you said to me yesterday—I really don't. 'Live and let live,' that's my motto. But I had no idea George was near, and he minds those words something awful. But don't worry!" She strode forward, and the crowd gave way before her. "I will take care of this! I've controlled him before, and I know I can do it one more time!"

She ended up by Phoebus. He put his arm around her again. "What do you need, Lady Celeste?"

"Time, my brother," she said. "I brought all the supplies with me. I need time. And the help of some powerful spirits."

He led her gently to her cabin, Madame Zoe following behind. I was reminded of James Brown being led offstage by worshipful attendants. Lady Celeste needed a shiny, spangled cape to complete the picture. I was sure Phoebus had several options in his wardrobe.

"I could use some powerful spirits too," Lenny muttered. "All right, we've got a trail ride coming up. Let's get these horses in and saddled, boys."

The crowd broke up, carried on the wave of excited murmurs. Bob came down the path next to a young man who had to be his son, Wolf. I nudged Rose and she looked up. They'd come to see what the commotion was about, and they got the update from Lenny. Abbott and Costello found a shovel and set off with their grim burden across the pasture, jumping at every shift of the wind.

Wolf didn't look much like his father. Caucasian, mid-thirties, tall, fit. Dark hair and a mustache that could have won competitions. No distinguishing marks visible from a distance. No obvious ink stains on his fingers, to my regret.

The Moonglow Mystic looked in our direction until Celeste grabbed her hand and pulled her into their cabin, following Phoebus. The door slammed shut. No doubt they conspired within.

Wolf and Bob disappeared into the barn. "Shall we follow?" Rose asked me.

"No good reason to do it. We'll meet him after breakfast at the trail ride, anyway. No, don't look into the barn as we pass. We'll get in there when we're less obvious. Let's get cleaned up."

We headed to our cabin, down the porch from what was surely a brain trust of "prophets" in the adjoining suite.

We'd hardly entered the room before a firm knock sounded from the connecting door.

Evadne's door. Not that I cared.

I unlocked the door and pulled it open. Lady Celeste, Phoebus at her elbow, peered in. "Well, if it isn't the Eagle Guy and Running with Rosie," Phoebus said with a beaming smile.

Celeste pushed past him. "Let me look out your window," she said. "Hey, little girl," she greeted Rose familiarly.

I stepped back, and they (followed by Zoe, barely coming up to anyone's shoulders) eased toward the window. Evadne was the last to slip into the room behind them.

"Look at those boys go," Celeste said in satisfaction. The figures of Abbott and Costello shrank from view as they crossed the pasture. All traces of terror or a Southern drawl were gone. "You'll think twice before you disrespect me again, you ignorant bastards."

"You should have told me," Phoebus said. "I would have backed you."

"You did, Brother Phoebus." She turned and regarded Phoebus and Zoe with a grin. "You both did well."

Zoe nodded. "I didn't get it at first. You kinda scared me."

"That's the point, little one. Don't worry—you'll get it. And you did fine."

"Nice touch with the Mississippi," Phoebus said with a grin.

"What was that about?" I ventured a question. Apparently, Celeste trusted Rose and me, because she favored us with an even larger grin. I fought to restrain my answering smile. Her satisfaction was contagious.

"Used to be said witches couldn't cross running water. People forget the details. If I suggest zombies are foiled by water, they'll believe it. And now, two good old boys are picking their way across several fields of horseshit to throw a dead prairie dog in a river because they think they can mislead the zombie into following the charm." She regarded us all with a fiendish smile. "But that isn't going to work, I'm sorry to say."

Phoebus threw back his handsome head and laughed. "Where'd you get the prairie dog?"

"Caught it last night. Nothing to it—I brought the trap with me. I can always use a random varmint when I need to shake some people up."

"You're a real pro, Celeste," he said, clapping her gently on her shoulder.

"You hired the best, you get the best," she agreed.

"Hang on." I had questions. "Voodoo is a peaceful religion. Why would anyone buy this act? You're a stereotype. It's so . . . fake."

Celeste agreed. "That's right. Now you've got it. If they're stupid enough to believe in zombies and horror-movie nonsense, why shouldn't I make money off that? It's not my job to educate them. People see what they want to see."

"Well," I mused, "I guess that's true. And why are you telling me this?"

Celeste jerked her head to the side, somehow clearly pointing to Evadne without even taking her hands out of her pockets. "'Cause of her. She says you're okay. And that's good enough for me."

"She says I'm—" Again, I was left with no way to get out all the questions that statement inspired. Evadne was still on the fringes, her large violet eyes lowered, as if she wanted to escape notice. She did not look like a woman determined to con people for money, but that probably made her more of a success.

"Don't worry about it." Celeste broke my train of thought. "You either believe in her or you don't. You don't, and I do. So we'll leave it at that, right, little man?"

"Come on." Phoebus ushered his psychics to the connecting door. "Let's get out of these people's hair." He turned to me. "I can count on your discretion?"

Confusion pinged around my pinball brain, but at least I knew how I felt about Phoebus Apollon: he amused me. I nodded. "And I can count on you to stop listening in on us?"

Phoebus paused in the door and regarded me with the light of calculation in his eye. Then he laughed and walked to the lamp. "You're good," he said as he pried the microphone from the base. "And Celeste is right: Evadne says you're okay. Can I assume I'm not the one you're after?"

I glanced at Evadne. It was the briefest visual connection, and yet I felt her on my skin. Against my professional judgment, I was drawn to her and found I believed in her essential innocence. This was why she was an excellent con artist.

"I'm not after you this time," I said to Phoebus. The message was clear: Rose and I had bigger fish to fry. For now.

"Okay, then. That's good to know. Well, I'm sure we'll see more of each other."

"I'm sure we will."

Before I closed my side and Phoebus closed his, my gaze darted past him to look to Evadne once more time. As the door closed between us, a clever smile crossed Phoebus's handsome face.

He knows I'm interested, I thought. *That's bad. What a man wants can always be used against him.* I had a weakness I would need to guard against. *Fuck.*

"Let's focus," I said briskly to Rose. "All of this is a distraction. Let's get showered and changed for breakfast and the damned trail ride with Wolf. We've got things we need to do."

"What's up first?" She moved to the bureau to retrieve her clothes.

"First, we've got to get a look at that barn."

FOURTEEN

DASH

DESPITE RUNNING FOR A SOLID HOUR, ROSE ONLY ATE CHUNKS of cantaloupe with yogurt and pumpkin seeds for breakfast at the lodge. She was soon drawn off into a conversation with Running with Rosie fans who had admired her form in her underwear—I mean, her running clothes. Would she be willing to start a running group for the week, or maybe a fitness class?

I was enjoying my pancakes and bacon (did I mention we'd run for a solid hour?) when some of the mystics concluded their readings. Three prophets slipped out a side door, and three guests came out the Hall of Mysteries aglow with the hidden secrets revealed in their private readings.

Outside, Elbert and Annette walked along, unconcerned, chatting easily. But Evadne was silent. She glanced to the side, not as if she was scanning the area but as if she knew what she was looking at.

And what she looked at . . . was me.

I was caught again for a moment by her otherworldly beauty, by the attraction that pulled me to her. She'd been silent during Lady Celeste's scene by the barns and later when she came with the others into our suite, but I could feel her in my skin all the same.

That was foolish. I'd *heard* her admit she scammed people for money. Maybe the state law protected what she did because of the "for entertainment purposes only" clause in the guest agreement, but she was a criminal just the same. And I made my living putting criminals behind bars.

Then she looked away, and they were gone, down the path to do whatever mystics do after they make thousands of dollars off of willing victims—perform a celebration dance naked in the moonlight, maybe. Annette and Elbert were welcome to engage in that theoretical ritual without witness, but I thought that whether or not she was a con artist, I'd offer myself as bodyguard, should Evadne need any help in that particular practice.

Not the thoughts of an old man or an agent who needed to be retired from fieldwork. I felt smug about that until I wondered if I was fooling myself.

"Come on, lover boy," Rose said. She'd finished her conversation with her fellow fitness nuts (prebreakfast yoga on the lawn in front of the lodge was the consensus). "Let's focus. Heard from Bob yet?"

No sign of him at breakfast, and no emails either. No need to panic. I'd get into the Triangle-K's computers.

On a positive note, there were no emails from Owen asking for my decision either. "Nothing," I reported after checking my phone.

"Then it's time for our trail ride. Let's go meet our boy."

This would be our first chance to interact with Wolf and the other ranch hands, and I looked forward to that part. But there were aspects I wouldn't enjoy. "I hate horses," I grumbled.

"Oh, come on," she said. "What have you got against horses?"

"I'll have you know I came off a horse badly when I was eight."

We joined the slow tide of people heading to the corral. "Well, that was three decades ago, old man. Maybe you can give it another shot."

"You're unsupportive for a wife."

"I'm a wife who bucks up her man."

"Yeah," I said. "It's the bucking that's got me uneasy."

"Inner thighs, Dashiell. They're not just good for what you think they're good for. You've got to grip the *horse*."

"Inner thighs for *you*, wifey darling. You're trying to squeeze in—I'm all about the outer thighs. The pushing apart."

Our spousal banter made others around us smile.

We came around the barn and into the organized chaos of a corral with saddled horses and curious guests. The ranch hands paired riders with mounts and kept the unwary away from the kicking end of horses. Well, obviously. I stood on the barn's low porch, out of hoof range.

"Things are pretty busy here," I murmured to Rose. "Think I'll go check out the barn. Wolf's got his office back there, and I want to take a look."

She put out a hand. "Dash. Let me go."

I looked down at her. "You sure? You ready?"

She nodded firmly. "Authority comes from experience, right? Besides, I'm smaller. I can slip through these people below eyesight. And I'm way better at playing dumb than you are. I can do it."

Her courage had me biting back a smile. Rose was coming into her own. "A peek. Don't take anything, don't open anything —anything we learn has to hold up in court."

"I know."

She played it perfectly, walking through the barn door like she owned the place. I eased back until I could see her out of the corner of my eye. Just in case.

I watched her walk through the dim barn, silhouetted against the light from the office window. She walked in, peered around, and turned to leave again.

Bad luck. Lenny the ranch hand appeared with an assortment of leather straps in his hand. Bridle, reins, whatever.

I watched as he slid a stupid hand down to grope her ass.

And I watched as Rose did a takedown that would have made her Quantico instructor proud.

She wheeled, shrieking, and pushed against his shoulder. Unnoticed by all but those who knew the move, she also planted her foot behind his, hip-to-hip like a redneck tango.

People turned to see what was going on. Small Rose had pushed big Lenny off-balance, so he stepped back to regain his footing, only to trip over her foot. Down he went like a felled ox, and Rose took the opportunity to fall, too, landing on top of him.

She "accidentally" crushed her forearm across his throat in a move guaranteed in hand-to-hand combat to incapacitate any attacker. I winced. That would do some damage.

Lenny, on the ground, uttered a sound that would have been a shriek if he'd had a working voice box.

"Oh my god!" Rose cried. "Are you okay? Hey, mister—can you breathe?"

People crowded around. Lenny was gasping. Rose pushed off him (she planted a determined knee in his gut to rise and he grunted in pain) and turned, flustered. "He groped me! He grabbed my butt, but I didn't mean to hurt him. Are you okay? Mister? Are you okay?"

I put my arm around her, and she clung to me. Wolf appeared, large mustache preceding him like a Western movie.

"He grabbed you?" He didn't sound surprised. When Rose nodded, Wolf looked at Lenny. "Get up. Apologize. We've talked about this."

Lenny had a hard time rising, and Wolf finally realized his ranch hand might be injured. He helped Lenny up and nodded at a teenager. "Dalton, take him up to the lodge. Someone up there can run him into town to the doctor." He glared at Lenny as they left, and he turned to us.

"I apologize, ma'am. I promise he'll be reprimanded."

"I didn't mean to hurt him," Rose said weakly.

"He shouldn't have groped you." I played the injured

husband, swelling out my chest, which was in no way as large as Wolf's. But I was a paying guest, and he had an abusive employee. We both knew who had the upper hand here, and Wolf made his apologies.

As we walked into the sunlight, Wolf glanced into the barn toward his office. "What were you doing in here, anyway?" he thought to ask.

"Bathroom?" she said weakly.

He nodded, his suspicions clearly aroused. "No bathrooms here. Isn't that your cabin right there?" He gestured up the path, and we turned, feigning surprise.

"Oh. Yeah. I guess I forgot."

He eyed her and then me. Then he gave us a big false smile and told us he'd wait to saddle us up until she got back.

I walked Rose to the cabin, where she confessed she'd acted on impulse.

"He made me so mad, Dash. I'm sorry. I went with instinct."

"You acted like a fitness trainer who'd been assaulted. Don't worry about it. What did you see?"

She blinked. "Laptop on the desk, closed. Regular office printer. Calendar on the wall. Books and ledgers on a shelf. An old saddle. Coffee cups. Lots of coffee cups."

Not surprising. Only rarely did counterfeiters leave towering stacks of fake bills in the office until needed.

"Okay. Ready to go back?"

We rejoined the guests in the corral, most still milling around on foot. We weren't the last ones up, and suddenly I had lost the upper hand. A horse is a damned large animal when you're sure it wants to kill you.

And I'm such an old, old man.

"I'm not happy about this," I said.

"That makes you one obvious tenderfoot."

"What makes you so sure you're going to be better at this than me, Rose?"

We were drawing smiles again. "I had riding lessons when I

was little. I can ride anything," she boasted. "I've got inner thighs for days."

Women cheered and men blushed. One of the local teen hands led up an enormous palomino. "Miz Williamson? This is Sunshine, and I'm Lucius."

The horse eyed Rose with what seemed to me to be an unwholesome hunger, but Rose was not intimidated. She rubbed velvet on the nose far over her head and cooed, "Aren't you a fierce beast? Yes, you are! Oh, I'm in love!"

The teen blushed, but he helped Rose into the saddle. She had no problems and moved her leg back as the kid shortened the stirrups.

I watched as Rose proved her point. She and Sunshine already moved as one. She was a damned centaur.

I hadn't yet been singled out to be put on a horse, and I was fine with that. Instead, I watched young Skip attempt to persuade Bart the bearded ranch hand that Skip ought to ride a very large, very red horse standing by itself in a corral to the side.

"That's the one I want," Skip stated.

Bart laughed. He had an impressively vigorous beard. "Not that one. That's Rocket—he's a bronc. He busted two guys all to hell at the rodeo, and now Wolf's gonna break him." He nodded to where the ranch manager talked Colleen Rettinger from Tallahassee onto a pinto pony. "Now *that* guy really can ride anything."

"Me too," said Skip sullenly. "I rode the bull at an amusement park longer than anyone. I can do it."

Bart took pity on the kid. "Sure you can. Maybe next year. Come meet Daisy."

"Daisy?!" Skip was horrified by the name. It was worse when his sister trotted up on a pony named the Kraken. "How come she gets a cool name?"

The ranch hand with Melanie laughed. "That pony is gentle, but come to a stream? She'll stop dead right in the water. Won't move an inch. Miss Melanie is going to be firm with the Kraken, aren't you, miss?"

Melanie nodded happily. "I told you, João. Kracky and I understand each other."

Bart refused to look at the Latino hand, but João and I exchanged a look of appreciation. The kid was cute.

And then a huge equine nose cut off my view. Wolf himself was leading a large black horse up to me.

"Mr. Williamson," he said in greeting, "I hear you don't like horses."

"It's not that I don't like them—" I started, and he finished it with me.

"—they just don't like me." Wolf's smile didn't reach his eyes. We assessed each other, and neither of us found a reason to feel comfortable. "This is Ferd."

"Ferd?"

"Short for Ferdinand, because he looks like a bull. And because all he wants to do is stand in the meadow and sniff flowers."

"Well, that sounds good to me. Why don't you let him go and he can sniff all the flowers he wants?"

"Come on," Wolf said. "You can do it. Put your foot here."

He raised an eyebrow and nodded when I used the foot farthest from the horse.

"Good for you. Lots of new riders put the wrong foot up first time."

"Not my first time," I muttered as I fought off irrational panic. "You hold his head now."

"I've got him."

I grabbed the saddle horn and stepped up as high and as quickly as I could to get into the saddle before the horse decided to bolt.

Ferd stood. Buildings had more movement.

First challenge passed. I was on the horse.

Wolf lengthened my stirrups. "This should be easy for you.

You've got a lot of leg. Grip with your thighs. Remember, if you wrap your shins up against the horse, he might take it as a sign to go faster, so try to use your upper legs—not that Ferd here has ever gone faster. Right, you big cow?"

Ferd flicked an ear, and Wolf slapped the horse's neck with force. Ferd whickered and heaved a great breath, his ribs bellowing out under me. I clutched the saddle horn and wished this was over.

"He's testing the cinch. I'll tighten that up for you." Wolf pushed my leg and hauled on the strap around the horse's belly.

Suddenly, Wolf kneed the horse and Ferd let out a big breath, allowing the cinch to tighten.

"Big faker," Wolf muttered. "Now, I'd teach you to neck rein, but it won't do any good. Ferd is going to follow everyone else. You sit tight, Mr. Williamson. Enjoy the ride."

He had a pleasant smile, did Wolf, but it was betrayed by his cruelty in small things. It occurred to me that wherever Wolf went, the big bronc, Rocket, tracked him. *There's a backstory there.*

"Everyone up?" Wolf called.

The last horse had a rider. We were ready.

"Now, this is the beginner trail ride, and everyone has a buddy. And we don't have enough hands to match each guest, so some of the more experienced guests will be pairing up with the first-timers."

He made a vague gesture at me as he swung onto his own horse and moved to loom over Colleen on her pony.

And then I felt it before I saw her: the invigorating fizz of an ice-cold soda on a hot day.

The Moonglow Mystic rode up next to me. Her pale-silver horse matched the pale-silver hair flowing from beneath her dark hat. Her eyes smiled at mine. "Mr. Williamson."

"Dash, please," I managed to croak.

"Then call me Evadne," she said. "I'm going to pair up with you, if that's all right."

I lost any cool I had. Skip the teen was more mature. My

tongue was stupidly thick in her presence. "You know how to ride," I said stupidly.

"I do. I've been riding for years. I think you're going to enjoy it."

Suddenly, my mood shifted. Enjoy it? She might be right.

"Everybody got your buddy? Okay. Let's lead them off, Mrs. Rettinger." Wolf and Colleen led us out the corral and up the barn path to certain disaster.

FIFTEEN
EVADNE

RIDING HAS ALWAYS DELIGHTED ME. I FEEL A PARTNERSHIP with my horse. I left behind on-the-ground concerns and any feelings of isolation or loneliness when we started out. I'd been given a sweet-tempered horse named Blissful . . .

. . . and I had Dash at my back.

It took him a few moments to get used to the movement of Ferd underneath him, but Dash was naturally graceful. I knew he'd adapt. Soon he became used to the rhythms of riding and could broaden his awareness beyond Ferd's broad back.

And it didn't take long until I felt his eyes on me.

He was interested; I could feel it. It made me sit up straighter. It made me hope my hair looked nice, that my jeans fit well . . . and it made me sad. Because men had looked at me with interest before, but it never lasted. I had to stay under the radar, hide too much of myself. Too much of what I know about them that they didn't want me to know. And endings are always painful.

I pushed away my longing and resolved to keep my head on straight.

I turned in the saddle to check in with him. "Doing okay?"

He blanched like a high school kid caught ogling his teacher. "Ferd and me, we're coming along."

"You're doing great."

"Thanks."

The path twisted through the trees and slowly climbed the hill behind the ranch. The air was fragrant with balsam and stands of aspen shone in the sunlight. It was a gorgeous day, and that alone was reason to have a light heart.

The trail broke from the woods and ran through a meadow. It was a perfect spot for beginners to try a faster gait, and Wolf led the beginners at a faster pace. I watched as Dash's "wife," Rose, took off with a delighted yell, trailed by Lucius, her guide. They were around a bend and out of sight in a few thundering paces.

Time to test the courage of my student.

"This looks like a good place for a lope," I said to Dash. "Want to try?"

"*Lope?* Is that the same as *canter?*"

"Canter is more of an eastern word. Out here, we don't canter—we lope. We don't trot—we jog."

"Shouldn't we trot, er, jog before we run?" He eyed the far-off ground nervously. Ferd was quite a large (if exceedingly placid) horse.

"Loping is much more comfortable than trotting. You can do it. What do you think?"

He gathered his self-possession. "All right. What do I do?"

"Kick Ferd with one leg."

He had a brief explosion of dislike at the thought of hurting an animal, which made me like him all the more. "I don't want to kick Ferd."

"It's okay. At that angle, it's hard to hurt him, and you're not wearing spurs. It's the signal he's been trained to respond to. Kicking with both legs will get you a jog. Kicking with one leg is a lope. Now lean forward and kick with one leg."

Dash gave his horse a tentative nudge. Ferd was indifferent.

Dash frowned and tried again. Again, Ferd ignored him.

My mouth curved up as I watched. There was a distinct moment when Dash's unease was overwhelmed by his annoyance. Ferd was supposed to lope but wouldn't. Dash's brows grew together, and his forehead wrinkled in concentration.

Soon he was kicking Ferd. Finally, he worked up to kicking Ferd with authority. As he became more determined, Ferd became more deaf. Their pace never varied from a dignified walk. I stopped being able to hide my smile. It was a test of wills, and stubborn Ferd wasn't going to surrender.

"Come on, Ferd, let's go." (Kick.) "Let's go. Giddyap now." (Kick.) "I'm not kidding, Ferd. You're making me look bad." (Kick.)

By the end, Dash was straightening his leg in the stirrup and bringing it down with force. Ferd was utterly indifferent. He would walk, and nothing Dash could do would change his mind.

I couldn't help it. I broke into a burble of laughter. Dash's frown was too adorable.

Finally, I came over and reached for his reins. He passed them over, and I clicked to Ferd, nudging Blissful forward. "Kick now! Kick hard!"

At that point, Ferd decided he wouldn't even walk. He dug in all four determined hooves and planted himself like a tree. I almost came out of Blissful's saddle and was left stretched impossibly back, hooting with laughter as I struggled to drag Ferd into unwilling movement. The reins pulled taut in my hand and Ferd's neck stretched out, but he was not persuaded.

"Kick hard! Harder!" I called to Dash through my giggles.

Ferd all but shook his head. Nope. He was walking, and that was that.

I almost fell off my horse from laughing. Even Dash chuckled. Ferd was not going to be led, and he was not going to be ruled. Ferd knew his mind, and even though the rest of our group had long since disappeared around the bend, Dash now projected an irrational wave of affection for his horse.

I circled back and handed Dash his reins. "It's not you," I said. "That horse wouldn't run if his life depended on it."

"How do you know?"

Because despite what you clearly think, I am not a con artist, I thought. *I can read that horse as easily as I can read you.* "I know."

"Huh."

Wolf came thundering in on his big bay, easy competency in the saddle. He looked as if he'd have a John Wayne drawl, but he spoke normally enough, "Hey, Eagle Man. You okay back here?"

Dash was irritated by the nickname, but he covered with an easy grin.

"We're good," I said. "Ferd is going to walk, it seems."

"Of course he is. Well, I got to keep up with the group, and the path is pretty easy to follow. Every time you come to a fork, go right. Take you in a big circle back to the ranch. There're a couple of picnic tables set up closer to the end if you want to take a break. Want me to get someone to stay with you?"

"That's okay," I said. "I think we'll be okay. We'll get back to the barn sooner or later."

"Okay. Your phone should still work this close in. Call if you get in trouble. Have a good walk."

Dash's annoyance flared for a moment as Wolf galloped easily back to the rest of the group now disappearing into the forest on the far side.

"I'm sorry," Dash said.

I shrugged. "I don't have any more readings. This is my free time, and I can't think of a better way to spend it. It's lovely out here."

It was indeed.

"What's the deal with you and horses?" I asked as Ferd agreed to resume a walk. I had vague intimations of his problem —his left thigh throbbed, in an emotional sense—but I wanted to get him talking.

"Well, not that it covers me in glory, but a horse threw me when I was eight and then came back to stand on me. He broke my femur and I was in a cast for two months. But I've gotten more manly and impressive since then."

He swelled his chest cartoonishly, and I laughed.

"Oh, I can tell." I smiled. "Ferd clearly thinks so too." I liked his wry sense of humor and had to remind myself that as fun as meetings were, endings were miserably hard, and I could save myself heartache if I curbed the crush I was developing.

"Well, it set up a phobia for me. I'm not a fan of horses."

"Makes sense."

"No offense to you, Ferd." He stroked along Ferd's neck, and the horse whickered obligingly. In Ferd's place, I might whicker too.

This kind of thinking wouldn't help me.

We walked along, moving from shade to sunlight, from warm air to cool shadows. The silence was smart. It would be wiser to keep Dash at a distance to avoid notice. But even knowing that, I got a jolt of pleasure when he spoke again.

SIXTEEN

DASH

I NEEDED TO FOCUS ON THE REASON I WAS HERE, WHICH WAS the case. Not on the graceful woman riding at my side. I cleared my throat and got back to business. *Scratch this itch, Moonglow Mystic. Tell me what I don't understand.* "What did you mean last night about ink?"

"Not here," she said without thinking about it. "It's back at the ranch."

I shook my head. The whole sensing-ink thing would never stand up in a court case. "What does that mean?"

She shrugged, her shoulders bowing. When she didn't answer immediately, I gripped the reins more tightly to keep from reaching out and nudging her—or shaking her. *Tell me what you're talking about.* Perhaps feeling the weight of my stare, she spoke defensively. "It's just something I know." But now I'd awakened her curiosity in turn. "Tell me what the ink means to you. Why am I sensing it? Why is it important?"

I shifted in the saddle. *Nope. This isn't how interrogations go. I ask you questions.* "Just interested."

"Sure," she said, and I knew she knew—and she knew I knew —that was a lie. But she opted not to push it. For now.

We rode in silence. It was lunacy to expect a "psychic" could tell me something about my case. And yet until we met with Enrique and he could tell us which buildings he'd been able to search, Evadne's mention of ink was my most provocative lead. I went fishing again, trying to land a suspicious fish.

"If we played Twenty Questions, could I get closer to the truth?" I asked.

She smiled wistfully. "People rarely understand me when they try, but give it a shot."

"You're telling me you're used to being misunderstood?"

"Did you ever hear of Cassandra?" she asked. She rode next to me with unconscious grace, her body moving and shifting in coordination with her horse. "From Greek mythology," she continued. "Cassandra was cursed. She could see the future, but no one would believe her. She was forever telling people exactly what was about to happen, and they'd talk themselves out of believing her. Then they'd suffer horrible consequences, and she'd be left saying 'I tried to tell you.' I identify with her."

She kept her words light and casual, but I could hear pain underlying her words. This was, somehow, a review of her life.

"That would be horrible."

She looked at me steadily. I could almost hear her think, *You have no idea*.

"Is that why you pretend to be psychic?"

She flinched, and Blissful skittered under her. Evadne got control of the horse. When I drew up next to her again, her throat was working. "I'm not a con artist, you know. Despite what you heard me say to Celeste yesterday about making money."

I tried to phrase my comment delicately. "You're either a con artist or a psychic. And I don't believe in psychics—or I suppose you could be delusional."

Somehow, despite the fact she ran with a cluster of con artists claiming to be mystics, despite the fact I'd heard her tell Lady Celeste she was only at Prophecy Week to rake in some money—somehow, I'd wounded her. My words had hurt, and suddenly I wondered if there were possibilities I hadn't considered yet.

"You don't believe I have extrasensory perception?" she asked.

I hedged my answer. "Do you?"

She gave a huff of annoyance. "How else would I know about the eagle?" She glared at me. "I can already tell. It's like Cassandra. I should change my name. Go on—tell me. How have you persuaded yourself I couldn't have known about the eagle by occult ways?"

I winced. She waited me out, watching until I spoke.

"Maybe you did a Google search? Found it somewhere in a newspaper archive?"

"Oh." She nodded. "Of course. I'm that good at research."

"Hey, I think you can cut me a little slack. Phoebus has listening devices in every cabin. What am I supposed to believe?"

"I'm not Phoebus," she retorted, and I'd hurt her again.

I was at sea. What was I supposed to think? If you lie down with dogs, you get up with fleas, and I have the analytical, suspicious mind of an experienced FBI agent. All my training told me she lied. All my instincts told me she spoke nothing but the truth.

"I'm sorry," I said, and never had the sentiment been so true, "but I don't know what else to believe."

Her pink lips tightened into thin lines as she controlled her emotions. We rode along a rushing stream and then veered over a low plank bridge and into another meadow. *The case*, I thought. *Focus on the case. Emotion be damned. Be an agent.* I spoke again.

"Why would you tell Rose and me about the ink? I mean —why us?"

She gestured vaguely, the sweep of her hand taking in the sunlit grasses, as she chose her words carefully. "Well, you're here *because* of the ink."

I was taken aback. Why would she think Rose and I had

anything to do with some out-of-place sensation she'd espoused? Had I—had Rose—done something to indicate we weren't a happily married couple on an expensive vacation?

I'd let the silence draw on for too long and opened my mouth to protest that I didn't know what she was talking about, but she cut me off.

"I don't need to know why you're here or why the ink is important to you." She glanced at me as we shifted from sun to shadow. "You're filled with secrets, and I can certainly respect that."

"Huh."

She smiled. "Do you know about that?"

"About what?"

"About that 'huh' you just gave."

"What now?"

"It's what Phoebus would call your tell. When presented with a new line of thought, you say 'huh.' You might as well say, 'Hold on—new data—processing.'"

"I do not."

"You do it all the time. Terrible habit for someone wandering around in an identity that is not him and yet *is* him. Which— weird, by the way."

"Huh. Oh, shit. I *do* do that."

Her laughter was as silvery as her hair. "I should take a picture of your face. I could call it *Confusion.*"

I opened and closed my mouth a few times, but nothing came to me. My brow wrinkled. I sputtered and spoke. "I'm—"

"Vapor locked."

"Vapor locked. That's it. I should have a spinning icon over my head and a sign saying *Rebuffering.*"

This time, she threw her head back and her laughter rang through the woods. Con artist or not, she was a magnet. I had a hard time looking away.

I was compromised. It mattered less and less to me that she

was almost certainly lying to me and everyone around me. I wanted to stay by her, to watch her, to listen to her.

Whoa, boy. I wasn't here investigating con artists, but that didn't mean I could ignore the law. Or my mission.

I regrouped, mentally shook myself. "Okay," I said, trying again. "Let's get back to you sensing ink and what it's doing this far away from a supply store."

"Twenty questions," she said staunchly. "Give it a try."

"Right. Can you tell what kind of ink it is? Are we talking about a fountain pen or what?"

"No, it's more like a cartridge."

"Like for a printer?"

I was too intense. She was spending as much time eyeing me with suspicion as she was considering the question. "Yeah."

I knew I needed to back off (I was trying to narrow down a lead from a liar, anyway), but this was an itch I needed to scratch. "What kind of printer?"

"What kind?"

"Ink-jet? Laser-jet?" She looked at me, confused, as I listed all the kinds of printers that have ever been used in counterfeiting operations. "Offset? Dot matrix?" (All right, dot matrix was unlikely. I was grabbing at straws.)

"What's the difference?"

Good question. I had no idea what kinds of inks each press took. "Okay." I thought for a moment. Could I confirm my theory that Wolf was in this to his neck? "Is the ink sense tied to a person? Can you tell?"

She stopped my interrogation with a question of her own. "If you're taking me seriously, then let me ask you a question. Are you going to believe me if I tell you?"

I felt it in my skin: this was a turning point. She was asking if I could ever trust her, and it was a big question that deserved a true answer. I gave her as much as I could. "I'm going to try, Cassandra. And I do want to know."

It took her a few more steps down the snaky path between

the trees before she grudgingly volunteered an answer. "It's not tied to any one person—that, I can tell."

Damn it. It's not like I could have used her "sense" in a court case anyway. Questioning her was ridiculous.

So why did I keep asking? "What about a place? Can you tell where the ink is?"

She considered the question. "It's nearer the lodge than the barn."

"So you *can* tie it to a place."

"I suppose I can."

"Could it be *in* the lodge?"

She frowned, thinking. "Maybe."

"What about now? Can you sense ink now?"

"No," she said with perfect confidence. "It's definitely on the ranch. Nothing strange out here."

"Okay." Right. Silly mission. On the other hand, if she was an actual psychic, shouldn't she be able to sense things? Other things? Not ink?

This train of thought led me to ask what the hell was out here with us in these woods and meadows as we rode alone absolutely alone and isolated with no firepower or backup or elephant guns or anything. "Nothing strange? What can you sense? Any danger?"

She laughed. "What is it you fear, Dash? Something big."

Damn. It *had* been a turning point. I was now apparently counting on a con artist to keep me safe in the wild. I must have been losing my mind.

"You're remembering something," she said. "Something from this morning. Something you thought was safe but turned out not to be."

She was doing it again, without even putting her hands under mine. Reading me as she had in the so-called Hall of Mysteries. And again, she got it right.

"A moose?" she said. Shivers chased each other up my spine. How had she known *that*? "Dash, a moose is a really big deer."

I used bluster to hide my reaction. "It is not."

"No, really, it is. Same family. And deer aren't scary."

"Deer are a little scary. And a moose isn't a deer."

This entertained her and unnerved me. "Well, no. Okay, some moose are scary. They're a grumpy species, generally."

"Great. They're grumpy. That's good news."

Another bubble of laughter rose up in her. It was more fascinating than my questions, which ran in a litany around my empty head. How had she known about the moose? About the eagle? If she knew that, why wouldn't I believe her about the ink? How had she known about the ink? What did it mean to "sense" ink, because that was a phrase designed to drive me insane?

She ignored my sidebar into the brief crazies. "But it's not a moose. That's not what's got you jumpy. So what is it?"

The path had narrowed, and I rode behind her. She looked back at me, cocking her head as she considered.

I scowled as she attempted to measure the limits of my machismo.

"No, not moose—it's bears," she decided. At that point, I wasn't even surprised she'd read me so accurately. What was this, the fourth time? "I can promise you, Dash, there are no bears anywhere around here, although there's a large rattler sleeping in the sun over the top of that boulder."

Snakes are so much easier to dismiss than bears. But how the hell did she know?

"You're not going to check?" she asked.

"Check if a rattlesnake exists or not? I see no upside to that experiment. I believe you."

Her eyebrows disappeared into her hairline. Were her eyes suddenly bright with tears?

"What—what did you say?" she asked.

SEVENTEEN
EVADNE

My sight of Dash was blurred by the quick rush of tears, but I knew he watched me. He spoke softly when he repeated his statement. "I believe you, Evadne."

"Ah." I fought against and then finally surrendered to a smile. He couldn't have known how that easy statement touched my heart. The simple words *I believe you* were something for me to treasure. I was either discounted and dismissed or feared and shunned. Simple belief? That was rare.

As if I needed any more proof Dash was unusual. He neither rejected what I knew about him nor attempted to attach himself to me to bleed me of knowledge and energy and independence.

He believed me. And that was enough.

I was light-headed and clutched the pommel of Blissful's saddle while I waited out a brief dizzy spell.

Dash watched.

Worried about me.

Confused.

Curious.

And disciplined. He pulled a large lungful of pine-scented air into his lungs and returned to his questions. "Could the ink be *behind* the lodge? There's a vehicle barn back there, and Wolf's house, and the cook's."

I shot him a look. "You know the layout pretty well."

"I'm the question-asker here." He gave me a smile, but he was serious too. "What do you think? Could it be in one of those places?"

"Could be." I led our horses around a fallen log, holding back the long, whiplike branches that would have hit him or Ferd in the face.

"Will you check later? Go take a walk? Don't get too close. See what you can figure out?"

"You'd really believe what I told you?"

"Well," he hedged, "I'd be willing to listen."

After so many years, I no longer expected to have much success with people, but I suddenly wanted his approval. I wanted his simple *I believe you* to turn into trust. "I don't lie, you know. I don't always tell the whole truth, but I don't lie."

"I'm sure." The answer was rote, but I hoped it was the beginning of something stronger.

We came to the picnic tables Wolf had mentioned. "Look." I pointed to the clearing. "This is a good place to stop and stretch your legs. Your knees will thank you."

We were in a forest glade. Wolf had left a canteen on the table on his way through. *Smart.* The Triangle-K thought of everything for their guests. I dismounted and came to hold Ferd's head as Dash descended.

He hit the ground and groaned. For new riders, knees always feel strange after a ride. It walks off quickly, and Dash was athletic and fit. He moved gracefully about the space, towing Ferd behind him as he stretched.

"Most Western horses are trained to be ground-tied," I told him. "Drop your reins."

"He's not going to run off?"

"Not until the bears come." Now I was teasing him, and his grin told me he liked it. "Ferd won't bolt. He likes you."

"You can read horses too?"

"I can read all intelligent animals. They're easier than people." I sat on the table with my feet on the bench. He sat beside me, and I handed him the canteen. The cold tea tasted like nectar. We shared it, and I firmly did not think of him putting his lips where mine had been.

"I'm surprised you don't do something with that skill," he said after we'd both had a long, refreshing pull.

I nudged his shoulder with mine. I was too close but couldn't bring myself to move. "Other than reading people at Prophecy Week?"

"Right."

I looked at the canteen held in his long fingers. "The money I make here is going to pay off some long-standing bills. If there's anything left over, I'm hoping it will get me one semester closer to a degree in zoology. I know I'm old to be an undergraduate at thirty-two, but I'm all but homeless, so I can't get loans. I have to pay my tuition in cash at the start of every semester."

He was overwhelmed. "Why are you homeless?"

I avoided his eyes. It was stupid to invite him into my life, but I didn't want to stop. "Being able to read people isn't always an advantage, you know. People think I'm weird. Things tend to end badly."

"What do you mean?"

I shrugged. "I have to repress so much to be with people. Too often, I slip and tell them something they don't want to know—or don't want me to know. I get chased by fanatics who want to control or cage me, or I lose jobs. I lose friends. I'm down to about one friend, and he's an out-and-out con man named Artie who's currently calling himself Phoebus Apollon."

I gave him the side-eye. I was confessing that Phoebus was a con artist. This was foolish; Artie was my only family. I was risking his safety to open my soul to a stranger.

But he was the most honorable stranger I'd ever met. I took the risk, foolish or otherwise.

He was pleased with my trust. Since he didn't leap to his feet and immediately phone the authorities, I went on. "And I'm seven semesters toward a decent job with animals somewhere I won't have to interact with people."

I waited for his reaction. He clearly knew he was on delicate ground; both accusation and pity would end this conversation. "How come I get to hear the truth?"

"Didn't I tell you?" I asked. I looked away, but not soon enough to hide my blush. "I've never met anyone as honorable as you."

He liked that but didn't think he was worthy, and that made me like him even more. "You can't know that," he protested.

"I can." I'd spent my life trying to avoid attention, but Dash was different. Resolutely, I shifted so I could face him. "Here's what I know."

I held out my hands, and he faced me too. He put his hands in mine, palm-to-palm this time, with the sudden jolt of warmth that came from contact between naked skin. My desire made a surprise reappearance. When he curled his fingers around to hold mine, I swallowed, summoned my courage, and wrapped my fingers to clasp his hands in turn.

I paused to relish the sensation, then I gathered my reality around me and gave him as much truth as I could.

"I know you barely know Rose, that you couldn't possibly be married as you say." I cut off his protests. "And that delights me. Because I don't want you to be married to someone else, Dash."

His protests died away. My heart now thumped in my chest, and my ears buzzed. His grip on my hands tightened. I felt hope and curiosity battle with his need to maintain his cover. Sunlight laced through the pines and painted the planes and curves of his face.

I stiffened my mental armor and went on.

"I know you want me. And I know I want you back. But . . ." I tried to pull my hands away; he wouldn't let me. I looked at our clasped hands, and sorrow broke over me. "These things don't end well for me. I have a hard time trusting, so I'm afraid I have nothing to give you, Dash. I hate to be a cliché, but this is true: it's not you. It's me. I'm afraid this isn't going anywhere."

I was near tears. It wasn't just Dash—although he was rare enough to cry over. It was every boy I'd ever liked, every friend I'd ever hoped to keep, every time I'd risked trusting someone. All those attempts were suddenly close in my memory, and the pain of rejection, the sorrow of loneliness . . . they stung all over again.

He released one hand to draw his thumb, warm as sunlight, over my cheekbone. "Evadne," he said uselessly.

I turned my cheek into his palm and let him cradle my head. And then I put him from me. I straightened. "I'm sorry."

"Wait. You couldn't even trust the most honorable man you've ever met?" His protest was charming. I wanted to surrender to it, but I knew the pain of his ultimate rejection would shatter me. I laughed and got up, going to the horses.

"Not even for him," I said lightly. "Come on. I'll help you mount Ferd."

His lust flared again. The idea of mounting had triggered it, and his response excited me in return—but there was nothing to be done about it. He climbed onto immobile Ferd and watched as I swung onto Blissful. We set off again, both of us lost in thought.

"How does Phoebus make my skin tingle when you look at me?"

I eyed him, reading him with all my senses to attempt to understand. "How does he what?"

He clarified. "When I'm near you—when you look at me— it's . . . effervescent. What's he use? An electromagnet?"

I read him, and my smile faded to something soft and sad. "That's your nervous system, Dash."

"No, it's not."

"Sure it is. You're reacting to something in your environment."

"It's never done that before. It's only with you."

I nodded. "Yeah." What a tragedy.

My response frustrated him. "What do you mean, 'yeah'? Do you feel it too?"

"No. I feel you feeling it."

"Like an echo chamber?"

My smile was wistful. "It's not always easy being me."

"I guess. So you don't feel it?" That made him a tad pouty.

"I don't." After a bit, common sense was overwhelmed. Helplessly, I shared the truth with him, knowing I wasn't making things easier for either of us. "I feel something different than you do."

"What?" By not concentrating, he'd successfully nudged Ferd into a faster pace and drew alongside my horse. "What do you feel?" He reached one hand out to rest it on my wrist, the golden warmth traveling up my arm.

I looked at his hand on my skin and I closed my eyes to savor the sensation. I covered his with mine and whispered my answer.

"Safe. I feel safe."

EIGHTEEN
DASH

"HEY, DASH. I DIDN'T KNOW IF I SHOULD WAIT AT THE corral," Rose said when I collapsed in the seat next to her in the empty dining room. "Wolf was eying me, so I didn't think I should loiter, you know? Should I have?"

After revealing that I made Evadne feel safe (which made my nerve endings fizz with proud adrenaline), she had stayed well ahead of me and wouldn't let me draw up next to her again. She'd fled by the time I dismounted at the barn. (My staggering gait had earned a snigger from Lucius, the teen ranch hand.) But I needed to get my head right. Evadne wasn't my job—and working with my partner was. I eyed Rosie.

"Who was the badass I saw on that huge beige horse?"

She scoffed. "Palomino, Dash. Not beige."

"Right. What was up there? You were totally in charge."

"I like riding." I gestured for her to go on. "Well, it's—it's not about how you look or how big you are. It's all about the energy you bring to it."

I gave her the Look. The raised-eyebrow, put-the-pieces-together-rookie look.

She responded with scorn: "Dash. It's not that easy."

"Yuh-huh. It totally is. You're confident when you're Running with Rosie, and you were an ace on that horse. What made you so strong then?"

She ducked her head. "I don't know. It's—I'm not a cute little girl then."

I looked in vain for a server. Rose pushed the remains of a steak sandwich to me. I took it gladly and spoke around a mouthful.

"Who's called you a cute little girl in the past five years?"

Again, the defensive posture. This was a good time to make a point.

"Rose, you're hearing voices in your head. People called you a cute little girl when you were growing up, and that limited your view of yourself. But you're not that girl anymore." I dropped my voice in the empty dining room. "You made it through the FBI Academy. Did anyone make that easier because you're cute and little? Anyone?"

I knew the answer, and she did too. "No."

"Of course not. Half your classmates washed out, but you sailed through with flying colors. You're one step away from badass. Stop listening to your past. Think about the energy you bring." I held my hands up, miming holding reins, and she nodded reluctantly. She wanted to believe me, but it was hard to let go of a self-image. I'd seen it before: Rose needed time, and if I had anything to say about it, she'd get it.

"Well," I said, finishing her lunch, "experience leads to authority, and you did well today. You did. You handled yourself in that barn, taking out Lenny when he groped you. The next time you need respect, remember riding. Holding the reins. The energy. That's who you are now. You're a badass. Okay?"

She ducked her head, smiling. "Okay. Thanks, Dash."

"It's what I do, partner."

"I'm glad. My instructor was right. You're the best."

I turned my wince into a smile, and she didn't notice. Owen had said something similar, but I didn't want to get out of field-work. I liked tracking down bad guys—the smart ones even more than the stupid ones. I liked the hunt. The puzzle. The hours of painstaking research paying off in heart-stopping action. The mission of building a legal case so tight no judge could ignore it. I didn't want to train other senior agents to be better mentors.

Did I?

I shook off my navel-gazing. "Any sign of Bob?"

"Haven't seen him."

I'd already checked my phone. Nothing. I needed access to the ranch's accounts, but I couldn't make him sign my contract faster. "I did have an interesting chat with our mystic."

"Oh yeah? She know anything?"

"Maybe. She's going to have a look around later, see if she can narrow her scope."

"I guess it's a start," Rose said guardedly. "We're hardly going to get a warrant off it."

"I know. Could be a break, though."

"Well, I met Enrique on the trail ride. Did you see him? With Twig and Harry?"

"All I saw was a whole line of backs and horse asses."

"Nice view."

"What did he tell you?"

"Couldn't talk with everyone around. He's going to come to our cabin tonight if he can sneak away. Apparently, the bunkhouse is ruled by Lenny, who they're expecting to be on heavy painkillers tonight." She tried not to look smug. "I wonder why?"

"What was the doctor's diagnosis? Did you break his throat?"

"Give me some credit. Only a bruise."

"He's going to love you. We're not getting close to anyone that way."

"Right—not like you with your Moonglow Mistress."

"Rose." I shook my head in pain.

"Don't tell me you're not interested." She grinned, but I

grabbed the hand that wore our wedding ring. The dining room was empty, but there were still people nearby.

"I'm only interested in you, sugar lips." I squeezed her hand, and she made a *fine* gesture with her eyebrows.

"And I'm only interested in you . . . my weak-thighed husband."

I chuckled despite myself. After an hour of running and an endless trail ride, she was right. My thighs were rubbery.

"Bob's driving me up the wall. I wish he'd send me that contract so I could get to work."

"Well, I'm going to keep talking with the staff. This afternoon, I've got campfire cooking class with the cook and half the waitstaff to see what I can find out about them. Maybe someone's bragging about some new luxury purchase. And you're going skeet shooting, right?"

"Right. Nice, manly sport." I pushed out my chest to match her fake simper. "Finally, something I don't suck at. I thought I'd wander past that vehicle barn first, though."

"Ah. Get lost on your way to the gun range."

"Exactly. Do a little snooping."

"Good plan," she said. "All right. Get out of here. You smell like a horse."

"You got it, boss." I dropped a husband-like kiss onto her head, her smooth bob tickling my nose. "You do, too, by the way."

I was heading out the door to the porch when a voice hailed me from the registration desk.

Bob.

I resisted the urge to chortle and rub my hands.

"Hey there, Mr. Accountant! What do you say? Got a moment?"

My various old-man aches and pains vanished, and I got into the Western vibe by *moseying* over to the desk. At least, I thought I moseyed.

Rather than send it to me with an e-signature, Bob had

printed out my contract and signed it by hand. *Sweet. Undeniable in a court of law.* He handed all seven pages to me. "I checked out your website and even called a few of your customers. It's clear you're the guy for me. Here you go now!"

I gave him a hearty smile. "Well, Bob, you've put a whole new spin on my afternoon! Don't tell my wife." I looked around conspiratorially. "Let's get going on this!"

"Now?" Bob was startled. "I have a few things to do this afternoon—"

"This won't take long. Do you have a second chair?" I snagged a seat and pulled it up to his desk. "Come on and sit. You don't want me to be in your accounts without you watching."

"I don't?" He sat on the edge of his chair, as if he wasn't so sure he was staying. "You can't do your thing without me?"

"Well," I hedged, "I have to ask you some questions about your setup, your employment records . . ." I ran through an extensive list of accounting minutia, and soon a frown creased his forehead. He pulled the scheduling book over and thumbed through it.

"You've got skeet shooting this afternoon, don't you, Dash? Wouldn't want you to miss that."

I laughed and slapped him on the shoulder. "Last time I picked up a weapon, it was a Daisy air rifle and I shot my brother in the butt. Not on purpose, of course—I was aiming for a fence. Better for everyone if I sit right here!"

The last time I'd picked up a weapon was at the FBI's shooting range, when I'd proven to myself there was nothing at all wrong with my distance vision.

The memory made it easier to put on my dreaded reading glasses. The numbers on Bob's laptop sprang into focus. "This will be a lot more fun!"

I kept him beside me for almost half an hour, dragging him through his records. His wife, Marcia, happened by and exclaimed in delight. "Thank God you're taking over, Dash! Bob can't handle bookkeeping to save his life!"

Bob blushed and called her "Mother," and at last made an excuse to flee.

"You can take care of this, Dash. I've got to run into town. I'll be back in a bit. You do what you think is best."

"Sure," I said. *Verbal permission as well as a signed contract. Building a powerful case here.* "Of course. You go run your business. Let me get used to your setup, and I'll have a list of suggestions for you when you get back."

He took off, all long legs and elbows, as if I'd invited him to join me in a nice, relaxing colonoscopy. I settled in, installing a keylogger and replicating his information to a cloud-based account . . . as made legal by the agreement he'd signed.

Marcia was right; as bookkeepers went, Bob was hopeless. I didn't need to contact my guy at the IRS to come up with four entirely legal ways to lower his payments and streamline his systems. When he returned, I was ready.

"Here's how much you're going to save each month"—his eyes lit up—"but why aren't the ranch records on here? This is just for the inn part of the business."

"Yep—Wolf runs the ranch, and we split costs. He keeps his own records."

Really? I'm so surprised. "Well, let him know that if he wants me to check on saving him as much, I'm available. Especially if it's during a time I'm supposed to be riding with the wife!"

"You may not have much luck with Wolf. He's a real private guy, and he hates paying taxes even more than I do. But if you can save him money like you've saved me, I'll give you a five-star rating on Yelp!" We had a manly haw-haw over that, and I left him, hiding my grinding desire to get into Wolf's computer.

Take the bait, Wolf, I thought. *Take the bait and let me into your records. I've got a crime to solve, a legal case to build, a crowded, smoggy, overworked life to get back to.*

NINETEEN
DASH

IN KEEPING WITH STANDARD PROTOCOL, THE UNDERCOVER Secret Service agent stayed away from us until he could approach us without creating suspicion. He was good too. That evening, Enrique appeared at our suite's door. "Good evening," he said, his arms full of stovewood. "I was told you needed someone to tend the fire?"

"Oh? Oh, right. Come in." I closed the door behind him and checked that the curtains were drawn.

He offered us a blinding smile as he dumped the wood next to the already-full bucket and then turned to offer me his hand. "Enrique Martinez. US Secret Service."

I realized I had seen him around. He looked taller standing in our cabin, easier in his skin. Beyond these walls, he'd held himself differently. He'd looked shorter, less substantial. He'd held himself like a dog afraid of being kicked—and no intelligent human would lightly kick the man in front of me now.

"What can you tell us, Enrique?" I asked.

I figured I'd maintain his cover story by opening the damper and building a fire in the fireplace. We would have baked if I'd used the far-more-efficient stove, but the fireplace wouldn't warm up the cabin much, and smoke from the chimney would help to cover Enrique if anyone wondered why he was in our cabin.

Plus, us dudes would want a fire in the fireplace, right? Romantic?

"I wish I had more to tell you," he said. "I've been all through the barn, the stables, the bunkhouse. No printing equipment, no supplies, no indication of any counterfeiting operation. And I've been through the lodge pretty well too. There was a rainy day when they put us to work cleaning out the basement and a tiny attic, and that building is clean—not literally." He gave us a blazing grin.

"So what are you looking for?" Rose asked.

Enrique stood at ease as he answered her question. "First thing is ventilation. They can use a generator instead of having electricity, so the press could be in literally any building—but the generator would need ventilation. And unless the operator is fully masked, which is annoying over time, the inks can be pretty overpowering in a small space."

"What's overpowering about ink?" Rose asked, but she and I exchanged glances. Evadne had told us she sensed something.

"To fake currency, ink has to go on thick—more like a paste than what you'd find in a fountain pen. Plus, these guys are using color-changing inks, like the Mint does with real bills, and that has chemical properties most people can't handle."

"So they need power. What about water?" I thought I knew the answer, but it was good to get it from the horse's mouth.

"We think when they started, they bleached one-dollar bills and overprinted them to make fives. Back then, they'd need plenty of water to neutralize the process. But that's a low rate of return for a federal crime. Might as well go big. So now they're using a textured newsprint thin enough to sandwich a fake security strip between two sheets. It won't stand up over time the way the cotton-linen mix we use will, but they just need it to hold up long enough to pass it on."

"So now no water."

"Not much. They might thin the inks, but you could do that from a gallon jug."

"So they could literally use a hut hidden in the hills," I theorized.

"A pretty big hut, maybe. Once you print the bills, the sheets have to dry, so you need some room. We're not looking for anyplace too small."

"Okay." I envisioned the aerial views of the ranch as I tended my fire. "So a cabin like this one would be tight."

Enrique looked around, measuring the space. "You could," he hedged. "But why go small when you can go big? If you could print up a million dollars over the course of a week, would you settle for a hundred thousand?"

We all agreed that was inefficient.

"What about the vehicle barn behind the lodge?" I asked.

Enrique's eyes lit up. "Yeah," he said. "We're not supposed to go up there. Off-limits to ranch hands. So maybe you guys can get a look."

We reviewed the potential needs of a large-scale counterfeiting operation. "It's large, it's ventilated, it has power—electricity or a generator, probably water too. Hidden from view. Plenty of space to hang sheets of counterfeit bills to dry." Rose counted requirements on her fingers, and she turned to me, excited. "The vehicle barn has to be it! I know the presses are in there!"

"Hold on," I said. "It's a big ranch, and we don't know that. There's still the building to the west to check."

"What building to the west?" We brought Enrique up to speed on the ranch properties we'd identified through the thermal imaging camera. "That place is on Tri-K property? I didn't even realize it." He scratched his head and turned to gaze into the distance, as though he could see through walls.

"What is that place?" Rose asked eagerly.

"I dunno. I never paid much attention to it. Guess I wasn't

briefed as well as you guys were before I got the job here." He looked chagrined.

"That's why we're here to help you. We're a team. Right?" I stood from my fire, drawing nicely now, and chucked him lightly on the shoulder.

He gave me a grin and straightened.

"What can you tell us about the ranch hands?" My question restored his composure and he stood at ease again to reply. Military background.

"Wolf, you've met. He's the brains of the operation. He's smart and practical. He usually stops his men from injuring any of the Latino workers. It's because he still needs us to get the work done, so we have our value. But he's a fucking sadist. You can tell."

Enrique gestured toward the stables. "You should see him working that bronco they bought. Rocket. The horse is unbelievably fast and has a lot of heart. But he and Wolf are in a battle of wills, and Wolf isn't afraid to hurt the horse to win."

All three of us now wore sneers. An unconscious bias. Anyone who would hurt an animal must, by default, be a thorough bastard of a guy.

"And Bart is his number-two guy, right? I haven't dealt with him much," Rose commented.

"I was supposed to go skeet shooting with him and he came by to find me," I interjected. "He's smug and arrogant and has the biggest, messiest beard for miles around, but those aren't crimes. Too bad too."

That made Enrique laugh. "Bart is Wolf's mini-me. If Wolf told Bart to roll in horseshit, Bart would do it. Bart thinks Wolf walks on water. If Wolf is in this, so is Bart."

"And Lenny?" Rose asked with an arched brow.

That earned a delighted snort from Enrique. "Girl, you took the stuffing out of that man!" He high-fived her. "What I wouldn't have given to watch you take him down. He's in his luxury condo right now, stoned on pain pills and cursing you for the clumsy bitch you are."

They both cackled in delight. "What do you mean, luxury condo?" I asked.

"Oh, inside joke. The bunkhouse is divided into three rooms, each one with two beds. But Lenny won't share with a Latino. Abbott and Costello have the room closest to you, and Gustavo and João and I share the middle room. No side window. Lenny gets the last room at the end, and he lives in private luxury all his own. It's okay." He smiled at Rose, who tried to interrupt, her outrage plain. "None of us want to share with him anyway. It's not so bad. We've all been through worse."

"Is Gustavo the one they call Gussie?" Rose clarified.

"Yeah."

"So Gustavo is Gussie, João became Joe, and you're Rick."

"Good old Ah-MUR-cun names," he said. "My family has called me Rick since I was born, but they think they're insulting me. And make no mistake—they are."

Rose grimaced. "And Abbott and Costello? How'd they get those names?"

"Because Paul's last name is Abbott, and because they're inseparable. Bart came up with it, and it stuck. Those two aren't the brightest crayons in the box, but they're good followers. And that's what you need if you want to run a crime ring."

"You're sure they're in on it?"

"No, but there's no reason why they shouldn't be."

"So what's the motive here?" Rose asked. "Just greed?"

"Maybe. But a lot of counterfeiters aren't trying to make a profit. A bunch of groups have wanted to destabilize the United States over the years by screwing with the economy. Anti-government groups like the Justice Patriots believe the entire US government is illegal, and white supremacists have tried several times to flood the nation with fake currency to devalue the real thing."

Enrique looked proud, and rightly so. The Secret Service had an impressive record of tracking down those who wanted to hurt our nation.

Rose hadn't known the Service's history. "Man, that's evil—and smart. Who came up with that plan?"

Enrique relaxed. "How about Hitler? He was printing fake US money during the Second World War."

"You're kidding?"

"Nope. Who stopped him?" Enrique's pride was obvious.

"The Secret Service?" Rose asked with a grin.

"Proud to serve," he replied. "We were founded during the Civil War because the South was flooding the North with fake currency. We stopped that too. And we'll get Wolf and his boys."

His confidence was appealing, but as the senior agent in charge, it was my job to keep us focused on fact and evidence. Nothing would get through a court case without them.

"Anyone else on the staff who you think might be in on this?"

"I can't be sure, but it doesn't look like it to me. Wolf and his four guys are pretty insular. If he needed help with a job, he'd turn to Bart, Lenny, Abbott, and Costello. The rest are day laborers or teenagers working part-time. I don't think he'd bring in the cook or any of the cabin girls."

"At the least," I went on, "you can't discount Bob and Marcia. If Wolf is a ringleader, he had to learn that behavior at someone's knee."

"Bob and Marcia are both sweethearts," Enrique countered. "They intervene to keep Abbott and Costello from treating us Latinos too badly."

"Good for them." I wasn't as quick to write off the Ozzie and Harriet of the Triangle-K. "Still, we should keep an eye on them too."

"You said Bob wouldn't be able to hide assets, now that you're in his computer."

"I said it was unlikely at this point, but the analysts in DC haven't begun to track down all the leads his records provide. If we get anything, the judge will give us permission to use the pineapple."

Enrique looked blank. Rose filled him in. "It's the size of a soda can and duplicates a cell tower. We'll be able to monitor Bob's email, his text, his phone—anything in or out. If we have any luck, we'll have enough to get a subpoena for Wolf's computer. It's a whole cascade."

She'd done well. I smiled, and she preened. An A-plus for my brightest student.

"Okay," said Enrique. "What about Wolf's brother, Hank?"

Bob and Marcia had named their kids Wolfgang and Heinrich, which were the names of every cartoon villain, but that wasn't a crime. Definitely Nazi movie names, but hardly evidence of criminal tendencies. Hank was a long-distance trucker, and the working theory was Wolf was printing fake currency and Hank was distributing it across the nation.

"If we could find any evidence at all," Enrique went on, "we could get a judge to subpoena the GPS in Hank's rig, so we'd know where he is and where he goes. It could be the break in the case we need. But if we don't find any evidence, no judge will help."

"So we'll add that to the list of what we're looking for, plus large quantities of newsprint or other paper, supplies of several different inks, drying racks, and what else?" I asked.

"Printers. Several different kinds of printers. They can probably be desktop printers, but if they have a big, sheet-fed print operation, they'd be able to turn out more money, so don't assume one and not the other." Enrique fixed us with a stern eye. We paid attention.

"And we've got to get a look at Wolf's records." Rose looked to Enrique. "No chance you could get into Wolf's office?"

I waved that off. "It's not enough to steal Wolf's laptop. Remember, we have to build a case and acquire our information by legal methods. We need proof that will convince a judge to give us the subpoena—not a stolen laptop we have no right to access."

She nodded, chastened. "Everything aboveboard and legal. I'll remember."

Enrique's sudden laughter pulled her from her funk.

"Abbott and Costello, though—man, they are fit to be tied. That treatment they're getting is definitely not aboveboard. I mean, they are jumping at every creaking board. That voodoo queen has got those boys on their last nerves!" We shared a laugh. "João and Gustavo were nervous, too, but I explained about the psychics all being con men. I'm not sure they believed me, but they're more cheerful about this scenario than Abbott and Costello are, that's for damned sure!"

Lady Celeste earned some admiration. We spent a few pleasurable minutes reviewing how adroitly she'd worked her crowd, and then made our plans for the following day.

"Let's see if Wolf lets his dad's new accountant look at his books. I'll try to get a look at the vehicle barn. And I think you and I, Rose, should take our morning run in the other direction to check out that last unknown building."

"Right. I'll keep talking to the staff, cozy up to some people. Maybe I can get into Wolf's office again."

"Don't taint the investigation if you get the chance to look at anything. We need permission—either Wolf's or a judge's."

She felt good enough to roll her eyes at me. "Thanks, Dad. I might have forgotten from five minutes ago."

I grinned, but her tease was a dagger right in the reading glasses. She turned to Enrique. "Try to get near the vehicle barn, but don't blow your cover. I've got another trail ride, then I'm trying roping. Lenny apparently teaches that, so that should be fun. And Dash, you are . . . ?"

"Fly-fishing. I get Bart the Bearded Wonder. Maybe Abbott and Costello."

We were finishing up when we heard the sound of an entrance and then voices in the next suite. Lady Celeste and Evadne had returned from the evening's psychic presentation. Judging by the male voice, they'd brought company.

And then a muffled knock came on the connecting door.

TWENTY

DASH

Alert as I was to potential danger, I was not alarmed by the knock from the suite shared by Evadne and Celeste. That crew earned their money the old-fashioned way—by conning people instead of printing their own.

Rose opened the connecting door, and Phoebus Apollon beamed his high-wattage smile on her. "Good evening."

She stepped back and he came in, followed by Lady Celeste, Madame Zoe, and Evadne, who darted a glance at me and ducked her head.

Phoebus took in Enrique at the door. "I beg your pardon," he said. "We didn't mean to intrude."

"That's okay," said Rose as Enrique stepped forward and held out his hand to Phoebus.

"We haven't met. I'm Enrique."

Phoebus took the outstretched hand with a glad grin. No one had more warmth or charm. Phoebus was a con man first, last, and always.

"Very nice to meet you—oh." He looked at Rose and me, the light of suspicion dawning in his eyes. Finally, he turned to Evadne, who nodded to him. He beamed at us all. "This is a friend of yours, I take it?"

Rose finally nodded, and Phoebus's grin grew slowly across his face. "And you're all allies. Partners, as Evadne tells me." He hit the word *partners* with significance, telling us he knew we were at the ranch for reasons other than a vacation. "How very excellent. I wonder, Enrique, if you'd care to help us play a small joke on your friends Abbott and Costello."

Enrique had been working at the ranch for weeks. His deep tan made his grin look like an advertisement for tooth whitener. "I guess I'd like that a lot," he said.

"Well, that's excellent," Phoebus said. "Even better." He explained his plan. "This afternoon, by strange coincidence, I happened to drag a long branch into the no-man's-land between this cabin and the bunkhouse beyond."

He gestured to the curtained window, which, if opened, would face the window into the room shared by Abbott and Costello.

"Such a strange coincidence," Enrique said neutrally.

"Yes. Wasn't it?" Phoebus was as cool as milk. "This evening at our demonstration, I noticed your coworkers"—Enrique smiled to hear them so described—"paying rather a lot of attention to my colleague here." He put his arm gently around Lady Celeste, who remained impassive. "They couldn't look away. She fascinates them."

"Ma'am"—Enrique tipped an imaginary hat respectfully—"I don't imagine they're the only ones."

She nodded to him, a gracious queen before her subjects.

Phoebus regained the attention of the room. "Not five minutes ago, my friends and I watched Mr. Abbott and Mr. Costello retire to their bunks. I was going to slip out to that branch and scratch lightly at their window. As a tease."

"A joke," agreed Enrique. "A witticism."

"Exactly."

"And if that scratching branch should happen to sound like the scraping fingers of a bony, skeletal hand . . . ?"

"Oh, the frolic of it all!"

All of us were grinning. Even Evadne masked a smile beneath a waterfall of silky, silver hair.

"But if there were any smarts between the two of them," Enrique said, "they might think someone was playing a trick on them."

"They might, indeed!" Phoebus regarded him with approval. "You must be a good man to have at one's side."

Enrique acknowledged the compliment. "So if you people were all, say, outside on the path, having a nice conversation . . ."

Phoebus nodded, pleased to have such a ready ally. "If it was clear none of us could have scratched our fingers along that window . . ."

"Well," said Enrique. "What are we waiting for?"

In a sudden flurry of activity, we were all bustled out of our suite and onto the porch beyond. I pulled the screen over my fire and regarded it fondly. It would burn nicely for at least another twenty minutes.

After the fire's heat, the cool evening air was refreshing. Phoebus ushered us up the path, closer to the lodge but still within sight of the bunkhouse. I felt a cool tingle against my skin as Evadne's hand slipped briefly into mine. She'd chosen the anonymity of the group to reach out to me. I felt as though a butterfly had landed on me, and I moved slowly so I wouldn't alarm her. I closed my fingers gently around hers, and she held my hand for a brief, hanging, timeless expanse—and then she stepped away again.

"Okay. Good," murmured Phoebus. "Here we are, all having met on the path. And we're having a lovely conversation. And how was your day today, my dear?"

He laid his pearly-white smile on Rose, who goggled at the view but gathered herself quickly. "Very enjoyable. I got on a horse again for the first time in a decade. I loved it."

"Did you?" he asked in delight. The rest of us pretended it was a fascinating conversation, and I measured the emptiness between my shoulder and Evadne's.

It didn't take Enrique long. Soon we all heard the most horrific scratching from the wall of the bunkhouse, accompanied by a sound somewhere between a moan and a wail.

"Oh, that's a good sound," Lady Celeste murmured approvingly. "The boy has good initiative."

"Wait," Phoebus said. While still smiling at Rose and haloed in the glow of the pathway lighting, he counted softly to himself. "And three, two—"

Before he got to "one," the door to Abbott and Costello's room flew open and the two hands spilled out.

"We'll catch 'em! You go that way!"

They stumbled to a stop, confronted—to their confusion— by most of the psychics grouped halfway up the path.

"Hey!" shouted Costello. "How the hell did you do that?" He was angry, but it was an anger based in fear.

Abbott was warier. "Did you hear that noise?"

We'd moved forward as a group. The area between the cabin and the bunkhouse was empty. Enrique was fast.

"Hear what?" asked Madame Zoe with a squeak. I wondered if she'd been goosed into talking.

Costello zeroed in on me. He stepped forward. "Who's in your cabin?"

I blinked at him. "Our cabin?"

He pointed to the window opposite his own. "Who's in there? Right now?"

"I have no idea. No one, I suppose. Do you want to check?"

I walked him to the porch and let him in. He did a quick search and rattled the connecting door, finding it locked. *The fire looked nice on the hearth*, I thought contentedly. Coming out onto the porch, Costello shook his head at Abbott, who clearly couldn't decide whether to be annoyed or frightened.

We all stood there, looking at each other, when the scratching sound filled the air again, accompanied by the wail— louder and longer that time.

And we could look right at the window. No one there.

Lady Celeste compounded the excitement by offering her blue-ribbon scream, which made everybody jump. "Oh, Lord! Oh, Lord! My spell wasn't strong enough!" She turned her face up to the sky and cried out, "No, George! No! Not these men! They didn't mean it!"

Guests appeared from their cabins. They clustered on their porches or came down from the lodge, eager to catch anything mystical or interesting.

"You all get inside!" she shouted, her voice carrying in the night stillness. "You get inside and let *me* fix this!"

The whispers started. "It's the voodoo woman!"

"And the eagle man!"

What? I was just standing here. No eagles. How was I suddenly notorious?

The crowd disappeared, the lucky ones getting behind closed doors to watch through their windows. Celeste grabbed Abbott's arm (he was the closest) and got in his face. "You know what you need to sing, don't you?"

Abbott, now drawn with anxiety, nodded. His mouth worked a few times, and then he whisper-sang, "I pay my dues, time after time . . ."

"No!" screamed Lady Celeste. "That's 'We Are the Champions'! You don't want to sing that song—Lord knows! Not *that* song! You!" She caught Costello in her glare. He was pinned like a bug in a museum display. "What are you going to sing?"

"Uh—um—is this my real life, is that just fantasy . . ."

"That's the one!" Celeste cried.

On the other side of the circle, Rose shook her head. Not the right words. She was ignored as Lady Celeste went on.

"You sing that Rhapsody. And when you get to the Bismillah part, you sing out! You sing to save your souls! Now get inside! Oh, Lord—hurry up! You get inside and don't come out, no matter what you hear outside! Not until dawn, do you hear me? Not until dawn! You need that good sun's warm rays to touch you, not this dark of night. Are you listening? Oh, God!"

Abbott and Costello bolted, fleeing into their room. We could hear the bolt thrown on the door.

On the gently pitched roof of the bunkhouse, Enrique stood from behind the chimney and grinned, waving a long branch with skeletal fingers.

Phoebus hid his grin and ushered Lady Celeste and Evadne into their room, followed by an escort for us into ours. The fire's embers glowed cozily. "Thank your friend for me, won't you?"

"Most fun he's had in months," Rose replied, hiding her smile.

"Well. A very good night to you all!" Phoebus put a solicitous hand under Madame Zoe's elbow and towed her up the path.

TWENTY-ONE

EVADNE

LONG AFTER OUR SUITE HAD SETTLED INTO SOOTHING
stillness and Celeste's delighted chuckles had faded into the deep
breathing of sleep, I laid in my bed and stared into the darkness.
I was thinking about courage.

What was the nature of bravery?

For instance, if I were to draw comfort from holding a man's
hand when I was uneasy, and then if I were to break away from
that hand for fear of the harm that might come to me as a result
. . .

Was that brave? Was it the wisdom of experience?

Or was it cowardice?

My friend Artie was often foolhardy in his courage. One
might say he lacked common sense and survived on animal
instincts. No, it wasn't courage that defined him. It was self-
preservation.

Elbert and Annette, the other members of my temporary
Prophecy Week family, were meticulous about their cons. They
listened carefully when I told them about their clients. They
planned and spoke with forethought, always aware of the risks
and the rewards of everything they did. Was that courage? Or
caution?

Zoe . . . I waved my hands in the darkness to dismiss Zoe. She still didn't like or trust me.

And Celeste. Was she brave?

Perhaps more righteous than brave. She manipulated Abbott and Costello with consummate skill. They deserved it, to be sure —but their responses were so easy to predict that Celeste played them like a cello. She was a master.

Courage, yes. But not defined by courage.

As I laid there, I realized I valued courage highly. I would like to be brave in the face of danger.

And even in the face of rejection and ridicule.

Always close in my memory was the friendship I'd formed with a woman when I'd found a job in Wisconsin at a dairy. We'd worked side-by-side for five weeks, slowly building a friendship and sharing laughter.

She was as lonely as I was. I let down my guard. One day, I stupidly told her she'd forgotten to close the gas cap on her beat-up car. Brows drawn in confusion, she told our foreman she needed to take a break, and he let her. When she came back, she was still confused.

"How did you know?" she'd whispered.

I'd shrugged and tried to brush it aside. But she kept after me, needling and cajoling and teasing me. Two days later, I told her about the dream she'd had the night before.

After that, our relationship changed. She looked at me like I was her personal miracle. She began to call me at home and then to sit outside my tiny apartment all evening, all weekend. She told me she'd given testimony about me at her church, and others wanted to meet me.

On the day she showed up at my door with a man I'd never met, both of them reaching their hands out to me and begging me to tell them what I knew, I lost my nerve. When they finally left after calling imploringly through the door and alarming my neighbors, I packed up my car and fled without my last paycheck.

Fear or fanaticism—I'd even been called a witch. I learned to stay mobile, to never sign a long-term lease. And I stopped trying to make friends. My car was my only constant, and it was almost always in need of major repairs.

I'd been beaten down by the life I was forced to lead. I reacted to hurts even before I experienced them. I was, in short, a coward.

But that long-distant friend was not the only person—not the only kind of person—in the world. And the chance to evolve, to become someone who was stronger and happier, laid on the other side of the cabin's common wall. Was he lying there, thinking about me?

He'd let me hold his hand and then let me pull away. He hadn't tried to stop me or held on when I needed to let go. His fundamental decency and integrity were beyond question. If there was ever a time to hold my chin up, square my shoulders, and risk more pain, this was that time.

I would summon the courage somehow. I would try to be brave when it came to Dash.

Decision made, I turned to curl up on my side, pulled the covers up, and soon drifted off.

And when I awoke, I had a plan. I would be bold.

TWENTY-TWO
DASH

WHEN ROSE DRAGGED ME OUT OF OUR CABIN THE NEXT morning for our run to the west, we were startled by the entourage waiting for us, hoping to go Running with Rosie.

While none of them was dressed as sportily as Rose (today in a royal-blue running skirt and a blue-and-white shirt that glowed in the predawn darkness), five guests had gotten up to run with their idol.

They grinned up at us: Cheri and Jack, Suzette and John, and Milt of Milt and Oscar. (The fact that Oscar had clearly refused to get up before the sun for exercise made me like him all the more.)

"Oh," said Rose. "I explained this was private time for me and my husband."

"I tried to tell them," Cheri said.

"We know," John said. "We thought we could run behind you —you know, pace you. And you'd set the speed and the distance, and we'd stay out of your hair."

"Is that okay?" Milt asked earnestly.

Rose and I exchanged glances. This would make it harder to investigate the building targeted by the quadcopter. But protesting now would make things more awkward.

And there would be more of us to scare off any long-striding moose who might take it into their mooseish heads to wander across our path.

"Sure. Come on. We'll all run together."

Their fitness goddess had spoken, and her worshipers were thrilled.

The larger forms of wildlife had all opted (like Milt's friend Oscar) to sleep in that morning. I envied them. I would rather have been sleeping than running, but at least today's course was along the river. The land was flat, and as the sun came up, I settled into a comfortable rhythm. We drew close to the outbuilding we'd seen with the drone, but the presence of an entourage meant we wouldn't be able to give it any attention. I had an entirely glance-based communication with Rose and then fell back.

"I'm going to take a break," I said to the group.

"Oh, thank god!" Cheri said. "I'm out too!" *Damn it.*

"Um . . . yeah." She was not wanted, but I could hardly say so. "Okay."

Rose, hearing us, ran backward as easily as she ran forward to exchange a look of consternation with me. Cheri was a complication I would have to handle. Rose and her minions acknowledged our weakness, and then they were gone, running fleetly along a road that rose off the river valley floor as it swooped around the next curve. Another hill to run up. And then down. And then up. And then down. How satisfying. At least I'd picked the right time to investigate something stationary. Old age has its privileges.

The sun crested the mountains to our backs, and Cheri and I sat on the guardrail at the side of the road.

"What is this place?" she asked.

The building was plain and unfussy, a pitched roof over cinder blocks painted white. It was wired for electricity and looked like it would be large enough to handle many drying racks. There was a gravel parking lot and a driveway that curved around to the back. It also had at least two inconspicuous security cameras under the eaves.

That was interesting. What went on here that needed camera surveillance? I repressed a buzz of excitement. No good jumping to conclusions—it would distract us from facts and evidence.

"There's no sign," Cheri said. "Let's look in the window."

The minute I spotted the cameras—and there was a third one wired into a tree to show a view of the front door—I knew things had gotten complicated.

"Better not," I said. "It's private property."

"Oh, go on." She grinned. "There's no one here. I'm going to peek."

If the cameras were powered by a feed to Wolf and his team, Cheri would be walking into a hornet's nest. She would earn their suspicions as someone who was too nosy. The manufacture of fake money made people willing to commit violence. So did the potential for a long stint in a federal penitentiary. And it would be the fault of a federal agent—me—for letting her get involved.

"Cheri," I barked. "There are cameras."

"Oh, please. I'm just going to peek. No one will care."

"Hey, I'm not kidding. Come back." I used my most alpha voice. Criminals have backed down without firing a shot and people planning to do harm have changed their minds because of that authority, but Cheri was a different personality entirely. She lived in a world where good things happened to good people, and you could always explain your way out of a mess.

She was on the front steps, peering in the window. My authority was gone somehow. Probably lost it when I got the glasses and the offer of the so-called "promotion." I jogged to join her.

"It's a meeting room. Bunch of chairs and a pulpitlike place. That's nice."

No printers? No drying racks? I had her by the elbow and

dragged her off the stairs. "Really, Cheri. Let's go catch up with the others."

"Oh no. No way. I'm done running. I'll walk to the ranch. You can catch up with them. I won't mind."

There was no way I was leaving her here now.

"What's along this driveway?"

She ducked out of my hand and squirted away. *Maybe she was federal*, I thought glumly. No one else could be determined to explore where they were so obviously not wanted.

My options were limited. I could either reveal myself to her, forcing her to return to the road, or I could follow her and do my best to protect her from whatever happened.

I liked Cheri. She was cheerful and kind and didn't much like running. We had much in common. But she was also chatty, and not the sort you could confide in. I sighed and followed her around the corner.

More cameras. Of course. More electrical poles.

The driveway wound past a back entrance and bent into the forest. We were at the edge of the valley. The mountains rose with startling abruptness a few feet into the woodlands. Pines and aspen combined in a riot of greens, lit by shafts of the dawning sun. No moose—at least, no visible moose.

Great. Now I was thinking about moose armed with cloaking devices. Invisible, like George the Moaning Zombie.

"Isn't this pretty!" Cheri said.

"Sure is," I said with resignation. We strolled along. She admired the path before us; I listened for invisible zombie moose and counted cameras. Six so far.

At the bend in the driveway, Cheri exclaimed. "Look! The road goes right into the hillside. But there are doors across the way. It's like the hall of the mountain king!"

More like industrial-steel hangar bays with a conduit to bring the electric into the bunker. "Cheri, someone doesn't want us here. Let's skedaddle—what do you say?"

"You don't want to see if we can open the doors? No? I guess you're right. Let's go back. I don't want to do any more running, though. Can we walk to the Triangle-K?"

By that time, I could hear the sound of a motor coming toward us over the pasturelands on the other side of the meeting house. "Pretty sure that's not going to be a problem."

By the time we walked around to the front of the building, Wolf's second-in-command, Bart, was pulling onto the gravel from the field beyond. "Hey there!" he said with a grin big enough to show through the beard. "It's you guys. I'm so glad!"

"Ooh!" Cheri headed for the Jeep with a sprightly step. "How'd you know we were here? Was it the cameras? Dash here said we shouldn't trespass, but I wanted a look. Did I do something wrong?"

"Nah," Bart said easily. "Those cameras are for show. We had some trouble with the local teens partying out here, so we set them up. But there is a motion detector on the front door. And when it went off, Wolf sent me out to check."

"So you don't mind me looking here?" She shot a victorious glance at me, and I raised my hands in surrender.

"Sure don't. This is Tri-K property, and our guests are welcome everywhere."

I made a mental note of the exact phrasing. *That's permission a judge would accept. Thanks, Bart.*

"Aren't you the nicest thing!"

"You folks want a ride back to the ranch?"

Cheri was already climbing into the passenger seat beside him. "Are you going to run back, Dash?"

She blinked innocently at me. I could run ahead and meet Rose and her long-distance multimilers, or I could run to the ranch—or I could climb into a nice, comfortable Jeep and be driven back by one of my suspects, with whom I could have a casual conversation about a meeting hall with electricity and plenty of room to store bundles of twenties and hundreds.

I threw my leg over the side and climbed in. As it happened, chatty Cheri did all the interrogations for me with such obvious interest I knew Bart would not suspect her of covert investigations. Never was an "operative" less covert than Cheri.

She began with a cozy, "What *is* this place, Bart?" and went from there. She kept him talking all the way to the ranch.

It was just a local gathering place, he told her, used mostly in the fall and spring as a place for ranchers to coordinate cattle drives. And the "hall of the mountain king" was an old World War II fallout shelter—pretty big one too. Went back almost fifty feet. But it hadn't been opened in years, of course. No fear of the Big One now, right?

He and Cheri laughed merrily at the absurdity of nuclear threat, and I considered how neatly clipped all the surrounding foliage had been, considering the road led to a set of steel doors not opened in decades.

Bart dropped us at the lodge. Wolf came out the front door. He eyed me, and distrust rolled off him in waves. "Morning," he said to Cheri as she went past him to get a bottle of water.

She waved happily and was gone, the screen door slamming behind her. Then he turned to me, and Bart came up behind. I smiled easily and relaxed. It's always easier to act when your muscles aren't bound by tension.

"You get a good look at the community hall?" Wolf asked, his voice neutral and his eyes hard. I began to reply innocently, and he cut me off. "I hear you want to look at my books."

"Christ, don't mention it to my wife!"

Neither man offered the mild chuckle that deserved. "You looking for anything in particular?"

"I found some good tax deductions for your father and a streamlining macro that—"

"You're not getting a look at my books. I don't know who you are, and I don't need any help paying taxes to a government that doesn't deserve them." He was losing his neutrality. Anger crept into the set of his shoulders and the way he held his hands.

"It's okay with me," I said easily. I backed and "accidentally" bumped into Bart, who was knocked off-balance. I put out a hand to catch him. "Sorry, man—I didn't see you there."

Wolf looked at me without speaking. I gave him an innocent eyebrow lift. "Is there a problem?"

He shook his head slowly. "No problem. Come on, Bart."

He took the wheel of Bart's Jeep, and they left in a cloud of dust. Bait definitely not taken. I needed to make a few calls. If the fish won't nibble, then you change the bait.

On the other hand, Wolf acted like he had something to hide. I just had to figure out what it was—and prove it to a judge.

I watched them go. Then I turned and walked to the vehicle barn. Run of the ranch, huh? Might be a good time to reconnoiter an unexplored area.

TWENTY-THREE

DASH

QUICK SURVEILLANCE INDICATED NO ONE IN FRONT OF THE vehicle barn. I walked across the large asphalt apron as if I owned the place and peered in through the windows on the first of six large bay doors. The grime was too thick to see much inside.

Two electric gators were charging at a station on the side of the barn, and the gas pump was nearby. I was about to explore the back of the building when a Ford F-series pickup pulled in. Nothing looks guiltier than trying to avoid notice, so I stood there and waited. Bob Koenig parked and got out, an enormous grin lighting his face.

"Why, hi there, Mr. Accountant! Whatever are you doing back here where it's boring?"

"Looking around. Is that okay?"

"It's sure okay with me! Want to give me a hand?"

He opened the tailgate to reveal cases of bottled water. "We store 'em out here until the cook wants to move them into the walk-in. Grab a case or two, will you?"

He rattled open the first bay's garage door and stacked his cases next to other similar boxes. Together we unloaded half a dozen flats, and then I stood in the dimness of the garage and took a long, frank look around.

"You have quite an operation here, Bob," I said.

"Sure have! I guess this is one of my biggest line items, as you know." He stood next to me and flicked on the lights, lighting up a space the size of a small warehouse. Bob counted off the vehicle in front of us.

"Six off-road Jeeps to get our guests where they need to go. Only four here this morning—the boys must have a few out and about. There's the luxury bus you came in on; she's our newest purchase. Isn't she a honey? Behind her, a horse trailer. Wolf's truck is big enough to tow it. That catering truck back there turned out to be kind of a failure. We can't even drive it now. Turns out it can't get up the Jeep trail to Smuggler's Basin, so we're trying to figure out if we can fix the truck. Or fix the trail. Wolf's a fiend for problem-solving. We're still taking supplies up there in that old school bus. Doesn't look like much, I know, but that bus is tough as nails. Then my wife's sedan, the mower, pair of gas-powered gators, the tractor. We've got the plow attachment for the tractor to get us out of here in the winter." He listed them with great pride, and I exclaimed at each treasure.

There were a lot of vehicles. No Ferraris. Nothing flashy that one might buy with one's fake money. There were also only four garage bay doors in this large space, while I'd counted six doors on the other side. The far wall hid something.

Bob came to the end of his roster of nonflashy cars ("My dad's old Willys. Barely runs, but I can't bear to get rid of it"), and we walked back into the sunshine.

"Thanks for giving me the tour," I said.

"Thanks for asking! Most people only care about the horses—not the horsepower!" We laughed at his little joke.

"What's that odd smell, Bob?" I asked casually.

"You can smell that, can you?" He eyed me with approval. "You've got quite a nose on you. That's the medicine for worming the horses. Wolf keeps it up here because it spooks the stock if he stores it in the barn. Smells funny, don't it?"

"Sure does." Maybe it was wishful sniffing, but I thought I was smelling a whole bunch of printer cartridges.

He walked me to the lodge, and I still couldn't decide if he'd deliberately kept me away from the last two bays or if he thought of those as Wolf's territory, and he naturally gave his son room to run the ranch his way. Bob Koenig: Nice guy? Or counterfeiter?

Mentally, I shrugged. Could be one was an act to cover the other.

"I sure do want to thank you for the work you did for me yesterday. Going to save me a fair piece."

"My pleasure."

"I told Wolf he should talk to you, but he didn't like that idea."

"I know. I talked to him this morning. He seemed suspicious."

"Well, don't take it personal. That's his way. What's on your agenda for the day, Dash?" he asked.

"I'm on the fly-fishing expedition."

"Now that's a smart way to spend the day!" His delight was evident. "If I had the day off, why, that's where I'd be! You catch you a trout before lunch and the boys will roast it for you right there on the fire. You catch it after lunch and Cook will serve it up for your dinner." He leaned in to confide in me. "Now, our chef is a hell of a cook, but I'm telling you, there is nothing so good as a trout you pull out of a cold, rushing stream, cooked over an open fire. That's a slice of heaven right there."

He beamed at me with sincere goodwill. I began to be hungry for trout.

"And then you've got the square dancing tonight."

"Oh, well," I hedged, "that's off the property, isn't it? Rose and I sort of thought we'd stay here and watch the stars. You know—relax for the evening."

"Son," he said with a grin, "you take an old man's word for it: take that cute little lady square dancing. Now, I know it's silly. Even hokey. But I promise you are going to have the time of your lives. And aren't you going to Smuggler's Basin tomorrow for some glamping?"

I nodded.

"Best stargazing in the world up there. No, you go square dancing tonight and cuddle with your honey under the stars tomorrow. And here she is!"

We were standing at the lodge. Up the barn path came Rose, her coterie trailing out behind her in varying states of exhaustion.

"Why, hello there, Miss Rose!" he greeted her. "Don't you look like you could take on a pair of bears!"

She did too. A light sweat picked out her muscle definition, and her breathing was deep and regular.

"Hi, Bob. Hi, honey." She and I exchanged a quick buss on the lips. "I'm ready to tangle with your bears. Gotta save my man here. He's got a bear phobia."

"No," I clarified, "I have a *horse* phobia. My fear of bears is entirely rational and appropriate."

"He thinks Big Ben is going to get him," Rose explained to Bob, who smiled as he corrected her.

"That's Big Billy—and you're going to have to travel farther than you'll be going with us to come across him anytime soon!"

"Glad to hear it," I said. The two of them laughed at me kindly. Sort of.

"Let's go grab a shower," Rose said to me. We waved to her running buddies, now draped in assorted poses across the veranda, and took our leave.

"If that guy's trying to destabilize the US economy," Rose said to me quietly, "he's sure hiding it well."

"He willingly gave me a tour of two-thirds of the vehicle barn."

"Two-thirds?"

I'd learned a lot since we'd parted—more than enough to justify the fact I hadn't run ten miles and had even gotten a ride back from the two or three I had run.

Old, not stupid.

I ushered her into our cabin and made a quick electronics sweep. Still unmonitored.

I explained. "We've got a meetinghouse with cameras and electricity. A suspicious cave in the hills behind big doors, also with electricity. A third of the vehicle barn we haven't seen yet. A strange smell that may be ink."

"And your Mistress of the Mysterious says something unusual is going on."

"Don't call her that."

"Sorry." She ducked her head. "Her warning is the one least likely to get us a warrant anyway. No, we're going to need some evidence if we're going to have any chance of stopping these counterfeiters."

"But we've also managed to upset the balance here," I said. "Three of the ranch hands are either injured or terrified. That's got to help." Rose high-fived me. "They know I've been through Bob's books, that you've been asking questions, that we've been snooping around their meetinghouse and know about the bunker behind it."

"And if Daddy is in on it, then they know you've been snooping around the vehicle barn too."

"Safe to assume they don't like us, then. Wolf wasn't doing much to hide it. So, tell me, rookie: What would you do now if you were them?"

She whistled as she considered. "I'd do two things: first, take out the snoop and his busybody wife." She looked at me, and I nodded back.

"Given. What's the other thing?"

"I'd move whatever I was hiding in that garage."

"Ink and paper, maybe the printers . . . okay, so you move it from the barn to the bunker. When would you do that, if you assumed the snoop and his snoopy wife were undercover agents who might unleash the full force of the US government on you? Me, I'm betting if something were to happen, it would happen tonight, when the entire ranch is being nudged out to a square dance in town."

"That's when I'd move anything that needed to be moved," she agreed.

"We need camera surveillance."

"And a warrant." We both shook our heads. We didn't have enough to go to a judge.

"On the other hand . . ." I mused over the possibilities.

"You got something? What does the voice of experience have to offer, old man?"

"Well, we've got permission to use the drone."

"Sure."

"And you're pretty skilled at navigating with it."

She preened. "It's my generation. I grew up on video games—unlike you."

"I'll bet. What if you piloted that drone somewhere where it could accidentally run out of power with a view of the garage?"

She nodded. "Run the camera, ditch the flight. We could put it on Bob and Marcia's roof. Angled right, that would give us a view almost up to the vehicle barn."

"Enough to see what comes and goes."

"I'll do it after roping class, during lunch. Everyone will be at the lodge."

"Except us mighty fishermen."

"You should have seen the one that got away." She grinned at me, and we both finished the phrase, holding our hands far apart, "It was *this big*."

Rose's confidence was growing. *Ahhh. Satisfying.*

She swung her hand around to shake mine. "Not bad, old man. We'll go to a real, old-fashioned hoedown, they'll think they're safe, we'll record the whole thing. I like it."

"Me too."

I enjoyed the sense of power that came from a sound strategy and a young partner well-set on the path.

And then the fishing expedition happened.

TWENTY-FOUR
EVADNE

From my stuffy mini-Hall of Mysteries off the lobby, I watched as guests gathered after breakfast for the excursions. Lenny, still speaking with a notable rasp, saw Rose in the roping group. He gulped, touched his throat, and had an urgent word with Wolf. Wolf called Bart over and switched their assignments.

So it was Lenny who swaggered over to the fly-fishing group. That was where Dash was, and I was determined to live a life of courage. So I stepped up to interrupt before Lenny could greet the guests. "Is there room for one more?"

I avoided Dash's eye and smiled at Lenny, who turned bright red. Skip goggled at me and shoved his phone into his pocket. That was one I'd handle with delicacy. A teen crush was nothing to take lightly.

"Yes, ma'am," Lenny said. "I can fit five in my Jeep no problem. You can sit by me. That's fine." He realized he was spluttering and threw an elbow into Gustavo's ribs. "Gussie, get another pair of waders and one more pole. Go on now. All right," he said to the group. "Me and Gussie are going to drive you out to the river. We'll stretch the nine of you out so you're not on top of each other. You guys," he said to Charlie and Val with their teenagers, Skip and Melanie, "can be closer together if you like. Anybody here do any fly-fishing before?"

Quentin, the large businessman from Florida, stepped forward. "Lots of times. I love to fly-fish." Arrogant, competent, dressed in prefaded clothes for the dedicated-fisherman look.

"Well, that's great, sir. We'll put you between some of the newbies, if that's okay. You can show them the ropes."

Quentin preened.

"We've got equipment," Lenny went on, but Quentin interrupted him.

"I tie my own flies," he said grandly.

Skip looked up from his phone. "You tie up flies?"

Quentin laughed indulgently and opened the tackle box he carried. "I mean I tie these, son."

He and Skip peered in, followed by Melanie, who cooed over the different colors. That drew the attention of the other would-be fishermen, and Lenny found himself without his audience. He crossed his arms over his chest in irritation and directed us to the Jeeps as soon as Gustavo returned.

Lenny pushed the four-member family into Gustavo's Jeep, followed by Quentin. He put me into his front seat and barely acknowledged the three pushed into the back. Scott and Barbara —a young couple on their honeymoon—didn't mind the squeeze at all, and I felt Dash at my back like a warm ember banked in the fireplace. I would be brave today. I promised myself I would.

We drove through several pastures. (Dash was deputized to climb out of the back seat to open and close gates, and I tried not to stare. He moved like a cat.) The air in Wyoming was so clean that even after we'd been driving a good ten minutes, the lodge was clearly visible.

Eventually, we came to the flat, rocky banks of what I would have called a stream if I hadn't been informed by Lenny that it was a river—and I should respect it as a river. The water was thirty or forty feet across to the far bank, and the rocky bottom was visible through crystalline water.

"Most of it's shallow," Lenny told us, "but don't be fooled. There are parts you have to swim a horse across, so don't be stupid. That water is cold, and it's fast."

We were grouped around a campfire ring, and Lenny and Gustavo distributed waders and poles. (Neither Melanie nor Skip wanted to put on the saggy old waders, but their mother quashed their objections with a glare.)

"Don't we have to be quiet?" asked Melanie. "In movies, people who are fishing are always real quiet."

"Being quiet is an excellent idea," said their father, who, judging by the finger-combed wildness of his hair, was dad-harried already.

"That's not necessary," Quentin overrode everyone else. "The river is making enough noise. You can sing if you want. It won't help you fish any better, but it also won't scare the fish." He laughed at this witticism.

"Now I'ma show you how to cast," Lenny broke in, determined to get his audience back. "And then we'll spread you out so you don't hook each other."

We spent a few minutes getting our lines tangled in the brush. Skip was the one to spot the large bird hovering overhead.

"Look! It's an eagle! Dash, is that your eagle?"

Dash gaped, taken by surprise. I could feel his objections logjammed in his throat. *I don't have an eagle—my eagle was in Nevada—how long did eagles live, anyway?*

"That's a hawk," Lenny said dismissively. "And he'll steal every fish you pull out of this river. I have a creel here. You call me and I'll get it."

"Aw." Skip and Melanie both preferred the notion of Dash's own private eagle.

"Okay, that's enough," Lenny said, annoyed. "Let's get you spaced out on the river."

I ended up downstream of the group. I watched to see where Dash ended up.

He moved to stand near me.

Now there would be no excuse to not be brave. I felt fear and a fizzy burst of happiness.

One act of bravery, coming right up.

Quentin had stepped up to my left but was astonished to discover Skip had jumped Quentin's claim. I smiled at the boy, who ducked his head and grinned at me.

The teen stood a mere five feet from me, the cold water rushing shin-high over the heavy waders. "Too damned close," Quentin muttered and strode further upstream, where he could browbeat Skip's father, Charlie, about his casting.

I found myself lulled by fly-fishing. Casting required finesse and I botched it repeatedly, but after a time, I could flick my fly with reasonable accuracy.

The stones under my waders were loose and uncertain, but I never had to wade in much deeper than my knees. Beyond that depth, the water became a force to be reckoned with and threatened to pull me off my feet. The chill was profound.

But the sun was brilliant and reflected off the crystal waters. Low clouds were piling up in the south, but in this patch of icy river, the day was fine and clear. The clean air made the mountains look close enough to touch. I watched the hawk effortlessly ride the thermal currents rising from the warmth of the pasturelands. Horses in their fields grazed in the distance. It was serene and peaceful, and I found I'd relaxed.

The constant chatter of water over the rocks masked a lot of noise, but I could hear Lenny order Gustavo to go to the lodge to get lunch from the cook. I heard Quentin advise Charlie on his casting. And I heard Skip's shriek of joy when he was the first to pull a fat, silvery trout from the rushing waters.

Quentin *harrumph*ed his disbelief and favored both Skip and Skip's father with ample words about beginner's luck. Skip forgot his crush on me and moved upstream to lord his catch over his sister.

Lenny, standing on the bank and trying to talk to me, cursed when his phone rang. Then he cursed some more. The coolers for the lunch were in his Jeep, not in Gustavo's, and he needed to head back to pick up our meal. "You all okay here while I'm gone?"

"I'll watch over them," Quentin said arrogantly. We all agreed Quentin was welcome to try, and Lenny took off, muttering about having to open and close all those gates himself.

Stillness fell over the scene once again, and the various chatter and discussions faded into the background as I cast and reeled in, cast and reeled in, practicing the strange, supple whipping motion and slowly getting the hang of it.

And Dash stood nearby, also lost in the sunlight sparkling off the swift water.

No better time. I pulled on all my courage and eased over to him.

"You should cast over there," I said. "I think you'll catch something in that pool."

TWENTY-FIVE

EVADNE

I'D STARTLED HIM. HE TURNED, SURPRISED, AND HIS SMILE WAS the reward for my newfound bravery. Easing my way downstream was paying off.

"Are you reading the fish now?" he asked.

I laughed, watching the sunlight play across his face. "Fish are notoriously hard to read. Maybe they don't think much. Try below that rock."

I watched him cast. He had a natural grace and an economy of movement that was very attractive.

He caught me staring. "You're getting pretty good at this," I said, to cover the fact that I was eyeing him like lunch.

"Thanks."

We fished and I kept my eyes to myself. Mostly. Outwardly, I cast serenely. Inwardly, I tried to work out how anyone could possibly be sexy in hip waders.

Quentin had moved upstream to harangue Charlie about his rod etiquette. Dash and I were all but alone. The chatter of the river masked any conversation from nearby ears, so there was a sense of intimacy amid the vastness of open land.

He broke the silence. "Were you a little scared last night?"

Startled, I looked at him. I thought about my late-night

reflections on courage. How had he known? "Are you reading me now?"

His lean, handsome face creased in a gentle smile, and his kindness washed over me. "You took my hand. Maybe you hoped I would make you feel safe."

I could feel the heat of my blush on my cheeks. *Embarrassing.* I studied the water rushing across our feet. "I couldn't just want to hold your hand?"

"You can hold my hand anytime you want, Evadne. But then you let go. I wondered why."

I cast again, thinking about courage. At last, I formulated an answer.

"I don't like teasing those men."

"Who? Abbott and Costello? You don't think they deserve it?"

"No, they do. The pair of them are a nest of snakes. They're not good. But . . ." I reeled in my fly and then flicked my wrist, whipping it out into the middle of the river. So satisfying when done right. "Scared people do stupid things, sometimes violent things. And they're scared."

"Huh."

He caught me biting back a smile at his tell.

We fished as I mused on the value of courage. He thought about his investigation. And deep below his conscious thoughts, he wondered if he could trust me.

"When you read Abbott and Costello," he said, "can you tell what they're going to do?"

I shook my head. "I can't see the future. I see the truth of now and how the past affects that."

"Okay. Someday you're going to tell me how you do that."

I smiled to mask regret. "You won't believe me."

"Sure, Cassandra."

He'd eased closer to me. Or had I moved closer to him?

"I took a walk behind the lodge this morning," I offered with studied nonchalance.

"And?"

"I think the ink, or whatever it is, is in that back barn. I'm not sure. But it's not in the lodge."

"I think it's in the back barn too. But your reading and my hunch aren't going to get us a search warrant." He bit back a measure of frustration.

"And that's definitely the situation you're here for?"

I asked it carefully, but he knew it for the moment of trust that it was.

"Well—maybe," he hedged.

I nodded. "I guess that's good. Someone should do something about it. I'm glad it's you and Rose. And Enrique? He's . . . undercover too?"

He didn't look me in the eye. "Um—"

"That's okay," I said quickly. "I get it. Don't worry about it."

Somehow, the space between us had grown again. He stopped reeling in his line and turned to me, watching me directly.

"Evadne, I'm not exactly who I say I am, and you're not exactly who you say you are. But before I leave, I'm giving you my phone number and my real name. And you can call me whenever you want—to feel safe or just to talk. I hope you do. Because Phoebus Apollon is not your only friend."

I blinked at him. I had no words for the sudden rush of emotions—from myself and from him. I wanted so deeply to believe what he said, to find the courage to trust that more was possible with this good, handsome, sexy man. The weight of my deep-down loneliness wasn't the only reason I was drawn to him.

I felt his goodness. His surprising, glorious desire to protect me. Could I trust what I was reading about him? Was I that brave?

I drew in a ragged breath, scenting the wild freshness of the air, and then switched my rod to my other hand. Holding out my right to him, I willed my hand not to shake.

"My name is Eve Simons."

"Eve Simons," he repeated with a goofy smile that melted something calloused and hard inside me. "It's nice to meet you."

We shook, and I knew again the security that came from holding his hand. Our arms were awkwardly extended out over the water, but I didn't want to let go. "I'm Dash," he said. "That's really my first name."

I nodded. The heat of my blush flowed across my cheeks. Reluctantly, he let my hand drop.

"Eve's a pretty name. How'd you end up with Evadne?"

"Artie's idea, of course. Phoebus," I amended, looking at him to make sure he understood. He nodded. "Evadne was some woman in Greek mythology. She was . . ." My voice stumbled, and then I took a breath. "She was the mother of a famous prophet."

I know he saw my pain. He didn't understand it, but he wanted to reach out to me anyway. He took one long step toward me and found his footing on the rocky riverbed. He leaned over and slid one finger lightly across my flushed cheek, painting me in warmth and concern. "Now, why was that so hard for you to say, beautiful?"

I looked up at him and leaned in, my face turned up to his. He stopped breathing. I tried to summon the words. I tried to explain. They got jammed up inside me, and I knew I wouldn't be able to face my past. Not then. Not in the middle of a rushing stream with uncertain footing and glaring, truth-seeking sunlight all around me.

My defensive armor came up again. Breaking my own heart, I stepped from his touch. "You're reading me again?"

I cast my fly with an aggressive flip.

"Pain that obvious . . . you don't have to be psychic to read it."

"Just clever and observant, huh? I'll have to get better control of myself." All of my shields were up again. The sense of intimacy had been pushed brusquely away.

"Well, not on my account." He gave it a moment before voicing his assumptions. "Do you have a child, Eve?"

My sudden rush of tears betrayed how close to the surface my emotions were with this man. I turned away to hide the tears, but he saw them anyway. Those emotional shields I'd raised were made of tissue paper designed to look like stone. "No. No children for me."

There. That was the truth, if he cared to hear it.

"Okay." He wanted me to know he was backing off. "Now— do you want to ask *me* any hugely inappropriate questions?"

His change of tone made me smile. I read the zip of electricity my smile had given him, and I was deeply flattered. I waited until he was in midcast to ask.

"Why aren't you married, Dash?"

His cast went wide and snagged on a fallen log on the far side of the river. *Ah—not so easy to maintain your calm when you're the one getting the third degree, huh?* He tugged, but it was hopeless. He lost the fly and reeled in an empty line. I handed him one of my spare flies.

"How do you know I'm not?" he asked.

"I know."

"Well, you're right." He fumbled with the hook, and I realized he was embarrassed because his up-close vision was blurry. I reached out and took it from him, tying a quick knot in the line. "Except for Rose, of course."

"Of course. Go ahead. That's on now."

"Thanks." We both cast, and I waited to see if he'd open up. He brooded over a painful memory.

"Telling you this story is going to show you the ugliness of my past. You'll have to decide if you still think I'm so honorable."

I nodded and maintained a neutral expression. Maybe we were both fishing for more than trout today.

He paused and then spoke, "I was twenty-four and just out of the Academy—ah, just out of training."

Police academy? FBI Academy? Yes, I thought, *FBI feels right.* I kept a straight face. He went on.

"My girlfriend at the time, Danika . . . she was . . ." He fumbled with the challenge of expressing a complex situation in plain, simple language. "She was great. Funny, gorgeous, smart. But as time went on, she sort of . . . changed. I don't know."

Remorse from that time rose in him again. *You can think you're past it, but shame never goes away.* I know that all too well. It lies in wait like the La Brea tar pits, ambushing you when you least expect it and pulling you down into clinging, tarry oblivion.

"She became needy and kind of paranoid and—I don't know, bitter. It stopped being fun to go out with her. And I was stupid enough about the whole thing—"

His speech tapered off as he got lost in his memories. "What happened?" I asked quietly.

TWENTY-SIX

DASH

DREDGING UP ONE OF MY UGLIEST MEMORIES WAS NASTY. BUT offering it to Eve was, I realized, a last-ditch effort to push her away from me. I still wasn't willing to admit she might not be a con artist, so how could I become involved with a criminal? Me, the potential leader of the FBI's program to make better FBI agents?

I broke my narrative down to the barest facts. "I broke up with her. She begged me not to, and I did it anyway."

Just the facts, ma'am sounds so easy, but remorse swamped me. I stumbled to a halt, my fishing rod forgotten in my hand.

Eve laid cool fingers across my wrist. At her touch, my heartbeat slowed, my panic receded. What kind of effect did this woman have on me? "And then what?" Eve asked.

"Danika killed herself. Overdosed on her roommate's prescription medication."

Those two simple sentences came out easily. These were the facts; they needed no emotional packaging. And yet they hid a pit of horror in me. At my most fundamentally childish center, where pure selfishness lived, I was still shaken. Still asking, *How could she have done that to me?*

I blinked and realized how this must have sounded. I rushed

to clarify. "It's not that I'm so incredible women can't bear to lose me. I'm not saying that. I'm saying she was dealing with some form of mental illness and needed support. And I was too stupid to know. Too selfish to care."

I tried to keep my expression calm, my gaze over the river steady. I'd capped the gushing well of sorrow inside me, and now it had blown again, splattering my mind with stinging acid.

"I met with clients this morning who were swamped by emotion," Eve said. "I had to let them leave early, so they could run or dance or . . . something." Her voice was distracting and soothing me, and a light flush led my thoughts into an R-rated intimation of what the *something* might be. "You, on the other hand? You need to howl, to slam, to rip something apart."

There. She'd helped. I capped my shame again. "Hulk smash, huh?"

She grinned. "You do what you need to do."

We went on casting into the rushing river, and my pulse slowed. My breathing evened out.

"She didn't do it because of you," Eve tried, but I cut her off.

"Oh yes, she did. Maybe I wasn't the cause of her depression, but I was certainly the catalyst for her death. After that . . . I didn't want to have any relationships close enough to be able to hurt someone that badly again."

I looked at Eve, focusing on the present again. I surrendered to the pull I felt to her. I hoped she would recognize the warning when I spoke.

"The women I date know I'm interested in fun and companionship and sex—but not intimacy. Not the dangerous link that forms when you let someone inside far enough to be able to cause them pain."

"Wow," she said. "You and I need to talk about courage."

I grinned at her unexpected words. "You think I'm not courageous?" Should I be offended? Angry? Surprised? It didn't matter.

"I know I haven't been courageous," she said stoutly. "And I'm going to try to be braver."

I looked at her, confused. What was she saying?

"Okay," she said with a smile. She sent a fly whizzing sweetly out over the water, her reel singing with the success of her cast. "Now we know the handsome brooding guy's backstory. That explains some stuff."

"Oh, yeah?" I was grateful for the change in mood. "Like what?"

"Like why you're not running from me, for instance. Not yet anyway."

"What?" I forgot my fishing rod again. "What does that mean?"

"Well, most guys think I'm pretty, but I have a hard time trusting anyone. I scare them off by saying something they don't want spoken. For me, progress happens at a snail's pace. And with your unwillingness to get intimate, that would probably feel pretty good to you. Most guys end up going for someone easier pretty quickly."

Her words were smooth, but they didn't quite cover up the pain. She'd been hurt, and I wished I could have protected her from that.

"Easier how?"

"Oh, you know—falling into bed with someone else. That's what you should probably do, Dash." She grinned at my shock. "You're a classic. Tall, dark, and handsome. Half the cabin girls think you're hot. The other two are in a relationship with each other, and even one of them thinks it would be fun to take you out for a test-drive. Plus, there are plenty of wives here who would welcome you, you know."

She laughed outright at my astonishment. My days of attracting multiple potential partners had been left behind in the optometrist's office when my impending old age was confirmed.

Delighted by the effect of her words, she gestured with her

chin upstream. "Quentin's wife, Colleen, thinks you've got a gorgeous ass. She spends a lot of time imagining you naked."

I lost my metaphorical footing. I was still sputtering and trying to come up with a good response when Quentin's actual feet got swept out from under him.

We'd both turned to look upstream when she mentioned Quentin's wife. The older man had been moving further and further into the river, the water over his knees, when he must have stepped wrong. With a startled gasp, he fell and went under.

"Oh, God—that water's cold," she gasped.

Quentin resurfaced almost immediately, but the current flowed into his hip waders and dragged him down. He lost his footing again.

"Hey!" he shouted, making a grab for a passing rock. His fingers slipped on the wet surface, and he tumbled.

Past me, there was nothing but miles of fast river and hard rock. I stepped into deeper water and managed to grab Quentin's foot as he flashed past. I threw out an arm to counter-balance the moment and stop my own plunge into an icy nightmare, and Eve was there, anchoring me. Quentin screamed as we pulled him into the shallows.

"My leg!" I thought I'd hurt him, but Quentin's hands tried uselessly to hold his other thigh. Blood seeped out from the top of the waders. "I hit a rock!"

Adrenaline and basic first-aid lessons zapped through me. This guy was in trouble.

Skip and his father ran down the riverbank to help, followed by the others. Together we moved Quentin onto dry land as gently as we could.

I stayed calm, and that helped the others to avoid panic. I told Skip to call the ranch so they could send help. The call went through, but no one answered.

"Try again."

Barbara, the newlywed, arrived from her position the

furthest upstream and announced she was a physical therapist, certainly the closest among us to medical competency. We gently worked Quentin out of the waders and piled our sweaters and coats on him.

The bone sticking out of his thigh had gone through muscle, skin, and pants. "That's one hell of a compound fracture." Barbara smiled easily at Quentin, whose skin was clammy with pain. "We're going to stabilize you until we can get you to a doctor." She looked up at me and nodded, her smile still in place but her eyes grim. "We need that Jeep. Now."

Quentin grabbed Evadne's hand. "Am I going to die? You can tell, right?" He looked up at her in desperation.

"I can tell," she said soothingly. "You're not. You're going to be fine."

"Stay with me!"

"I will."

I rounded on Skip. "Still no answer?"

The boy shook his head, his eyes wide and his face tinged with green. Looking at Quentin's leg had made him queasy. This was more excitement than he'd bargained for. Actual bloodshed was nowhere near as fun as video games. *Welcome to my world, kid.*

"Okay." I eyed the lodge. In this annoyingly clear air, everything was magnified, and distance was untrustworthy. What the hell was I doing so far away from a city? The lodge was farther than it looked. "I'll get Lenny."

With her free hand, Evadne grabbed me. "In the pasture. Take that horse."

I looked to where she'd gestured. An enormous red beast watched curiously.

"That's Rocket," I said uselessly. "The one who broke two cowboys at the rodeo. I can't ride him."

"Yes, you can." She tugged my hand until I looked away from my nightmare—away from the huge, stomping hooves and overwhelming size, so much more powerful than me. The massive muscles bunched over shoulders, over hindquarters. Not an animal to trust.

"He likes you. He'll let you ride him."

"Evadne," I said desperately. "No."

"Yes. You can do it." She looked at me with hope, her eyes pleading with me to trust her. To, at last, simply believe her.

But it was a horse. A *horse*. No saddle. No reins. No stirrups. No knowledge. No skill. No way. I looked at her, apology dripping off me from every pore. *Believe me. I can't do it.* "With all the gates, I can run it just as fast. I'll be back."

I struggled out of my waders. I'd worn hiking boots. It would be a long jog.

Evadne looked down as her shoulders came up. A defensive posture. "You don't trust me."

Regret and anxiety welled up in me. But this was not the time for a heart-to-heart. The others were building a fire to keep Quentin warm, but the guy was going into shock anyway.

"I trust you—I don't trust the horse. I'll be back."

I took off, keeping an eye on Rocket as I ran through his pasture. Rocket watched me pass, bemused, but the monster never moved a muscle.

As I moved away at a steady run, I tried not to feel as if I'd crushed something new and fragile.

TWENTY-SEVEN

DASH

NONE OF US HAD FRESH-CAUGHT TROUT FOR LUNCH THAT DAY. On the other hand, almost none of us was medevac'd from the pasture to a hospital in Cheyenne.

Taking advantage of the excitement caused by a helicopter on the lawn, Rose got the drone onto the roof of Bob and Marcia's house without drawing any attention.

I'd learned Evadne's name was actually Eve, but I was too much of a wimp about horses to earn her trust.

In summation, the day had had its ups and downs.

Happily, my guy at the IRS approved a little-used, multigenerational, historic-properties provision Bob could legitimately claim to lower his taxes. Nothing a judge could say was entrapment—but most definitely a trap for Wolf.

"Once Daddy tells him how much he could save, Wolf should change his mind about letting me into his books," I theorized to Rose through the door as she changed in the bathroom. She appeared in the door in a swingy skirt held out by petticoats or crinolines or something. She looked like a cowgirl ballerina in a tutu. I goggled at her.

"What the hell are you wearing?"

"Didn't you see the website? Guests are invited to wear traditional square-dancing apparel for the big hoedown in town tonight."

She twirled, her white skirt flaring out to show off bands of red bandanna at the hem. Her short, red cowboy boots matched perfectly, and she wore a denim shirt tied at the waist.

"Where are you getting all of these clothes? You brought one suitcase. I watched."

"Lycra packs small." She bobbed in a cute curtsy, and I had to admit my "wife" was absolutely adorable.

"Stand there," I demanded. "I need to send a picture to your fiancé. Has Enos seen this outfit?"

She fluttered a wave at my phone. Enos, an agent with the Treasury Department, was a lucky man.

"Well, do I need to do something?" I asked her. "Find a coonskin hat? Steal some cowboy boots?"

"Oh, you're fine," she said dismissively. "Jeans and a T-shirt. Men have it easy."

"But we don't look anywhere near as gorgeous." I bowed to her as she grinned back.

"All right, sweet-talker. As we've been told repeatedly, dinner is at the lodge, and then everybody onto the bus to head into town."

I nodded. We'd been getting the full-court press from the entire staff about how we had to go to the dance. The unspoken *get out* message was clear.

Rose wasn't the only woman who'd pulled out the petticoats. It would be hard to board the bus with so many ruffles. Some of the husbands had been forced into shirts that matched their wives' outfits. The females cooed in delight. The males exchanged pitying looks and long-suffering grimaces.

The week's only family appeared in coordinated red, white, and blue jean outfits. Melanie and her mother were cute as kittens in matching skirts, and Charlie wore his Western-style snap-front shirt with good grace.

Skip, I noted, had been forced into his matching shirt but

had determinedly pulled a World of Warcraft T-shirt over it. He resisted his mother's anger radar by burying himself in his phone. More and more, I liked that kid.

But the most startling outfit belonged to innkeeper Marcia Koenig, who appeared in a bright-yellow getup with tribal ornamentation, lots of turquoise jewelry, and a fringed suede vest.

"Damn," whispered Rose in admiration. "Fringe. That old lady has got it going on."

Marcia clapped her hands. "Are we all looking forward to our evening?"

"Are you coming with us, Marcia?" someone called.

"Of course! I never miss a chance to square dance!"

"And Bob too?"

"My darling husband says he pulled his back today loading in cases of water. He's up at the house, making sure to moan occasionally." *Damn.* I wouldn't be able to give him the news in person about his tax exemption. I pulled out my phone to contact him electronically. Marcia went on. "Lots of complaining, but he looks pretty comfortable in his recliner in front of the TV!"

We all exchanged a hearty chuckle over that. *Men.* What can you do?

"So Lenny isn't only going to drive the bus. He's going to be my partner tonight!"

Lenny, waiting by the door, tipped an imaginary hat to her. He didn't look quite as excited as she did by the plan.

I felt Evadne on my skin as she entered the room. She and several of the psychics had been finishing up their private readings in the rooms off the Hall of Mysteries.

But it was Sister Annette who pushed to the front of the psychics. They scattered as she commanded the attention of the room.

"I have a message from Martine!"

Her high voice cut through the chatter, and the room fell silent.

"My darling Martine sees far, you know. She sees . . . beyond the veil." She cast a sweeping arm grandly toward the kitchen, and we all agreed this was far indeed.

"And now she is speaking to me. Tell me, Martine! Tell us all! Speak through me!" Her eyes rolled up in her head, she swayed on her feet, and then she spouted incomprehensibly.

"What's she doing?" I whispered to the square-dancing daddy next to me.

"Martine is from the sixteenth century. She speaks medieval French."

"Of course she does."

That's a pretty good dodge. If anyone here happened to speak French and caught Sister Annette in a clunker, she could claim it was the ancient form of the language. I had to tip my metaphorical ten-gallon cowboy hat to Professor Sprout.

"What does that mean, Sister Annette?" Phoebus Apollon stood behind her, his arms outstretched in benevolent protection of his psychic. "Translate for us, learnéd one."

Her eyelids fluttered as she came out of her trance. "Oh, such a message!"

She was wreathed in smiles and milking her opportunity. I, hungry for my supper, noted the servers at the kitchen door, ready to bring out the meal. *Let's get on with it, Betty Lou.*

She got on with it. "A baby!"

The room broke into excited whispers. "A baby?"

"She said a baby."

"Like a foundling in a basket?"

Sister Annette stood on her toes, bringing her up to about chin height for most of us. "A baby will be begun tonight! A happy, happy future, just waiting for . . ."

She drifted slowly about the room, people moving back to give her a circle. Some eyed her with eagerness, some with dread, and she teased them all, her hand painting ribbons of anticipation on the air as she roamed hither and yon.

Her sense of timing was pretty good. She didn't let them lose

interest before she came to a halt and went rigid. Her arms went
into the air and then moved in a teasing sweep . . .

. . . to point at Rose and me.

"An eaglet!" she cried. "Tonight you will create your future
together! A new eagle to share with the world!"

If I looked like Rose, I must have looked like a deer in the
headlights.

Around us, people grinned and applauded. Sister Annette
swooped down on us. "So lovely! A beautiful little eagle baby!"

"Excuse me?" Rose asked.

"We must have a toast with dinner!" Annette cooed. "After all
—you're not pregnant yet!"

Men shook my hand. Women crowded around Rose to
exclaim over the mystery of life. Over the crowd, the Moonglow
Mystic laughed at my astonishment.

Evadne waved at me with a smile. She turned to those around
her and ushered them to the dinner tables, and my tension bled
away. A ray of sun had broken through dark clouds. Maybe she
hadn't forgiven me about Rocket the Killer Horse, but she wasn't
utterly disgusted with me either.

Rose and I were seated together and made much of. Sister
Annette sat beside us and presided, preening in all the attention.
Everyone wanted to contribute to the general attitude of joy and
anticipation of our future child.

"Rose needs wine. This is her last chance. Shall we order
some champagne?"

It appeared I was expected to buy champagne for the table. I
studied my menu intently.

"Our table is the eagle's home! What's that word?"

"A nest? Our table is the nest?"

"No, there's a better word."

"*Aerie.*"

"Airy. You bet. Way up on a mountain."

"Not *airy*—*aerie*. That's the name."

"Of the mountain?"

"Of the nest."

"This table is airy, isn't it?"

"We can close the window."

"Can I get some wine too?"

"So Rose is going to have an egg in her nest!"

"You'd better leave the bottle."

"Hoo-haw! Do-si-do, pardners!"

"Martine says that 'do-si-do' is French. It means dos-a-dos, or back-to-back. But I don't believe that's how eaglets are made, do you, Dash?" Sister Annette dimpled at me. Professor Sprout leered over my purported sex life.

Hal, the schoolteacher, pointed out that eagles mate in air, in free fall.

"Gracious! I hope you'll take longer than that, Dash, dear!"

How had my wineglass emptied itself so fast?

"Don't you worry, Sister Annette." Rose had found her self-confidence and appeared to be enjoying the insanity. "He won't. I'll make sure!"

The women tittered as the men shifted uneasily.

"All right," I said uselessly, knowing I wouldn't be able to divert the conversation to anything less cringe-inducing. Maybe whether nails on a chalkboard were worse than lemon juice in a cut. We couldn't discuss European macroeconomics? A spirited chat on fungal patterns in industrial agriculture?

By the time dinner ended and we were loaded onto the bus, I would have sold my soul to the devil for a quiet evening alone in my apartment with all the doors locked and a dead battery on every electrical device. At least the annoyances outweighed the quiet voice at the base of my brain reminding me I was now too old to find someone with whom to have an eaglet of our own.

By public acclaim, we were enthroned in the first seat, and every guest had something to say about babies and prophecy and the importance of not making love while falling through the air from a great height. Skip was entirely too interested in that one.

My smile was frozen on my face when Lenny finally tugged

the door shut on a misting rain and pulled out. Rose leaned over to whisper in my ear, and I knew every eye behind us was watching.

She craned upward on one hip, and I leaned down to hear her.

"I know you're miserable right now," she whispered, "so I'm reminding you of two things. First, you're about to learn how to square dance."

I winced, which made her giggle.

"And second, there really are large, hungry grizzly bears out there."

Her teasing had the intended effect. I grinned and poked her in the ribs. She shrieked with laughter. From behind us, the entire bus sighed happily.

The ride to town took almost half an hour through increasingly heavy rainfall. By the time we arrived, I was glad there was a big, dry overhang for the bus to pull under. What with my expected eagle-making duties, the presence of counterfeiters, the silvery hum of Evadne's presence on my skin, and the need to grin while learning to square dance—for god's sake, the last thing I needed was to also be drenched in a rainstorm.

TWENTY-EIGHT

DASH

THE TOWN'S COMMUNITY CENTER SERVED DOUBLE-DUTY AS A square-dancing facility. An octet of spangly men and women in matching outfits greeted us with alarming enthusiasm. They and the caller walked the new people through the basics—*allemande left and promenade right, do-si-do and bow to your corner*. I thought I'd have flashbacks to rainy-day gym classes in high school, but the evening turned out to be fun.

The guests from the Triangle-K took up a fair chunk of the town's community center, but we were far from the only ones there. Milt and Oscar bravely paired with Lady Celeste and Madame Zoe, thus avoiding giving offense to anyone too conservative to endure the horrific sight of two men daring to bow to a partner of the same sex. Shocking. There was much in the world that needed correction, and bigotry was only the most obvious judgmental injustice at the moment.

But that wasn't what I was expected to focus on, so I kept my eye on the counterfeiting ball.

I couldn't make Bob read his emails and pass on news of great tax exemptions to his son, and Rose couldn't pick up the drone's signal from town. But our plans were in motion. The email had been sent. The camera was recording. We knew we'd have a good image of anything that happened at the back barn when we returned.

So we kicked up our heels (well, she did, anyway, her red boots flying) and danced.

Evadne, in jeans and a flowing gray shirt, partnered with Phoebus at first, but once all the Triangle-K guests were comfortable with the basic moves, they moved through our group, briefly breaking up couples and forming different squares, much to everyone's delight. Evadne was cool and tranquil, the goddess every man wanted to partner with. And Phoebus?

Phoebus was wearing a white Dudley Do-Right Stetson that must have been hell to put into a suitcase. With his square jaw and his flowing mane, he looked like a caricature. Somehow, he pulled it off. I suspected he'd worn boots without lifts, as he no longer towered over me (platform boots must have been a real ankle-twister during a spirited Virginia reel), but his smile was no less blinding. He bowed to each new partner, sweeping the hat from his head in a courtier's bow that deserved a musketeer feather at the least—and the ladies swooned.

"How does he keep from getting hat head?" I muttered to Rose on our next promenade.

"Huh? What?" She looked at Phoebus as he gallantly steered starry-eyed Suzette in a grand circle. Suzette's husband, John, wore a similar look as he partnered with Evadne.

The Moonglow Mystic was lovely, as cool and composed as the moon in a room filled with stomping, yipping people who generated far more warmth than the open windows could combat. *Perhaps*, I thought with envy, *she's a mythical nymph who doesn't feel the heat.*

In the next dance, they were in our square. Whenever our group went through the complicated pass where you perpetually reached for someone's hand, I always knew in the seconds before her slim hand slipped into mine because for a moment, I was fizzing with excitement.

The windows on one side of the community center had to be

closed because of the driving rain, and the room got hotter and hotter. We paused occasionally to laugh and pant and have a drink. I braved the refreshments table to get water for Rose and me.

"Don't use up all your energy," Skip's mother said to me with a naughty wink. "You've got more to do tonight!"

Stupidly, I thought she was referring to a review of the drone's recording before I realized she was giving me advice on impregnating my "wife." I attempted to end the conversation by smiling and ducking away, but there were too many people around who either wanted to chime in or explain to the assembled townsfolk about my uncanny power over any passing bird of prey and the important duties that lay before me that night.

"You say he can talk to eagles?"

"They're his spirit animal. I heard one brought him a fish from the river today."

"That's incredible! And he has to—you know—with his wife? Tonight?"

"Not for fun. It's destiny."

"Destiny. Wow."

"They're going to make a baby eagle. An eaglet."

Now every eye in the place followed me. I slunk back to Rose and sat beside her, trying to duck below observation. She took a long pull of the water and then leaned over to plant a wet kiss on my cheek.

"You blush so cute."

The room as a whole nudged itself and grinned.

"Don't look so smug. You've got to give birth to a bird."

"Nonsense," she replied tartly, "it's going to be an egg. And I'm going to percolate it."

"Incubate it?"

"Right. Incubate it and hatch it, and then I shall teach it how to fly and shit on the heads of bigots all over the world."

"The eagle of justice."

"The bird of preying on dickheads."

"This is a pretty good plan."

"I thought so."

Silly as it was, this banter with Rose further cemented our unity of purpose. Our partnership was strong, which was interpreted by the many onlookers as true love. Everyone was satisfied.

Across the room, Evadne smiled at me again, and I was washed in a glowing wave of satisfaction. I might have had a wife and an entire community center between me and the woman who lit me up like fireworks, but somehow, in that moment, Eve Simons and I were together.

Much beer was consumed by the Triangle-K guests, and who could blame them? They were on vacation. There was no late-night surveillance on their agenda. And many commented on how smart it was that Rose and I only drank water. We were advised you couldn't start too early being careful about a baby's health.

As the kegs went dry, I spent as much of my time next to teenager Skip and Melanie because then my new, happily inebriated best friends found it harder to give me increasingly graphic advice on the best way to make an eaglet. Rose, in a similar scrum of women, generally said something that would make all the females shriek in shocked delight. Truly, it was better for my ego and my gender if none of us ever learned what she said.

For the ride home, Rose and I were moved to the rear of the bus so we could, we were told, "start our intimate night of bliss." There was a great deal of hooting and joking about that, followed by tipsy singing and comments about fatherhood I thought were a bit much for the kids to hear. But Skip and Melanie were grinning along with their parents. Children today —it was a disgrace. I intended to raise my eaglet better than that.

Wolf and Bart waited at the lodge in Jeeps with their canvas tops in place to drive guests through the pounding rain to their cabins. Seated at the very back, Rose and I were faced with waiting until others had been delivered to their doors and Wolf or Bart returned to ferry us—or making a quick sprint through the rain. We were both eager to get our door locked behind us and check the drone's recording, so we opted for the rain. Naturally, this thrilled those still waiting in the bus.

"Look at them go!" someone hooted. "Have fun tonight, Eagle Guy!"

Finally out of the bus and in the cool, rainy darkness, I didn't smother my growl. Rose laughed out loud. We ran as fast as boots could take us down the slick and muddy path to our cabin, ignoring the glee of those who thought we were off on an entirely different adventure.

TWENTY-NINE

DASH

"Looks quiet in the bunkhouse tonight." Rose noticed the surrounding area, and I approved of her observation as I unlocked our door. "Where is everyone?"

She stripped off her boots and pulled out her phone.

I yanked the curtains shut and grabbed towels from the bathroom as she keyed in the password. "Okay. What have we got . . ."

I finished a quick electronics sweep and pulled out my hated glasses to peer over her shoulder.

"Look," Rose said. "There's that catering truck Bob told you wasn't working."

In the darkness of the recording, the broken, undrivable truck was clearly being driven out of the back barn by Wolf. The drone's camera had droplets of water on it, but the image was as clear as we'd need for a court case.

"So there's no way to know what's in the truck," I said.

She nodded. "Could be barrels of ink. Could be pallets of paper. Could be bundles of printed currency."

"Could be nothing at all."

We watched the screen together, counting the times the catering truck came and went over the span of two hours.

After the third trip, I began doing some rough calculations.

"If it's currency . . ." Rose finally said as the recording showed us a fourth trip away from the vehicle barn.

"Then it's a lot of currency," I agreed. "Let's say one big rig, like the one driven by Wolf's brother Hank, could hold three catering trucks' worth of boxes."

"Boxes filled with fake money." Rose nodded.

"And a fifty-three-foot tractor trailer is roughly six million cubic inches."

"How do you know that?"

I held up my phone. "Google. It also gave me the cubic inch of a single dollar bill, which is a little less than .07 inches."

"Yeah?" Rose watched me with dawning interest. "What's that come to?"

"Well, if you filled the truck with neatly stacked bills and had no boxes or anything to account for . . . roughly eighty-seven million bills."

Her eyes grew to round circles. "So—Hank the long-haul trucker could soon be driving around with eighty-seven million in his truck? Why don't these guys have more Ferraris?"

I corrected her. "They're no longer turning ones into fives, remember? Now they're printing hundreds. So it's not eighty-seven million fake dollars to dump into the American economy."

The flush on Rose's skin faded as she went pale. "It's—"

"Yeah. It's just under nine billion. Plus, they could put two and a half billion more in the catering truck and drive in a different direction."

She inhaled. "Eleven and a half billion dollars."

"Roughly. *If* that's what they're doing."

"Is that enough to—you know—destabilize the economy?"

"Well, the US economy is massive, but it won't help. More to the point, what would you buy with twelve billion if you had it?"

She shook her head, overwhelmed. "I don't know. Aruba?"

"Let's hope it's something so cheerful. We need to talk to Enrique."

"Yeah, we do."

But Enrique didn't answer my text. Given the vastly increased scope of the situation, that was alarming. I sent in our report to the joint task force while we sat on our bed, thinking.

"At the end of that video," I said. "After the last time the catering truck pulls out? I'll bet you Bob walks from the vehicle barn to his house."

"Bob with the bad back? Are you one of the psychics now?" She grinned, pressed play, and then swore impressively. "To the minute! There goes Bob, moving easily."

"That's because he's done helping his son load up the catering truck."

"Makes sense. So he's definitely in on it. Good to know. Got anything else figured out?"

"Wolf's got Dad helping him load in at the back barn and Bart helping him unload at the hiding place. So for the last trip back, Wolf won't be alone. Bart will be with him."

Rose fast-forwarded through the recording. "There's Bart in the passenger seat. Pretty good reasoning, old man." She nudged me in admiration. I pretended the *old man* didn't sting.

"After that, I'll bet they went to Wolf's house by the back path, and there's nothing until the Jeeps pull out to meet our bus."

"You're a wizard. Nothing happening until before the bus pulls in. Oh, wait—there's a bear."

"What?" My heart leaped, and Rose burst out laughing. Her teasing was a mood lightener after we'd walked ourselves through how serious the situation could be.

"You're a chicken for such a brainiac," she said. "I'm kidding. So, Mr. Wizard: Where'd they move the stuff?"

"You and I both know the answer. A round trip, including unloading, is about twenty-five minutes. So they're either going to that dirt bike pit where the kids go, or it's the bunker in the mountainside."

"I'm betting on the bunker."

"Well, duh. The only question is—where are Abbott and Costello?"

"Yeah. I didn't think of that. Where *are* those two?"

"Hmm." We both thought about it, and I offered a potential theory.

"How about this? Abbott and Costello have been left at the bunker to arrange things for the transfer to the trucks day after tomorrow?"

"So they might be there right now?" Her eyes lit up.

"The drone is going to have a hard time in this rain."

"Not the drone!"

Rose plucked a long, black scarf from her drawer. She shook it out. It wasn't a scarf—it was a full-length black running suit with a hood. She ducked into the bathroom to change and came out holding a roll of black duct tape, which she thrust at me. She threw out an imperious arm.

"You want me to tape you up?" I was confused. Why would I put black duct tape on a black suit?

"Look—right there. It catches the light differently. It's a reflector strip. Cover them."

She spoke with such natural authority that I spent the next five minutes using my hand to slick duct tape down the body of my young, pretty partner. It meant nothing to either of us.

"What am I going to wear?" I asked as I curled a strip of tape around her calf.

"Oh, you're not coming, old man."

"Come on. You can't go by yourself."

"The hell I can't. You'll slow me down. You told me to find my confidence like when I'm running, and here's my chance. I plan on going fast, and they'd definitely hear your huffing and puffing."

I must have looked chagrined. She went easy on me.

"You hate running. Anyway, we can't both go. You have to stay here in case someone comes looking. Tell them I'm in the bathtub."

"Seriously? There must be a better excuse than that."

"Whatever. Give me my running shoes. No, the black ones."

"Look at that energy," I said wistfully. "You're a badass. I've created a monster."

She stood. "Don't worry about me for an hour or so. If there's no one out there, I'm going to do some snooping in the hall of the mountain king."

"They've got cameras all over the meetinghouse, and Bart mentioned a motion detector."

She grinned. "They're not going to detect me. I'll be back."

She slipped out the door, leaving me standing there in reading glasses like a mournful dad. "It's raining cats and dogs," I said to no one. "You're going to catch a cold." Even though it was clear to me no cold would catch Rose.

I stood in the middle of the room and scratched my belly. What now?

I peeled off my damp shirt and kicked off my boots. Even the socks had gotten wet, and I took them off too. The young, speedy agent would go running through the darkness, and the old man would have a nice shower. That seemed about right. I found Rose's cowgirl-at-the-hootenanny outfit in a crumpled, wet ball on the bathroom floor, so I draped various parts over the furniture to dry. That made me feel domestic and sad.

And then I heard a knock on the connecting door, and I forgot all about being old and left behind.

THIRTY
EVADNE

To my amusement, Celeste had managed to sail through the square dancing with her stern dignity intact.

Others had yipped and hooted and grinned. Lady Celeste did her promenades and allemandes with perpetual suspicion, causing a delighted edginess among those who had paid to live on the margins of the dangerous afterworld.

But she was grinning broadly as I let myself into our cabin.

Celeste was hunched over yet another dead animal. She would be adding to her zombie reputation, no doubt. She looked up.

"You're sopping wet. Where did you go?" She stepped to the bathroom and tossed me a towel. "Did you never hear of coming in out of the rain? It's dark as the inside of your hat out there. What were you thinking?"

She didn't want an answer. She moved about me fussily, taking the towel from me after I'd blotted my face so she could attempt to dry my hair.

My reply was muffled by the towel coming down over my face. I grabbed the towel and tossed it on my bed. "What are you doing? Is that a porcupine?"

"Yeah. Isn't it gorgeous? I didn't know my trap was big

enough. Took me some work to get him out without sticking myself."

We bent over its form. My lab work in zoology kicked in. "Look at that deformed foot. No wonder your trap worked. Rough life in the wild if you're not whole and healthy."

"True, true," she muttered, not listening. "True in the wild and in civilization . . ."

"Do you want help skinning it? What are you going to do with it?"

"George is going to express a little wrath, the heartless bastard." She looked up and grinned again. "Literally heartless. His heart was removed during the zombie process, right? All the black-and-white movies agree."

I wasn't up on my horror-movie lore, so I had nothing to offer. Her eyes cleared as she came out of her revenge fantasy and looked at me.

"No, of course I don't want you to help," she said.

I was surprised. She and I had gotten on so well. I inhaled to venture a brave question and she cut me off.

"No, you don't want to help. You're entirely upset by the gutting of woodland creatures. Aren't you?"

"Upset? No, I'm not. I've dissected—"

"You misunderstand me." Her eyes cut to the connecting door beyond which lay all of the integrity and beauty that was Dash. "It makes you sick to even be around this. Doesn't it?"

"Oh. I—" Panic suddenly fizzed up in me. Was I ready to be with Dash?

Celeste wrapped her hands around my shoulders and bustled me over to the connecting door. Not giving me a chance to respond, she knocked boldly.

Dash opened the door. I briefly forgot how to breathe. He was shirtless with a towel around his shoulders. His long, lean torso seemed even more naked than if we'd caught him fully nude rather than in jeans and bare feet.

Ruthlessly, Celeste pushed me through the connecting doors.

"Take this," she said shortly. "I caught a critter in my trap. I have to do some light taxidermy. I can't work if she's going to turn green on me."

I protested, but Lady Celeste cut me off, nudging me further into his suite.

"I'll have it all taken care of in an hour or so. You can wait here with Rose and Dash."

As she closed her door, she looked past me and mouthed the words to Dash: *You're welcome*. She smiled wickedly, and then the door clicked shut. My face was superheated by my blush.

He closed his side of the door and turned to me.

"You've been had," he said. "She doesn't need you gone. She's setting you up to be with me."

He was glad I was there, his pleasure easy to read. And yet he informed me Celeste had put us together under false pretenses. It was such a purely good thing to do that I relaxed, trusting in his good nature. The heat faded from my face, along with my blush, and I shook my head with a smile.

"God, you are so honorable," I said.

"I'm sorry?"

"I know that's what she's doing. I can read her, too, you know."

"Huh." The room was spiced with his growing interest. Flattering. "And you don't mind?"

I summoned my courage. "What makes you think I don't want to be here?" His eyes widened slightly. "Where's Rose? Bathroom?"

"Ah, yeah—no. Um, Rose is . . . not here."

"Not here?" I looked around the empty suite, bewildered. "Oh. Is this something to do with . . . ?"

"Yes," he said. "About the stuff I can't talk about."

"Okay. Gotcha."

"She should be gone about an hour. I'll get you a towel. Why are you still wet?"

I followed him to the bathroom door. "I went up to the back barn."

"Tonight?" He turned to me sharply, concern radiating off him.

"Just now. I wanted to make sure. It's okay, Dash. The strange sense—it's gone."

I was eager to share my news, but he was more concerned about my safety. "Did anybody see you?"

"I don't know. I don't think so. It was raining pretty hard."

I caught sight of my reflection in the mirror. My hair was wet, and my skin was goose bump-y. I looked drowned and realized every movement of air blew across wet skin and damp clothes. I shivered from the cold.

I had clean, dry clothes on the other side of the connecting door, but when he pulled a T-shirt and sweatpants out of his bureau for me, I didn't protest. The idea of wearing his clothes . . . it was a delicious, daring intimacy I couldn't resist.

"Go put these on. I'll wait out here."

"But did you hear me? The strangeness is gone."

"I heard you. We think we know where it's gone. That's what Rose is checking out."

"Oh—so it's not really gone? Just moved?"

"That's what we think." He nudged me gently into his bathroom and shut the door. "Towel off and get dry, and then we can talk."

I hadn't been to high school, had never gotten ready for the prom or a date. I'd never felt these foolish, cresting waves of anticipation, anxiety, stress, excitement. I'd never before allowed myself to hope, to trust that something . . . romantic might happen to me this evening.

I stripped, toweled off, and slid into his clothes, clean and dry and smelling of laundry when I wanted them to smell of him. A comb lay beside the sink and I ran it through my hair, attempting to restore some sense of order.

"Do you want coffee?" he called through the door. "Or tea?"

"Tea, please," I called, as if everything was normal. "Thanks. That would be wonderful."

I stared at myself in the mirror, astonished to discover my face hadn't changed. I still looked like me, even though I felt like someone else entirely. I pressed my cold hands to my hot cheeks. No, not a fever. Just a determined flush.

I couldn't stay in the bathroom much longer, couldn't avoid attention or stay below the radar. It was time to be brave. Steeling my courage, I opened the door.

He smiled when he turned to me, and I got his appreciation. Instead of baggy sweats, suddenly I was in the finest couture.

"I used someone's comb," I told him. "I hope that's all right."

"That's fine. Want me to light the stove?"

"That's okay. I'm already warming up."

"Yeah, I'm not buying it. One log—it'll be toasty in here in no time."

He handed me a mug of tea from the room's brew pot, and I sat nervously in the armchair. He built his fire in the prosaic woodstove. The fireplace would have been more atmospheric, but now that I clutched that warm mug of tea, I realized how cold I'd gotten. The woodstove would warm the room quickly. I needed warmth.

He sat miles and miles away from me, on the bed.

There wasn't a closer spot without cuddling with me in the chair, and I knew he wouldn't presume. The gulf between us, though, felt vast, and I was awash in awkwardness.

I cupped my hands around the tea and blew on it. I wondered what an adult would say in this situation, since I had clearly not yet gotten through the lessons any high schooler could have passed.

"You were saying you wanted to be here tonight?" His voice was warm and kind, but I jumped at his words all the same.

"Well." I looked into my tea and knew my blush was back. *Courage*, I thought. *Be brave. Trust in his kindness.* "I do want to be here . . . and I don't."

"Huh."

That was his confusion response. He was trying. I needed to help him understand why I acted like a terrified virgin. Okay. I could do this.

I shifted uncomfortably. "I think you know I like you. I hope you do."

He was relieved. "I'm glad. I like you too. But you can read that on me, I'm sure."

Maybe he would think my fierce blush was caused by the tea. "I can read that on you, and kindness and honor. All kinds of good things. So . . . I guess it's silly to be afraid . . ."

When had he gotten off the bed? Suddenly, he was kneeling beside my chair. "What are you afraid of? It's not me, is it?"

"No," I said. "And yes, I guess."

He sat back, and a ghost of a smile played around his mobile lips. "Is this as confusing to you as it is to me?"

I pursed my lips around an answering smile. "Not so confusing. I can explain better."

But then I couldn't explain. The bitter truth I'd hidden away for so long was painful to reveal. I knew it was important to share my truth with Dash, but speaking the words would take all the courage I had.

Dash gave me time. He didn't push, and I could read his concern and his down-deep goodness. I darted a glance at him.

"Most people hate silence," I said. "When I can't think of how to say something, they start talking, guessing what I'm working on saying. You don't do that."

"Is that bad?"

"No." I shook my head. "No, it's nice. I can take my time."

"Good. I'm interested in what you have to say."

I cocked my head as I regarded him. "You really are."

"I know."

The smile became a grin. "I know you know. I wanted you to know I know you know. You know?"

The teasing settled both of us. My stomach muscles

unclenched, and his shoulders came down from around his ears. I tried to envision exactly how I would feel safest and most able to tell him my story.

"I can explain better," I said slowly, my words coming with a blend of caution and trust, "but I'd like a favor first—if you don't mind."

"If I can make it happen, I will."

I closed my eyes. "When I tell you, I want to be lying on that bed with you holding me so I don't have to look at you. And I want you to know that's all I'm offering." I opened my eyes. "Do you understand?" *Could he understand?*

THIRTY-ONE
DASH

THIS WOMAN WAS SO WOUNDED. SHE WAS PERPETUALLY BRACED for disappointment. It called on every fiber of my protectiveness. I smiled gently to let her know she had nothing to fear from me. "You want some physical comfort while you tell a hard story," I said, "and you don't want that physical comfort to imply you're ready for anything more intimate."

"Now you're reading me."

"Good. I want to get this right. Do you want me to put on a shirt first?" She shook her head, and her eyes fell to my naked chest. I repressed my flash of lust.

She was frozen in her chair, awkwardness icing over her movements. I could help her with that. I stood and took the mug and then her hand to help her up. I led her to the bed, and she laid down with a passivity that alarmed me. My job here was to let her know she was free to leave at any time with no shame or guilt.

I was unfolding the quilt at the foot of the bed when I was snagged by the thought.

That wasn't my job here. Had I so thoroughly forgotten that she was a con artist, and not a part of my mission?

In the time it took to shake out the quilt and spread it over her, an entire dialogue played out in my head.

The case had proceeded with increasing urgency, but my partner was undertaking the investigation with confidence and strength, as I wanted her to do.

There was nothing more I could do that night.

Eve's situation called to me as a human, not an agent, and if I could help her, I would.

And I wanted—I ached—to slide beneath the quilt and hold her to me and listen to her story and feel her against me. Whether she was a con artist or not.

So I did.

I lay back, opened my arm to her, and—as if we'd done it a million times—she nestled into my side and laid her head on my chest.

Her warmth, her scent, her living body beside me . . . I was overwhelmed. It was probably the most innocent thing I'd ever done with a woman in my bed, but it was deeply intimate.

I stroked her hair lightly with the arm around her. The other hand, I kept by my side. I was determined to let her know I would not hold her, that she was free to go or stay as her mood and needs dictated. I wouldn't scare her by grabbing and pawing at her.

"Is this okay?" I murmured.

"It's very, very okay." One hand crept up to lie lightly on my chest. I felt like I'd won a prize. "I'm not too heavy?"

I laughed. "You feel great. You feel like warmth and peace."

"Okay." I felt her smile against my shoulder. "You feel great too."

"Good."

We let the silence cover us like the quilt. We got used to being so close, slowly relaxed into the stillness, and both my heart and hers settled.

Then she sighed, and after a determined inhale, launched into her narrative.

"When I was seventeen, I caught a cold."

She stopped again, all the forward progress in relaxing against me lost to the emotions that halted her speech.

"A cold?" My question was gentle. I wanted to help but didn't know how.

"Yeah. Don't ask me about that, okay?"

Confusion. "Um—okay."

Her muscles had gone taut against me, like a woman preparing to endure something hard.

"The cold messed with my ability to read people. I was working in a bar in Little Rock. I was underage, but the bartender liked me and he let me take some shifts." She rambled, but I didn't try to refocus her. She was gathering her nerve. "Most of the time, I did pretty well. It helps to know who's flirting for fun and who's angling for more."

I couldn't control the growl that rumbled in me. I felt that rush of protectiveness again.

She ducked her head and hid her face in my side—as if that would let her hide from the truth—and spoke. "There were these two guys. Really, three, but I didn't know about the third guy then. Greg and Kenny—those were their names. And later, Bango. I never learned his real name. And I had that cold, and I couldn't read them, and I was stupid."

I could feel her heart thumping against my ribs, and a few hot splashes on my skin told me she was losing the struggle not to cry.

I soothed her, "It's not stupid to not have an extrasensory perception to save you from assholes, Eve."

Her hand flexed when I used her real name, and she smoothed her fingers over my chest.

"I know that in my head."

"Yeah. The heart's harder to persuade, huh?"

"Yeah. Anyway." She wiped at my chest but couldn't make the tears disappear. She presented the facts baldly: "Greg and Kenny abducted me and kept me locked up for nineteen days and seventeen hours. Almost three weeks, chained by the ankle to a radiator. They would tie me up and take turns on me, and later, Bango did too. They said they liked having a live-in."

I throttled the horror inside me. My fury wouldn't help her now. I took her hand in mine and gave her the only gift I could think of: the silence of my listening.

"And pretty soon, my head cold went away. I was a slave in their house, and I still managed to get over my stupid cold. It's like my immune system didn't know how badly we were in trouble."

She offered a watery chuckle. I huffed a laugh to let her know I listened in sympathy.

"By then, I knew Greg and Kenny were fully unbalanced. Greg was off his schizophrenia meds and thought he was God, and Kenny had some personality disorder that made him believe anything Greg told him. I guess when it came to Kenny, Greg was right. Because he really was God.

"And then Bango arrived, and I could tell he was scared of Greg, but he needed a place to stay. And he liked having a live-in too."

My muscles were bunching up with the longing to rise and act. No action would help. "Were there no parents to look for you? No one to help?"

She shook her head. "I never knew my dad, and my mother hasn't been around in years. I went into foster care when I was nine."

"Okay." I stayed calm because I knew she needed that from me, but I wasn't happy.

"Then one day, they brought home this guy—some random carny or roustabout from a cheap traveling circus. They were going to play poker because the carny had gotten paid and everyone else was broke. Probably they would have robbed the guy; they'd done it before. And Greg said to him, 'You want a piece of the live-in first? You can have her for twenty bucks.'"

I felt her lip curl against my side as she spoke the words. Her tone had automatically lowered as she aped her captor's voice. I stroked her head, and she went on.

"And the guy looked at me, and by that time, my cold had cleared up and I could read him. He was a total lowlife, but there was still something in him that was kind. So he told Greg he'd bet his motorcycle against their live-in at one hand of poker—which, because he was better at cheating than they were, he won."

"And you were there for the game?"

"Right there. They liked me to sit on a pillow by the radiator. I watched the new guy win the hand, and I saw him beat the crap out of Kenny when Greg told him they wouldn't give me up. He beat Kenny while Greg howled and Bango ran away. And then the guy took the key from Greg, unlocked my ankle, and put me on the back of his bike. And we drove away."

She sniffed back her tears again. "And that was Artie. Arthur. Now known as Phoebus Apollon."

"The man you say is your only friend."

"Well, now one of two friends." She smiled into my ribs, and I pulled her closer to me, thrilled she knew she could count on me.

"That's right," I whispered.

"Anyway, Artie didn't have much, but he helped me get back on my feet. And he held me when I lost the baby." The words came out of her in a monotone.

"Oh shit."

"Yeah. I don't even know which one was the father, and I hated all three of them like . . . I can't explain how deeply I hated them."

Uselessness swirled in me, maddening and frustrating. There was no way to reach back and help that woman, no way to serve stern justice to her captors. I murmured wordlessly.

"But the baby—that was pure innocence," she said. "The baby deserved to live. And I messed that up."

"What happened?"

"Miscarriage. The doctor said it was no one's fault; it happens a lot of the time with first pregnancies. But I felt like a failure. I still feel like a failure."

"Shit," I said again—uselessly—and stroked her hair. "That's why it was so hard for you to say you had no kids when we were fishing."

She nodded. "My baby would have been fifteen now." She was torturing herself. "The same age as that teenager, Skip. I might have had a boy who played games on his phone. Or a girl like Melanie, who loves anything to do with horses."

Her voice trailed off, clogged silent by what might have been. Then she swallowed and finished it up.

"Anyway, now I'm helping Artie con rich people out of their money so I can fix my car and pay some back bills and maybe get that last semester of college. And everything is normal—as normal as it can be for the Moonglow Mystic. But relationships? That's harder. I mean, with men."

"I understand."

"Not only can I read inner intentions—which, I'm sorry to say, is not a flattering thing for most guys—but add my total fear of sex and intimacy and getting close to people, and that makes me *real* fun at parties."

She tried to turn her wounds into jokes. Her resilience humbled me.

So I told her so.

THIRTY-TWO

EVADNE

"You're the strongest person I've ever met," he said.

I lifted my head off his chest to look at him. It would have taken the slightest movement for our lips to meet, but he didn't press the issue. Not after hearing my story.

"I'm *so* not strong," I protested.

"You *so* are," he said determinedly, nudging my head back onto his chest. "You go through all that, and you're still kind and caring and funny and smart. They tried to make you a victim, and you became a survivor. Strong as hell."

He saw me so differently than I saw myself. I was lost in thought and tracing unconscious patterns on his skin. I could lie with him forever.

"Let me propose a new plan," he said. "I don't mean to tell you how you should live your life—you've clearly done a better job than I ever would." I tried to protest, but he shushed me. "For our relationship, we do it this way: from now on, you're in charge."

My fingers stilled. He definitely had my attention. And he spoke as if we *would* have a relationship. Like it would be that easy.

"If you decide you want to kiss me, then you kiss me. If you don't want to, you don't. I'll know that if you kiss me, that doesn't mean you're offering anything more. And you'll know that while I'd love to kiss you, I don't expect you to. And I don't expect anything more if you do kiss me."

My head spun. He was offering to let me play the many-times-raped virgin? He would wait patiently while I waged epic mental battles between fear and desire, with no guarantee of which side would win? I shook my head minutely against him. "It could take years."

"I'm not in a hurry. I'm acting like I'm in high school, but really, I'm entirely grown-up. Old, even. I have reading glasses. I promise I won't die if I get excited, and then we go no further."

He felt like this was high school too. Remarkable. How kind he was. "Wow," I said. "You'd do that for me?"

"I'm pretty sure I'd do that for anyone. It's no fun to have sex with someone who doesn't want to."

He spoke of sex so casually, as if it wasn't an obstacle in the path of happiness. His attitude was so different from mine. Hope bubbled up weakly through the thick sludge of my past. I sat up and crossed my feet next to him. His chocolate eyes studied me intently.

"God. You really mean it."

He smiled. "I really do."

Could I take him at his word? Did I dare hope for the impossible amount of patience it would take for desire to win out over fear?

Here he was in front of me, bare-chested and luscious. His kindness was a golden haze that covered us both. Did I want him? Did I want to try? How much courage could I muster?

"Okay," I said.

"Okay?"

"Yeah. Okay. Let's do that."

"Good."

"And when this vacation is over—or whatever it is that you're doing—you're going to give me your number?"

"And my real name. And you can call me whenever you want. Or come and stay with me. I can help you find a place in DC." He smiled, not wanting to pressure me. "There's a great zoo in DC. You can do your zoology there."

"Dash." I grinned. "Zoology isn't the study of zoos."

"Yeah, but someone with a degree in zoology could surely get a job at a zoo, right? And be near her boyfriend?"

My heart threatened to explode at the word. "Is that what you'd be?"

"I'd be anything you want. I'll be your boyfriend or your friend—so long as the word *friend* is part of it."

"But you're gone a lot, right? I mean, like now?" The thought made me nervous. This was a man who would put himself in the path of danger to save others. I admired that—but I feared it too. If he became so important to me, could I survive if . . .

"I've kind of been offered a desk job, though."

He spoke calmly, but he was suddenly awash in confusion—with shame and anger and pride wrapped into the emotion.

I watched him. "Want to talk about it?"

He cleared his mind. "I want to talk about us. About spending more time together, however that works out, as long as it's good for you."

I'd been alone for so long. For *so long*. His words hit my nerve endings, and I trembled in response. "Well, that was like a key in a lock."

"What was?"

"I'm reading you. You are good and pure and honorable, Dash. And so damned handsome."

"Stop. You're making me blush."

"It looks good on you. I'm going to kiss you now."

I had my hand on his naked chest, so I felt his heart speed up. I was a teenager once more, and this time, I would do some exploring.

"You are?"

I nodded. I studied his mouth, his lips. I touched my finger there, and he pursed his lips in a tiny kiss. I needed to move; I needed to follow through. And yet I was hung up, unable to accomplish the simple, monumental task of leaning forward.

"Don't do it if you're not ready," he said, his protectiveness outweighing his desire.

"Shut up, Dash."

"Yes, ma'am."

I decided I was thinking too much.

He seemed to agree. "It might be easier if you don't concentrate so hard."

My pulse thudded in every inch of me. "Shut *up*, I said."

"Right. Sorry."

I wet my lips, and he wet his. And then I leaned over him.

My hair came down on either side. It happens every time I lean over—only this time, there was another face inside the curtain with me. It was the antithesis of loneliness.

When our lips were almost touching, when I could feel his warm breath, I paused.

"I'm sorry," I whispered. We were so close that the movement of his lips disturbed the air between us as the words slipped out.

"It's okay. You don't have to do this."

Fear and desire waged a war in my brain. And then his kindness, his willingness to wait, tipped the scales in favor of desire. "I *want* to do this."

Low-voltage electricity thrummed around us. I felt as though I could have seen every contour of his face with my eyes closed, limned in nothing more than the energy between us. That made me smile inside—

—and that was when I dipped my head that last fraction of an inch, and his mouth touched mine, and peace filled me like a minor chord resolving at last to a major. The celestial spheres clicked into a new, better alignment.

He kissed me lightly, barely brushing against me. It was warmth and intimacy and excitement. I had the power, the right, to nibble with my mouth, sandwiching his lower lip between mine. He sighed in response, and I echoed that sigh. For a moment, our lips were parted and together and I was so close to tasting his tongue.

But I was overwhelmed. I couldn't handle another sensation. I sat back. I was victorious and scared and not quite as pathetic as when we first lay down.

"I did it," I said.

"You did. And it was good."

I put my fingers to my lips, checking to see if they'd been changed by the experience. "It *was* good. Fifteen years, it took me."

He was stunning. He took my breath away; he was so handsome. And I had kissed those lips. I'd done that. "You are astonishingly beautiful," he said.

His desire and admiration no longer frightened me. Now it felt wonderful. I looked at him with a near-wink. "I know you think so. I can read you."

"Should I be embarrassed?"

"You should be proud. I know you wanted more, but you still let me decide. And now I think *you're* the strongest person in the world."

Happiness lit me up. My mood had morphed to flirtatious and teasing. With one kiss, I'd taken back the desire, the cravings—yes, the outright lust that had been brutally ripped from me by three subhumans. I'd gotten back some of the power I'd allowed them to have over my life since that long-ago nightmare.

It was my right to feel this way. I could say yes and I could say no—and I could trust that Dash would hear and respect that.

I felt . . . powerful.

"I want to kiss you again."

He didn't move, except for the cheeky grin. "I'm agreeable."

"It wouldn't be too much of a tease? To kiss you and do nothing more?"

"Eve, I'm begging you to tease me. Tease me as much as you like. Start now, why don't you?"

I laughed outright. This time, bending forward was simple. Easy. Filled with joy. And this time, when our mouths parted gently, I slid my tongue cautiously forward, touching his. Alien. Strange. Wonderful. Delicious.

His desire grew, but his hands remained at his sides. And then I heard an actual moan from him, which sent a bolt of excitement through me. *I made him moan.*

I sighed with pleasure and stroked my tongue along his.

"Teeth are funny things," I murmured without breaking the kiss.

"Funny," he agreed without minding—or even noticing.

"Yours feel like mine, but I can't feel me feeling them. That's odd." My assessment had ended the kiss as I smiled into his mouth. "I'll try that again."

"Oh, good," he sighed.

I ran my tongue along his teeth in a slow sweep. He groaned again.

"Now you feel mine," I murmured, and that was permission for him to kiss me back.

He was gentle and restrained, and I realized I wanted more. I was hungry for more. The thought made me dizzy with relief and adrenaline.

"Dash," I sighed, "I want you to touch me."

"You're sure?" Our voices were hushed, our mouths were touching, our air was shared. We were in a place of warm intimacy. Like heaven.

"I'm sure. I want your hands on me."

"Where, beauty?"

"I think . . . my neck. Yes—that. Oh, you're warm."

"Can I kiss you here?"

"On my neck? Yes. Do that. Oh . . . oh, that's good. I want to do it to you."

I kissed his neck from the tendon under his ear to the junction with his shoulder. It was deeply erotic. I'd never wanted to taste a man's neck before, and now I couldn't stop nibbling.

"Oh my god, you feel good," he crooned, and I rewarded him with the tiniest nibble on his earlobe. It made him shiver.

"That was good?" I asked. "Do that to me."

I presented my ear to him, and he took the lobe in his mouth and sucked on it gently. I writhed against him, lost in the sensations.

"Wow," I admitted with a gasp. "That's—it's—those nerve endings are connected in surprising places!"

"Long, silvery nerve endings lacing through your beautiful body," he said as he nibbled along my neck. "All for you to enjoy —whenever you're ready."

"Honestly, I'm readier than I'd expected."

He stopped and looked up at me. I looked down at him.

"You don't have to do anything you don't want."

"I want—I want you. I've been working with the wrong guys is all."

He was lost to a primitive wave of adrenaline, a caveman urge to conquer.

I grinned at him, flush with the trust he'd inspired in me. "That won't work, you know. You won't scare me off."

"What?" he asked, confused.

"You wanting me is still not as strong as your honor."

"Shit," he said. "I can turn the honor off for the night if you want me to."

"No, you can't. And that's what makes this so much fun."

I shifted my legs around. I half lay on him, feeling the sensation of my breasts fully against his naked torso. *It would feel better if I had my shirt off too.*

The thought, unexpected, was a cry of freedom. Perhaps I wouldn't have to be alone forever. Perhaps I, too, could have lovely, wonderful, toe-curling sex like normal girls. I laughed out loud and dropped my head, capturing his mouth with mine. "Use your hands on me more, Dash," I demanded, and he was delighted to comply—

—when there was a sudden heavy banging on the cabin door.

"Mr. Williamson? Mr. Williamson. Open up!"

It was Wolf Koenig.

THIRTY-THREE

DASH

SHIT.

I'd been so caught up in making out with Eve that I'd forgotten I was an FBI agent on a case, forgotten that my partner had put herself in harm's way. And in my humiliation and fear, I came up with the ideal response to his shout.

"What the fuck do you want?" I called.

His answer was immediate. "I think I saw your wife on the road. I'm worried about her. Where is she, Mr. Williamson?"

Evadne read me almost as fast as I formulated the thought. She nodded and threw the quilt over her head.

I halfway unbuttoned my jeans. My hair was tousled from her fingers, and my mouth was probably smeared with what was left of her lipstick. I yanked the door open, the only time in my life I was glad to be seen with a raging erection.

Wolf blinked in the sudden light, Bart at his shoulder. He looked past me into the room. An obviously female form stretched under the quilt on the bed, one bare leg sticking out. Rose's cowgirl outfit and my clothes were scattered all over the room. I did my best to look like a man interrupted in the act.

"Excuse the fuck out of me? Who do you think I'm trying to make love to here?"

They both gaped at me. This was not the way they'd expected their arrival to go.

"I'm sorry—I—I'm sure we saw her out running."

"At this hour? In the pouring rain? Could you please get the hell out of here? I'm trying to make an eaglet."

Hysterical feminine laughter came from the bed. Wolf creased his brow in confusion.

"An eaglet?"

He hadn't been on the bus trip to town. *Well, let him figure it out.*

"Is there anything else?"

"Uh, no, sir. I'm sorry to disturb you. Have, uh—have fun."

Bart was now leering through his beard over Wolf's shoulder. I half expected him to ask if I'd be willing to share. That would have been a serious mistake, as, primed by Evadne's story of her enslavement, I was looking to take out some anger on the nearest male jaw. But Bart wisely opted to say nothing.

They stomped off the porch, and I slammed the door. Adrenaline and testosterone raced through my veins. I'd never felt less old.

"Oh my fucking god," I said, but Evadne sat up and put her finger across her lips. She pointed to the door and shook her head. They were still listening.

"Rose," I said, "I'm sorry for that interruption. Now, where were we, baby?"

I landed on the bed and bore her down under me. Mindful of our agreement, I didn't kiss her. She was the one who lifted her head to me. After that, it was a pretty even distribution of authority. Her arms were around my neck, and she arched upward as I slid a hand up her rib cage. Just before I satisfied my hand with the curve of her breast, I regained control.

She uttered a mewl of protest that did my soul a world of good.

"Still listening?" I whispered.

"What?" she said thickly.

"Wolf and Bart." I nuzzled her ear, and she turned her head to give me better access. "Are they still listening?"

"Oh. No. Gone. Sorry—I didn't want to stop."

I grinned at her. "Me neither."

"They didn't buy it. They don't know what happened, but you're . . . someone they need to do something about. Watch out, Dash. I think you're in trouble. They're planning on harming you."

"Huh."

We lay together, and I relished the warmth of her under me. My belief that she was a con artist had taken a serious beating. I wanted her in my life, but I had a mission. "I'd like to stay right here, but I have to find Rose. She might need help."

"Right."

With suddenly clearer heads, we both sat up. I reached for dry socks and my boots while Evadne ran her hands through her hair.

And then, with a rush of relief, I heard the bathroom window slide open.

I got there in time to help Rose slither in without crashing into the tub.

"Thanks," she said. "I almost got caught!"

"Closer than you know. I had a visit from Wolf and Bart demanding to know where you were."

"Shit! How'd you handle it?"

She grabbed a towel to dry herself and came out of the bathroom to find Evadne standing by a rumpled bed. Evadne waved awkwardly.

"Hi."

"Hi," said Rose, turning to look at me. I held my hands out in protest.

"Hey, it worked. They don't know it wasn't you."

"Uh-huh," she said, not believing it.

"I pulled the quilt over my head," Evadne offered.

"Yeah. I guess. Well, do we have any secrets left?"

Evadne gathered up her wet clothes hurriedly. "I'll leave. You need to talk."

She passed closer to Rose on her way to the door and then stopped. She looked at Rose intently.

"You've been with the strange thing. The ink."

Rose and I looked at each other, and then at Evadne.

"I didn't get inside. How do you know that?" Rose asked quietly.

Evadne shook her head and shrugged. "I know."

Rose watched her. "Okay. But we can't go to a judge for a subpoena based on the readings of a psychic."

"She's telling the truth," I protested, and Evadne shot me a grateful smile.

"Oh, I know she is," Rose surprised me by agreeing. "I've seen enough these past few days to be a believer—in her, anyway. But no judge is going to agree."

"Then we'll have to get the evidence some other way," I said. "I could still get into Wolf's computer if Bob plays his part tomorrow morning. If not, we've got the camping trip tomorrow, and all the ranch hands are going on that. Our best bet is to stay with them."

"We'll have Enrique with us. The three of us against Wolf and his four ranch hands. We can handle it."

I was about to point out we had no idea if there were only five counterfeiters when Evadne spoke up.

"And me," she said. "I'll help. I don't know what's going on, but I'll help."

Rose and I protested, and the caveman in my brain gibbered in panic at the idea of risking Eve in a struggle with people who might possibly commit violence to protect their eleven billion counterfeit dollars. "That's sweet, Evadne," Rose demurred, "but it would be better for everyone if we didn't get civilians involved."

"Civilians. Huh." Evadne huffed in annoyance. "We are *professional psychics* skilled at reading the human mind." Rose didn't buy it. Evadne laid her case bare. "Con men. We're hardly a flock of innocents."

"I can appreciate that," Rose said, "but we'll keep you out of this if we can. Understand?"

Rose's natural authority got Evadne to back down. I made a note to compliment Rose later on her energy. To Evadne's credit, she asked no questions. "I'll go now," she said simply.

"Let me walk you to your door." I escorted her the three feet to the connection between our suites. She smiled, and then, with a glance at Rose, she leaned up and kissed me softly. "I had a wonderful time."

"So did I." I meant every word.

"Don't forget," called Rose, and Evadne and I startled apart guiltily. "No matter what happened here tonight, he's my husband tomorrow. No smooching where anyone will see."

"I promise," Evadne replied. She gave my hand a squeeze and turned to the door.

"Sweet dreams," I said.

"I know who they'll be about."

"Mine will be the same as I've been dreaming for the last few days," I countered.

"Jeez," Rose carped. "Get a room, you two."

"We *had* a room until you came back!" I made both of them smile, and Evadne winked at me and closed the connecting door behind her.

"Don't think you're getting into bed with me in that state, mister." Rose was charged up and assertive. "Go take a cold shower or something."

I winced. "Tell me what you found."

"I found jack shit, but I had a great run. The proximity alarm must have been real because I hadn't been at that bunker door for but ten minutes when Wolf's Jeep screamed into the parking area. I climbed a tree. They checked all the locks and kicked the door and generally made nuisances of themselves. Shone their flashlights all around, but they never looked up. They thought they'd find you. You're the counterfeiters' number-one enemy, by the way, for snooping around their clubhouse and trying to get into Wolf's records. Congratulations."

"Thanks. How'd they spot you?"

"Must have been the duct tape. Supposed to stay on when it's wet. Or maybe I pulled some of it off climbing that tree. Everything was locked up tight, so I left. I knew I'd make better time on the road coming back. Night running over fields is an invitation to a sprained ankle. And they doubled back on me and must have caught a reflection strip in their headlights. I was off the road before they got close enough, of course, and they never found me. Tell me about your evening, old man. Looks like you had a pretty good time."

I ignored her suggestive face and told her the details of Wolf and Bart coming to the door so she'd be able to handle any questions the next day. She howled with laughter at the line about making an eaglet.

"So you had fun with your mystic," she said. "Do you need protection? I hope you're being sensible, Dash. Safe sex and all that. You don't know *what* astral plane she's been hanging out in."

"Should the need arise," I said coldly, "I am prepared to use the proper protection. Thank you for your concern, and now shut the fuck up."

That sent her into gales of laughter. Rose's experience was giving her authority. Score points for the rookie. She went to take a hot shower and bury her black running suit deep in her luggage, and I went to bed where I could still smell Evadne's wild, fresh scent on my pillow.

Sweet dreams indeed. Until the morning began with an out-and-out disaster.

THIRTY-FOUR

DASH

IT WAS THAT ONE-LOG FIRE I'D BUILT TO WARM EVADNE THAT saved us.

Rose slept past five thirty that morning. Even she couldn't ignore the strain of an evening of vigorous square dancing, followed by an hour-long night run in the drenching rain.

So, for once, I was the first to stir.

And once I moved, I heard a sound.

Still drowsy, my brain chased the thought around like a butterfly on a summer's day. It was even chances I'd stop chasing the noise and go back to sleep. But something caught my focus, and I woke up enough to pay attention.

I shifted my foot under the covers again, and again I heard the sound, like a tiny steel band playing an atonal trill.

What was that?

This time, I stayed still, pried open my eyes, and reached out slowly to turn on the lamp.

The answer was coiled on the flagstones under the stove, where it soaked up the heat from last night's fire.

I nudged my wife. "Rose."

She grunted. She sounded like me when she dragged me out of bed the last two mornings. *Payback's a bitch, sweetheart.*

"Rose. We have a little problem."

"How little?" she mumbled.

"I'd say three and a half, maybe four feet."

She turned over to question me and heard the miniature steel band herself. She propped herself up on her elbow and looked around.

"I'd say," she said, "that there's a big damned snake in our suite, Dash."

"I'd have to agree with you, Rose."

"Well. Will you look at that."

I did. I looked at the snake. She looked at the snake. The snake looked at us.

"Any chance that's not a rattlesnake?" she asked.

"I'm no snake expert," I replied, "but the rattle in the tail seems conclusive."

"Agreed."

We did some more looking. "What would you say our options are?" she asked.

"I've got my service weapon in the closet safe."

"That's problematic," she said.

"I know. The minute I fire a gun, our cover is pretty much blown."

"Right. Plus, it would be pretty clear to the bad guys we're onto them, while now they only suspect it."

"I'd guess they suspect it pretty strongly, given that they put a venomous snake in our bedroom."

"Yeah," she said. "I've asked too many questions, and you want into their computers. Looks like they're going to try to take the snoops out now. So much for your pantomime with Evadne." We thought about that, and then she added, "Think maybe the snake wandered in on its own in search of a little heat?"

"Maybe," I allowed. "Did you leave that window open?"

"I did not."

"Neither did I—and yet it's open. It's a smart plan. You or I, hot from a long night of eaglet-making"—Rose smothered a giggle—"opens the window. A passing rattler thinks that looks better than being out in the rain. He slithers in and makes a nest at the foot of the bed. Bang—one extremely sick or possibly dead snoop, and a spouse who sure isn't going to stick around to go glamping."

"Accidental death. No reason to suspect anything else."

"Right. A terrible, terrible tragedy."

"Okay. But we're still in this bed, and that stove has to be getting colder." Rose cautiously sat up, the covers falling away from her sleep shirt. "Did you know rattlers are pit vipers?"

"Is there a reason you're telling me this now?" Cautiously, too, I sat up. The rattles from the snake grew louder, but it made no move.

"It's interesting. I saw it in a documentary. There's a pit in the rattler's head that senses heat. It can strike accurately at a mouse in total darkness because it 'sees' where the heat is."

"That's charming. Thank you for sharing." I felt less defenseless sitting up, but not much. "So if it hadn't been for the stove, the warmest heat source in this room would have been—"

"Yeah. You and me. We could have woken up with a rattler on the bed."

"Or under the covers with us."

"Or curled around a head. Like a hat. A big, thick, venomous hat."

We weren't doing ourselves any favors with this speculation. I thought about the length of floor between us and the snake, and how very naked Rose's legs and feet were. And mine, too, of course.

Rose was still going on with her animal kingdom lecture. "You could say a pit viper has extrasensory perceptions. It should be right at home here at Prophecy Week."

"We're going to need to take care of this ourselves," I commented.

"This is what is termed 'a firm grasp of the obvious,' Dash."

"I wish we'd slept in boots and pants."

"You think that would have helped?"

"If a snake strikes at me, I want the venom running down the inside of my jeans, not the inside of my leg."

"Yeah. We're not going to get the chance to armor up before taking that thing on."

Given that the snake had lifted its head and now tasted the air with its tongue, I assumed she was right.

"How about we throw the covers over it? Slow it down?" We both thought about her suggestion, and I was the one to voice the objection.

"Me, I'd rather know where it was and not have it moving around angry where I can't keep an eye on it."

"Excellent point."

More thinking. Eventually, I got tired of lying there.

"Maybe I've got a plan."

Rose looked at me. "Go on, Father Time. What you got?"

"We both leave the bed at the same time on different sides. The snake will have two things to focus on. Maybe that will keep it in one place."

"Good. Then what?"

"Grab something."

"Any suggestions?"

"You get that little shovel on the fireplace they use to clean out the ashes."

"It's got a pretty short handle."

"You want I should order something better on Amazon?"

"Don't get testy." She put up a hand to soothe me, and the snake added its own punctuation to the conversation.

"I'm going to grab my boot there, and then get to the lengths of stovewood Enrique left by the door."

"Fair enough. Ready?" I nodded. "Go."

I was closer to the snake, and it zeroed in on me, but Rose tapped her bare foot on the ground. Now the snake's attention was divided. Indecision worked in our favor.

"Go slowly," she said. We both eased apart from each other, me going for my boot and Rose making it to the fireplace.

Every time the snake focused on me, Rose would move. Every time she was at risk, I'd shift around. By working together, we both ended up with our chosen weapons. Teamwork.

"Okay," I said. "Stop moving. Let me have its attention now."

"What are you going to do?"

"Hang on."

I held my boot by its laces at arm's length and slowly swung it back and forth, a pendulum that caught the snake's focus. Its unblinking black eyes never wavered. I was able to ease over to the lengths of wood by the door. Once I had a stout piece in my hand, I whispered, "Get ready."

"Oh, I'm ready."

And then I launched my boot toward the rattler.

It took the bait, uncoiling in a flash of movement too fast to see and striking at the tough leather with shockingly long fangs.

With my other hand, I aimed to slam the length of stove-wood down on the snake's head, but it was far, far faster than me, and all I succeeded in doing was pinning it to the ground. It coiled and uncoiled, working to free itself from my inefficient trap.

"Okay," I gasped to Rose. "Use the shovel."

The snake was getting too much leverage, so I slammed my bare foot down on its writhing body. Immediately the snake coiled around my leg to press for traction. I was fighting a pure, muscly tube of evil. "Rose! The shovel!"

"Grab it behind its head!"

She'd moved up and was right next to me.

"Why? The wood will do it."

"You'll get a better grip!"

"I am not getting my hand near that snake or your shovel! Kill it!"

She struck with the confidence of the young and athletic. In one moment, I was fighting with a nightmare. In the next, two limp pieces of meat lay bleeding on the ground.

Rose and I regarded our vanquished foe.

"Oh, look, honey," I said when my breath returned. "It's bleeding out on your cute hoedown outfit. What a pity."

"Easier for cleanup, anyway. The blood's all contained in one place and not on the rug at all. Nice." She stooped and picked up the body with impressive calm, turning it to admire the snakeskin pattern on the back and pale belly. "Damn. I'll bet there are bigger snakes out there, but this one will do."

I took the shovel from her and scooped up the malevolent, triangular head. "What are we going to do with this?"

"I'm thinking . . . nothing. We go on about our day happy and let them go slowly crazy, wondering what happened to their snake."

"I like it. But at some point, a cabin girl is going to come in here and make the bed. It's asking a lot to assume she'll ignore the dead rattler on the rug."

"Right. We could burn it in the stove? Or no—wait! Let's give it to Celeste! You know she'll have a good use for it!"

"The minute a headless snake shows up, they'll know where it came from."

As if summoned by Rose saying her name, there came a knock on the connecting door.

"Everything okay in there?" Celeste called out. "We heard yelling."

"Bah," I said uselessly. Rose was more put together than me.

"We're fine. Dash had a nightmare. Thanks for checking!"

"A nightmare," we heard through the door. "I guess."

In the silence that followed, Rose and I looked at our snake.

"How about we throw it out the bathroom window into those bushes and let Mother Nature handle the body removal?" I asked.

"Love it." She disposed of the body, I did the head, and then together we cleaned up any evidence of the struggle. "And look at that. There's still time for our morning run, honey!"

I laughed outright. "Not this morning, drill sergeant. You'll have to make do with your running posse. They should be here any moment."

"Yeah. I'm wiped out. This morning it's going to be yoga at the lodge instead of Running with Rosie. Because . . ." She struggled to come up with a good excuse for not running. Amateur. I scoffed.

"Because it's too muddy this morning, obviously. You could twist an ankle."

"Good one," she said admiringly.

And that's exactly what she told her fans when they arrived at our cabin. They followed her happily to the lodge, where they no doubt found robust, transcendent health from the Downward-Facing Dog position.

Evadne was at breakfast, but we were both well-behaved. We sat on opposite sides of the dining room, and I never let on that I could read her presence on my skin.

Bob waved at me from the registration desk and fanned out the papers in his hand. He'd printed my email and wanted me to know he was grateful. Next to him, Wolf watched me from stillness. Not taking the bait. Planting venomous serpents. And yet Bob was so enthusiastic about his tax break, I had to wonder. What did he think he'd been helping his son load up the night before? Was Bob a coconspirator or a dupe? A few billion stored in the garage ought to make a tax break seem insignificant.

The psychics set up for their morning readings, leaving Rose deep in a cluster of women who wanted to talk about pregnancy and childbirth. I walked out of the lodge on my own to head to the suite.

And I knew without turning that Evadne had slipped out behind me.

So I paused to take in the view, which, on this golden morning, had the brilliance of a post rain freshness. After last night's storm, droplets of water in the air added radiance and magnification to everything. The mountains were polished, the grasses gave out their sunny-day perfume, the birds overhead had it going on in terms of twitter and call. The entire world was washed clean and new.

It would be a nice place to build a big, robust city. With paved streets and Lyfts and thugs trying to look tough.

"There was danger this morning," Evadne said from her place many feet away.

I continued my assessment of the wild world beyond the porch and responded neutrally, "There was. We handled it."

"It's not over."

I turned to look at her, startled. She frowned.

"I'm not sure what it is," she said, "but something is wrong at the cabin."

THIRTY-FIVE

DASH

"Trouble at the cabin? Is it more snakes?" I said thoughtlessly.

"More? Is that what that was?" Now she faced me too. There was no more pretending we weren't having a conversation. "It's not that. This is something different. Be careful, Dash."

I nodded to her. I couldn't look into her eyes without feeling the ghost of her lips on mine, the weight of her head resting against my chest. She blushed and bent her head to hide a smile. "Be careful," she said again, and then she went into the lodge.

Be careful, huh?

Well, she'd proven her value. Maybe not a con artist. Definitely not delusional. Perhaps something else. I would be careful.

Instead of walking to the cabin on the barn path, I cut across the lawn to get to the driveway. Hidden by a fringe of trees, I walked behind the cabins until I reached ours.

And from that angle . . . sure as shit, there was bearded Bart crouched in the bushes next to the large tree that hung over the path. He was hidden from view between cabins and had a rope looped around a branch over his head.

One large, bearded hand (well—not bearded, but grimy at least) held that rope.

I eased around until I could figure out his plan.

The tree limb was splintering near the trunk. Did last night's storm cause damage? Or had someone bearded and determined climbed up to weaken the connection? It looked to me like Bart could wait until someone came along the path, haul hard on his rope, and drop a massive branch on the head of whatever victim wandered past.

Then he'd untie the rope and take off, allowing the injured (or dead) victim to be found by whoever came along next.

Again—a terrible tragedy. No reason for anyone to suspect an innocent ranch hand.

And now I was caught in a dilemma.

I could confront Bart, even arrest him, but that would most definitely blow my cover and set the investigation back—possibly until after Wolf's brother arrived with his truck to distribute enough fake money across the nation to be a problem.

I could ignore Bart, leave him crouching in the bushes, but he'd wait for Rose to wander by. He'd like to kill or disable either of us because when one went to the hospital, the other could hardly stay happily on vacation.

Or he could drop the branch on Evadne.

What to do?

The best idea would be to trigger Bart's trap early before anyone got hurt. But how to do it without letting him know I was onto him?

I was crouched behind our cabin, near the bathroom window shared by Evadne and Celeste. That reminded me of my bathroom window, under which was . . .

I crept back quietly until I found what I was looking for. A flash of unnatural snake belly, white in the bushes under the window.

I picked up three thick feet of dead rattler and carried that with me.

Why not? About time that snake did me some good.

Bart never heard me coming. But he sure noticed the snake I flung like a lasso, which easily wrapped itself around his neck.

He leaped up, screaming, and flung the snake into the woods. As I'd hoped, his convulsive surprise made him yank on the tree limb.

What I hadn't planned was that he would back under the branch.

The tree gave with a mighty *crack*, and he fell back as he looked up. The branch caught him squarely on his chest and slammed him into the wet ground.

Damn, Bart.

I stepped forward, astonished by the success of my ploy. Bart was groggy and losing consciousness, but both his feet and hands were still moving, so he'd gotten off lucky—no spinal cord damage. Still, his ribs were probably stoved in, and it was unlikely he'd escape without some internal injuries.

I regarded him coldly. And then I turned on my heels and left him lying there in the mud.

I climbed in through our bathroom window and was coming out our suite's door by the time Abbott and Costello came along the path and discovered Bart under a fallen tree.

"What happened?" I called to them. "I heard something. Oh, Lord! That branch must have fallen on him! Look—he must have been trying to clear away some storm damage with that rope. Is he okay?" Bart was unconscious but breathing. His color was bad. "Stay with him. I'll run up to the lodge. He needs medical attention. Don't move him."

People arrived in twos and threes, eager to not be left out. They were followed not long after by the medevac helicopter from Cheyenne.

"Good gracious," Marcia said to no one as she wrung her hands. "That's twice in two days. This is the most accidents we've ever had—and right on top of each other."

The EMTs loaded an unconscious Bart into the helicopter on a backboard and in a cervical collar under the froth of beard.

One of the cabin girls was deputized to go with him, and we watched them fly away.

Rose appeared at my side. "What happened?" she asked *sotto voce*.

"Tell you later."

"I knew it. I knew there was something to tell."

Marcia struggled with her anxiety and then remembered her duty as hostess. She clapped her hands. "People, I don't want this accident to upset you. We'll still be leaving at eleven for the wonderful glamping trip in Smuggler's Basin. And I have the greatest news: I checked online, and there are solar winds above the earth. The evening will be clear, no clouds, and that means . . . the northern lights! Oh, it's a perfect night for glamping!"

She did a good job of selling it. Frowns and concern were overwritten. People turned to talk and smile at each other and discuss how long the northern lights had been on their bucket list.

"And," Rose said quietly to me as we walked to the cabin, "now we're three of us against four of them. You, me, and Enrique against Wolf, Lenny, Abbott, and Costello. The odds are getting better!"

"Huh."

However, the morning wasn't done with us yet. There was still one more challenge to overcome.

THIRTY-SIX

DASH

ROSE AND I WERE IN THE SUITE SENDING OUR DAILY encrypted email with our report and begging for information from the analysts working on Bob's computer (and, on my part, ducking Owen's questions about the mentoring program), when we were distracted by shouting at the bunkhouse next door.

We looked out the side window. Wolf Koenig stood on the porch, yelling into Abbott and Costello's room. He was so angry he didn't notice when I eased the snake-entrance window open and then stood back so I was invisible to him.

"Motherfucker, Abbott!" Wolf yelled. "You couldn't have waited a few fucking weeks?"

"It was Costello's idea!"

"The hell it was!"

We couldn't see the two ranch hands, but it sounded like they were right inside the door. Wolf continued his rant, his manly mustache quivering in anger.

"I've got Bart in the hospital and thirty-eight dudes to get up to Smuggler's Basin by nightfall. And you decide it's the perfect time to kick those Mexicans out of the country?"

Rose and I exchanged confused looks. Where was Enrique,

and how had Abbott and Costello managed to deport him from his own nation?

"Fuck, boss," Abbott said, and then clearly ran out of things to say.

"All right," Wolf said. "Spill it, Costello. What happened last night?"

Costello shuffled out onto the porch, possibly trying to increase his distance from Abbott. "We drove up to Malta like you said and got the two things—you know."

"Yeah, I know. I'm the one who sent you. Get to it. What about the Mexicans?"

"Well, Abbott says—"

"That's a filthy lie!"

"I ain't said it yet!"

"Shut up, Abbott. You had your chance. Go on, Costello."

"Well, Abbott says we won't be but two hours to the Canadian border, and we could get rid of three Mexicans right away."

"That was your idea!"

"Shut up. Go on."

"So we jumped the big guy—that Rick—and got him tied up, and Abbott put a washcloth in his mouth and tied it off with a bandanna. It was real neat."

"You're lucky as hell you didn't suffocate him. Go on."

"Then we got the other two. They were even easier. We put them in the back of my truck. You know it's got that cap on it so no one could see, and we drove off to get the devices from the guy."

"I got the devices. What I don't got are trail hands. Get to the point."

"We drove into Canada. The guys at the border were real nice. We told 'em we wanted to get some of them doughnuts."

"Tim Horton's." Abbott sounded sulky.

"And they all laughed and said we could bring 'em some back on the return, and we did too. They were real glad."

"You had conversations with border guards while you were

kidnapping Mexicans. You brought them doughnuts so they couldn't possibly forget you." Wolf's contempt dripped out and pooled on the floor between his well-worn, hand-tooled boots.

"Well, we thought . . . you know. Be nice and all."

Wolf vented his rage in an impressively varied string of profanities. When he ran out of breath, he turned to the pair and heaved a huge sigh. "Where'd you leave my trail hands?"

"There was a utility shed out back of the truck stop. We put 'em in there. Someone'll find em 'ventually."

"And you think they won't identify you as their abductors."

Abbott and Costello had come far enough onto the porch for me to see the nervous glances they exchanged. "Well, boss, you'll swear we was here all night, right? I mean, you was going to do that anyway because of picking up them devices."

Wolf shook his head as he looked at them. "You better hope they keep their traps shut or we get past this before anyone tries to piece this mess together."

"That's what'll happen, Wolf. I'm sure of it!"

"Shut up. I got enough trouble dealing with those snoops." He glared at our cabin, but we were beyond his vision in the shadows.

Costello heard the warning, but his partner kept talking. "They ain't got no money, no wallets, no ID." Abbott snorted in amusement. "Good luck getting back into our country."

"You didn't keep the wallets? I know you kept the money."

"Didn't have much on 'em. We used the money to buy the doughnuts. You want one, Wolf? We still got some."

"Shut the fuck up. I'm going to have to call in the part-time help and maybe a few cabin girls. The pair of you are assholes, and maybe I'm gonna fire you after this is over."

"But them federal laws don't apply to us, right, boss? Whole new world soon? A better world? Like you said?"

"Get to work. You got to saddle horses for thirty-eight guests, the four of us, and two more I'm going to have to dig up.

You fucked with my morning, boys, and it ain't been going so well before you two laid this shit on me."

"We're sorry, boss."

"Yeah. We're real sorry."

"I know you are. You're damned bigots and too fucking dumb to know any better. Go on, get to work. I need to make some calls."

They went their separate ways, and Rose and I stared at each other.

"I'll call in right now," she said. "Tell headquarters someone's got to get Enrique out of that shed. Where the hell—"

"It'll be the closest border crossing from Malta, Montana, and then the nearest Tim Horton's. They'll find them."

"Shit." She was dialing and cursing.

"Better tell them there's someone in Malta making 'devices,' too—possibly the kind that maybe go *boom* to destroy any evidence."

"Right. You know what this means?"

"Yeah. It means we're not getting into Wolf's records. And we're down to you and me against Wolf, Lenny, Abbott, and Costello. The field office had better have some people on stand-by for this."

"I'll tell them. Good thing we're such badasses."

"Good thing."

THIRTY-SEVEN

EVADNE

I'D FELT SOMETHING WRONG AT THE CABIN CELESTE AND I shared with Dash and Rose, but not knowing what it was maddened me. And Dash, endlessly curious and afraid only of wildlife (as far as I could tell), had taken off to investigate with a barely contained hunger.

But I swallowed my concern. I had a private reading in my little office with Hal at nine o'clock. We'd barely begun when Dash ran past my small window.

He moved quickly and easily. Clearly healthy. Whatever danger Dash had had to confront, he'd overcome it. I hadn't realized I was half holding my breath until I saw he was all right. I turned to Hal, relieved.

Hal, however, was on his feet, peering at the activity brewing in Dash's wake. He shot me an apologetic look and took off, following the crowds that flowed toward the barn to see what was going on.

By the time the helicopter took off, carrying Bart to the hospital, there wasn't much of our session left. I didn't need much time, though. Hal's conflict had been apparent since he'd arrived at the ranch. I didn't waste time once we were in my tiny, temporary office.

"Hal, you've embarked on an affair, even though you love your wife."

He slumped in his chair. "You really are amazing."

I got not guilt but relief from him. "Are you hoping I'll force you to stop?"

He covered his face. "I don't know why I did it. I was bored, I suppose."

I'd been used as a confessor before. Often, good people need to admit their mistakes. Hal and I spent the last few minutes of his time discussing how he would end the relationship and strengthen his ties to his wife.

Humans are so . . . human, I thought after he left. We act against our own best interests and sabotage the best things in our lives out of boredom, or curiosity, or fear.

I was guilty of it myself. I'd allowed the fear of rejection to keep me from making connections to people. I vowed I wouldn't sabotage my connection to Dash. I would continue to be brave.

Zoe had finished her palm reading early and sat near my door. She smiled brightly when I came out, clearly thinking I couldn't read her.

Of course I could. I knew immediately there would be no salvaging her future at Prophecy Week.

"Zoe," I said, my accusation hardening my tone. "You'd do that? To Hal? You overheard enough to know he's going to end his affair. Why would you do that to him?"

She leaped up, her posture defensive. "You don't know what the hell you're talking about. I haven't done anything!"

Elbert came up beside me and laid one skeletal hand against my back in support. We looked at Zoe together.

She was cornered. "You can't know anything! There's no such thing as an actual psychic, you freak!"

Elbert hissed, checking to make sure she wasn't overheard.

"Zoe," I said sadly. "You could have done well here."

"I can still do well here! You're not in charge!"

She scurried out, heading for Phoebus's cabin.

"Want me to go after her?" Elbert's offer was chivalrous, even though there was nothing he could do.

"That's okay. She's not going to find him. He's out back, doing his workout. I'll talk to him."

Phoebus had been using the glade in idle moments since we'd arrived. It was out of sight of the guests, which allowed him to maintain the illusion that his physique came naturally. If no one ever saw him doing an endless series of crunches, sit-ups, and chin-ups, his godly image would remain intact.

"Hi," Phoebus said when I arrived. He was doing a side plank. I took a moment to note that his naked chest, although impressive in sculpted detail, was nowhere near as interesting to me as Dash's. "What's up?"

I sighed as I sat on the leaf litter. I could have wished for a lush lawn, but his glade was not well-groomed. "Zoe thinks she's going to blackmail Hal."

"Why? What's Hal done?" He rolled his torso forward and changed arms. I now looked at his back.

"Nothing you need to know about."

"Oh, come on, Eve. Winters are long and cold, and somehow the money from Prophecy Week disappears as fast as it comes in. What am I going to live on until we come back next year? Some extortion could tide me over."

Amoral. The man had no ethics at all. He was only redeemed by his cream puff of a heart.

"She has to go. And now."

He collapsed and turned to me. "We can still make money off her," he protested.

"She leaves, or I do."

Artie grimaced as he lay on his back. (He had a nice yoga mat. I was on dirt.) "That's an empty threat. Now that you're finally here, you'd never leave me."

He was right. "But you'd never hurt me," I countered, "and Zoe staying would hurt me."

He bridged upward, his crotch obscenely thrusting to the sky as he marched his legs up and down. "You're sure?"

I nodded. "And tell her to leave Hal alone or I'll hex her."

He winced. "You have no hexing powers. Do you?"

"She doesn't know that. Get her out of here, and keep Hal safe."

He sighed and pulled himself to his feet. Time for squats. "I'll get someone from town to drive her to the airport today. There's that guy who says he's got a taxi . . ."

I left him lunging across the clearing, clenching his glutes. *Fitness like that isn't worth the effort.*

True to his word, Zoe was gone before we left for Smuggler's Basin. I was handing my overnight case to Marcia when I saw Zoe getting into a ratty pickup "cab." She glared at me and forked the sign of the evil eye. Wasn't the first time.

"I'll have a private tent tonight," said Annette. "Thanks for that."

"You and Martine can sprawl." I knew she wasn't angry with me.

"Yes, well, Martine doesn't take up much space . . ." She winked at me, adorable in her mom jeans.

"You girls have fun on your ride," Marcia enthused. "By the time you get up there, the cook and I will have a feast ready to go!"

"You're going to have a perfect journey in that bus of yours," Annette said with a smile. "Martine told me so!"

"Isn't that wonderful! Thank her for me!" Marcia was wreathed in smiles. She confused me. Phoebus had done his thing for three years at the Triangle-K; it was safe to assume she knew the forecasting was smart guesswork, not actual prediction. But people saw what they want to see. That was why con men existed.

"Come along, Evadne, dear," Annette said, linking her arm in mine. "Let's go saddle up."

We arrived at the barn as Wolf led a horse to Dash. Wolf was angry and suspicious. His intentions toward Dash were not at all kind, and the horse he led up was part of that.

THIRTY-EIGHT

DASH

"This is Kettlebell," Wolf said and handed me the reins to a prancing, dark-gray monstrosity. "We don't take Ferd on long trail rides. It would take him months to get up to Smuggler's Basin. Bell here will have you there in no time."

His smile never reached his eyes as he slapped the horse on its neck. The horse snorted and shook its head, stomping big hooves in irritation. Horses have leg-snapping feet and huge teeth. Sometimes they bite. I hoped this one would bite Wolf before he bit me.

I did my best to cover my panic. "I'm sure he will."

"She, Dash. Bell is a mare. She's a real sweetheart, aren't you, Bell?"

Bell regarded me with a definitely skeptical eye.

Lucius brought Blissful up for Evadne, standing nearby. "I can get Dash up, Wolf, if you want to get to the others."

The teenager's innocent attempt to be helpful drew down some of Wolf's manic intensity. He nodded at the boy, gave me a glare poorly disguised as a smile, and he was gone.

As if to prove the depths of my failings, Evadne greeted her horse, Blissful, and stepped up easily into the saddle. *Show-off.*

Bell and I studied each other. Neither of us liked what we saw.

Time to face the inevitable. "This is too much horse for me, Lucius," I said to the teen.

The boy's brow wrinkled and he shuffled his feet, caught between a guest and his boss. "She really is sweet, but she hates to be left behind. She's a runner, and you need a strong hand to hold her in. You're okay with that, aren't you, Dash?"

"Huh."

I glanced at Evadne, who shook her head at me. Her message was clear. *Don't do it. Don't accept that horse.*

I squinted at Bell, who let out a sudden snort of air, which I took as prelude to an attack. I fell back a few feet, and I swear that horse laughed at me.

Deliverance rode up at that point. Rose was high atop her mountainous palomino, Sunshine. She took one look at the situation and slipped gracefully down the many feet to the ground.

"Switch," she ordered. "Lucius, you can help us with the stirrups, right?"

"Are you sure?" I protested as Rose nudged me bodily over to Sunshine, a far larger but definitely more placid animal. "You're no more experienced at this than I am."

"Are you kidding?" She and Lucius worked together. Before I could resist, the teen had thrown her up into the saddle. Her firm hands calmed Bell immediately. "I'm miles better at this than you will ever be."

"She's a runner, Rose," Lucius said as he moved to lengthen the stirrups on Sunshine. His tone was different. With me, he'd issued a nervous warning. With Rose, he passed on useful facts. "She'll want to be at the head of the pack, so hold her in."

"A runner, huh? Excellent."

Lucius nodded to me. Sunshine was ready for me. I bit my lip and set my shoulders. Courage, it was said, was action in the presence of fear, and damned if I wouldn't show courage now. I scaled the heights of Sunshine with as much dignity as I could muster, forcing back the panic.

Once seated, I looked around. Sunshine was a big horse, and I was far from the ground below. I looked at Evadne on the smaller Blissful, and then at Rose, also below me. "This is a big horse."

"Yeah." She grinned. "And that one gallops. You're going to have more fun on this ride."

That statement was questionable, but I kept my views to myself.

We stood quietly in the crowded corral as our fellow guests mounted up.

Phoebus Apollon was on Blizzard, one of the few horses bigger than Sunshine. He'd insisted on the ranch's only white horse and knew he looked good. Annette sat stolidly atop her mild roan. It would take the apocalypse to shake her from the saddle.

Celeste was on a sorrel. She rode with the same implacable calm that characterized everything she did. She looked like she could conquer the West single-handedly.

The entire ranch had emptied out for the event. There was organized chaos around us as riders were paired with their mounts, but the process went swiftly. Then Wolf returned his attention to our group and saw I wasn't where he'd placed me.

"You changed mounts." His tone of accusation was barely hidden behind a veil of politeness.

"I wanted Bell," Rose enthused. "I hear she's a runner."

Wolf moved his attention to her. His contempt was obvious; it was in his eyes and in the way he held his shoulders, gripped the reins. His big bay snorted and danced, and Wolf checked the horse with a swift jerk. "Sure you did," he said. "Woman like you *needs* a good gallop."

Nothing was wrong with the words. It was the attitude that turned it into an insult. I bridled and leaned forward to speak, but Rose cut me off.

"Always," Rose agreed, as if she'd heard nothing wrong. But a glimmer of challenge straightened her spine, and a new alertness bled through her happy-housewife persona. Her sunny smile had a lot of teeth.

"Well," Wolf said dismissively. He looked at me. "You're a novice, so I'm going to have Lenny ride along with you."

Lenny rode up and gave us a thick, mean grin—but he kept me and big Sunshine between himself and Rose. He'd learned his lesson there.

Wolf went on, "Lenny, you're responsible for Dash. You stick with him, hear?"

THIRTY-NINE
EVADNE

IN MY MIND'S EYE, THE ENTIRE PLAN SPOOLED OUT LIKE dropped wrapping paper, falling past my grasp in a broad and shiny path. Dash was supposed to be on Bell and unable to control her. She'd run away with Dash, Lenny would follow, they'd move far in front of the group . . . where anything at all could happen without witnesses.

Pitched over a cliff. Thrown to crack his skull on a provident rock. Wiped painfully from his mount by a low-hanging branch met at far too great a speed.

If he'd been on Bell. Rose had foiled that plan neatly. I felt a burst of relief.

"You got it, boss," Lenny said. His twisted smile said he was annoyed at the change in their plans. "I'll be his shadow today."

"So will I," Rose threw in.

"And I'll watch out for him too." I nudged Blissful forward and only then realized young Skip was behind me. I couldn't help but associate the child with the baby I'd lost, but Skip didn't feel that way. The boy was awash in adolescent lust and didn't know if he wanted me or Rose more.

"Me too!" He gulped. "I'll ride with this group!"

Rose laughed. "Looks like Dash will have a lot of helpers. It'll be a parade! Are you sure you need Lenny to stay with Dash, Wolf?"

We'd arranged ourselves alongside Dash in a line of solidarity. We looked like an inept Three Musketeers posse—or four, rather, because Melanie rode up on her horse, Kraken. "What are we doing? Can I be with you guys?"

Wolf's smile was choking on profanity. "I guess you're in good shape, Dash. Come on, Lenny. You ride the line, help out wherever you're needed. If anyone gets run-away with, you go after them." He shot one last look at Rose, who smiled at him, and then they were gone.

"Okay," Dash said. "Thanks."

He said it to Rose and me, but it was Skip who answered. "You got it, man. What crawled up inside him and died? Am I right?"

We received a brief lesson on trail etiquette and what to do if we got in trouble. As Wolf addressed the crowd, Lenny pursed his lips and eyed Rose, clearly hoping she'd get into trouble so he could avoid helping her. Then we took those first steps beyond the fencing and into the open world.

Sunshine wasn't Ferd. He moved out alertly, and I explained to Dash about neck reining. Sunshine decided he liked Dash, so he was alert and responsive. The more he listened to Dash, the calmer Dash got. Optimism rose in me.

"I feel we can create a tentative partnership," Dash said as he stroked the powerful neck. The horse twitched an intelligent ear in response.

The ranch hands had panniers on the backs of their horses to hold our lunch, but the rest of us rode unencumbered. The overnight bags we'd packed would be driven to Smuggler's Basin by Marcia in the tough old school bus. Our horses were unburdened, and we worried about nothing but enjoying ourselves.

Those who could enjoy themselves on horseback, anyway.

Rose's firm hand kept Bell pacing along eagerly from her position in front of Dash. Then we reached that first long, skinny meadow where Ferd had refused to lope previously, and horses in front of us were kicked into genteel lopes.

Bell lost her mind.

My anxiety rose as I watched, but Rose was firm. She wasn't allowing her horse to pursue the disappearing pack—and to my astonishment, she was also laughing. As Rose reined Bell back further and further, the horse managed to break into a trot, but painfully slowly. I watched, astonished, as Blissful and I passed her at a walk. Bell trotted so tightly that every step went up higher than it went out, and Rose bounced on top of the horse until she was all but helpless with the giggles.

"Oh no, you don't," Rose insisted between her bursts of amusement. "We don't go until I say we go."

I turned to look behind me. Their battle of wills raged, and Bell now trotted in place like a show pony. Skip and Melanie cheered.

"You're right to be the one in charge," I called to her. "Stick with it, Rose!"

"It's all about the energy," she said. Dash grinned.

At last, Bell came to a halt. Rose made her stand there, trembling, for a moment. Then, once she knew she'd won, Rose gave a tiny flick with one heel and released the reins. With a scream of pure joy, she leaned in as Bell leaped forward and all but flew down the meadow. Skip and Melanie followed, the girl's pony trotting with bone-jarring briskness.

I wasn't the only one watching them disappear. Sunshine leaned forward, politely not pulling but clearly interested in catching up.

"So much for your parade." I was at Dash's side. "Ready? Remember how to ask him to lope?"

He inhaled deeply. His courage was brighter than the sun. He was determined that old fears wouldn't rule him.

He leaned forward and nudged Sunshine with one heel.

The huge muscles in the horse's mighty shoulders bunched. His rear rose. He threw out one leg . . .

. . . and then they were loping.

Blissful and I leaped to join them. I couldn't help my grin as I watched Dash conquer long-powerful fears. He was an inspiration. "Nice!"

It took him a moment to get used to the changed pattern, but soon his spine loosened up, and he began to roll with the gait. The speed alarmed him at first, but the rhythm was so enjoyable, his fear soon fizzed into excitement.

Loping was exhilarating. Like a waltz, but faster and more powerful.

He let go of the saddle horn and risked a glance to make sure I was still with him. He looked back in time to duck under a whippy branch reaching out from the woods.

"You can move away from those branches too," I called. "Don't forget the reins."

He gritted his teeth and laid the reins gently over Sunshine's neck. The horse responded, moving away from the woods and deeper into the meadow. Dash grinned.

"I feel like I'm in a Western," he called to me.

"You are!" I laughed, picking up on his intoxication.

We'd come up against the group, slowing to a walk as they approached the end of the meadow. Dash pulled back experimentally and gently on the reins, and Sunshine dropped briefly into a painfully bouncy trot and then to a walk.

He'd done it.

He tried to mask his relief and felt silly that he was so proud.

Face your fears, I thought, a reminder to myself—a philosophy far removed from my typical plan of staying unnoticed and hidden. *Be brave. Summon the courage to trust. I can do that too. I know I can.*

The trail returned to the cool shadows of the forest, and we went single-file to negotiate twists and turns on the path. Rose had jumped well ahead in the line, and Dash's entourage had scattered.

I stuck with him, though.

Blissful and I were behind him, quite literally watching his back. He checked again to make sure I was there, and then a tendril of lust and desire reached me. His excitement had turned into something more intimate.

And I was lost in the memory of his mouth on mine, the slight scruff on his cheeks and chin, the taste of his tongue. My heart beat faster. My mouth was suddenly dry.

Whoa, girl. Down. You're like a cat in heat.

The realization made me proud. I was facing my fears, too, and getting every bit as much excitement out of it. Dash and I were both facing our fears today—and it was exhilarating.

We had several more lopes across mountain meadows, and with each one, Dash's confidence grew. We followed the long string of horses making their way up and down slopes and valleys and across the stunning landscape. The country unfolded before us, and we either forded babbling streams or crossed them on sturdy—if rough-hewn—bridges. The forests were fragrant and deep, the meadows filled with swaying, waist-high grasses. Birds sang, and the breeze tasted wild. Wildflowers bloomed in flashes of brilliant color. Mountains ringed us, and the air was crystalline-clear, brilliant with sunlight, cool and dry. *Paradise.*

By the time we halted for lunch, Dash had mostly lost his fear. We sat in a clearing on logs and gladly took the canteens and cold beef kebabs Abbott and Costello passed around. And even though Dash ate his lunch sitting next to his wife, he and I were together.

Cheri remarked the clearing was like a little room, and I explained how a beaver's dam would slowly turn a forest into a meadow. Years of zoology came out of me under her interested questions, and before long, the entire group was listening.

I was startled by the attention. *Keep your head down, avoid notice* . . . but Dash smiled at me, and I gathered my confidence and kept talking.

"The beaver makes a dam to back the water up to the trees. Sediment settles in the pool. Many years later, maybe decades, the sediment builds up until the land is flat and dry and the grasses come. Voilà: mountain meadow. It *does* looks like a little room. Cheri's right."

Young Melanie wore a frown. "But what happens to the beavers?"

I smiled at her. "They go downstream or upstream and start again."

Melanie wasn't the only one clapping in delight.

"Are all mountain meadows made by beavers?" Suzette asked.

"No, certainly not. But some of them are. I think this is one of them. Don't you?"

"Well, I'll be damned," said Wolf. He grinned readily, a man of charm and action. It would be easy to believe the false front he presented and assume he had no violent urges.

Abbott and Costello passed around cookies and chilled grapes. We sat in the sun and took a moment to be content with our lot. It would be good to be a person of means, I decided.

We moved out not long after, and Rose retook her position by Dash. In the meadow, we could ride three abreast as our horses walked along, long grasses brushing against our boots.

"You're a good teacher," Rose said.

I smiled sadly. "Do you know that was the first time anyone listened to me about something other than prophecy?"

"How did you know that? About the beavers?" Rose asked.

"Seven semesters as a biology major. Zoology, actually."

"Wow. That's cool. Is that so you have something to do when . . ." Rose nodded ahead of us to where Phoebus Apollon sang "Don't Fence Me In" in a rich baritone, to the delight of the women riding near him.

I nodded, and Rose didn't press. "Well, it was impressive," she said. We rode along in quiet unity, and I was warmed by more than sunshine. Courage was leading me to expand my tiny circle of friends, and splashes of hope landed on my loneliness. What would the next day teach me?

FORTY

DASH

Smuggler's Basin was enormous. You could build a major metropolitan airport in it with all the runways, if only any plane could have dropped straight down to land amid the mountains ringing the basin like a stone crown.

"Good Lord," Rose muttered as we emerged into a vast meadow. "The hills are alive with what now? That's right—the sound of music."

"It does look like the Alps," I agreed. "Bigger, though."

"Damn. Hey, Evadne—was this place all beaver-built?"

Others turned to hear the answer.

"I don't know." She laughed. "But it's possible. It would take a lot of beavers, though!"

The discussion flashed up and down the line. Someone said because they liked to garden, they thought their spirit animal was a beaver, which added fuel to the fire of heated discussion. And then an eagle was spotted far overhead.

"Look! Look, Dash! It's an eagle!"

"Is that your eagle, Dash?"

"Think it knows about Rose's eaglet?"

"That's a good sign. It's good luck—I know it is!"

"Eagles don't eat beavers, do they?"

"Wait. Do beavers eat eagles?"

"What if a beaver ate the tree where an eagle lived? What would happen then? Dash, what would happen then?"

"How do we know anything about beavers? Eagles, yes—but are beavers the spirit animal of the Moonglow Mystic?"

"She should have something more, you know, moonish."

"What's a moonish animal?"

"A bat."

"A lunar moth!"

Lenny came back to find out why the train of riders had come to a halt as this fascinating discussion ground on. The riders behind us had bunched up around us. He glared at me and said, "Get up, now. Camp's not too much farther."

Slowly, the knot of riders untangled. We stepped along a creek running through high meadow grasses.

"Don't you worry about her spirit animal," Suzette said. "You can trust the Moonglow Mystic."

The conversation flowed around me. I breathed in air definitely holding extra oxygen. It was invigorating. The sun warmed the grasses, which exhaled a dry, wild perfume: hay on a bender. My muscles had gotten used to the movement of the horse under me. I'd passed from anxiety to competency to vague, unspecific discomfort. I was ready to get off and stretch.

And it was Suzette's words that rolled around in my head. Trusting Evadne was like a stone in a rock tumbler—or in a rushing mountain stream. The longer the thought sat in my head, the more the rough edges got buffed away. It took a good twenty minutes to reach the camp, and by the time we rode up to the horse pen, I had a smooth river stone of truth:

I could trust Evadne.

More, I *wanted* to trust her.

I put that truth through some mental tests as we dismounted and turned our horses over to the trail hands.

Was it only attraction? Was I drawn to Evadne because she

was beautiful? Because the feeling of her lips on mine was a ghost of a sensation, even now?

Was it a protective urge? Did I want to care for her because she was too often sad and alone? Or because she apparently admired me?

Was it temporary insanity? Had I drank too much of this oxygen-rich mountain air? Did I need to wait for sobriety to return to me? That morning, I'd caused serious harm to a man by flinging a dead snake at him, and yet I felt no remorse. That alone troubled me. Was I competent to decide who to trust?

Probably not.

So I resolutely ignored the question of giving honesty to a woman who made her living conning eager dupes. I toured the glamping site to get the full measure of glamorous camping.

It was worth the look.

Marcia had arrived with the cooking staff. There was a track through the trees to the Jeep trail Bob had mentioned, but they'd kept the vehicles well-hidden to preserve the Wild West vibe.

The camp was arranged in a large half circle along the bank of the stream. Tents on sturdy wooden platforms were scattered across the landscape with enough room to maintain a sense of privacy. Inside, real beds were made up with fresh linens. Kerosene lanterns added a primitive touch to opulent luxury.

"Each tent has panels to open so you can see the night sky when you're in bed. If we get the northern lights tonight, you'll want to open those!"

Marcia's grin was infectious. We all hoped for a radiant night.

She showed us the kitchen area, where the cook and her helper handed us cookies and Mason jars of lemonade. The smell of dinner roasting in a clay oven made my mouth water.

"There's a bunkhouse back there for us workfolk. And here's the washhouse. There are four potties over here and a nice shower. It's stream-fed, but the tank warms in the sun all day, so it's not too bad. I've made up a schedule for showers. Ladies first, gentlemen! You boys can smell like horses for longer, right?"

A large fire pit sat in the center, ringed by Adirondack chairs. "This is your living room," Marcia said. "You come here when you want to be social. And when you want alone time, you can be in your tent and no one will bother you. Welcome to Smuggler's Basin!"

We got our tent assignments. Rose and I were in a tent tucked up against the mountains, almost in the woods. It was cozy. If we hadn't been watching Wolf and Lenny, I'm sure Rose and I both would have enjoyed the camp had we been with different partners.

"My shower time is in half an hour," Rose said once we were alone. "After, I'll grab a quick nap here and then take the first watch tonight. Sound good?"

"Sounds good. I'll keep an eye on our boys this afternoon. Make sure they stick around up here, away from any presses or color-changing ink."

"Right."

I wandered over to the fire ring and took a seat with a view of the far-flung camp. People came and went over the next hour, and we chatted easily. I realized I'd grown quite fond of many of them.

And I was particularly fond of the woman who folded herself into the chair beside me.

"Hello," Evadne said.

Her hair was wet, and she smelled good. It made me all the more aware I was still sweaty and gamy, my jeans stiff with dust and essence of trail ride.

"I joined the FBI right out of college," I said by way of a greeting, and then came to a halt.

FORTY-ONE

DASH

I'D JUST ADMITTED TO EVADNE THAT I WAS FBI. I'D STARTLED myself. So much for putting a sobriety waiting period on my desire to trust her.

"Oh yeah?" she said neutrally.

We were in one of those pockets of solitude that developed unexpectedly. There was no one to overhear.

"Yeah. I've been there for seventeen years. I'm the senior agent, and Rose is my partner."

She didn't run away or scream. She didn't jerk in her seat in surprise. "What are you investigating? Not false prophets, I'm guessing?"

I exhaled with surprise. It sounded like my horse laughing at me. "No. A counterfeiting operation. Joint task force with the Secret Service."

"Ah," she nodded, her eyes going to Wolf. He was in the horse pen, checking hooves. "So that's what the ink is for."

I regarded her. "You're not startled," I said.

"That's true, I'm not. I knew you were in some kind of law enforcement. I didn't know what flavor."

"How? How did you know?"

She raised her eyebrows and gave me an enigmatic smile. "What I can't figure out, though, is why you're telling me."

"Yeah." I shifted in my chair. "That's a good question." I sifted through my own confusion. "Because I don't want you *not* to know. You know?"

Silence was called for as I kept thinking. She gave me that silence. With too little forethought, I gave her my confession.

"I kind of caused Bart's accident this morning."

"You were a part of that?" I nodded. "He was the danger I warned you about?" Another nod. "And why do you feel guilty? Do you think it's your fault he got hurt?"

I shrugged my shoulders, uncomfortable. "Well, he planned on hurting me. Or Rose. So . . ."

"Ah—there it is. The conflict in you. I knew there was something. What's got you upset?"

I spoke the answer before my conscious mind had time to consider my response. "He was a threat to Rose. And he might have hurt you. And maybe I shouldn't have sprung his trap."

"Hmm. Well, thank you, then."

"Thank you," I repeated in wonder. "I caused him grievous harm. Doesn't that—I don't know—doesn't that unsettle you?"

"It sounds like you were helping. I trust you, Dash. Whatever the situation, I'm sure you read it right."

"Huh."

I was having trouble getting my feet under me, metaphorically speaking. It wasn't only her calm acceptance that unbalanced me. I was still reeling from my own decision to present Evadne, a woman I'd known for a mere handful of days, with the bald truth of my existence.

Among the many reasons why I shouldn't have spoken was the reality that this was not a smart way to remain undercover.

And yet I knew she wouldn't betray me. As Suzette had said, you could trust the Moonglow Mystic.

I was a wooden version of Dash, unable to think of anything to say. The tortured silence was mercifully cut short when Skip launched himself victoriously into the chair on Evadne's other side, beating out his sister with a whoop of victory. Both were clean and neatly groomed.

The afternoon passed, and neither Wolf nor Lenny did anything remarkable or suspicious. Abbott and Costello remained similarly engaged, helping the cook, setting up tables and benches, scurrying to do Marcia's bidding.

Rose appeared as a large roast was sliced for dinner. She was rested and relaxed, laughing with her growing cadre of fans.

Phoebus Apollon, in a gold mylar windbreaker that caught the light of the setting sun in a blinding display, intoned a mystic, Druidic prayer before we dove hungrily into our meal. Campfire songs and s'mores took up the rest of the evening until the sun finally set beyond the mountains.

And then, as darkness fell, the sky was filled with glowing ribbons of light.

"The aurora borealis!" Marcia exclaimed, as proud of the display as if she'd created it.

Coos all around. The night sky was a huge hit. As the darkness deepened, the colors became more intense. The predominant color was green, glowing and shifting overhead, but there were slivers of rose and sometimes blue.

The chairs were adjustable. We all reclined, gazing straight up and marveling at the show. Wolf and his cohorts cooed along with us, so it was easy to keep an eye on them.

Of course, people couldn't ride all day and then recline comfortably in darkness without paying the draining price of miles in the saddle. Charlie and Val were the first to gather their two sleepy kids and announce they would watch through the panels in their tent roof.

Their departure triggered a general exodus of weary, overfed, contented guests. Rose and I walked to our tent, paired up like any other loving couple but aware Bart had tried to harm or kill one or both of us that morning. We were targets, and it was only wise to keep that in mind.

"I'm going to change into my black running suit and take a stroll around the camp to keep an eye on things," Rose said. "You get some sleep. I'll wake you up when I get tired."

She bounced on her toes in rested and eager anticipation of spying on Wolf. I wasn't tired, but her plan was sound. "Be careful. And if something goes wrong, remember to bring the right energy to the situation—the Rose on Horseback energy. The Running with Rosie energy."

She nodded. The idea had been brewing in her, and she stood straighter. I gave her room to find her way. "Shower time for me at last. I'll be back."

"I'll watch over you from afar."

The shower was chilly but enjoyable. I scrubbed off layers of dust, sweat, and horse and gloried in the sensation of long-forgotten cleanness. I left in sweats and a T-shirt, unlaced sneakers on my feet. Celeste waited at the washhouse door.

"We've been talking about you," she said in her low voice. Dangling from her finger was my shaving kit.

"Who?" She'd caught me by surprise.

"Rose and me. And Evadne and me. And now Annette and me too."

I goggled at her. Hard to believe this would be a good discussion for me. "Um—why?"

"We're planning out your night. Making a few adjustments to the sleeping arrangements." She smirked.

"Like what?"

"I'm going to bunk with Annette. She has an extra bed in her tent, since Madame Zoe's on her way back to New Jersey. You're going to take my place and sleep with Evadne."

My eyebrows disappeared into my hairline. Celeste thrust the shaving kit into my hands.

"Um," I said, taking it from her. "Thank you?"

"Rose says she's got the energy she needs, and you need this. Stop gasping; you're not a fish. It was her idea."

"Rose's idea?"

"Evadne. I told you—we've been talking about you. Go sleep in my tent with Evadne. Do I need to give you further instructions, little man?"

Her sudden grin startled me, and then she was gone.

Huh.

There are moments of paralysis when a decision can't be made. I was overwhelmed.

Then I shrugged and went back into the washhouse to shave. That wasn't why Rose had sent the shaving kit. She got it to me because I keep condoms in there. But since I had a razor, why not go to the lady with a smooth jaw?

Evadne was cross-legged in the middle of the bed, a thick braid of silver hair hanging over her shoulder.

She looked up as I peered uncertainly through the open flap.

"Come in," she said.

FORTY-TWO

EVADNE

I craved privacy for this evening, so, quite boldly, I'd dimmed the lamp. We would cast no shadows on the tent walls for any passing viewers to see. This was my own evening, for me and Dash alone.

More light came from the northern lights overhead than the lantern, but there was enough for me to realize the truth:

Dash was nervous.

This beautiful, experienced, capable man stood inside the tent and shifted from foot to foot. His anxiety calmed mine.

"Close that tent flap, will you?"

He turned to comply. I blessed Celeste for nudging me in this direction. She'd rapidly become . . . yes, another friend. This had been the most remarkable week for me, and if things went according to my vague plan, I would leave my emotional virginity behind this very night.

He turned back, his small task completed, and held one elbow with the other hand.

"Wow," I said. "There's tension rolling off you. Was this a bad idea?" I sat on the edge of the bed.

"No," he protested, but his tension remained high. "Not at all."

I smiled and raised a skeptical eyebrow.

"I'm not sure why I'm here," he said. Given that desire came off him as cleanly as tension, that was not an entirely accurate statement.

I looked pointedly at the shaving kit in his hand—the kind of place a man might keep a few condoms. To my delight, the embarrassment of a blush heated his face. He was more nervous than I was.

I took pity on him. "You're here because you said I was in charge. So I'm being in charge."

That sparked a smile from him. His tension faded while his desire came at me more strongly.

And still his dominant characteristic was protection. He didn't want to scare or rush me. My body reacted before my mind. Some muscles went looser and longer, some tightened up in tingling anticipation.

"So," he said, "how would you recommend I play this?"

"Play this," I echoed. I tested my appeal by leaning back on my hands, knowing my shirt would follow the contours of my breasts. His gaze dropped where I wanted them, causing my heart to race. "You're not sure what to do, huh?"

"I mean—I know what to do. It's—" He gestured awkwardly between us.

The practice of bravery was getting easier. I put my cloudy vision into words. "So what if I seduce you? Would that be okay?"

His desire leaped. "Yeah," he breathed. "That would be okay."

I stood, and he paid me the compliment of a quick inhale in appreciation. He was immobile in his mental box by the tent door, so I went to him.

"You're not nervous at all," he noted.

"I'm not. I feel completely safe with you, Dash."

I slipped my hand along his jaw to cradle his cheek and was rocked by the waves of peace and joy he gave off. It was the most flattering thing that had ever happened to me. It gave me the push I needed.

"I've never done this before," I admitted, "so please pardon me if I make any mistakes."

He turned to press his head into my palm. "I don't think there are any mistakes."

He wouldn't laugh. He wouldn't reject me. He wouldn't call me a freak or walk out, leaving me defenseless and ashamed. I knew it. It made me smile as I moved closer.

"You'll tell me what you want me to do?" he asked.

"I will," I assured him. "And you tell me what you want to do, and I'll tell you if that's okay."

"Okay." His word ended with a sigh as my hand slipped to the back of his head and I stretched up to press a kiss to his jaw, smooth and warm and undeniably male. "Nice."

"Good."

He let me go at my own pace. My other hand slid up from where it rested against his pounding heart, and I boldly tilted his chin up.

"You taste as good as you smell." I nipped and licked along his jaw to the long, corded tendons of his neck.

He stumbled through an answer. "I—I had a sh-shower . . ."

"No," I said. "That's not it. It's you. Just you."

"I want to hold you."

I paused from the nibbles I took along his collarbone. I didn't want to be a tease, but I also didn't want to lose my nerve. "One hand on my waist. Lightly."

We both experienced the heat of adrenaline as his hand rested on my body. I wanted more. I wanted to explore his chest, to stroke the skin over his muscles, to run my hands across his warmth. I tugged on his collar impatiently.

"I can't," I complained. "Take this off."

His shirt disappeared. He might have whipped it off; it might have incinerated under the heat rolling between us. He tried to put his hand on my hip, but I backed up. I needed a moment to experience this.

"Dash. You have a beautiful chest."

He fisted his empty hands, then he opened them and calmed himself.

"I never understood the fascination with six-packs," I went on. I trailed my fingers over his stomach. He sucked it in, as if he needed any more definition. His mild insecurity made me smile again. "But I have to say, this is gorgeous."

My fingers went lower and lower, tracing the line of each muscle. He gritted his teeth, remaining passive beneath my touch.

"I'm sorry," he said. "The sweatpants don't do much to hide things."

We'd gotten to the form jutting out from the cloth. I regarded it with wonder. It didn't fill me with fear; evidence of his arousal didn't make me shake. On the contrary, it made me want to preen. Here was physical evidence of his desire. Of my desirability. I was proud.

"I don't mind." I wanted him to know. "I like it."

I stood closer, bringing my body up against his and pressing my stomach to his cock. No fear. No panic. A rush of excitement. The welcome weight of him made me close my eyes and sigh.

More.

I ran my hands into his hair and tugged his head down. At last, we kissed.

At last, his mouth on mine. At last, his tongue connecting us.

Euphoria. I was turned on and not scared. I moved against him, brushing back and forth over his groin.

"Hold you?" he murmured through the kiss.

"Hold me," I agreed.

His arms slid up around me. He held me as if I was fragile, as if I might break. As if I was precious. He made me feel treasured, that my safety was his priority. I purred as one of his hands stroked my braid and the other looped lightly around my waist.

My own sexuality was being restored to me. I was glad to cling to him. My head spun.

Lost in sensations, I told him, "You feel good against my nipples."

His lips curled against mine. "You feel good against my cock."

I arched my spine to push my breasts more closely into him. No fear. No shadows of confinement or violence. I brought my hips forward. It made him growl. My pleased laugh broke the kiss.

"Sit," I demanded and pushed him onto the bed.

He did as he was told, stepping out of his sneakers and once again fisting his hands to keep from tugging me to him.

I turned out the kerosene lamp. The only light came from the flickering ribbons of the northern lights through the transparent panels overhead. I could still see him, but vision was secondary to being able to touch him.

I unbuttoned my shirt slowly, a mix of nerves and hunger and the need to feel my naked breasts against his naked torso.

"Am I going too slowly?" I asked as the shirt slid from my shoulders to the floor.

"Yes," he replied, not reaching for me.

He held himself with impressive restraint, but he clearly wanted me. Somehow, he'd given me exactly the right answer. I unhooked my bra, but before I dropped it, I probed lightly at the edges of my control over him.

"Am I driving you crazy?"

"Crazy," he agreed. Excitement fizzed through me. And then the bra followed the shirt. "Christ, you're beautiful."

My breasts had become sensitive—to the cool air, to the heat of his regard. My nipples were eager peaks, and I was suddenly mad to know what his lips would feel like on them.

"I want my breasts against your naked skin," I said.

"Well, come on."

I held my breath and straddled him, still standing.

Now my pebbled nipples were at mouth level. He panted with need but never touched me unbidden.

"You're so patient," I said. "Thank you."

"Take all the time you need." He sounded as if his mouth was dry.

"And what if I need to stop?"

"Then we stop."

"Really?"

He looked away from my breasts and caught my eye in the dim light. "Really. I'm like steel right now, but it won't kill me. I can take care of that myself. Don't you worry about it. If you need to stop, tell me. We'll stop."

I stroked my fingers through his silky, dark hair and felt him shiver from the sensation. His goodness filled me with trust. *I can do this.* "Okay," I breathed.

And then I lowered myself onto his lap.

FORTY-THREE

DASH

AT LAST, THE WEIGHT AND HEAT OF HER SETTLED ONTO MY cock. I sighed at the sensation.

Eve almost purred, but her back was awkwardly arched. Her legs were badly placed to straddle me as she stood at the side of the bed.

"Back up," she said with newfound confidence in her voice. Here was a demand, and it was glorious to hear. "Sit in the middle of the bed. Cross your legs."

She stood with liquid grace to let me move.

This time, she switched her pose so her legs came on either side to wrap around me. Without preamble, she nestled her butt between my legs and slipped her arms around my neck. *Ahhh.*

"Now," she said. "That's better."

I could only hum in agreement.

"Your hands on my waist, please. Am I too heavy?"

She all but sat on my fully erect cock. All that separated us from the bliss of fucking were our clothes.

"What?" Overwhelmed, my tongue was thick in my mouth.

"Too heavy?" She took the opportunity of my continued silence to lean forward and drag her nipples across my chest. We both shivered. The sound from her throat was a cross between a purr and a growl. My lips were too empty.

"Kiss?" I suggested.

"Oh, yeah," she said, and then we were laced together. My hands were filled with the velvet of her skin, my ears listened for the tiny moans she made, my mouth was flooded by the flavor of her tongue.

We were both panting when she pulled back. "You aren't grabbing me."

"I want to. Do you want me to?"

"No, I'm grateful. This is—" She bit her lip. "This is sort of my first time. The first time I get to do what I want."

The light was too low to see her blush, but we were so close, I felt the heat. "Then do what you want. I won't grab you. I promise."

"I believe you." She kissed my cheek. It was a sudden flash of innocence and trust in the raging storm of desire, and it melted my heart.

But she was focused on lust, and I was more than willing to accommodate that. "Lie back, Dash. Please."

"I'm going to turn to put my head on the pillows. Okay to hold you for that?"

She nodded and gasped as I held her closer to me and shifted.

"You're strong," she said.

I'm a fucking caveman. But she needed to know that the power in my arms and back would never be used to hold her down or force her. This experience needed to be the exact opposite of what she'd been through fifteen years before.

Those bastards had not broken her permanently. She deserved to know that she, too, deserved passion and safety. My determination to protect her grew.

"Now lie still," she said. "Let me explore."

"Go crazy," I said, as if my heart wasn't pounding in my chest. She straddled me, kneeling atop my hips, and her fingers once again stroked the muscles of my chest. "You're beautiful, Dash."

"I'll tell you how beautiful you are if you let me."

"No. Not now. This is what I need—just to touch you. Okay?"

Her hands slowly moved lower as she unfolded a fragile new sensuality.

I fisted my fingers into my hands to keep from touching her. I wished my cock could somehow attract those wandering fingers like a magnet drew iron, but I held on. "Okay," I replied shortly.

She tilted her head in the dim light, her eyes losing focus as she assessed the situation. Then she shifted back a few inches, freeing my cock to stand and jut up beneath the cloth. How far would her explorations go?

And then she answered that question.

She took hold of the waistband. "I want these to come off," she said.

Praise all the gods. "Rise up a little."

She rose far enough for me to tug the sweats down and kick them to the darkness beyond. Past this bed, there was nothing. The world ended at the mattress. There was nothing left except Eve, watching me. She leaned forward to examine every inch of me. She bit her lip in concentration, and I jerked in reaction. She grinned as the head bobbled.

Trust, I thought. *Not a weapon of pain—instead, something to enjoy, to please and be pleased by.*

She sat, now at my knees.

"This is my first invited cock. My first wanted cock."

Her fingers trailed down my hips, and my breath came in short pants of anticipation. She was working up her courage, and I'd endure this torment for decades.

"It's pretty," she said, and that surprised a laugh out of me.

"No cock is pretty. They're odd-looking and ugly."

"No. Not yours. Yours is—"

She didn't finish, but her fingers slipped inward. And then one finger ghosted up the length. I inhaled sharply and gave her a reassuring smile.

"Is this okay? I'm sorry I have to go slowly."

"You're going exactly the right speed," I told her. And I meant it.

She nodded, and this time, her fingers lingered. She stroked. She caressed. And she made me moan. Her pleasure at that was deeply erotic.

"Like this?" she asked. She wrapped her fingers around me gently and slid her hand up and down.

"Mmm," I said. Anything she did would light up my nerve endings like a pinball game.

"No, I can tell that's not right. Show me, Dash."

My eyes popped open. "Excuse me? Show you?"

"Show me. You do it."

I was suddenly shy. But I didn't want her to think it was wrong to ask, and she was brave. I could not deny her courage. Before the situation could get any more awkward, I took my cock into a practiced grip and groaned at the relief of a firm squeeze.

"So tight," she marveled. "Doesn't that hurt? You're tugging hard."

"It doesn't hurt." I dropped my hand. "It feels good. But so did your hand. Try again?"

Now that she knew what I liked, she was eager. She took my cock in her hand, this time much more firmly. I was the luckiest man on the planet.

Her hand was smaller than mine. She wrapped both hands around me, and I couldn't help the gasp. "Yeah—that's good."

She grinned. Showing her what I liked had freed her in some way . . . and it was certainly a thrill for me.

Then an idea bloomed across her face.

She stopped tugging. I barely resisted the urge to beg. Barely. "There's more, right?" she asked. "I mean—my mouth?"

I goggled, unable to believe my ears. Was this paradise? Had I died and gone to heaven? "What?"

"Yeah. I've never done it before. But I'd like to try."

My cock jerked in her hand, and she wriggled farther down the bed. "The guys who took you, they didn't—"

"Told them I'd bite it off if they tried," she said with a degree of satisfaction.

"Good for you." My voice was hoarse, and I would cut crescents into my palms from clenching my fists so tight. This lust was intoxicating.

"I want to taste you. You taste so good, Dash."

My eyes rolled back in my head as she placed a soft kiss against the head of my cock.

Her confidence was compelling. She swept her tongue along the head, sending electric shocks through me.

I groaned and shivered.

"You taste good. I want more."

"All you want," I muttered through clenched teeth.

She hummed in satisfaction as she drew my cock into her mouth. The vibration of that hum went right through me, lighting up an entire switchboard of nerves.

But I was so close, and this woman didn't deserve what was about to happen. Not for her first time. As much as I wanted to finish in her mouth, I had to warn her. "Evadne. Baby."

She didn't listen. Her growing excitement fed my need.

"Eve."

The situation was becoming critical, and my tone was sharp. The use of her name got to her.

"What?" she said, lifting her head and licking that tongue across slightly swollen lips. I jerked in her hand again.

"You're going to make me come."

"Isn't that the goal?"

My groan was a battle between *hell yes* and *hell no*. She grinned in triumph.

"I'm thirty-eight years old, Eve. I'm not a teenager."

"You think you can't go twice in one night? You're not geriatric, Dash. Let's put that to the test."

"Oh, fuck."

She lowered her head. Apparently, she'd learned by watching me stroke myself, and she set to work. Her pull was firm, her determination obvious.

"Eve—"

"What happens if I combine techniques?"

God save me. She used her fist to cover the part of my cock that wasn't making it into her mouth and held tight. I was gasping.

"Come off," I gasped. "Come off—I'm going to come. Lift your head."

She shook her head and sucked harder.

I gasped—she refused to let go—and then I came with a sizzle of galvanic energy that lifted me, bucking, off the bed. "Jesus Christ!" I yelled.

She drank me down like victory and then looked up at me with a catlike smile of satisfaction. "Shhh. You'll wake someone up."

I still shuddered with aftershocks. "Crawl up here and let me try that on you," I managed to say—but it was bravado for the moment. I couldn't so much as lift my head.

She grinned. "I did good, didn't I?"

My strength bled back into me, and I watched her crawl up my body to lay her head on my shoulder. I needed to hold her as much as I needed air to breathe.

"I'm putting my arm around you. Okay?"

"Okay."

We lay for a few moments while our heartbeats returned to normal. "You did magnificently," I added, too late to make sense. But she understood anyway.

"You don't have to tell me. I know."

I chuckled. She was right. The evidence had been obvious.

I drifted for a moment, and then she spoke. "I want more

from our evening. I want to regain all of me that was a woman, that was strong and brave and capable."

My eyes were open, and my heartbeat picked up again. I listened breathlessly as she finished her thought.

"I'm ready for the final step."

FORTY-FOUR
EVADNE

"So, Dash. Do you still think you can only go once in a night?"

I slipped from his side and stood by the bed. Catching his eye, I unbuttoned my jeans and gave a shimmy.

They slid downward. I stood in the uncertain light in nothing but panties.

And then I hooked my thumbs in the sides and slowly slid them down. I stepped from the pooled clothing and stood by the bed, legs spread.

His cock was hard again, and his lust was undimmed. I smiled at him.

"Not as old as you thought, huh?" I said.

"Can I touch you?"

He was one slightly stretched arm from me writhing on his hand, but that was a loss of the control I needed. I stepped back. "I'm not ready for that."

His eyes cleared, and his protectiveness overtook the lust. "Okay." He crossed his hands behind his head in a pose that showed me he would neither rush nor scare me.

"Really?"

"Really. But clarify—what aren't you ready for, exactly?"

"I'm not ready for . . ." I moved back to the bed and sat, trying to put emotions into words. I shook my head, struggling for the words. "I'm not ready for you to . . . do what I did to you."

"You don't want me to make you come?"

"Yes. I'm sorry. That's silly. But I don't—I don't think I can. Not yet."

"Okay. Let's go slowly. One day, you'll trust me to give it a try, and that will be good. But we can sleep now. I'm good with that. I can hold you, right?"

"Oh, don't misunderstand me." I rose to my knees and straddled him again, this time the soft furze of hair at his crotch catching and ticking my crease. "We're going to have sex. I'm dying to do that, to own that. Do you see?"

He nodded, even though he didn't understand. It didn't matter. I could trust him. I went on.

"I've been to therapists. Most of them didn't help much, but one told me if I worked on it, I could have a normal, fulfilling sex life, and eventually, I'd need patience and a partner I trusted. And now I have a partner I trust, and I'm ready to get past . . . the past. So ready."

He rose on his elbows—slowly, so he didn't alarm me.

"You're a strong woman. I'm honored to help, and not only because I'm going to get laid."

I grinned at his words, and he smiled back.

"Take your time, Eve. I think I could help you enjoy sex more, but we'll do this exactly as you want to."

"I know. But to have you touch me or lick me . . . it scares me."

"Thank you for telling me. We'll do it any way you want, or not at all."

"This thick cock I'm sitting on notwithstanding." I grinned at him.

He shrugged. "I can't always control that reaction. But I hope you take it as a compliment."

262

"I do." I leaned forward and kissed him. It was a kiss filled with hope and courage and innocence and pain . . . and then it was a kiss filled with tongue.

I released him and pushed him onto the pillow.

"Just lie there. Let me do this."

I thought about what I wasn't yet brave enough to let him do. My hands rose and teased my nipples. His cock jerked against me.

"Oh," I sighed, "that's good. Do you like the way this looks, Dash?"

He nodded, watching me intently in the low light. His cock leaped under me. I smiled.

"I see you do. What if I do this?"

I centered my hips over his cock and ran the groove up and down his shaft. Wetness slicked onto him, and he groaned. He fisted his hands over his head to stop himself from grabbing me. The sight was an aphrodisiac, and waves of lust built in me.

"Yeah," I said to myself, "oh, yeah."

I ground onto him. We both moaned.

"I want it, Dash," I panted. "I feel empty. I want you to fill me."

He wasn't so lost that he didn't recognize I wasn't inviting him. I was challenging myself. "When you're ready," he said.

The taste of electricity filled my mouth. The soft sheets were rough against my skin. My nerves were worn almost to pain by the tension.

"Oh," I gasped. "You really wouldn't make me, would you?"

He ground his teeth together. "We can stop right now. I'll survive."

"And you won't grab me."

"I won't grab you." I was still grinding against him. His words were stilted and dry, but they served their purpose.

"I believe you."

I dove off him and retrieved his shaving kit. I handed it to him with shaking hands. "Hurry. Do it."

He fumbled with the zipper, fished around for a condom, and threw the kit to the floor as he ripped the foil packet with his teeth.

Clenching his jaw in concentration, he rolled the rubber on. And then it was up to me.

"Okay," he said, and I knocked his hands away.

"Behind your head again." My tension turned my words into an involuntary command, and he obeyed. His surrender thrilled me.

I took his cock in my hand and slid him through the wetness now seeping from me. *This is it. This is my choice. I want this.* And then, with a deep breath, I slid the head of his cock inside my body.

We both froze as I hung my head.

And then I tilted my hips and slid down another inch.

"Oh . . ." I breathed. He filled me; he opened me. "It's good. It's so good."

He had no answer, and I didn't need one. I was centered entirely on the heat, the size, the rightness of him inside me. He controlled the urge to move. Distantly, I regretted testing him. But overwhelmingly, my brain was focused on the sensations rippling out from my core.

I slid further, and then further still.

And then, with a shudder, I had him fully inside me.

I sat on his hips again—but now with his cock buried deep within me. I could barely control the shivers filling me, the joy and glory and relief.

I hung forward a minute, getting used to the stretch. *There. I did it. The rest is purely for pleasure. I made it past my own fears. I was brave . . . and I love it.*

"Okay?" he asked.

I nodded—a gesture I could feel deep inside me, where he was hidden. "You're huge."

He grinned. The caveman thumped his chest. "Thank you."

"Thank *you*." I smiled.

And then I slid back and down.

"Up and down, right?" I breathed hard. He'd forgotten to breathe.

"Yeah. That. Oh—yeah."

I moved slowly, experimentally. My breathing quickened, and then I sped up my hips slightly. *Yes. A little faster.*

"It feels . . . good . . ."

"Yeah," he agreed, lost in the slickness.

"Faster . . . deeper . . ."

I suited my movement to my words as I explored this new universe. Dash grabbed his forearms to hold himself back.

"Faster. More." I coached myself and closed my eyes in concentration. Something was building. Silver arched out away from my core, zinged back in. "Oh my god."

My eyes flew open. I looked to Dash, overwhelmed and alarmed.

"That's—what's—"

"Eve. Evie. Touch your clit. Please. If I can't do it for you, you do it. Stroke it. Yeah—like that. How's that?"

"Ah—" I'd become inarticulate. The silver zings arched from my fingers to my core, rebounding and multiplying. My hips moved faster. *Orgasm*, I thought distantly. *I'm going to have an orgasm.*

"Press harder, Eve. Press harder. Like you stroked me. Hard. Hard."

He and I were caught up in sensations. I gasped. His jaw clenched, and he held his own arms in a death grip.

"Yes," I gasped. "Like that. Oh, Dash—yes—"

I discovered the thrill of a circular moment of my hips, and then the all-consuming, shocking change when I leaned slightly back.

"One finger," I gasped. "Put one finger here. Dash—here."

I guided his reaching hand until his broad, strong thumb landed on my clit. The relief was epic. I braced both of my hands against his chest and slammed my hips over and over onto his cock.

We came together. I was transported by the sensations he'd helped to create in me with his lust and patience and kindness. He groaned in his release, and my orgasm swept me silently. I made no sound but shook around him for an endless moment.

And then I collapsed against his chest, limp.

We lay together exhausted, his cock still buried inside me.

His strength returned first. He gently turned me and retrieved the condom, leaving the bed to dispose of it. The night was still and quiet, strangely lit by the northern lights, and peaceful.

He returned. Sleepily, I made room for him. Slowly, giving me the chance to object, he took me in his arms. I nestled against him and felt bliss to my toes.

"My god," I said. "That was . . . I had no idea."

A chuckle burbled out of him. "I think you got your own back."

"I'm going to get *you* back," I teased. "We need to do that again. Tomorrow, though."

"Good. Tomorrow."

We drifted. I didn't want to go to sleep because I didn't want to waste any of my time lying next to him. And I marveled at the trust he'd built in me.

I could be braver this evening. I could tell him the truth.

Hidden in darkness, I spoke.

FORTY-FIVE
DASH

"When I was four, I started having headaches."

She was telling me a story in a tone of voice that let me know it was important. I came out of my blissful haze.

"Okay," I said to encourage her.

"Know how rare it is for little kids to have headaches? It's unusual. It means something's wrong. When I started crying from the pain, my mother scraped up enough money to take me to a doctor."

She definitely had my attention.

"And the doctor took me to a hospital. And the hospital took me to a CAT scan. Turns out I had a brain tumor."

She spoke quietly in a normal tone of voice, but her calmness hid ancient fear.

"The surgeon told my mother he'd do the best he could, but there's a lot about the brain they don't understand, and my tumor was in the part of the brain that controls the senses."

"Shit."

"Yeah. Well, he got it all out and it turned out to be benign. Just one of those things. Nothing to worry about. Except the bills, of course. Those were worth worrying about."

"I bet."

"My mother was a waitress, and my father was long gone. We never had much, and when the hospital bills became impossible, she packed up what little we had, and we snuck out of town. And that became our pattern: settle for a while, then run from creditors."

The memory made her muscles grow tight under my hand. She moved away from me and sat up, facing me.

"So I never had the follow-up I was probably supposed to have. And that turned out to be a good thing. Because that surgery did something to my brain."

In the pale northern lights, she looked at me to gauge my reaction.

"Something like what?" I'd noticed nothing wrong with her brain.

"My sense of smell."

"What about it? Do you not have one?"

"The opposite. It's hyperaccurate. The surgeon was really interested before we left town. Mom told me later he talked about tests and protocols and studies. She knew we couldn't afford it, so off we went. But I bet he looked for me for years afterward."

Her voice in the darkness faded, and she sat quietly, lost in memories.

My impatience grew. I nudged her lightly.

"What's that mean, you have a hyperaccurate sense of smell?"

"Nobody knows this. Okay?"

"Okay."

"Not even Artie. No one. Just you."

She was trusting me with her most hidden secret. I was determined to protect her.

"I understand."

"Well, I can smell things no one else can. Plain as cookies in the oven."

I thought back. "Like—you could smell Kimber's cancer."

She nodded. "There are dogs who can do it. Why not a

human? I knew Kimber had cancer before she ever spoke to me at the vet's office."

"So you *did* save her life."

"You know what's funny? If I tell people I smell something wrong, they think I'm a nut. If I say I'm a prophet and an extrasensory reading tells me something's wrong, they drop everything and rush to the doctor. It's the only way I can get people to listen to me."

"Holy shit. Have you ever been tested?"

She shook her head. "Pretty sure that wouldn't be a good idea. A lot of poking and prodding and who knows what else in my future. Not so great for a zoology student who wants a quiet life with animals. Right?"

"Right." She was correct. Any researcher presented with a skill like Evadne's would immediately attempt to lock her in a lab for as long as they could keep her. The thought made me reach for her hand, and she let me take it.

"Wait—how did you know about the eagle in my childhood?"

"I'm telling you my theory, because I don't know, but I think big things change our body chemistry. Something major happens in your life; it changes your scent fractionally. But it's enough for me to smell it. I've worked in raptor programs, and all the people who were mad for the big birds of prey—they all have the same scent you have. Yours has faded, so I took a guess and chose early adolescence."

"It was more than a guess."

"Yeah. I guess it was."

"And you got abducted when you had a cold."

"Colds knock out my sense of smell completely. It's like going blind."

"So you can smell things like . . . honor?"

She chuffed a soft laugh. "Honor has a smell. It's part of your DNA. All emotions have a scent. I guess they release hormones or something, and I can smell that. Honor is probably the best smell of all. And you . . . mmm."

Now she held my hand as enthusiastically as I held hers. She inhaled deeply and gave me a slightly drunk smile.

"What does it smell like?" I asked, fascinated.

"What does it smell like," she mused. "It's hard to describe a smell, you know? But . . ." She paused. "Okay," she tried, "say you're in a desert—some arid, dry place with nothing around you but sand and scrubby, ugly bushes and a lot of sun. Hot sun. Can you picture it?"

"That's what I smell like?"

"Shut up. Can you see it in your mind?"

"Yeah."

"Now see a waist-high wall in a circle with a small roof over it. You walk over and realize it's an artisanal well, pulling water up from the bedrock. It's a nice well, too, with straight, clean walls and a spiral stone staircase leading down into the blessed darkness to where the water is, cold and black and refreshing. It's life in that desert. No well water, no survival. Can you envision it?"

"I can."

"Then stand at that wall and lean over. Let the cold, damp air slip over your sweaty face and thread through your hair. Let that sense of life and strength course through you and restore your hope and your courage and your will to go on."

She'd painted such a vivid picture that I was lost in it.

"That's how you smell to me, Dash. That's the smell of honor."

I opened my eyes, moved and touched and almost alarmed. "Jeez," I said stupidly.

"Yeah," she agreed. "I was lost for you the minute you walked into the lobby. Long before I saw you."

I was speechless.

"Do you want to leave?" she asked.

"What? Why would I want to leave?"

"I'm a freak. You don't have to stay."

I tugged on her hand and persuaded her to lie with me again.

I wrapped my arm around her and then dared to turn into her to wrap her in both arms.

"I don't want to leave you," I said. "I'm falling in love with you."

The words were out of me before I could measure the stupidity of saying something like that to a woman I'd just met. But, like telling her I was FBI, I couldn't regret it once said. I wanted her to know.

She rose up on one elbow. "Are you teasing me?"

I smiled at her. "You can tell if I'm teasing, can't you? What do I smell like?"

She inhaled, then she cocked her head in wonder.

"You smell like—like you're in love. With me."

"There. You see? I love you. And I'm not going anywhere."

I pulled her down again and we lay silent. The wetness on my shoulder told me she was crying.

"Wait—sweetheart. Is it so bad that I love you? Do you *want* me to go?"

"No!" She clutched me to her, and the fear that had leaped up in me died. "It's . . . I never thought anyone would love me once they knew. And I never thought I'd fall in love with them too."

"Hold on," I said, and this time, I was the one pulling back. "This is a pretty important point, so let's be clear. How do you feel about me?"

I heard the smile in her voice, although her face was buried in my neck. "I'm in love with you, Dash. I'm sorry. I can't help it."

Laughter welled up in me. Dancing and sunlight and foolish rainbows surged through my blood. "Well, of course you can't," I replied gruffly, trying to play it cool. "I'm wonderful." I settled next to her and pulled her into my heart. "I'm in love with you, and you're in love with me," I tried out. It felt pretty great to say.

"We are. We are in love with each other," she clarified.

We were having trouble wrapping our heads around it, but

our hearts kept up. And then she kissed me, a sweet, full-of-love kiss that might have been the first true kiss of my life.

Tomorrow would be soon enough to worry about logistics: about the case, about living arrangements, about the desk job and introducing her to my family, about Evadne's life as a con artist (without actually conning anyone; the situation was twisty). For tonight, we were content to drift in a happy cloud of tangled limbs and soft kisses and the chance to breathe the magical phrase *I love you* in foolish and frequent repetition.

And that was how we lay until the gunshot rang out.

I was out of the bed and jerking on clothes while Evadne took a deep inhale. Her shoulders hunched as she said the words.

"Dash—bear."

I froze. Adrenaline slammed into my heart. "Bear? A fucking bear? Are you kidding me?"

A second shot cracked across the night silence. My ears automatically sorted the sound—weapon type, direction, distance. Shotgun. Not Rose's service weapon. Not that she had it with her. Not that I had mine with me. I was a fool. An unarmed fool.

"Bear. Angry bear." Evadne was pulling on her clothes now too. "Lace up those shoes. You're going to need good footing."

I'd thrust my bare feet into the sneakers and was about to fly out of the tent when her words stopped me. Cursing, I took the time, the precious ticking seconds to lace the shoes tightly.

"You'd better stay here. Turn on a light. That should keep the bear away."

I spoke calmly, but that was out of my ass. I had no idea what would keep a bear away.

"Seven semesters of zoology, mister. I think I know more about bears than you do. I'm coming with you."

At least I'd know where she was. I could get between her and any bears. "Where is it?"

We came onto the deck, and she pointed with confidence. "Over there."

"Shit. That's my tent."

"Rose!" Evadne kept up with me as I ran under the faint light of the aurora borealis. The paths were smooth, but it was foolish to run in the dark. Still, my fears drove me on.

"She's watching Wolf and Lenny," I said. "She's not at the tent. Can you tell who's shooting?"

"I think it's Costello, but I'm not sure."

Lights were coming on in the tents we passed. "Stay inside!" I roared. "Keep your lights on and stay inside!"

People called out from tent to tent, and my orders were relayed throughout the huge circle. From the bunkhouse, Marcia echoed the order to stay inside. But people peered from their doors and watched me race past, Evadne in tow.

"What's going on?"

I ignored the questions and kept running. The third shot was answered by a deep, meaty, earth-shattering roar. Primitive muscles on my scalp rippled into motion. I was trying to raise hackles mankind hadn't had for thousands of years.

"Was that . . . ?" I asked Evadne.

She nodded. "I can smell blood. Someone winged the bear."

"So it's harmless now?"

We slowed as we got closer. It would take a fool or a heavily armed platoon to approach the sound of that roar without caution.

"Not harmless. Angry."

FORTY-SIX

EVADNE

THE NIGHT WAS WILD AND UNCONTROLLED. SCENTS SWIRLED around us as we ran, the air pushing against me, begging to be read and understood. I raced after Dash across the broad clearing ringed by platform tents. I tried to sift the scents into order to make sense of what I got from the night air.

Dash pulled me with him as we crouched behind a boulder with a view of the tent, and I took a deep breath to confirm what my sense of smell told me.

His voice was surprisingly calm. "Is it Big Billy?"

There was no doubt of what I was getting from the darkness. Heat. Size. Fur. Anger. And . . . cubs. "Big Billy is actually Big Betty. And she's protecting her babies. Dash, she's furious. That is not a rational bear."

Dash blinked at the concept of a rational bear, but he let it go.

Rose popped up from the other side of the boulder, sending a bolt of panic through me. Dash swiveled at her movement and shoved me behind him before recognizing his partner.

"I would have shot you if I'd been armed."

"Glad you didn't," she whispered. Her fragrance was bright with stress. "Glad you're here."

"What do you know, Rose?" Dash asked, and his natural authority calmed her. I saw the trust and partnership they'd developed.

"Plenty. Wolf and Lenny are gone. They took a Jeep and left about fifteen minutes ago, but not before giving directions to Abbott and Costello. Those two jokers grabbed shotguns and headed out behind our tent."

"The bear's den is over there." I could smell it clearly now, in the forested foot of the mountains.

"You couldn't have mentioned that a little sooner?" Rose tried to remain evenhanded.

"I didn't come over this way. I'm sorry."

Dash held one hand up to Rose and laid the other on my wrist. "Doesn't matter. Safe bet Wolf knew where Big Betty liked to hole up."

"Big Billy is a female with cubs," I said in an aside to Rose, "and they've stirred her up."

"We were given this tent for a reason," Dash said.

"A tragic accident, again." Rose nodded.

"That does seem to be their go-to," Dash commented dryly. "It would be the end of glamping in Smuggler's Basin for a while, but they'd be rid of some pesky snoops."

This plan had flaws, and I felt I had to speak up for Big Betty. "Even an angry bear won't attack a tent," I said.

The fourth shot cracked out, making us jump. The crashing and breaking tree limbs came closer, the sound of impending danger.

"Unless someone drove the bear on, making it crazy." Dash's pronouncement filled me with dread. We were crouched behind our boulder when a new voice spoke up beside us.

"What the hell is going on out here?"

Rose uttered a scream and Dash whirled in the new direction, once again getting between me and the unexpected.

Celeste looked down at us. "What are you doing?"

We pulled her down. Rose glared at me, and I held up a hand

in a back-off gesture. "She came from downwind! I didn't know she was out there!"

"Some help you are," Dash grumbled and reached to hold my hand.

"What's going on?"

"Celeste, didn't you hear me say everyone should stay in their tents?"

"I am not everyone, mister. As Phoebus would say, there are sheep and there are wolves. I'm not a follower. I want to know what's going on."

"Christ. Don't mention wolves. That would be all we need."

Rose updated Celeste. "Abbott and Costello are driving a bear into my tent—a wounded bear. A wounded, angry bear. Stay here with us until we figure out what to do about it."

We listened to the bear drawing closer and closer. Another shot rang out. Another roar of fury shredded my eardrums.

"There will be witnesses," I said, "who will know the gunshots came before the attack. What about that?"

"No. That's easy," Rose hissed. "They saw the bear coming and tried to chase it away. But alas."

"Shit," said Celeste shortly.

We were lined up like children in a cartoon, peering over the boulder. And we all shivered when the tent suddenly shook and then collapsed, canvas billowing out. The roar of the bear was now an extended assault of sound, and mad thrashing shredded strips into the fabric.

And then a huge, shaggy head appeared in a hole.

The sight confirmed what my nose had already told me. Even in this uncertain light, I could see it was a grizzly, a big one. We were none of us a match for that force of nature—even if it did have Rose's plaid shirt dangling improbably from one ear like a vast pirate's eye patch.

The bear bit at the fabric, maddened by the remains of the tent now wrapping itself around the bear as the convulsive movements went on. Canvas shreds caught in its teeth and flowed down like an old man's beard.

The sight was alarming . . . and, quite horribly, I found I was holding back a gust of unhinged, nervous laughter. The plaid shirt had been flung over the bear's shoulder but was still hooked on its ear. I had a vivid image of a privileged teen flinging her hair over her shoulder in a huff.

Big Betty was having a tantrum.

And I, who should have been looking for a hole into which to shove the people I loved, had a case of the giggles about it.

The bear was out of the tent now and lunging back in to bite madly at anything that came to mouth. A pair of jeans flew up into the night, and a pillow broke in a feather explosion that added to Big Betty's appearance.

She chased the feathers. Rose muffled an unwilling chuckle.

And then there was crashing from the forest on the far side of the clearing.

"What the hell is that now?" Celeste asked.

We turned to look. The bear turned to look.

The crashing got louder, and instead of a roar, a horrible, drawn-out wail of a moan rose into the night.

I blanched. We all blanched. The bear blanched.

And then they all (except the bear) turned to me.

"Downwind!" I cried. "I don't know what that is!"

Rose eyed me suspiciously before turning to the new line of attack. "What does the wind have to do with it?" she muttered.

"Don't worry about it," Dash said. "What are we going to do now?"

The moan rose in pitch and volume and then became horrible, insane laughter. The crashing continued.

"Jesus Christ," said Rose. "That's not . . . is that . . . ?"

She hadn't finished her sentence before Abbott and Costello burst out of the forest and flung themselves behind the boulder with us.

"It's George!" Abbott whisper-screamed. "Save us!"

Celeste regarded him with a sneer until the laughter turned into hysterical shrieking.

Costello moaned in horror and didn't notice when Dash calmly reached out and took his shotgun. Abbott had the presence of mind to resist Rose when she reached for his after Dash nudged her, but when the shrieking mutated into desperate, gasping pants, he dropped the gun and shrank behind Costello.

"George! That's George! Lady Celeste—save us!"

Celeste was caught between her contempt and her confusion. She knew there was no George, but something horrifying was definitely crashing through the forest toward us.

FORTY-SEVEN

DASH

Our situation remained uncertain. We were not in control yet, and civilians were at risk. On the now-stripped deck, Big Betty's head had lowered. All of her focus was on the noise approaching us, and she backed slowly away, still dressed in shreds of the tent and frosted with feathers.

"Well, now, what the hell *is* that?" Celeste asked no one.

"It's George! It's George!" Based on the whites showing all around his bulging eyes, Costello was on the edge of outright hysteria. He would have fired at anything if I hadn't taken the shotgun.

Celeste's brow wrinkled. She peered uncertainly into the forest. I risked a quick look to make sure Evadne was still okay, and she shook her head at me. She had no idea what was coming. Rose had a good grip on Abbott's gun. We watched the bear, now almost into the woods and peering into the darkness at — well, at George's approach.

Lady Celeste made up her mind. "I guess you boys better start singing."

Abbott and Costello both looked up at her, wide-eyed and hopeful.

"I've taken the vows, my curtain call," sang Costello shakily.

"You gave me fame and fortune and all the things that go with it—" Abbott chimed in, but Celeste cut them off with a hiss.

"Not that one! How many times do I have to tell you?"

She duckwalked behind them. Putting a large hand on either shoulder, she faced in the direction of George and sang, "Is this my real life? Is that just fantasy?"

They joined her, panic making their voices squeak. "Caught in a slipslide, no escape from reality—"

From behind me, I heard Rose mutter, "Man, those are still not the right lyrics," but her griping was drowned out as Abbott, Costello, and Celeste stumbled through the verse, gaining in strength and confidence as they went on.

I did a rapid assessment and deployed our resources. I had Rose focus on the bear while I aimed toward George, who was now shrieking as he came along.

"Don't be distracted," I said. "No matter what, you stay on the bear. Right?"

"Right," she said through gritted teeth. She was focused and calm. Rose would make a great agent. Assuming she lived through this.

The sound of "Bohemian Rhapsody" drowned out the zombie wails as people in the nearby tents took up the song, hoping to keep George from their doors too. The song spread from tent to tent. By the time they got to "Mama, I killed a man," the entire camp was singing. Loudly.

I wished they would stop. It was getting hard to track George by the sound, and—as if the music was having its effect —he'd gone silent. But the crashing came on, branches breaking before a massive presence.

Abbott, Costello, and Celeste were heartened that George had fallen silent. Their treatment was working. They were smiling. I was getting tighter and tighter, the calm of prebattle madness focusing my attentions on the forest, shadows and forms shifting in the variable northern lights overhead.

Then, as my finger pulled back on the trigger, George resolved into the figure of the attention-seeking grandstander Phoebus Apollon in all his glory, stepping from the trees, wreathed with a massive, white-toothed grin.

"Hi," he said easily, apparently not caring that I had come within a few ounces of pressure to putting a spray of pellets through his massive chest. "Thought you could use some help. Here I am."

"Phoebus!" Abbott was having the nightmare where you scream but can barely make a noise. "Get over here! George is out there!"

Phoebus shook his head and gestured with a thumb over his shoulder. "No," he said, "that was me—" but it was no use. Abbott, Costello, and now apparently Celeste, too, knew what they knew. "Bohemian Rhapsody" was coming to its big crescendo, and they were going to repel zombies with the power of Queen.

"Dash." Rose got our attention. "Look."

Without the threat of madness coming through the forest, Big Betty had turned her attention to the cluster of humans behind the boulder. Her neck bunched up, and the feathers on her shoulder had gone dark. Her wound was bleeding—not enough to slow her down. Just enough to make her mad.

And she was now ready to be mad at us.

Rose, to her credit, had not let her attention be distracted by the King of the Con Men, but her shotgun (and mine) would not be enough to kill the beast. Make Big Betty angrier, definitely. Put her down, unlikely. I calculated potential firepower, assessed weak points in her defenses (the eyes?), and spared a glance at what used to be a tent. Her massive claws had ripped it to shreds.

"Don't shoot her," Evadne breathed. "She's got cubs."

"*I've* got cubs," I barked. "Well, you know what I mean. If it's between us and her, I choose us."

"I do too. But let me try something. Does anyone have a phone with them?"

Caught up in the drama, the Freddie Mercury Trio had fallen silent, although the song continued from tents in the large circle. It turned out all of us had our phones with us.

"Artie," Evadne said. "I mean, Phoebus. Get up on this stump, please."

She made him clamber up until he towered over all of us.

"Everybody, turn on your flashlights, but cover the lens with your hands until I say. Rose, you and Dash get ready to fire into the air. Not into Big Betty—not yet. Promise?"

Guarded, Rose and I looked at each other, and then we nodded.

Evadne waited for a painfully long time. I kept my eyes on the bear as Big Betty drew closer. The camp now bellowed out a guitar solo, warbling "nanala-nanala-nanala" in place of the instrumental.

The camp sang "I saw a little silhouetto of the man," the bear reared hugely on its back legs, and Evadne shouted, "Lights on Phoebus!"

The night lit up.

The camp screamed, "Thunderbolts and lightning! Very, very frightening!"

Rose and I fired our shotguns into the sky.

And Phoebus Apollon, arms outstretched and leonine head roaring, was caught in the painful glare of white phone flashlights in his gold mylar windbreaker.

The bear shrieked. I didn't know a bear could shriek, but she did. She toppled over in astonished fear and took off into the woods as if the devil himself was after her.

In reflective gold mylar.

"Nothing truly mattered," sang the camp. "Nothing truly mattered to me."

"Christ. Those lyrics are just wrong," grumbled Rose.

282

Evadne turned to me with a smile. "Any way the wind blows—"

"Hush."

She'd done it. Big Betty was on the run. I surrendered to temptation and gathered her into a left-armed hug, the shotgun still held ready in my right. Adrenaline burned its hot way through my nervous system.

"Is it safe?" Costello gasped.

Eve nodded. "Big Betty has had enough. She's gone to the den, to her cubs."

"Jesus Christ," Rose said.

There was a moment of silence. "Now what?" cried Abbott.

"Now you two follow me with those phones, please."

Phoebus Apollon jumped lightly from his stump and strode to the fire pit at the center of the circle. Natural followers, Abbott and Costello trailed after him, lighting up his blazing goldenness with their phones. What the hell was that showboat up to now?

FORTY-EIGHT

EVADNE

MY FRIEND EXUDED CONFIDENCE, ADRENALINE, AND excitement. Phoebus loved to live on the edge of danger and rarely minded when he fell over that edge. His mood was excellent, and I could tell he relished his chance to stand in the spotlight.

"Well done, camp!" Phoebus called. His impressive I-am-a-prophet voice rang through the broad meadow. "You have vanquished the enemy. This camp is safe once more!"

Cheers went up from around the ring.

"Sleep, now. The dawning sun will all too soon bring its glory to our humble lives. Sleep. Sleep, and remember your dreams— for we can read the future in them! Good night!"

There was a murmur of chatter and the occasional question-and-answer called from tent to tent, but in a surprisingly short time, the impromptu warrior chorus became a sleeping camp again. Marcia and the kitchen staff clearly thought better of wandering around in the night. They never left the safety of the bunkhouse.

I watched with a smile as Phoebus strutted back, his new attendants in his wake. He, at least, was having a wonderful time. He spoke. "This has been awesome. What do we do now?"

Dash, backed by Rose, fixed Abbott and Costello with a glare. "Give me the shells to these shotguns. Hurry up."

With muttered curses and lowered eyes, they did as they were told. He filled his pockets. Rose tucked shells down her cleavage.

"What?" She'd finished tucking away light ammunition in this highly inappropriate place and looked up to the fascinated gaze of every man. "You see any pockets in this running suit? Please."

"Best purse there is," agreed Lady Celeste. Dash returned his attention to the two ranch hands, now open-mouthed in appreciation of Running with Rosie in a catsuit.

"Where did Wolf and Lenny go?"

They shuffled their feet and wouldn't meet his eye.

"Do I have to tell you what happens if you cross me?"

It wasn't the shotgun he held that persuaded them, but the "prophets" lined up at his side, one of whom could summon zombies and one of whom, judging by his predatory and blinding grin, apparently wanted to bite them. Hard.

"You tell us what we want to know," Dash added, "and we won't tell what you did with Enrique, João, and Gustavo."

"The Mexicans," breathed Costello, now regarding Dash with the same nervous awe as he gave to the prophets. "How did you know?"

"Oh, we know. We know about Tim Horton's, and how you paid for the doughnuts, and the storage shed out back."

"Fuck, Costello." Abbott had thoroughly lost his nerve. "Tell 'em."

Costello straightened, but he still wouldn't raise his eyes.

"Wolf 'n' Lenny are going to load the trucks."

"Which trucks?" Dash's authority calmed the two hands, natural subservients.

"Hank's big rig and the catering truck."

"Hank? Wolf's brother? He's here?"

"Back at the ranch, yuh. He's due tonight. Should be there now with an empty semi."

"Not empty for long," his companion chortled. They both nudged each other and grinned.

"What are they loading up?"

Abbott and Costello eyed each other, and Dash pointed to Lady Celeste, who fixed the ranch hands with a furious gaze.

"The money!" Costello cried.

Abbott nudged him to shut up but nodded at the same time. "The hundreds," he agreed. His eyes were large. "So many of them. Man."

"And where are they going?"

"Hank's going south, and Wolf's going west."

"You don't know where?" Dash was stern but calm.

"Lotsa places." Costello was eager to help—eager to avoid Celeste and her zombie pal.

"Yeah. Lots. And then we get our money!"

"Shut up, Abbott. We ain't in this."

"Oh, right. We don't know nothing. Nothing to do with us."

"Yeah. Nothing." The two pasted on innocent looks, but I didn't need my hypersensitive nose to read their low and stupid cunning.

"You're part of a plot to destabilize this nation," Dash said flatly. "You're in it up to your grimy necks."

"Not us!" Costello was insulted by the insinuation. "We love this country! We're protecting justice for the people, not the feds!"

"Yeah," Abbott chimed in. "We're good Americans! Patriots! Wolf says we're real patriots."

"Sure you are. What did you pick up in Montana?"

The ranch hands blinked at him. "Huh?"

"You went to Montana on an errand for Wolf. When you were done, you went to Canada to abandon the three Latino ranch hands. Remember that?" Dash's sarcasm bled through his calm.

"Oh, yeah."

"So what did you pick up for Wolf in Montana? You called them *devices*."

"How'd you know that?"

This time, Dash gestured to my oldest friend. Phoebus didn't know what was going on but had never been one to turn down the chance to posture. He straightened his spine and glared at the cowering men.

"Anti-theft stuff!" Abbott cried. "To keep people out of the trucks!"

"Anti-theft," Dash clarified. "What kind of anti-theft devices?"

They examined their boots and scuffled in the soil before Costello offered a grin. "Well, the explosive kind."

Dash rolled his eyes. I could read his annoyance. "So Wolf and Hank are arming the trucks to blow up if anyone other than them tries to open them."

"Well, yeah."

"This just gets better and better," Dash muttered.

"Gonna be great," Costello offered. "We're ending the federal government. It ain't constitutional. This'll be a better world."

He nudged Abbot, who grinned. "I'm gonna finally pay off my shitty truck. And then I'm gonna get me a Ford like Wolf's."

"I'm gonna get me two!"

Both Rose and Dash restrained themselves. *Years of training*, I thought. *I'd like to drive a firm knee into two different pairs of balls.* "You're part of the Justice Patriots." They nodded. "And you're both idiots," Dash said shortly. "What's left back there to drive?"

"Two Jeeps and the supply bus."

"One Jeep," corrected Costello. "Wolf's got his."

"Right. Marcia's Jeep and the bus the cooks came in."

"Good. I oughta tie you up, but you've got a job to do." Dash fixed them with the glare of authority. "You get these people out of here safely at first light. Put them in the bus and drive them down. One of you drive; one of you takes the horses back the long way. Don't stop for anything. I want to see you at the ranch when I get back."

"Where are you going?" Costello was getting braver.

"You don't need to know. Get these people home."

"What if the zombie comes? Or the bear? Give us our shotguns."

"Fuck off," Rose said succinctly. It wasn't professional, but it was satisfying.

Abbott responded with a sneer. He called Rose a reprehensible name, but Rose was upright and powerful. She wouldn't be baited into a response.

Celeste, however, had no such limitations. She sent her fist into Abbott's nose with a crunch that sent him reeling backward until he suddenly sat, his hands uselessly attempting to hold back the gush of blood.

Not to be left out, Phoebus turned to Costello, gave him a charming smile, and drove a knee into the smaller man's balls.

Ah, I thought. *There it is. I bet that felt good to do.*

Costello lost the ability to breathe for a moment, and then turned to vomit in the grass.

"Girl did that to me once," Phoebus said. "That guy is going to have one miserable ride home tomorrow. Horseback's going to be a bitch. Bet you twenty bucks he'll be the one to drive the bus down. So." He returned to the matter at hand. "What's next?"

"Next, Rose and I are going to take the Jeep and go after Wolf," said Dash.

"Right. Obviously. And I'm going with you." Phoebus was smiling. Dash might have faced down bigger guys than Artie, but it was unlikely any of them grinned quite as broadly. Phoebus looked like he'd been invited to a kegger.

"This is not a place for civilians," Rose tried. "We're FBI. You're not."

"Oh, it's FBI, is it? Well, FBI, you need backup. Come on. You know you do."

Abbott and Costello had staggered away, leaning on each

other, and Phoebus had used his magnetic personality to get us all moving toward the Jeep trail.

Rose and Dash had a silent conversation conducted entirely with raised eyebrows.

"Okay," he said. "You shouldn't come, but I think you're right. We'll need help."

"Good thing we're all coming then," Celeste said stoutly.

"No." Dash might as well have been talking to the trees. Celeste and I kept up with them. "Really. Please stay here. We don't want anyone getting hurt."

"Let me get this straight, little man." Celeste got in front of us and stopped. "You'll let Phoebus here come, but not the womenfolk?"

Dash recognized the proverbial hairy eyeball when he saw it. She kept at him.

"You've seen my right hook. You think I'm going to get a fit of the vapors in a harsh moment? Maybe get my period and have to go lie down for a few days? Boy, get out of my way, and let's get the hell off this mountain."

She stomped ahead of us, cursing under her breath, and we trailed after her.

"They grow 'em mean in New Orleans." That was Rose's announcement of concession.

"Girl, I'm from Ann Arbor. And you have no idea." All the South had drained from Lady Celeste's voice.

I slipped my hand into Dash's, comforted by his strength. I was determined to not be left behind. He looked at me. "Don't worry. I'm not even going to try."

"Good," I said with a smile. "You need me with you."

"Yes, I do."

FORTY-NINE

DASH

Marcia's keys hung in the ignition. Why not? Who was going to steal a car out here?

Other than us, of course.

The Jeep was sporty. Its doors and the canvas roof had been removed, revealing bright-yellow roll bars to hold its occupants safe.

The aurora was fading. It was getting harder to see. I made a snap decision and nudged Rose to the driver's side of the car.

"Dash—are you sure? You should drive," she sputtered.

"Eyesight plus reaction time over age equals better driver," I said. "Get in. We don't have time to argue. Give it the Running with Rosie energy. You'll be fine."

The hardest part of mentoring is letting go when the time is right—*not* driving when that's the smarter decision. Rose set her shoulders and got behind the wheel. I only hoped I'd made the right choice, and that her speed and the lack of any doors wouldn't turn the Jeep into a rolling deathtrap.

Evadne was comparatively safe in the back seat, wedged in tightly between the bulk of Phoebus Apollon (who was grinning) and the height of Celeste (who was muttering). I rode shotgun—quite literally, as I held Costello's gun at the ready. Rose had offered hers for Phoebus to hold, but quickly corrected herself and handed it to Celeste, who uttered a short "that's right" before taking her seat.

The headlights cut an all-too-small path through the darkness, showing the rut-laced trail ahead and thick stands of trees to either side. What was probably a sylvan, lovely forest in the daytime was filled with the menace of night. What were we passing? Bears, probably. Beavers. Eagles. All of them lusting for human flesh.

"So what did you call them back there?" Phoebus asked. "Justice what?"

Rose replied. "Justice Patriots. They believe the entire federal government is unconstitutional, and the highest law enforcement officer in the nation is the county sheriff."

"Damn. Can I believe that too?" The con man was grinning at the thought. I wasn't. There was a lot of fanaticism in the Justice Patriots. Some leaders deplored violence; some didn't. We were obviously dealing with a faction that didn't object to killing to further their cause.

We flew down the mountain, thumping across the endless ribbons worn in the dirt by years of rain and snow. The night air was moist and filled with the scent of living things—mostly carnivorous living things. I decided I was ready to get back to the city.

"Ah, hell," Rose said. Her foot went to the floor. The Jeep fishtailed slightly as we shuddered to a stop. The headlights picked out impenetrable woods before us. We were at a T intersection. The tracks to the left were as rutted and well-worn as the ones to the right.

"Which way? We choose wrong now, life gets more complicated."

"To the left," Evadne said. "I can tell."

Rose looked at her and then at me. "Where do you come down on this, Dash? I'm all for the mystic mumbo jumbo, but if Wolf went right—"

"Go left," I said.

A large hand fell on my shoulder companionably. Phoebus Apollon showed his approval of my words.

"Believe her," he said. "She will not let you down."

Rose heard the certainty in my voice and in the prophet's. She swung the wheel over without another word and we were off again, a roller coaster without rails, running through black nothingness from whence huge trees too often loomed up to make us all jump in our skins.

Twice more, Evadne chose the path, and twice more, Rose followed her guidance.

We rattled over corded patches, over rough-hewn bridges, and once we forded a stream, the Jeep nearly upending in the water as Rose took the curve too quickly. Water splashed up, soaking my sweatpants and making me long for the simplicity of doors. And then, with a bang, we were through it and back on the track.

At least now I knew enough to be grateful the path was dry. That was something.

The bitter taste of adrenaline never left my mouth on that long and rattling trip, but my rookie held her own. At last, we came out onto a paved surface. The Jeep slammed to a halt on the edge, our hood sticking out into the road as Rose waited for Evadne's next direction.

She sat behind us, breathing deeply, her eyes closed. "It's hard to tell. Several cars have been by here—go right. Go right, and I'll let you know if I'm wrong."

Rose shrugged. "Can't argue with that."

The tarmac was indulgently smooth after a ride that could have dissolved kidney stones. The night-dark forest's looming sense of menace fell away. My death grip on the roll bar loosened. I was reluctantly coming to appreciate the natural world, but pavement would always be my home. It was good to be back.

"This is right," Evadne said, relief and excitement audible. "Keep going."

"I'm going, I'm going. Can't pedal any faster than this."

Headlights came from around the corner, and a car passed us.

"Nothing," said Evadne. "Not part of this."

None of us questioned her. We were all seasoned pros by this time, hardened and indifferent to the occasional pothole or the gleam of wildlife eyes caught in the headlights.

"Slow down," Evadne called across the wind of our passage. "We're getting close. Maybe two or three curves ahead . . ."

Rose pulled to the side and stopped. She fumbled about until she found the toggle for the headlights, and then we were in darkness, lit only by the faint light from the instrument panel. "What's our plan?"

"Wait a few minutes," I said. "We'll need our night vision. Let your eyes adjust to the darkness."

We sat. The sudden stillness was shocking after our descent. The blackness ahead of me was marginally darker than the blackness above it. From the corner of my eye, I could see the silhouettes of trees against the sky. The night was ending. Dawn approached.

"How sure are you we're close?" Rose asked Evadne.

"Pretty sure. They're not far ahead."

Our pupils slowly dilated, and Rose took stock of the landscape around her.

"I know where we are. I've run this road. We're about to come up on the community hall you and Cheri investigated, Dash."

"That right?"

"Okay. The road dips from the top of that curve up there," she said. I could see the curve if I didn't look directly at it. "How about I shut off the engine and we roll down on them in silence? They'd never see us coming."

"Make sure the steering wheel doesn't lock once the engine is off." Phoebus Apollon offered that tip. I turned around to look at him, my spine creaking agreeably at the stretch. "I boosted a few cars in my youth," he said with his sunny grin on full wattage. "That's a mistake you don't want to make too often."

Rose checked. "We're good. I'll be able to steer."

"Hang on," I said. "I'm going to get out here and go through the woods. Sneak up on them from the side while you come in the front."

"We're splitting up?" Rose's nerves were audible.

"You can do this. You've trained for this, and I'll be there when you arrive. Use a dominant, assertive energy. Let them know you're in charge. Remember: you're a badass."

"I'm a badass." She inhaled and said it again with more confidence. "I *am* a badass."

"Shit, Dash," Phoebus said. "You're volunteering to go through the woods? All by yourself? What if you meet a bear?" He grinned.

"Aw, I've met a bear," I said with brio.

"Been there, done that," added Celeste.

"Who's coming up front?" I said as I unfolded to stand beside the car. It was a glorious relief to be unbent.

"Celeste," Rose said, "come on up here with that shotgun. Let's show those assholes what kind of trouble a couple of cute girls can get into."

I estimated how long I'd need. "Give me fifteen minutes before you roll."

Rose checked her phone. "At last—I've got a signal. I'll call in the cavalry while you get into position." Backup would be welcome, but it would take time for them to scramble. It was up to us to delay Wolf and his plan.

Before I moved into the woods, I tugged lightly on Phoebus Apollon's arm as it lay over the side of the Jeep. "You're going to want to take off that jacket and sit on it. Otherwise, you're going to be pretty easy to spot if anyone turns on a light."

"Shit. Right."

Evadne watched me. My eyes had adapted. I could see the frown she wore, and I waited to hear what she would say.

FIFTY

DASH

Evadne pointed into the woods on an angle to the road. "Go that way."

I nodded. The adrenaline rush of finally, *finally* bringing this case to resolution faded as I looked at her. I didn't want to leave her.

Nothing to be done about it. I had to go. I touched a finger to my lips, and she raised her own hand to her mouth. Message sent and successfully received.

I left them squirming around, arranging seating and hiding gold mylar. The pause to let my vision adjust had helped, and the palest light filtered down to the forest floor. I moved fairly quickly. Thankfully, the woods weren't as thick nor the hillside as steep as the trail we'd come down.

I never heard Rose start the Jeep again to get to the point where she could roll it in neutral, and I listened for it, which gave me reason to believe neither Wolf nor Lenny would know we were coming.

It's tough to judge distance in the woods at night—even harder to hold a straight line—but I'd slowed to approach with caution when I was brought up short by the sound of voices from the bottom of the hill in front of me.

I flashed to an open-field training I'd had several centuries before. (I was a city dweller. Why did I need to know how to avoid slipping on pine needles?) Dredging up what I could remember, I rolled from heel to toe slowly enough to feel a branch under my feet before it broke. This gave me time to consider the challenges of approaching men who were likely armed.

My mountain-man attempt at silence turned out to be unnecessary. I'd come out on the stone lip over the bunker entrance, and the light had grown enough to see an eighteen-wheeler backed up to the open doors. It was parked so close to the edge that it was barely a stretch to step onto the roof of the trailer.

That explained why my ears had identified them before my eyes had. There was a strip of light about a foot or so wide between the truck and the mountain. The bunker might have been constructed specifically to fit the dimensions of a semi-truck. Probably was.

I stood on the roof of the trailer and peered cautiously through the gap.

They were rolling flats of currency up a ramp and into the truck. They'd skipped boxes and simply wrapped stacks of hundreds in clear plastic. Lenny alternately speculated on what he'd buy and bitched about loading it all in. Wolf was growling. We were dealing with at least two men.

And I was standing on a tractor trailer, so that meant Wolf's brother Hank was around somewhere too.

Rolling heavy-loaded hand trucks wasn't a quiet sport. I didn't have to guard my footfalls as I walked to the front of the truck. Still, I was grateful for the sneakers on my feet instead of the boots I'd used for horseback riding.

I was charged-up and calm (I've been told it's an unusual combination), but a portion of my brain still focused on the fact that my shoes were laced over bare feet. Not long ago, I'd been naked in bed with a woman I loved, one who sizzled my skin and made me want to make her a top—*the* top—priority in my life.

I stood at the front of the trailer and considered the situation.

The catering truck was visible down the hill, past the white bulk of the meetinghouse. I would bet the catering truck was already loaded with its share of cash, plus a powerful round of explosives.

No sign of Wolf's Jeep, unless it was parked at the front of the meetinghouse. Did Wolf and Lenny ride here with Hank in his truck? It didn't make sense. I filed the loose end away.

No evidence of anyone on watch, but that wasn't surprising. If Wolf kept his operation entirely based on the ranch, then most of his allies had been disposed of. Abbott and Costello had been left behind to tend to the guests in Smuggler's Basin (although by now, I hoped they had their charges in the supply bus and were heading home), and Bart was unconscious in the hospital.

Nope. Still didn't feel guilty about that.

Hank might have picked up a trucking partner, and Bob was still unaccounted for. Now we were up to maybe five people.

Unless that meetinghouse was used to rally counterfeiters from throughout the community . . .

As usual, there were too many variables to make forethought and preplanning more than an academic exercise. I'd learned pretty quickly to think on the fly. That was a lesson Rose was learning through experience.

I heard nothing but the sound of rolling money and Lenny's rumblings and grumblings, but I caught sight of faint movement on the driveway.

In low light, it's easier to see things if you don't look directly at them—something to do with the rod and cone cells in the eye. I let my peripheral vision gather data.

The Jeep came silently along the driveway, rolling impossibly up a gradual incline.

Then a foot slipped on the gravel, and my brain made the connection. I was seeing the Jeep being pushed up the hill by Phoebus Apollon, with strong Celeste at one side and slight Evadne at the other.

Rose, smallest and lightest, manned the wheel.

I grinned. Rose had come to an obstacle (even if it was only a gentle slope) and made a badass decision. *Atta girl.* I tucked the shotgun into the corner of my arm, pulled out my phone, and shone its flashlight on the front of the truck. Now she knew where I was and what she was up against.

They moved to twenty, thirty feet in front of the truck, and she eased the emergency brake on with an alarmingly loud creak.

No one came running at the noise. No watchman had objected to the flashlight. I switched off the light and texted Rose.

At least three men. Maybe more. Loading truck.

She read my text and responded: **I called help. Will be here soon.**

We couldn't wait for the cavalry to ride to our rescue, though. The loads being rolled into the truck weren't rolling far. They'd filled the trailer and would be leaving soon.

I put my phone away. She did too. It was light enough now to see all four of them watching me. I distributed my army.

I pointed to Rose and closed my fist. *You stay there.*

I pointed to Phoebus and then to the woods at my right. I put Evadne against the wall of the meetinghouse and sent Celeste into the woods on the left. Now all the civilians were deployed where they could be useful but were also out of the line of fire, as safe as I could make them.

Once they were out of sight, I nodded to Rose and gestured as if I was holding reins. The unspoken message: *use that strong energy.*

Giddyap.

FIFTY-ONE
DASH

ROSE TOOK A MOMENT. THEN SHE FLIPPED ON THE JEEP'S headlights and stood on the driver's seat with the shotgun raised, her belly braced against the roll bar. She shouted in a voice ringing with confidence. "FBI. You're under arrest. Come out where we can see you, hands over your heads. Do it now."

I faded back to midtrailer, close enough to hear the havoc caused by her call.

"Motherfucker!" That was Lenny.

"Shut up." Wolf's voice was low and laced with menace. "Goddamnit, it's that snoopy bitch. That fucking bear should have taken care of her."

"Fuck, Wolf!"

"Shut your damned mouth, Lenny. Not another word out of you, or I'll shoot you myself."

Armed then. No surprise.

"The question is," Wolf mused, "did the bear get anyone? Where's her fucking husband?"

"Come out," shouted Rose. "You're surrounded. There is no escape. Come quietly, and maybe no one gets hurt."

"Fuck that," muttered Wolf. "Lenny, go in front of me. Hold your hands up."

"I ain't nobody's human shield!"

"Motherfucker, do as you're told. Damn that Bart—he woulda understood. You're hiding my gun, Lenny."

"You shoot them, they shoot you, I'm in the middle. No fucking way!"

"You're going to get shot either way. I'll do you myself. Get ahead of me."

"Fuck, Wolf!" Lenny was whining, but he'd judged his threats and decided Wolf was more dangerous to him than the FBI. They edged their way carefully past the truck.

"We're coming out!" shouted Wolf.

"Don't shoot me!" screamed Lenny.

Unseen above them, I aimed the shotgun at Wolf's hand, hoping everyone would stay still if he drew on Rose.

And then I felt a tingle on my skin. I looked up.

The side of the meetinghouse was still dark with shadows, and I couldn't see Evadne until she moved. She pointed to the other side of the truck.

Right. Third man. I was about to meet brother Hank.

I reluctantly left my overwatch on Wolf and moved to the other side of the truck. Hank was ahead of the two on the other side. He had a trucker's cap, a silent step, and a large pistol.

The Koenig brothers were Justice Patriots and counterfeiters, but they weren't stupid. Their two-prong attack probably would have worked if I hadn't slid down the windshield with the shotgun held like a baseball bat. Landing on the hood of the truck, I wound up and hit one for the fences, cracking Hank across the head as he stepped from the shadows and took aim at Rose.

This was not a silent occurrence. Wolf and Lenny clearly heard my "oof" of effort, the sickening sound of Hank's skull clanging from the impact, and then him thumping to the ground.

They didn't hear me land on the ground next to Hank, but they probably heard the low moans he made. I was dragging him into the woods when Phoebus Apollon appeared beside me.

"I got him," he whispered.

We hid Hank in the bushes.

"Watch him," I said. Phoebus nodded with an excited grin.

I went back to the truck but couldn't find Hank's pistol in the low light.

Under the truck, Wolf's and Lenny's legs shone in the Jeep's headlights. They'd stopped, but now Wolf prodded Lenny ahead.

"Go on," he urged. "Get me closer. Move, Lenny."

"Don't shoot me!" Lenny was shouting. It was unclear who he was pleading with, but it didn't much matter.

"Few more feet . . . few more. I can see her. Stand still."

By the time Wolf had maneuvered himself into place, I was in my own spot, belly-down under the truck.

Wolf took that one last step, and the pistol came up. I tripped him on the shotgun barrel and watched with great satisfaction as he toppled over, taking Lenny down with him. The gun fired, the bullet burying itself into the ground.

I was kneeling on Wolf's back, realizing I had no handcuffs or other restraints, when I winced away from something cold on the back of my neck.

"Get up."

It was Bob, the sweet innkeeper. Not so sweet now.

"Well, Mr. Accountant. Get off my boy."

Wolf had twisted under me. Together, he and his father wrenched me up, and Wolf buried a fist in my gut. I doubled over, riding the waves of nausea.

"Son of a bitch."

"FBI," I gasped. "You're under arrest."

"The fuck I am. Your law has no authority here. Lenny, what do you see?"

"Don't shoot me!" Lenny had one line, and he was going to say it.

"Damn it, you moron!"

"Stop it, Wolf!" Bob pulled his son from a murderous rage.

"We've got one chance to make this right. Let's think while we can."

"They've got Dash!" Lenny screamed to the multitudes he imagined were arrayed before him.

"We've got Dash," Wolf roared in agreement. "So you stay where you are!"

Rose was silent. Then she called, "We've got Hank. Dash, you okay?"

Bob shook me, and I called back to her. "Real fine. Meeting three old friends. How are you?"

Wolf clocked me, slamming a stone fist into my jaw. I grayed out for a minute.

By the time I could make sense of things, I was lying face-up on the ground, Wolf's fancy-tooled boot slammed into my chest. He and Bob were having a heated conversation.

"Either the FBI is out there, or it's just the bitch. Either way, you've got to make it out of here."

"Dad—no."

"Son, we only have this chance. You take Hank's truck. Don't stop for anything."

"You come with me."

"I'm staying here. Me and Lenny. Right, boy?"

"What?" Lenny wasn't having an easy time focusing. "Me?"

"That's right. You and me. We're going to cover Wolf."

"But Dad—what if there's more than one agent out there?"

Bob sucked on his teeth and then straightened. "Go slow out the driveway. Lenny and me and this sack of shit are going to walk alongside the rig for cover. Get me to the catering truck. I've got the detonator. If it comes to it, I'll blow it and all of the FBI to hell where they belong."

"But what about you?"

"We're all prepared to be martyrs for our cause, aren't we, boy? Isn't that how I raised you? We're making a better world for all of us. Justice for the people. We're the good guys here."

"Dad." Wolf was moved to tears. "You're a true patriot. God bless you."

"If they come for you, you take out as many as you can."

"I swear I will!"

"Go on, then. I love you, son."

"I love you, sir!"

"Well, don't get all sappy. Get on now. Slow out the driveway, hear?"

I was dragged up and I staggered, leaning on Lenny more than was strictly necessary. Wolf made it into the cab of the truck, and the big diesel engines fired up.

"Halt!" Rose called. "You're under arrest! Shut off that engine!"

Wolf called her bluff. She shot into the engine block, but it did no good. Rose leaped to the side, and the truck crunched slowly and deliberately into Marcia's Jeep.

"Go on, my son," Bob whispered from behind me. "I'll buy her a new one. Crush it."

And crush it he did. Wolf pushed the hulk forward until he came to the first turn, and then he backed and turned, detaching from the wreckage and rolling slowly and unstoppably up the driveway.

We walked alongside, the truck between us and Rose's shotgun. Bob had a good plan.

But he hadn't counted on the long arm that shot out of the woods and snatched Lenny, jerking him off his feet.

Fortunately, I had.

I whirled and drove the heel of my hand into Bob's nose. He shrieked and dropped the pistol.

Even as his own tears of pain blinded him, Bob reached for his pocket. I knew he was going for the detonator to blow the catering truck.

I punched with all my strength, getting him in the nerve bundle of the upper arm. The impact flew up my arm and into my throbbing jawbone. I'm not sure which of us hurt more.

Regaining my balance, I kicked his feet out from under him and had his hands pinned on the ground when Rose got to us.

"Detonator," I said. "That pocket. Go carefully. It's armed."

She reached into his pocket gingerly and teased out a small plastic box. All the fight went out of Bob. I collapsed on him for a moment of blissful peace. Rose pried off the back and removed the battery.

From the woods beside me, I listened to Celeste and Lenny.

"Little man, you don't want to cross me."

"Save me, Lady Celeste! Get me out of here!"

"I will hit you again, you try anything."

"I know! I know! I ain't never killed anyone! Save me!"

It appeared that situation was well in hand.

I stood slowly. Rose and I looked at the remains of the Jeep, then at the truck now approaching the head of the driveway, about to pull onto the road.

"We'll call in the description. Let the local police take care of it."

I shook my head, a loathsome skim of regret and urgency coating my brain.

"He's got a detonator, too, and he's willing to be a martyr. We've got to stop him out here, where he can't kill anyone else."

"Shit." The truck gained speed in the slow, elephantine way of a loaded semi. "But how?"

And then Evadne called to me.

FIFTY-TWO

EVADNE

ROCKET THE HORSE WAS PASTURED IN THE FIELD BEYOND THE meetinghouse, and he'd come to the fence when chaos broke out. I sensed him there even from the other side of the building and filed away his presence without paying much attention.

But when Wolf began shouting, Rocket's agitation got stronger. His scent reached me, and I realized he was furious.

I crept around the meetinghouse as Wolf's huge truck slowly rolled down the driveway. Rocket stood next to a gate, his huge body straining forward.

Time to be brave. This was our solution.

I had no idea if horses could read scent as I could, but at the sight of me, Rocket gave off waves of immediate satisfaction. I opened the gate. He waited patiently while I climbed the fence as a mounting block and got on his back.

"We'll need help," I whispered.

I urged him forward, and when Rocket spotted Dash, he aimed for him at a trot.

"Dash! Over here!" I called. *See me. Time for me to be noticed.* He looked up and saw me. More, he saw Rocket—without a saddle or reins.

"Jesus Christ," he said. "Evadne . . ."

Wolf's truck negotiated the tight turn onto the road. We didn't have much time. "Get up! Come on—we can catch him!"

He gaped at me. "That horse is naked."

Hysterical laughter bubbled out of me. "Dash!"

"Take Rose. She's a much better rider than I am—"

I cut him off. "Rocket wants you. Give me your hand!" *Trust me. Trust me, Dash.*

Rose grabbed Bob's pistol and thrust it at Dash. "Go on! You're our best shot at this!"

He'd faced down men with guns, but this made him go pale. He shook his head but reached out for me. I took his hand, but he wouldn't move. "Do you trust me, Dash?"

Dawn was growing, birds sang, and a truck rumbled down a long country road. Rocket quivered, snorting with eagerness, and I could tell his soul was like cool, crystalline water in a desert well. Dash tightened his grip. "I do."

"Come on then."

Rose grabbed his ankle. Together, we boosted him up behind me.

"Hold onto me—here we go!"

He gripped my waist, one hand still clutching a large revolver. And Rocket showed him the difference between a lope and being run away with.

Rocket knew it was up to him. I didn't have to be a mind reader or be able to scent his determination. He got lower. Somehow, he got longer. He wasn't running for joy or at someone's command. That horse pounded along with the unquestioned determination of a hunter.

Dash got used to the rhythm and caught the pepper of the chase. He relaxed and became more alert. And we flew.

Wolf's truck lumbered up the steep hill. I was right. We could still catch him.

My heart pounded. I could feel my pulse in my ears, in my toes, in my gut. I was alive and terrified and exhilarated. Rocket kept up the speed, sprinting so fast Dash had to hold my hair from his face in the wind. I hoped he was reviewing the best ways to disable a truck.

Soon the license plate was clearly visible. Then we sped through a stinging hail of tiny pebbles spat up by the huge tires.

And at last, I could have reached out and touched the side of the rig.

"I'm going to shoot. Is Rocket ready?" Dash called.

"Do what you have to do," I panted.

He took careful aim. From this close, it shouldn't have been hard, but Rocket was moving beneath us. Dash shot and brake fluid sprayed out. Rocket veered away but kept pace.

Next, Dash shot into the wheels, aiming for brake calipers. He hit two and shredded several tires. At the top of the hill, Wolf began his descent and realized how much damage had been done. He pulled ahead of us, gaining speed . . .

. . . and then it was clear he'd gained too much speed.

I had to give Wolf credit. His brother was the long-distance trucker, but Wolf was able to ditch the truck in the loose gravel, and then soft soil, at the side of the road without tipping over. It was neatly done. But he was stuck fast.

Sides heaving like bellows between my legs, Rocket had slowed. We approached the truck carefully.

The landscape around us was bare and barren. If he detonated now, few lives would be lost. And at least I'd die with Dash.

He slipped off Rocket as we got to the back of the trailer. I dismounted behind him, but he made me stay behind the truck.

"Stay here. Keep down. We know he's armed." He looked at me and made me look at him. "Please stay here. Don't make me worry about you. I'll get distracted."

"I'll stay here. Be careful."

He touched my cheek and then crept around the corner of the trailer.

I crouched to peer after him.

FIFTY-THREE

EVADNE

REVOLVER IN HAND, DASH WENT QUICKLY ALONG THE driver's side of the truck until he got to the front of the trailer. Then he crouched behind the nearest set of tires.

"Okay, Wolf," he called. "You're stuck. Come out peacefully and make this easy on yourself."

"You mean easy on *you*!" Wolf hollered out his open window. The barrel of his gun searched for Dash. I drew back in alarm but had to keep watching. It would have been worse, not knowing.

Wolf was in an awkward position. To search for Dash, he had to crane backward in the driver's seat, and he did some shifting so he could get a better angle on his enemy.

No luck. Dash was tucked almost under the truck and out of Wolf's line of sight.

They were at an impasse, and silence hung thick and suffocating. Then the truck's door eased open. How far out would he stick his head? Would he spot Dash? Could Dash shoot Wolf faster than Wolf could shoot him?

I got raw anger from Wolf and icy control from Dash. The intensity was evenly matched. My heart was in my throat, and my grip on the trailer's bumper was painfully tight.

Then, as the door creaked open above Dash, a sudden flurry of movement at the side of the truck flashed through my system. Adrenaline spiked.

A large red body reared up and slammed into the opening door.

I jerked upright in surprise.

It was Rocket, out for his revenge.

Caught by the weight of a very large horse against the door, Wolf was slammed into the side of the truck. When Rocket's front feet fell back to earth, the door sprang open again, and Wolf fell out.

Rocket reared again, and then landed on Wolf's thighs.

The crack of the bones was a crisp, horrible shot of sound. Wolf shrieked, and Rocket uttered some horrible horse scream of victory.

Forgetting my promise, I rushed forward and held my hands up to Rocket. The horse saw me coming and backed down, his huge body trembling. He gave Wolf's hip one last massive stomp, and then Rocket allowed me to push him away.

By the time I turned around, Dash had Wolf's gun in one hand and was patting him down. Wolf writhed in agony.

The scent of Wolf's pain was bitter and sharp. He was having a hard time breathing because his agony was so bright. But long before I would have thought it possible, Wolf's hand reached for the pocket of his jeans, a powerful wave of determination coming off him.

Dash held up the remote.

"You'd like to take me and her and the damned horse out with you, wouldn't you? But there's no easy martyr's death for you. I've already taken out the battery. You're caught. It's over. Relax. We'll get you some help as soon as someone shows up."

"You'll never win," Wolf gasped.

Dash didn't bother to point out the obvious. He looked at Wolf with contempt—and, I realized, a small measure of empathy.

"I know how that feels," he said. "Horse broke my femur when I was eight. Hurt like a bitch."

"You're a bitch," Wolf gasped. It wasn't a good comeback, but I gave him credit for trying while his legs and probably his pelvis were in too many pieces.

"Okay. Well, this bitch is going to read you your rights now. Are you listening?"

Dash went through the memorized paragraph methodically while looking at his phone. No cell service.

"We're too far from your ranch, Wolf," he said. "Too far from any form of decent civilization. Well, that's okay. Rose called the field office. Someone will be along."

A pickup truck came toward us. I went to head it off—a nice rancher who wondered if I needed any help.

Wolf, Dash, and even Rocket were hidden from view by the bulk of the tractor trailer, so I drew on the experience I'd gained by running with professional liars and sent him on his way.

"That's okay. We've already called someone. Thanks, though."

The guy waved and passed on, never knowing how close he'd come to the ripping violence of an explosion.

I went to Dash, who leaned against the front of the truck.

"Rose did call this in, right?" he asked. Wolf's moans drifted across the morning.

"While we were in the Jeep. That was hours ago. Surely someone should be here by now?"

He smiled tiredly and reached for my hand. "Maybe twenty minutes ago. Time is sneaky, huh?"

"Twenty minutes?" I couldn't believe it. Her call was a lifetime ago.

"It won't be long," he reassured me.

Rocket had wandered away and idly lipped some bushes. I sat next to Dash on the truck's bumper.

"You're pretty good with a gun," I said. He shrugged. "Didn't need your reading glasses to shoot out the hydraulics, huh?"

DASH & THE MOONGLOW MYSTIC

He winced at the reminder. I kept thinking.

"Dash, if I can find a wildlife vet with a tranquilizer gun, could you put a dart into Big Betty?"

He gave me an astonished laugh. "After all this, you're worried about the bear?"

"She's got cubs. And it's not her fault some assholes tried to use her to kill you. She probably needs stitches and a whopping dose of antibiotics. It's not fair, Dash. We can't ignore her."

He shook his head, marveling at me. "You find a wildlife vet, and we'll find Betty. You're amazing. We'll have to dart the cubs too. This is going to be impossible."

Dash was so handsome. I was aware of him on a primitive level. Now I knew how he tasted. And he tasted good.

He suddenly grinned. "You're standing upwind."

I raised an eyebrow. "What, you're smelling me now?"

"I don't have to. I can hear you thinking."

"Yeah? What are you getting from me?"

He hit me with a smile that weakened my knees. "You're happy. Overwrought and your nerves are all jangly, but you're happy."

"A safe guess. Thank you for trusting me, Dash."

My comment surprised a burble of laughter out of him.

"You're thanking *me*? You're the reason this truck isn't going to kill anyone or distribute a smack to the economy."

"Not me. That was Rocket."

"Yeah. Let's talk about that. What the hell is up with that horse?"

I smiled at the bronco, now loose and free in the world. We'd need to recapture him and keep him safe.

"Wolf hurt him—consistently. Rocket hates Wolf. He's been looking for a way to get even. Rocket hates you, Wolf," I called to the crumpled body on the ground.

"Fuck you." He had enough spirit left to call out his rage. "Fuck that horse too. I should have shot him."

"Next time," Dash said soothingly. He didn't mind Wolf's

pain at all. I wondered how Wolf's father, Bob, was faring in Rose's care.

A sedan crested the hill and started for us. No, two sedans. No—three.

The cavalry had arrived.

FIFTY-FOUR

DASH

THE FIRST FACE OUT OF THE FRONT CAR WAS A WELCOME sight.

"Well, hey, Dash," said Enrique. "I hear you're to thank for getting me out of that Tim Horton's storage shed."

"That was Rose," I said. "She called it in. Welcome back from Canada."

"So what do we have here?" He wore a Secret Service vest. All the agents pouring out of the cars were similarly branded with their agencies.

"Truck full of fake hundreds and a nice packet of explosives. Here's the detonator. I took out the battery. And here's someone you might know."

I led him around the truck.

"Fuck. Hey, Wolf. What the hell happened to you?"

Wolf blinked up at the ranch hand he called Rick. "You goddamned beaner. What are you doing here?"

"US Secret Service." Enrique introduced himself. "Wolf Koenig, you're under arrest."

"Fuck you, you wetback."

"You're a loathsome human, Wolf. I'm happy as hell to take you in."

Wolf cursed impotently as Enrique read him his rights again. Nobody was taking any chances with this one. Wolf's skin had gone gray. Definitely in shock.

"We need an ambulance for him," I pointed out. "A prison ambulance, if you have one."

"I'll see what I can do. Let these guys take care of this. Tell me what's going on."

I made a verbal report to the agents on hand, who very much enjoyed the telling.

"Looks like you didn't need us at all," Enrique said with an admiring grin. "Let's head to the ranch and make sure Rose is still doing okay."

We left one car to watch over Wolf, the billions of fake dollars, and the explosives until the summoned experts arrived—medical care for Wolf, bomb experts to dismantle whatever the detonator went to, a tow truck to impound Hank's rig, and (at Evadne's insistence) a horse trailer for Rocket.

Evadne and I crowded in with the other agents. I passed a pleasurable moment enjoying the soothing rise and fall of her rib cage against my arm. *It was*, I thought distantly, *good to be alive.*

There was no one at the meetinghouse. No Hank vomiting from the concussion I'd given him. No Bob screaming from the broken nose. No Lenny clinging to the woman he'd formerly hated and begging her to protect him.

No prophet.

No Rose.

Somehow, she'd gotten them all out of there. Found Wolf's Jeep, probably. Maybe he'd parked it inside the bunker while they loaded up.

There was room for a Jeep in there amid empty pallets and one hell of a printing operation. Huge drying racks covered the large ceiling, where industrial fans would speed the drying process.

Two agents were assigned the task of watching over the

lethal catering truck until the same bomb experts could render it inert.

That made more room in the cars, but Evadne rode back to the Triangle-K still snugged up against my side, where she belonged.

But our day wasn't over yet.

Wolf's Jeep was pulled up behind the bus. Good. Abbott or Costello had gotten the guests home.

All the guests were still crowded on the lawn in a large U shape. I pushed through to see what held their attention.

It was a shotgun.

Of course it was.

And it was aimed directly at my partner.

Marcia stood over the slumped forms of Bob and Hank, both of them moaning. Bob was bloody from the broken nose, and Hank was gray. Judging by the crossed eyes, he was having trouble focusing—signs of one whopper of a concussion. He needed immediate medical attention.

And Marcia didn't like it.

The sweet, plump, happy woman was lost inside a screaming harridan. One look and I took her threat seriously. This was a woman looking for an excuse to shoot Rose. I couldn't have that. Rose was my partner, my friend. I felt it in my soul: no one was going to hurt her.

The distance between them was unfortunate. Rose was trained in disarming an attacker if she could get close enough, but Marcia wasn't letting her within ten feet of the bodies she was protecting.

Like Big Betty, I thought. A mama bear protecting her cubs is more dangerous than a regular old killer bear.

Only this bear turned out to be a drooling, slobbering fanatic. We were in trouble, and the civilians needed immediate protection.

I pushed Evadne behind me.

"Be careful," she whispered, her voice icy with fear. I nodded.

Marcia screamed.

"FBI, my ass! You are all alone here, girl! You have no authority here! Get off my land! Look at what you've done!"

Marcia's face was red and flecks of spittle flew from her mouth. Her guests were grouped in frozen horror. Rose saw me and her spine crumpled in relief, but I was too far away to step in. I held my hands as if I was holding reins and mouthed the word to her. *Energy*.

She nodded and swallowed her fear. Then she straightened and focused. "Marcia, I *am* FBI, and you *are* under arrest. Put the shotgun down."

"I will not! This is my place! You can't come in here like this!"

"Marcia, Bob and your boys planned to destabilize this nation. We had to stop them."

"You don't know a thing! That was *my* plan! It was me! And you hurt them! Where's Wolf?"

I moved closer and spoke calmly. "Look, Marcia. Our colleagues are here. It's over now. Put the shotgun down."

"I will not! Stay back! Nobody move!"

She swung the gun in a short arc, and the agents froze in place. They'd been easing around me, attempting to circle Marcia and move civilians to safety, but she wouldn't have it.

"There's no way out of here that works well for you, Marcia, unless you put down the gun." Rose's voice was soothing and strong.

"Shut up! Shut up! You people have no authority. The entire federal government is illegal! You get the county sheriff out here and maybe I'll listen. You federals are ruining this country! We've got friends all over this nation, and when they get that money, you're going to see a change. We're protecting the freedom of the people! We're making a better nation!"

"What kind of friends, Marcia?"

Rose's question pulled Marcia up short. Her eyes narrowed. "You'd like to know, wouldn't you?" she asked slyly. "Well, don't you worry about it. They're patriots like us!"

Marcia's eyes darted about. She tried to watch everyone at the same time, and at last, she focused on me. I'd made it to the front of the crowd.

"Where's Wolf? Where's my baby?" she shrieked.

"He's getting medical attention, and then he's going to jail for a long time. This is over now, Marcia." Like Rose, I kept my voice calm, reasonable, and strong—assertive behavior designed to make her surrender to us peacefully.

She wasn't going along with the plan.

"Not until I shoot the bitch who hurt my sweet boys!" She refocused the shotgun on Rose. "And that's you! You are all alone here!"

She'd said that before. That isolation was important to her. I spoke, drawing her attention again. It was like keeping the rattlesnake's attention split—only with something much more dangerous and vile.

"She's not alone here." I stepped up slowly but deliberately until I stood at Rose's side. "I'm with her."

Marcia blinked at me, confused.

"Are you going to shoot me, too, Marcia?"

My question hung in the still air. And then there was movement to my left. We were all so jumpy, Skip was lucky he wasn't shot.

The teen avoided his mother's clutching hand and stepped forward to stand at Rose's shoulder.

"Me too," he said with a brave gulp. "I'm with Rose. She's not alone."

Rose tried to pull Skip behind her, but he refused to be budged. Melanie tried to join, but her father stopped her with an iron grip.

As the sun came out from behind a cloud, Phoebus Apollon stepped up and threw an arm around Skip's shoulder. The boy didn't even notice when the leader of Prophecy Week turned the boy and moved him back.

"I'm with Rose too," he said.

Rose and I together took the step forward that kept us in the front of the group. We crept slowly closer to Marcia, who didn't seem to realize it.

Now the Running with Rosie fans were moving. They, too, stepped up to stand in a line with Rose.

"Are you going to shoot all of us, Marcia?" Cheri asked in a gentle voice.

With each new addition to the human wall, Rose and I eased further forward. Kimber and Perry from Indianapolis were the next to join Rose's defensive line. They'd been the first people we'd met on the bus ride in, and they stood with their friends now. Rose tried to persuade them all to back up, but no one moved.

At last, Rose and I were within arm's range of Marcia. Rose reached up a slow hand and gently pressed on the shotgun until it was aimed at the ground.

"I'm not the one who's all alone here, Marcia. You are. Give me the gun."

Marcia was living a nightmare. She trembled as she surrendered her grip.

Once the shotgun left her hand, all the strength ran out of her, and she fell to the ground next to her husband and son.

It was a family affair. Too bad there were no family-friendly federal prisons.

Rose stood next to me, looking at the pile of Koenigs.

"You're a badass," I told her.

Her grin was immediate, relief and satisfaction evident. "I really am!"

I smiled. She would be a great agent. Her evolution was my crowning glory. I could leave fieldwork behind now—in victory.

Enrique stepped up to us.

"You people don't ever do things the easy way," he said with a grin.

I found Evadne's hand. She was reaching for me. Adrenaline's crushing grip on my muscles and nerves eased as soon as her fingers wrapped around mine.

Marcia looked up. "*Rick?*" she spat in disgust.

"Enrique Martinez, US Secret Service," he identified himself to her. "Marcia Koenig, you're under arrest. I'll now read you your rights."

"You disgust me. A damned fed. You betrayed us. We gave you a home here!"

"Thanks," he said sunnily. "You have the right to remain silent."

He read her rights to her. I turned to Rose. "Did you explain Bob's and Hank's rights to them? And where's Lenny? I never read him his rights. Shit."

We discussed legal matters as she pointed to Lenny on the porch, now flanked by agents but refusing to let go of Lady Celeste, whose scorn was clear on her face.

Melanie had broken away from her mother's clutches. She pointed to the FBI badge pinned on one of the agents' vests. "Look at that," she said to him. "You're an Eagle Guy too."

My head snapped up. How many times had I looked at my own badge—the symbol of my career in justice—and never actually noticed that a bald eagle, wings outspread, guarded the crest?

Had Trap—*my* eagle—been with me all along?

I was thrown off-balance by the thought. It was welcome but strange, like Trap himself. Then Phoebus Apollon pushed through the crowd.

"This was the best Prophecy Week we've ever had. You guys are signing up for next year, aren't you?"

Rose laughed at him outright.

"Slow your roll there, brother. Dash and I are in financial crimes. You're going to want to change up your game, or we're going to come after you."

Phoebus looked at me in astonishment, and I nodded.

"I'd give you a head start, though," I admitted.

"Ah. That's all I'd need! Thanks, man."

We shook hands, which meant I had to briefly let go of Evadne, but that situation was quickly remedied.

I took her hand, pretty sure I wasn't going to be letting go again.

I could feel her in my skin.

AFTERWORD

What happens next for Dash and Evie?

I wrote an epilogue and I'm dangling it in front of you. Mm —looks good, dunnit??

All you have to do to download it for FREE (don't you love that word?!) is sign up for my authorial newsletter, *Bliss & Giggles*, in which I mostly amuse the hell out of myself. When you sign up, I'll send you the link to download the epilogue.

The response email will come to you as soon as you confirm the subscription, so watch for that in your spam folder if you don't see it quickly. Then you can download the epilogue. Like, right now.

So easy!

How do you do it?

Go to https://pruwarren.com and there the sign-up will be. Right on page one. Like I was waiting for you. Honey!

PS: You can unsubscribe immediately, if you want. But why? We'll have fun!

AND MAY I TEMPT YOU WITH DESSERT?

I love Dash & Evie's story—but honestly? I think Artie's story is even better!

I fell in love with Phoebus Apollon. I couldn't help it. He's such a scoundrel.

Turn the page for a sneak peek of ELLYN & THE WOULD-BE GIGOLO, which will be published on Oct. 19, 2021.

SNEAK PEEK: ELLYN & THE WOULD-BE GIGOLO

Chapter One—Ellyn

The guy at the front of the line had one hell of a shiner coming up around his eye.

He was trying to hide it. He kept his head ducked so the side of his face was covered with a lot of long blond hair. But I've been fascinated with bruising since I studied stage make-up, and I'm always on the look-out for good bruises.

He turned from the counter, a cup of coffee small in his large hand, and I abandoned my place in line to follow him.

He ducked around the corner of the coffee shop, moving like more than his eye hurt. He found a bench at a table on the wall. Good light from the front window.

"Hey."

He looked up, and a hit of electricity zipped through me. The black eye was so fresh the skin was still puffing up. This guy must have been hit within the last ten minutes. I shifted on my feet in eagerness.

"Mister, can I photograph your eye?"

"Fuck off, girlie."

He dismissed me from his attentions by concentrating on his coffee but winced at the sip. Too hot.

Undeterred, I pulled out the chair. My camera bag went between my feet and I unzipped the main compartment.

"Won't take a minute," I said. "Although if you let me, I'd like to take one photo every five minutes for an hour or so. Are you busy right now?"

"Am I busy," he said woodenly.

I reached past the GoPro. (*What if I'd had the right tripod and could film the black eye coming up?! Would he have sat still for an hour? That would be awesome. My kingdom for a tripod; why didn't I rent it with the video camera?* And me priding myself on always being prepared.) My trusty Nikon slipped into my hand like an old friend.

"Yeah. Are you busy." I sat up and faced him, camera in hand. "I want to photograph that black eye coming up. I make movies," I explained. "I study bruises. Like that one."

I gestured to his cheekbone and calculated the light from the front window. The dreary February day was overcast. No need for a diffuser.

"No, you can't photograph me. Fuck off, I said."

I grinned. I love New York.

"I'm not going to publish it or anything. Just going to capture the light coming off that massive shiner. For the good of the film industry. I'm sure you understand."

"You take my picture and I'll rip that camera out of your hands and..." Words failed him and he splatted his very large hand against the brick wall next to him. I winced at the implied violence to an innocent camera.

"All right," I said, ready to negotiate. "What do you want?"

"Want." He repeated me, not understanding.

"How much to photograph your face?"

He grinned, winced, and groaned. *Cheek muscles a tad tender, there, guy?*

"Aspirin," he muttered. "It will cost you aspirin."

I was already fishing in the medical pouch. "Advil or Tylenol?

I don't have anything with codeine at the moment. Sorry about that."

Now I had his attention.

"You actually have aspirin in that suitcase?"

"I'm a DP. Director of photography. I have everything. Well, I don't have actual aspirin. But acetaminophen, yeah. Does Advil work on you? Here—how many?"

I shook out two pills into the large palm that was suddenly reaching for me, and thought about it. I popped out a third one.

He grunted and made an impatient gesture with that reaching hand. "One more."

"You want four Advil?" I said. "Are you sure? This stuff will get to your liver eventually."

"Four. I'm a big guy."

That was true. I put the final pill into his palm (which was warm, slightly rough, large; how would a good director visually convey the faint frisson of heat that brushed my fingers with that faint touch?) and capped the bottle. It was in its pouch and my camera was in hand by the time he'd chased the pills with some still-scalding coffee. He goggled at the heat, but swallowed it anyway. "Thanks," he said.

I'd use my elbows as a tripod and remain consistent in my placement. "Pull your hair back. Look straight ahead."

He grumbled but complied.

The lighting would do. Through the lens, I saw he was handsome. Square jaw that would look good on a fifty-foot screen. Sharp cheekbones to catch the light; if we'd used video, I'd have had to use a matte powder to stop the light from bouncing. Broad forehead. Way too much hair worn long in a ridiculously blond mane.

And a mouse of a bruise coming up below his left eye. The guy who hit him was right-handed, and with a pretty big fist. Big end bone of the middle finger against the cheekbone, prominent first knuckle making itself seen next to the eyebrow. Blood seeped under the skin into the damaged tissue. Black and purple. Angry. It was gorgeous.

Click.

And it was mine.

I checked the shot; perfect.

The timer on my phone would remind me; I set it for five minutes.

"Now you can fuck off," the guy said, letting his hair fall over his face.

"Every five minutes," I said. "For at least an hour. What'll it take?"

"More than Advil."

I looked at the small coffee. "How about something to eat? Something bigger than that to drink? My treat."

He looked up, interested but not persuaded.

"And I'll make you an ice bag."

That did it. He nodded. "Fine."

The camera went around my neck (my usual necklace) and I picked up the camera bag. "Stay here."

"You can leave that here," he said. "It looks heavy."

"Yeah," I laughed. "Right. You're funny."

He was still sitting there when I returned.

"Where's my ice?"

"They're getting it. It's been five minutes. Pull your hair off your face."

Click.

The two images, one after the other, should have been put in a textbook. The black eye had spread, and the edema was increasing, all the lymphatic system's attempts to swell and protect the area making his eye puff up nicely.

"You're a good subject. The camera likes you."

He grunted. "I'm handsome."

And vain. "Nah. Plenty of handsome people look like shit on camera. You were born lucky."

He scoffed. Apparently he wasn't feeling lucky at the

moment. But I was. Best black eye study ever.

I went back to the coffee shop's waiting area, thinking it would be a shame to ice that bruise. On the other hand, it was hard to imagine a scenario in which a character in a film would not ice a bruise, so I was still going to get a realistic series of photos even if He-Man Jungle Jim insisted on suppressing the swelling. It would be okay.

"I got you soup. I thought maybe your jaw might be tightening up."

I'd also gotten him a venti iced tea and a cup of ice. I pulled a Ziplock baggie from my stash and poured the ice into it. He reached for my impromptu ice pack.

I pulled it away. "It's been more than five. Hang on."

Used to the routine now, he pulled his hair off his face with a big, affected sigh.

Lighting was still good. Photo acceptable. Bruise beginning to darken. He'd been hit by a *big* hand.

I surrendered the ice and reset my timer. He made an inarticulate noise as he gingerly laid the bag over his eye.

"So what's your story?" I asked.

One large, blue eye regarded me. "The fuck?"

His reply had been conversational; the ice was helping. I helped myself to the baguette that came with his soup. "Yeah. Who hit you? How come? What's the backstory, here?"

He snorted. "What's the backstory on your hair?"

I had to think to remember today's style. Right—black and white stripes. It looked good. He attempted to get the drink straw out of its plastic wrapper with one hand (the other hand being used to plaster a good chill over his eye).

He was going to crush the straw. I took it from him, pulled it out, put it in the iced tea, and handed the cup back. He took a long pull and the big shoulders came down.

"Someone put the major smack-down on that camera-ready face. I'm just wondering what the story was."

"You bought the right to photograph my bruise. You didn't buy my backstory."

"That's true." I reached out one long arm (it's always useful to be tall) and pulled the cuff of his jacket away from his wrist.

He jerked his hand from me, but I'd already seen the ligature marks. "You were tied, weren't you? When you got hit?"

The side of his face not hidden by the ice bag glared at me.

"I'm not surprised," I added. "Big chest, broad shoulders, obviously you work out. You've got muscle, and you look like a scrapper. You could probably throw down in a fight, and there aren't any marks on your knuckles. Not fresh ones, anyway."

I had a good look at his right hand, cradling the ice against his head. A series of crescent scars, silvery and pale, showed where he'd landed blows on at least one mouth (probably more than one) and the teeth had cut him—but those marks were old. He favored his ribs but not his fingers. He hadn't hit anyone in the last few hours, and he sure as hell had been hit himself.

"So someone jumped you, tied you up, and tagged that big blue eye. If you pulled up that sweater, I bet I'd see some nice bruises on your ribs, huh?"

I got the full glare now.

"Yeah. That's what I thought. I wasn't kidding. I study bruises. And your oversized body is telling quite a story." The timer went off. "Ice down. Pull back your hair. Ooh, that's looking beautiful."

The black blood under the skin had spread, and the eyelid was swollen almost closed. I couldn't help but grin.

"You're very odd," he said as he re-applied his ice.

Four perfect shots in a row. The light was holding. "I've been told. I'm Ellyn. What's your name?"

"Why?"

I laughed at his suspicion. "Because I've got you for another eight shots. Why not be civil?"

He thought about it for a while. "Artie," he said, grudgingly.

"Guarded much? How many names did you have to go through before settling on that one?"

Surprisingly, the question gave him the flash of a grin. The guy used way too much whitener on his teeth. "A few."

Right. Stage names, pseudonyms, aliases? This guy began to interest me.

I froze, suddenly seeing a possibility.

He didn't notice. He spooned in beef barley soup and eyed the remains of the baguette, still in my hand.

I assessed him coldly. Too tall, no doubt, but definitely handsome enough. Great shoulders, wide chest. Moved well, given that he probably had a few cracked ribs. Age? How old was he? Could have been anywhere from twenty-five to a thirty-five-year-old who took good care of his skin.

Aliases. Possibly violent past. Dressed in jeans, a camel sweater, a nice leather jacket. Way too much hair, but that could be fixed.

It would be risky. But what wasn't?

He'd noticed my silence. "What?"

I shook my head at him, still thinking. A text message pinged onto my phone from Mock.

Hello? Are you coming?
With my cappuccino?
Shit. I'd lost track.

Get down here now. Starbucks

My Starbucks or yours?

Yours. Hurry

You owe me coffee
"Who's that?" Artie asked.
"Friend of mine. Okay, ice down. Pull your hair back."
You can say a lot about Mock, but no one would say he was

slow. He appeared in the coffeeshop before the sixth photo, an Asian man weaving gracefully between tables. He'd spotted us quickly and couldn't look away from my new companion.

"Girl—who is this?"

His interest was obvious. Mock has an eye for beauty. He stole a chair from a nearby table and pulled it over to sit next to me. "New friend, Ellyn?"

"Mock, meet Artie. Artie, this is Mock, the best stylist in Manhattan."

Mock waved dismissively with his hand but he beamed. "Oh, go on with you. Hello, Artie. Aren't you *big*!"

Artie's one visible eye rolled between me and Mock.

"Wait until you see what's under that ice pack. We've got... thirty-seven seconds to a big reveal."

Mock clapped his hands eagerly. "I love a big reveal! Ellyn, you always find the *best* things! She's got such a good eye," he confided to Artie, who seemed not at all impressed.

"Oh, I'm going to *show* you a good eye," I assured him.

Mock and I both studied the timer ticking on my phone, our mutual anticipation building. I wasn't prepared for Artie's reaction when the timer went off.

With a flourish, he whipped off the ice bag and leaned forward toward Mock, angling his head so his swollen black eye was foremost. "Ta-daaaa!" he sang.

Mock grabbed my arm and gasped in wide-eyed amazement at the darkness spreading across Artie's eye. "Ooooh! Look at that!"

Artie settled with a grin. *Streak of the showman in that guy.* The Advil and the ice were working; his aches and pains had eased.

"Now that is a black eye," Mock said in admiration. I knew he'd understand. We'd taken stage makeup together.

"Wait until you see my series," I boasted. "Hang on. Every five minutes. Artie, pull back your hair, please."

Artie complied. By this point, we had a routine.

"Look at that bone structure," Mock said appreciatively. "Are you in the business? Actor, I mean. On stage? Heroic star of the silver screen?" Artie shook his head. "Why not? Everyone else in Manhattan is, and you're a looker, no doubt. Camera loves you. Here's the proof. But sweetie, what's with all that hair? That cut is entirely wrong for you."

Artie looked at Mock, confused.

"That's what I thought, too," I said. "Now, look at this series, Mock."

I showed him my collection and Mock had nothing but praise. "Look—you can see each knuckle coming up over time. And look at that color. How would you do the puffiness? Prosthetics, maybe?"

We discussed how we could recreate the effect on camera and Artie watched us do it, impassive but alert. But this was no longer the reason I wanted Mock's opinion.

"We've got a few minutes until the next shot," I said. "How about you and I get your cappuccino, Mock?"

Mock's my close friend. He got my message but responded with nothing more than the lift of one mobile, beautifully-shaped eyebrow. "Yes, girl. I need my 'chino. What about you, handsome? Can I get you anything?"

Artie received the decided leer without objection. "Venti Americano. Thanks."

"Venti," Mock said with a wink. "I'm sure."

Artie made a "what else?" gesture with his hands.

"Nothing in it?" Mock asked. "You don't want...a splash of soy milk? Something maybe a little Asian?"

Artie laughed out loud, which was impressive. Most butch guys don't know how to handle Mock's come-ons. "Not today. Thanks, though."

I snorted. "Come on, Mock. You can flirt in a minute."

I dragged the stylist over to the line at the counter and he fanned himself with his hand.

"Honey, I can't tell, and I can always tell. Does that guy play for my team or yours? Because yum."

"Calm down. What do you think about using him for the Aunt Cor situation?"

Mock snapped his attention to me. More than my career depended on this one. "Aunt Cor?" His clever brain already leapt ahead of his "gay Thai stylist" persona. "What are you thinking? You want to hire him to be a ringer?"

Now he studied Artie like the man was a job, not a bedmate.

"Well, I thought it was worth discussing."

"Do you even know him? How did you find him?"

"Met him right here, half an hour ago" I said promptly. "I know no more about him than you do."

Mock's known me for nine years; we met on the very first day of film school. "You already know more than I do. What have you seen that I haven't?" He waved away my dismissal and we moved up a place in line. "Hurry up. We don't have much time. Tell me."

I considered. "A history of brawling, but not recently. He's got a flare for the dramatic. He's reasonably intelligent and speaks well. He's camera-ready in terms of physical beauty. He's healthy. There are no signs of drug or alcohol abuse visible, although both could be early stages. And he's in trouble. Someone tied him up to beat him within the last hour. So he might be looking for an opportunity, too."

Mock nodded. We both stared at Artie, who stared at us.

"Final assessment?" Mock asked.

"Scoundrel," I replied. "Complete scoundrel."

Mock high-fived me. "That's what we're looking for."

We abandoned our place in line and returned to Artie.

"No Americano?" he said mildly.

"Artie," I said, "I have a proposition for you."

He looked at me. "I don't fuck for money." He leered at Mock. "Not anymore, anyway."

Mock fanned himself again and made a cooing noise.

"Not a sexual proposition. Would you be willing to come with us? Mock lives upstairs. We could have a discussion in private." I looked to Mock to make sure he was fine with my offering his apartment as our temporary headquarters. He nodded eagerly.

Artie caught his lower lip between strong, white teeth and considered us.

"I've been beaten once already today. I'm afraid I'm not available for violence. What would be in this for me? And I'll tell you right now, it'll take more than a venti Americano."

We didn't have a moment to waste. I cut through his concerns.

"How about a quarter of a million dollars? Would that make it worth your time?"

"Are you kidding?"

"I'm definitely not kidding."

He stood, unfolding from the seat, and I backed a step. I hadn't realized just how tall he was. Mock made an "eep" sound of alarmed delight.

"Then let's get out of here."

SCHMOOZING STRANGERS

I'm not supposed to wink and giggle with total strangers; Mom said so. But I'm winking and giggling at you. Because, obviously, you got my book. So we are strangers no longer!

Since my goal is nothing less than a GLOBAL PUBLISHING EMPIRE (ma-hah-hah-hah-hah, evil laugh), it would tickle me like going over the top of a roller coaster if you'd leave a review on the website where you bought my book. Wilya, huh?? (Winking at you in a coy fashion.) Every review makes that massive "smile" retailer (you know the name) rank me just a little higher in the "If you liked this, you'll also like this" algorithm. So is it any wonder I'm longing for your feedback?!

And let's keep this going! Sign up for my newsletter, Bliss & Giggles. It's supposed to be the author's IDEAL MARKETING TOOL, but mostly I use it to rant and snort and amuse myself. I think it might amuse you, too! You can sign up on my website at https://www.pruwarren.com/
    Plus—don't forget: You'll get the epilogue to DASH & THE MOONGLOW MYSTIC as my smooch to you for subscribing. Free!

ABOUT THE AUTHOR

Pru Warren (who is writing this in the third person as if simply too modest to toot her own horn) bores easily and thus has been a daydreamer since roughly the Bronze Age.

She is addicted to writing because in a novel, you can make things come out the RIGHT way. Life and karma really ought to take note; there are BETTER SOLUTIONS to these pesky daily annoyances!

Beside her in-the-laptop God Complex, Pru laughs often and easily, loathes cooking, and plays way too much solitaire. She's plotting world domination even as you read this, as long as she doesn't have to wake up too early to accomplish it.

ALSO BY PRU WARREN

Cyn & the Peanut Butter Cup

Dash & the Moonglow Mystic

Ellyn & the Would-Be Gigolo (October, 2021)

Farrah & the Court-Appointed Boss (November, 2021)

Love Gone Viral ("Joan's Journal")

Made in the USA
Middletown, DE
30 September 2021